My Ruined Life

Beth K. Belliveau

Cover by: Christopher Ramos

Copyright © 2021 Beth Belliveau

All rights reserved.

ISBN: 978-1-7373945-0-1

Special thanks to my husband, Phil, and my mother, Marie, who spent hours listening to me read the stories as I wrote them, chapter by chapter and offering their guidance and encouragement to make my lifelong dream come true; to be an author. Also, thanks to my son, Matthew and daughter in law, Jessica for help with the "technical components".

I am also truly grateful to the rest of my family and friends, who encouraged me and supported my passion to write a story (or two in this case) that focused on the lives, thoughts and emotions of middle school aged youths as they cope with real life scenarios.

Nina's Story –

Chapter 1

Torn… ripped into a million pieces...scattered on the wooden floorboards and across the green and white striped carpet. The black letters were shouting to me from the crisp white pieces of paper. Some words are still intact. I spot the word "always". What a bunch of crap...that means nothing to me. He is not part of my world anymore. I see the word "forever" staring at me. My stomach lurches and I just want to puke all over the words...all over HIM.

I reach for my iced tea, warm now, and has been on my table for hours, since before I read it. Those words were screaming through my mind. I want to hit a mute button and make them vanish, but that doesn't exist. My grandmother says, "Time heals all wounds", but she is wrong. I will never be the same again...never will my wound be healed. I will live with this open cut in my soul forever. So much has left my body. A magnet has drawn out all aspects of trust, security, happiness, love. Love is gone, and I know it's never returning.

How can I ever trust anyone anymore? Happiness is a foreign, unwanted feeling to me.
What about security? Nothing is ever secure in life. It's all lies...greed...selfishness. That's my world. My wall is being built, brick by brick. It is surrounding me. It is enclosing my world. There are no windows, just darkness and solitude. There is nobody to speak stupid words to help me understand who I am or why I feel this way or telling me how to "cope". It is such garbage. People and their words, their actions

are just a bunch of useless trash. I don't need anyone. Anything they offer me is a fake. A temporary band aid on a gaping wound in my soul. Go away, just GO AWAY!

The shadows in my room grow longer and the sky slowly fades into darkness. I hear the TV and murmur of voices in the living room. I want to go out there and tell them all to shut up, but I worry that the silence will be louder to my ears. I replay the words from the tattered pieces- as if being read by "his" in his voice. I try to block it out...I hum...it doesn't work. I try adjusting the voice so it sounds like someone I don't know...someone from another town, state or country. I've read about stuff like this happening and never once even thought it would EVER happen to me - my family- my world.

I must have dozed off. When my eyes open, only the streetlight shines through the window. Everything's quiet. Here it comes...the deafening silence...the pressure of nothingness building in my ears, like someone pressing the palms of their hands against my ears trying to squeeze the brains through the top of my head. I clear my throat just to make a noise. It breaks the pressure, but then it slowly returns, building...even more intense this time. The silence takes me, until wheels crackle along the street, slowly, then stopping in front of my house.

No knock. The front door opens. Someone comes inside. Mom or grandma let them in. I look at the clock. It's 2:47am. Who's at my house now, at this time? I listen closely. I hear adult voices. They belong to Mom and Uncle Vinnie. Why is he here now? The car pulls away. Someone dropped him off. Why? He has his own apartment. I hear mom crying and Uncle Vinnie speaking softly to her. I

can't make out what he is saying.
 I drift off again to wake with soft daylight streaming through my window. I've gotta pee. I haven't left my room in 12 hours. I walk quietly across the hall. Nobody is up yet. Uncle Vinnie is asleep on the couch. Why is he here? Why did he show up so late? As I return to my room, he sits up. "Hey Bug", he whispers. I wave my hand in his direction and continue into my room. He lies back down. After a while I hear his mild snoring. I don't know what to do...I want to just stay in my room forever. I know that won't fly with Mom.
 I get up, grab half a candy bar from my secret sweet stash I keep hidden in my room. I grab my backpack, throw my hair into a quick messy bun...thank God those are still in style...nobody will ask my questions...and I sneak to the front door. As I am closing it, Mom whispers, "Where are you going?"
"School", I reply
"It's two hours early," she says.
"I'm walking today", I answered. Then I closed the door behind me.

Chapter 2

It's cool out, early October. I'm cold at first, but as I keep walking I warm up. I arrive at school an hour early. The 5 mile walk woke me up a bit. I eat half of my candy bar for breakfast and wash it down with a few sips of water from the fountain next to the soccer field. I sit by the side door of the school tucked into the corner, waiting for the doors to be unlocked and students to be allowed to enter. The sky grows brighter but my mood doesn't.

I must have fallen asleep...a car door shuts and wakes me up. Ms. Lack, my history teacher spots me and walks in my direction. Her long brown hair with streaks of wiry grey woven throughout bounces as she approaches. She doesn't seem that old, but I heard she is retiring soon. She is very passionate about history and people who want to make "big changes" in the world. Some kids make fun of her because she doesn't wear much makeup or dress in fancy clothes and high heels. She is nice and only lectures you if you are disrespectful to anyone or if you don't at least attempt the work that is assigned. I like her because she isn't fake...what you see is what you get with her.
"You're early today." She remarks.
" Mm hummm," I respond
"Dropped off?" she asks.
"Walked." I mumble.
" Exercising or thinking?" She questions.
"Both." I comment.

She doesn't need to know my personal matters....and I definitely don't need the counselor or social worker calling me into their offices and grilling me about anything. It's none of their business.
"Come on in with me if you want. You can wait in my room until the buses arrive if you'd like." she offers.
I follow her in. My butt is asleep from sitting on the concrete...a chair will be more comfortable.

I sit and watch Ms. Lack as she unpacks her bag. She tosses an apple to me. "Here...breakfast or a decent snack...whatever you need it to be." she comments. I thank her and take a bite. That candy bar is already out of my system and my stomach is hurting with hunger. It is tart, but good. I get up and grab a paper towel. She is writing the daily message on the board.

The buses arrive and the kids start to trickle in. I quickly leave and head to Homeroom so nobody notices that I was somewhere different than usual. I don't want any questions. I don't trust myself to answer with a reasonable response. I just want to "blend" today. I just want to walk through the day and go through the normal motions without anyone noticing me at all. It is kind of like being invisible, but not getting marked absent. That is the only reason I am here today. Mom doesn't need another issue to deal with in her life, so I just do the bare minimum, like go to school. That doesn't mean I will pay attention to what is being taught or raise my hand in class, it only means that my physical body will be present wherever it is supposed to be based on my schedule.

I enter my homeroom and sit in my usual spot and take out a book. No phone out today because some teachers get mad and question what you are doing on your phone...I don't want that attention. A book is safe. I am not reading it, just faking it to avoid contact with anyone. I know most of the people in my homeroom, but am not close with anyone who would say anything about me "reading" before classes start. Announcements...I stand for the pledge and moment of reflection. Then the principal comes on and reminds us that 3rd period is an assembly for 8th graders. Great...that's me. I will miss math class. Math is "OK", I wish it were Science Class. I like Science, but Mr. Willis is bubbly and hyper and always calls on me and jokes with me. Neither one is a good idea today.

First period...Spanish Class. Not too bad. Doing minimal work on the computer program for intermediate level...just enough to keep the teacher from questioning me about not working.

Second period is History Class. Ms. Lack talks to us about a long term partner project that has to do with saving the world in some way. I half listen. It isn't starting today so no biggie. She walks to my desk while we are reading an article about a water issue in Michigan. She catches my eye and silently points to the door. I know what that means. She wants to talk with me privately, in the hall. Great. I sigh, stand, and head out the door.

The fire alarm sounds and I am saved, for right now at least. I usually hate fire drills, but not this one! Outside I keep my head down, pretending to be looking at something in the grass. Avoidance tactic works. We head back in and it's now time to share our thoughts on the article. Keep my head down like I am still reading the article, or looking for something to share kills time until the bell rings. Success! Now I head to math class.

Math Class starts with a "try this" problem on the board. I sit, open my notebook and pretend to work until the announcement to come to the auditorium comes over on the loudspeaker. I get up, line up near the end of the group, and follow the crew downstairs. I sit next to the wall so I only have one person to deal with, and luckily, it is a boy in my class who is next to his best friend. The two of them converse and I am left in peace. My phone has been vibrating with texts all morning. I quickly check. It is Mom making sure I got to school safely. I quickly respond with a "thumbs up" and put the phone away. I need to stay invisible.

Mr. Turbino, our vice principal, comes on stage and announces our guest speaker. Chuck Finster, a pitcher for the local semi pro baseball team walks on stage. Why do we need to know about baseball? Sports aren't my thing. I don't hate sports, but I am not someone who is very athletic, and don't like watching sports on TV. Anyway, Chuck starts talking about how he had problems in his family, school and with his friends when he was in middle school. He made bad choices, but didn't let them define who he was.

He started talking about how someone in his family had done something really bad and had moved back to Ecuador, his mother's homeland, to avoid going to jail. He wasn't told where the relative had gone and wasn't allowed to have contact with the person ever again. I started thinking about the torn pieces of paper on my floor; the empty words and promises that just wasted the ink and paper. My chest felt tight and I was having trouble breathing. I needed to get out of there...fast!

I climbed over the back of my chair to the empty row behind me, went up to Ms. B, my math teacher, and said I had to use the bathroom because I felt sick. She said yes and I escaped. I stayed in the bathroom for quite a while. Then I took my time and slowly got a drink. I waited outside the door of the auditorium to listen in on what Chuck was talking about. Once I heard it was babble about baseball and college, I stepped back in and went to my seat. Even though my situation isn't exactly like Chuck's when he was in middle school, it was close enough to give me a panic attack. Nobody seemed to notice, so my quick thinking of an escape was a success.

The rest of the day I just went through the motions of "school" and avoidance. At lunch I sat with a couple of friends. I told them I had a headache and stomach ache so they wouldn't bug me about being quiet and not eating too much. I wasn't really lying. My head hurt from over thinking and over planning every move I made so as not to be noticed. My stomach hurt from not eating much.

***

The bell rang. I went to my locker then my bus. I wasn't up for the 5 mile walk home. I sat in the middle by the window and put my backpack on the seat next to me to keep someone from sitting with me. It worked. Finally I have some peace and quiet. Well, at least as quiet as a middle school bus ride typically gets.

I got off at my stop, but didn't go straight home. Walked a block over to the park and sat on a bench to people-watch. It usually soothes me. My mind usually starts making up stories about the people there….where they live…how old they are….what their family life is like. When I got to the last part, my mind started to race back to my family….our lives would never be the same again. I didn't want to think about it, so I stood up and began walking. Only this time I went to Jasmine's house.

Jasmine is my closest friend. Her step dad answered the door and let me in. She was in her room making a Tic Toc video. When I walked in she was trying to get her dog to move his lips while she sang a new popular song. She was using dog treats to try to get him to cooperate, but all he did was drool and jump at the treats. Epic fail. I sat on her bed and took out my phone and pretended to answer a text that didn't exist. She knew me pretty well.

She started with questions like, "Why didn't you sit with me on the bus today?" "Are you mad at me?" "What did I do to piss you off?"

I replied, "This world isn't all about you. You did nothing wrong except ask too many questions just now."

Jasmine replied, "So what is going on?"

I started to cry. She came over and hugged me and said, "Everything will be alright."

Now I am mad…"No it will not...my life is changed forever and I HATE it! You always think everything will be fine. Well that is not how life works. You need to grow up and get real!"

I grabbed my book bag and stormed out of the house. She is so clueless it isn't funny.

Chapter 3

I walked in the side door and into the kitchen. My grandmother and younger brother, Jeancarlos (most people call him JC), were making dinner. The kitchen was filled with the aroma of pasta and garlic bread. My stomach rumbled. I truly felt hungry at that point. I dumped my book bag in my room and headed back into the kitchen. I wanted to check in with my brother and make sure he is OK. With grandma there, I couldn't ask him the questions I wanted to ask, but I would know how he was doing by his body language and whether or not he was talking. He was a really talkative kid when he was happy, but would totally go silent if he was sad or angry. I could always get him to talk, though, when it was just the two of us. He was pretty quiet, but would answer grandma's questions and follow her directions to help with dinner prep. My guess was kind of sad, but not too angry.

   The doorbell rang and grandma went to answer it. It was the FedEx driver dropping off a package. I was in luck. He is from Colombia, like grandma, so they often have conversations for a few minutes.
"How was school today, JC?" I wondered aloud.
"Fine," he replied.
"Were you able to pay attention and get your work done?" I questioned.
"Yup, most of it." he responded.
"Did you talk to anyone at school about what happened this past weekend?" I inquired.
"Well, I told Mr. Christian, the art teacher, that I had a bad weekend. He asked what happened, so I told him. It felt good to tell someone about it." he admitted.
"What did he say to you?" I asked.
"He asked me if I wanted to talk to the guidance counselor at school. I told him no, I just wanted to tell him. He then said he was going to let the guidance counselor and social worker know about what happened so that if I decide to go talk to either of them, that they will know the story already." he explained.
I said, "Were you mad that he was going to tell someone else?"
JC sighed and said, "Not really. It isn't a secret, is it?"
   I explained that it is a personal family matter and we should only talk to certain, trusted people about it. He agreed, saying he wasn't going to tell his friends because they might make fun of him. I got

mad, thinking back to how Jasmine didn't understand and thought everything would be fine without even knowing the issue that upset me. I told JC that keeping the information from his friends is probably a good idea. At that point I heard grandma closing the door and heading back into the kitchen. Our conversation was over....for now.

***

    Mom and Uncle Vinnie pulled into the driveway just as I was setting the table for dinner. That was one of my daily tasks. Mom didn't have her uniform on, so she hadn't been at work. Uncle Vinnie hadn't gone home yet. I had to know what was going on. I was quiet through dinner until Mom started talking about her day at the police station and then with some lawyers. I told her to stop talking. I explained how JC had already shared information with a teacher at school and that the teacher was going to tell the social worker and the guidance counselor. Mom seemed pleased that JC had talked about what happened with someone outside our home. She said some junk about how talking it out with a trusted adult helps you deal with it. I disagreed and told her it is nobody's business what happens in our family. I dumped half of the dinner that was left on my plate into the trash, put my plate in the dishwasher and went to my room.
  I put out my books and notebooks on my bed so if anyone came in it would look like I was doing homework. A knock came about ten minutes into my fake homework session.
"Come in" I mumbled.
It was Uncle Vinnie. He kind of surprised me. I thought for sure it would be Mom.

"Bug...you need to understand." he said softly.
"Understand what?" I replied in a snotty tone, "That Dad had no choice? That Dad did this for his family? That Dad is truly the 'victim' in this situation? Just go away...I don't want to hear any crappy reasoning or kindness towards him. He has WRECKED our family."
Uncle Vinnie sighed, replying, "At some point you will understand, but right now you don't seem ready to try. There will be a time when you accept what has happened and learn from it. The sooner this happens, the quicker you will be able to resume living a normal, happy life."
He walked out and gently closed my door.

My mind started racing with thoughts.... I don't have to accept anything....I will never have a normal life...Happy? What does that feel like? I've forgotten that emotion already.

I felt so alone, yet knew that I was choosing to be alone. I had pushed away everyone who tried to talk to me. Nobody understood how I felt so how could I expect them to say anything that would help me feel better. And to be honest, I don't want to feel better. I just want to sleep and wake up with things back the way they were...Dad, Mom, JC and Grandma here with me in our home. Our home....with Dad not here, will we have to move...will I have to go to another school...will I be away from my friends? I pushed that thought out of my mind enough for me to fall asleep.

***

I woke up around midnight. I was hungry and thirsty. My mouth was nasty because I haven't brushed my teeth. All was quiet. I went into the kitchen and opened the fridge, got a glass of milk and grabbed the chocolate sandwich cookies from the cabinet. I moved slowly so as not to wake up Uncle Vinnie who was, again, sleeping on the couch. I was half way through my glass of milk when I heard soft footsteps from the side room. Grandma shuffled in and sat down across the table from me. She reached into the package of cookies and began her routine way of eating them. Pulled the top off of two, ate the chocolate cookie part, then put the centers together to make a double stuffed version. Slowly she began nibbling on the self made cookie. I didn't pick my head up...didn't want to make eye contact with her. As I finished the last of my milk, she reached over and put her hand atop mine.

   She had soft, small hands. Her fingers had bumps on them from her arthritis. Her touch was gentle and calming. I started to tear up. So did she. She didn't offer me words of advice. She was just there for me. The first physical human contact since everything happened. My heart softened a bit, but only for a moment; then I pulled away and said, "Goodnight".

   I put my glass in the dishwasher, wiped the crumbs from the table and put the rest of the cookies away. I walked to my room, knowing she was watching me until I was out of sight. When I got back in my room I felt like garbage, but blamed it on the fact that I forgot to brush my teeth. Chocolate cookies and toothpaste don't mix well anyway. I lied in bed for another hour with flashbacks of the night I will never forget, then drifted off to sleep.

MY RUINED LIFE

***

 I woke up and the bright light in my room led my eyes directly to my phone to check the time. 9:13am. Shoot. I was late for school. Why didn't my alarm go off? I checked my phone...it was set, weird. I put my books back into my backpack from the night before and changed my clothes. I slept in yesterday's outfit. I stepped out of my room, trying to sneak out the front door unnoticed. Mom was in the kitchen and came out asking, "Breakfast?".
"No thanks...I am late. My alarm didn't go off for some reason."
"Yes it did….you were sound asleep, so I went into your room and turned it off. Figured you could use the extra sleep today. Have some breakfast and I will drive you to school." she replied.
 I didn't want to upset her, so I sat and ate the scrambled eggs and toast she had just made. It tasted so good. I finally had a full stomach and it felt better. Mom wrote a note to excuse my tardiness...saying I had overslept. Not a lie….Mom didn't lie about things. She was honest to a fault sometimes. We drove in silence...no radio playing, no conversation. As we pulled up to the school it hit me...she wasn't at work again. "Mom, do you still have your job?"
"Of course I do. I just took a few vacation days to deal with some legal matters. I go back to work on Saturday."
Some way to spend vacation time….thanks again DAD!
I kissed my Mom on the cheek and thanked her for the ride. None of this was her fault. I can't be mad at her.

Chapter 4

As I went into school the bell rang. 10:05. Third period. I didn't have to think about Ms. Lang wanting to talk because I missed her class. I entered the office, handed the secretary my note. She wrote me a pass to class and off I went.
   I was almost at the door to English Class when Mr. Coster, the school social worker waved me over from his office doorway. What did he want? I slowly walked toward him, with his big grin beaming on his face. Why was he always so happy? Sometimes it annoyed me because how could anyone always seem happy and positive? He pointed into his office and I went in; directly to the comfy blue chair shaped like an opened hand.
 He started with, "How are you feeling these days?" I rolled my eyes....a bad habit I've had since I was a little kid, "What do mean by that?" I replied.
"I heard there was something going on at home, just checking in with you."
"Where did you hear about it?" As soon as I said it, I remembered my conversation with JC.   JC had blabbed about it to Mr. Christian, who I suppose had to report it to guidance. This is the first year we've been in the same school in a few years. I got used to my business being just my business but now whatever JC shares about home will involve me. This really stinks. He needs to learn to keep his mouth shut about private family matters....it is nobody else's business. I will have a few words with him when I get home today.
"This is something I don't want to talk about because it isn't anyone else's business. If I want to talk, it will be with my family, not you or any other

adult outside my home."

I was shocked at how rudely I said this. I am typically a polite and respectful person, but I wanted Mr. Coster to know that he wasn't needed in this situation AND I didn't want him to bug my brother about it either.

My jaw dropped when he replied that he had already called home and spoke with my Mom and she had suggested that maybe I would want to talk to him about how I was feeling. Why did he have to call Mom? Why did SHE think I would want to talk with him about this? Nobody understood how I was feeling, what I was thinking, so they should just back off.

At that point I ended our "session" by saying, "I already missed a few classes and really don't want to fall behind, so can I just have a pass to class now?"

How can he refuse my right to want to be the learning environment?

He obliged and wrote out a pass.

***

It was half way through English Class. I gave my pass to Ms. Tamirro and went to my seat. Jasmine sits next to me. She gave me a hesitant smile. Luckily, she is the type of friend who doesn't hold grudges for long, so our episode at her house yesterday is out of her mind already. I fake grinned back and opened my notebook to try to catch up with the notes on the board about the novel we were reading. I was just finishing them when we moved into groups to discuss the author's purpose for the ending of the novel. I had already read the book over the summer, so I at least knew how it ended. I made a few general comments so I would get "participation credit" from Ms. Tamirro. It is ¼ of our grade so I want to keep that part of my grade up for this marking period. Just before class ended, she announced that our next unit is based on writing short stories.. Good...a break from a long novel for a while. I like to read, but hate being told what to read. This will be a good change for me. The bell rang....off to lunch.

I sat with Jasmine and a few other friends at the large round table. Most of them brought their own lunches. I hadn't made mine, so I got a sandwich from the daily deli option. I wasn't too hungry, but ate a few bites of the sandwich before slugging down my chocolate milk. I took the bag of chips with me for a snack later.

The conversation was about Ms. Lack's upcoming project ideas. Today when I missed class, they came up with topics of modern day issues in the world that kids could help improve. Tomorrow in class, we need to write down our first and second choices and then will be partnered up with someone else who is also interested in that topic for the project. Those of us in the same class chose what topics we would pick with the hope that we would be partnered with each other. All the topics were important, but having a partner you liked was more important to us.

***

The rest of the day I just pulled my "avoidance" tactics until the bus ride home. It was raining and after school sports were canceled so the bus was pretty full by the time I got onto it. All the seats were taken so no chance of getting an empty seat to myself. I sat with Mark, a quiet kid from my math class. He wouldn't try to have a conversation with me. He was very smart, always getting A's on the assignments and tests, but he was VERY shy. It was the safest choice for me.

Across from me was Jessica, the captain of the cheerleading squad. She was pretty on the outside but super cliquey and would only talk with her fellow cheer buddies outside of class. She spent the ride texting, then reapplying her lip gloss. As she did this, we hit a bump and the gloss went across her top lip and into her nose. I grinned and muffled my giggle.

She heard me, looked over at me and commented, "Really mature", then dug into her backpack for a tissue to clean her face. I didn't want to get into anything so I kept my mouth shut, but kept my grin intact.

She looked at me again and snorted, "What's your problem?"

My reply flew out of my mouth before I could stop it. "Gee, didn't know laughing and smiling wasn't allowed on the bus."

She replied, "If you minded your own damn business that would be helpful."

I came back with, "If you saw this happen to me, you would probably laugh, too."

Her comment was, "I don't pay attention to you, so I wouldn't have noticed."

What a ... Nope, I wasn't going to say that word. I am not big on swearing, or confrontation for that matter. At that point the bus was at my stop so I simply stood up and walked off the bus.

What is her problem? She is worse than I thought. She is just mean and nasty on the inside. Glad I only have one class with her each day.

Chapter 5

I went straight home. Felt like helping Grandma prepare dinner. She knew what I needed last night. Just to be there with me for my midnight snack. No pressure to talk. For the first time I thought about how she must be feeling...she is my dad's mother. What is she thinking about all of this going on? How did she feel about her son? I need to be there for her, too. Our family needs to stick together more than ever. I just need to talk to JC about keeping our situation within the walls of our home.

   Nobody on the "outside" needs to know our business. They will just judge who we are based on my dad's actions. It feels weird to love and hate someone at the same time. That is how I feel about my dad right now. It is a battle inside my mind and I know one has to win over the other, but right now, I don't know which emotion has the advantage...the strength to override the other.

***

   After dinner I followed JC into his room to discuss his actions at school.

   As soon as I closed the door behind me, he questioned, "What's up?"

He didn't have a clue why I was there to talk with him. I explained how I had gotten summoned into Mr. Coster's office to share my feelings and perhaps give more information about our family "situation". JC didn't seem surprised, nor bothered by this occurrence.

  He said, "So."

   He just didn't get it. This was a PRIVATE matter

and he was not keeping it private. I explained that the more people that knew about our situation, the more judgement that would come to our family. The more likely our friends and classmates would find out and start asking questions.
Again, his response was, "So".

I don't get the fact that he was so open to discuss all that happened with ANYONE. This was going to be a problem. We weren't on the same page with how to handle this issue. I really love my brother, but he was so wrong in his thinking about all of this. I flat out asked him if he is even upset about this. He said of course he is, but talking about it made him feel better. He also said that when the tension builds and he feels very upset that he goes for a run. He says running helps him sweat out his "worries".

JC is very athletic, so he can run with little effort. I, on the other hand, have asthma and don't do a lot of physical activity besides walking somewhere if I don't have a ride. I felt as if I got nowhere with our conversation because we didn't feel the same way about it. I asked him to please, at least, just keep his conversations between him and adults at school. No sharing this with his buddies who will spread this like wildfire throughout school. He agreed and I went to my room to attempt some math homework.

***

I worked for a while, took a shower after realizing that I hadn't taken one in a few days. I must be smelling pretty bad and just didn't notice it yet. I hope nobody else noticed. As I looked into the mirror I studied my face. I was a true blend of my parents. I had my mom's straight black hair and narrow face. I had my dad's nose, which was turned up slightly at the tip. I also had his piercing deep brown eyes with a few flecks of gold which made them almost shimmer in the sunlight. I also had his smile. I wasn't a super smiley person, but he was, until the last few months. I started thinking about why, maybe, he didn't smile so much, or seem as happy-go-lucky before his choice to wreck our family was made.

My anger started building. I stepped away from the mirror and walked to my room. I put in my airpods and blasted my music, trying to drown out the thoughts about my dad. Music was a great escape I used. It helped me adjust my thinking and focus on the words and blend of instruments. It brought me into another world of my own, where nobody else could be except me. It was working great until a song I usually love came on and as the lyrics unfolded, about a father's life choices hurting his family rang in my ears. My reaction was totally unlike me….I pulled out my earbuds and threw them across my room. One of them broke open. I didn't care.

I turned off my light and tried to sleep. The stupid words from that song kept running through my head. I started to hum. It was nothing particular, just hum to drown out the lyrics. It worked well enough for me to fall asleep.

***

Awake again at midnight...up for a snack. This time I just grabbed an apple from the bowl in the middle of the kitchen table. No grandma tonight to comfort me, but Uncle Vinnie came in from off the couch.

I decided to question him. "Why are you staying

here?"

His response surprised me. "I am here to help support all of you during this tough time."

I reacted with, "What do you mean by support?"

He replied, "Your Mom asked me to come and help you all deal with what is happening. I also explained to my friends that I live with, that I will be staying here for a while so they need to find another person to share the rent with."

I reacted with, "Are you moving in here?"

"For now," he said, " I am going to bring my bed and clothes and share JC's room until we can figure out something more permanent."

My head buzzed with all the thoughts and questions running through it. I wasn't sure if I was happy or not about this change. Uncle Vinnie is nice, but he is used to living with his friends, not someone with kids and an older "mother" figure. I didn't know how to react, so I just said, "Oh" and went back to my bedroom.

Chapter 6

I woke up to my alarm. My first thought...Friday, Finally! I needed a break for my brain and its constant scheming to remain unnoticed at school. I got ready, grabbed a pear to eat at the bus stop. I am not hungry in the mornings, but if I don't eat something I am usually starving by the time I get to school. I don't like the school breakfasts on most days, so a pear will usually keep my stomach from growling until lunch.

I hop on the bus and sit with Jasmine. She looks happily surprised. I haven't sat with her all week. She starts talking about some new show she watched on TV last night and how cute the guy on it is. I don't watch that much TV, but once in a while a new show catches my interest and I keep up with it for at least a few seasons. As she babbles on my mind starts to wander.

I am thinking about how my mom is doing. She's been very quiet and not talking too much more about how things are going to be since the episode earlier this week. I want to be there for her, but don't know what to do to help her. Does she need help? Does she need to be left alone? Does she need to talk things out about how she is feeling, what she is going to do with Dad not working and helping with the bills? Wow. I just thought about that for the first time. She doesn't make enough money to pay all our bills. Will we have to move? Will Uncle Vinnie pay part of the bills since he is moving in? If we have to move, will we all move together? My mind is racing with all of these "What ifs". Jasmine hasn't even noticed that I am not listening to her ramblings. The bus stops at school and I walk toward my homeroom and wave bye to Jasmine quickly so she thinks I was still "with her" from the bus ride.

I walk by the door to my homeroom and into the bathroom. I go into a stall, hang my backpack on the hook and just stand there. My breathing is shallow and I gulp for air. Another panic attack has set in. I try to calm down but my mind is still racing with a million unanswered questions. I start to hyperventilate. I sit on the toilet seat. My head is foggy. The room gets dim and I put my head down to my knees and focus on my breath. I inhale, count to 3 slowly, then exhale. I continued this pattern for a while. The room becomes brighter and I am more aware of noises around me. The bell rings and kids' voices fill the hallway. Homeroom is over....shoot I skipped homeroom. I have to figure out how I can get out of trouble for this.

***

I wait until the bell rings again and the hallway is quiet. I head to Mr. Coster's office. He has another student in there, but when he sees me at the door, he writes a pass for the other kid to go back to class and tells him that he'll set up a meeting time for later in the day to look at his schedule. I am relieved that I didn't have to wait in the hallway for long. I didn't want to see any of my classmates and explain why I am waiting to see Mr. Coster. It is none of their business.

I step into his room and he hands me a cup of water from his bubbler. I took a sip and then said thanks. He just sat there and gave me a few minutes to either decide what I wanted to say or to just calm down, I'm not sure which. I actually needed time for both. The water helped clear my foggy brain. How did he know that would help me? I've got to give him some credit for that move. When he started to smile, I knew he was going to ask me to speak. I was surprised when he gave me paper and pencil. He said nothing.

I started drawing...question marks...large ones, small ones, dark, thick marks. Some I smudged on the paper with my thumb. As I continued to smudge them, I got angry. All of these marks were questions in my head. Nothing was clear to me, so I smudged them until I had a paper full of grey marks that were unrecognizable. I stood up, tore the piece of paper into at least 20 pieces and threw them into the air, all over his office. Mr. Coster didn't move. He had stopped smiling, but didn't look mad, just concerned.

   I didn't know what to do at that point. I truly thought about running out of his office, out of the building, but to where? Where did I want to be? Nowhere; just nowhere with nobody near me. I wanted to have my world filled with nothingness, if there is such a thing. I didn't want to be happy, didn't want to be sad, and didn't want to be angry. I had stunned myself with my actions. My thoughts seemed to just push my body back down into the chair in his office. I wanted him to say something; anything, to break the uncomfortable silence. He just sat there. Letting me be who I had to be at that moment. I don't think he was judging me. Was I losing my mind?

   After a while I picked my head up off the table. My face was tear stricken. Sadness had won in my inner emotional battle. Why was I sad? Who was I sad for? The thoughts started whirling in my mind. Was I sad for my mom, brother, grandmother, dad? NO! I wouldn't allow myself to be sad for my dad. He had made his choices and wrecked many lives starting with our family, now a "broken" family. Was I sad for me? Yes...and my brother, Mom and Grandma.

   We were all victims; just helpless victims because of Dad. I didn't want to love him anymore. I wanted to build a barrier around the part of my heart that cared for dad and not let him or my feelings for him penetrate my heart.

   I made eye contact with Mr. Coster. He was just sitting so patiently. He has a casual smile as if he knew I was thinking things out and that I was helping myself and maybe ready to talk. I wasn't so sure of that. He was nice, but could I really trust him? If he knew, he could tell anyone...everyone...and my world would crumble around me. Maybe I could just talk about my worry for my family and be general about my father's part in all of this, even though he was the leading star in my now dramatic life. I'm sure he knew all that my brother had shared with Mr. Christian, but I wasn't going to bring that information into the conversation I MAY have with him.

I bent down and started picking up the mess I had made throwing the paper all over his office.
He asked, "Can I help you with that?"
I replied, "OK".
As we worked together to clean up the pieces, I said, "Sorry about that."
He said, "No need to apologize. You are cleaning your own mess. That is a first step."
I questioned, "What does that mean?"
He replied, "You'll see."
I was confused. I sighed and said, "I was just so angry, I needed to take action on my anger. The paper was my target at that point."
He came back with, "Why were you angry with the paper?" and kind of smiled.
I half smiled back, knowing he was joking and replied, "I was mad at what was on the paper."
"Why? It was just a bunch of question marks you drew. Why did you smudge them?" he asked.
"I have a lot of questions, but I know there aren't solid answers at this point, or if there is, I am not sure I want to know the answers." I admitted.
"Do you want to share some of those questions with me?" he offered.

"No. You wouldn't know the answers to them anyway." I concluded.

"Who would know the answers?" he questioned.

"Probably my mom may know some of them, but some probably don't have answers….yet." I replied.

"Do you want to call your mom and talk to her? I will gladly step out of the office to give you privacy." he offered.

"No. I am not ready to talk to her about all of this yet. I need to be stronger first." I admitted.

"What do you mean by stronger?" he inquired.

"I am not sure that I know what I mean by that. I need more time." I added.

He then asked something I wasn't expecting.

"Do you want to have me call for your brother so you can discuss your situation together and perhaps I can listen so I understand where you both are coming from?" he suggested.

"No", I replied, "I already talked to him at home privately. He knows to not blab about it to his friends, at least."

"Well," he answered, "If at any time you want to meet with your brother, or even your mother, I can set it up so you can have a third party to listen and weigh in on the discussion if necessary." he offered.

"What do you mean by a third party?" I asked.

"Someone who is not personally involved in the situation your family is going through who may see things in a different way than you or your mother or your brother. They may be able to give some insight about how to manage feelings and connections between people involved. It could be me, or I could set you up for some family counseling outside of school." he explained.

"My family doesn't need counseling. We aren't

crazy. We get along, too." I informed him.
"Counseling is not just for people with mental issues. Actually, most people who go to counseling just need someone to talk to that isn't directly involved in their lives. Those people look at the situation differently and can offer different perspectives on how to manage the stress of the situation and work together to cope with whatever is happening." he offered.
"Well, I don't think my mom would go for that. We are private people who mind our own business and stick together in both good and bad times." I shared.
"If you change your mind, or want me to call you Mom and discuss this option, just let me know. I am going to call and check in with her. I have to let her know you were here with me. I won't tell her about our discussion, just let her know we talked." he notified me.
"Do you have to? I don't want her to worry about me. She has enough to deal with already." I explained.
"Trust me. I will just be casual and tell her that you are stressed, but making good choices by coming to school and taking a break from the day when your mind is more focused on your situation at home by coming to my office and talking with me." he let me know.
"If you have to...I guess it is alright. Can I have a pass to class now?" I half-begged. He gave me a pass and I was about 30 minutes late to English Class.

***

Ms. Tamirro was just finishing reading some short stories that ranged from ones for very young kids to ones I didn't even understand the meaning of, based on the last one I heard her read as I came into class. We then discussed how short stories sometimes gave a big picture, but used fewer words. They also were sometimes written for self expression of a topic or situation you have deep feelings about. We came to the front table and chose a short story to read.. We were to read it through and analyze what message the author was trying to share with the reader. I played it safe and grabbed a short story that I knew was funny. I didn't want any sort of deep, emotional plot or outcome in the story. I had enough "deepness" in my own life right now.

***

The rest of the day was a typical Friday. Last class of the day was History. I haven't really spoken with Ms. Lack since the morning she let me into the building early. She was really busy explaining how our partners were going to be chosen for our projects. We wrote down our first and second choices on slips of paper then put them into the box labeled for the topics we were most interested in.

When everyone was finished, she called up students at random and they had to pick from one of the boxes they had put their names in. If you chose your name, or one that was already chosen by someone else, you got to pick again. If you chose someone whose name wasn't on the board, who hadn't been chosen, then he/she was your partner for the project with the topic that was first or second choice for both of you. When she called on me, I walked up and chose the box for my first choice. Most of my friends hadn't been chosen so I was sure I would get one of them. I reached down into the box and grabbed two slips. I realized this and dropped one back into the box before lifting my hand out. I opened the slip and did a total double take at the name. Jessica Dupont. NO WAY! Before I could throw it back into the box and try again, Ms. Lack carefully took it from my hand. She saw the expression on my face, which said it all....THIS CAN'T HAPPEN! She wrote Jessica's name next to mine on the board. The look on Jessica's face was the same as mine when I first read her name. She was clearly as unhappy about this as I was.

I said to Ms. Lack, "This is not a good match for either of us...can I draw again?"

She replied with a gentle smile, "No, that wouldn't be fair to everyone else who has accepted their first pick."

I replied, "But they didn't pick HER."

Ms. Lack reminded me that Jessica and I had chosen the same topic so if we just focused on the work to be done on the topic we BOTH chose, then there should not be an issue. I walked slowly back to my seat in total defeat. Jessica just put her head in her hands and stared down at her desk. When everyone was finished choosing their partners, Ms. Lack handed out the rubric for grading on the project so it would be clear as to how we could get a good grade. I don't know what kind of student Jessica was, so I truly had no idea how the work part of this would go. Next week we would start our planning in class then we could meet with our partners during common study hall time or before or after school in the library or at each others' homes.

No way was she coming to my house. Didn't want her to have any hint as to why my father was never around. I could lie and say my parents aren't together, but I am a terrible liar and always seem to get caught when I lie, which is not very often. Well, so much for a brain-break for the weekend. Now I had to figure out how she and I could do this project together without spending any time together. As I read through the rubric, it was not going to be easy to produce a good project if we truly didn't work together in person. More complications...just what I don't need.

Chapter 7

Jessica wasn't on the bus for the ride home. She was probably at cheer practice. I sat with Jasmine. She was talking about what her and Mark might do for a project. Mark was sitting behind us, but had his earbuds in, so didn't hear a word about Jasmine's plans. She and Mark weren't friends, but he was nice enough and definitely smart enough to be sure they would get a good grade, no matter what Jasmine planned. He is the type that would let her take the lead on what to do, but he would make adjustments to be sure they got an A. She told me she was surprised that I reacted so badly to getting Jessica for a partner.
"She isn't THAT bad", she remarked. She didn't know about the scene on the bus earlier in the week between me and Jessica. I didn't bring it up.
I just said, "Well, she is just so into her own group of friends and cheerleading that I don't know when we will be able to work on the project together."
Jasmine suggested that maybe we could work before school. That would mean me having to walk to school in the morning because tomorrow Mom

started back at work, so she leaves by 6am. That is just too early for me. The library doesn't even open until 7am. I would have to wait outside for 45 minutes until the building opened.

***

I got off at my stop and walked home with JC. He didn't have track practice on Fridays because they had most of their meets on Thursdays, so the coach gave them Friday's to have fun with their friends, then back to the school track on Saturday mornings. JC would run from home to school on Saturdays to "warm up" for track. He had so much energy.

I asked JC if he minded Uncle Vinnie moving in. He said it didn't matter to him. He seemed so unaffected by all these changes in our lives. As we walked into the house, my mom was in the kitchen making homemade pizza. My favorite! She didn't make it often, but it was awesome when she did. She asked us to sit down at the table while she worked. Oh no…. What now?

"I need to speak with you about a meeting I had with the lawyer's today." This couldn't be good. "It looks like your dad has agreed to a plea bargain for when the trial begins. He is willing to describe the entire incident for a reduced sentence."

JC spoke up, "What does that mean?"

"It means that if he cooperates and gives all the information the lawyers and judge asks for, that he will not have to be in jail for as long."

JC replied, "How long will he have to be in jail?! He didn't do anything compared to the other two guys involved."

My Mom responded with, "Your dad was a part of this incident. Right now there are no witnesses, so if

your dad helps put the pieces of this together, his reward is a lighter sentence." It was my turn to speak up, "So Dad has to snitch on his friends?"
 Mom's reaction was, "He is not snitching...he is doing what he thinks is best for him and our family. The lawyers promised to protect him."
 I said, "Right now I don't care if they protect him...he deserves what he gets for ruining our family." I stood up to leave.
 My mom raised her voice, "Your dad made a bad choice. He knows that. He is willing to do what he needs to be back here with us. We need to support him with this decision."
 I spoke back, well, yelled back at Mom, "Why do we have to do anything for him? He is a criminal! I don't want him back here pretending nothing ever happened. He has messed up this family so badly and thinks at any point he can just waltz out of jail and back home with us? He is out of his mind!"

***

 I hadn't realized that was how I was feeling until the words flooded from my mouth. I stormed out of the kitchen to my room and slammed my door shut. Mom didn't follow me. She knew I needed to calm down before I would be ready to talk to her, or listen to her. About 20 minutes later I could smell the pizza baking. Damn! I wanted to go out and get some. Not now. I'm sure she was ready to lay into me for yelling at her and talking that way about Dad. I don't get it. How can she be so supportive of him when he is putting her, and all of us through this? Love does dumb things to people, I guess. How can she still love him? How can she talk about letting him back with us when his sentence is over?

How long will he be in jail? What are his "friends" who are also in jail going to think of him when he rats them out? My mind was in a total spinning mode when a knock came. "Mom, I am not ready to talk yet." The response was not what I expected.

It was grandma. "It's just me, honey. Can I come in?" How can I say no to Grandma? I opened the door. She shuffled in and sat in my desk chair. She always looks so little and cute. She was only 4'9" and pretty slim. When I looked at her now, she looked older. She looked tired. She looked frail. Had she lost weight? Why wasn't her hair arranged perfectly, like always? She had no make-up on. She was wearing slippers. She only wore slippers when she got up during the night.

"Grandma, you look different." I commented.

"How so?" she asked.

"You just don't look like YOU." I remarked.

"I am just sad, sad for everyone. My son made some bad choices and it has hurt so many people. Some I love, and some I don't even know." I walked over, bent down and hugged her. When I did, I started bawling like a baby. She was crying too, but quietly. She let the tears run down her cheeks and drip into her lap as I let go of her to face her. I blew my nose, offered her a tissue and we wiped away our tears.

"Grandma, I am so confused. I love Dad but I don't want to love him. I can't love him right now. I just keep hoping to fall asleep and wake up to this being a terrible nightmare, or a huge misunderstanding and have Dad back here with us."

Grandma softly replied, "This is reality. It is not a happy part of our lives, but it is real. We need to help each other out. We need to love your Dad. He needs us now more than ever. When I spoke with him yesterday, all he kept saying was 'I'm so sorry'".

I looked up from the floor…"What? You talked to him? How did they let you talk to him?"

"He is allowed to call home once a week for 5 minutes until the trial. He is not allowed to speak about anything that happened related to his arrest. He called while you and JC were at school. Your mom and Uncle Vinnie were meeting with the lawyers. I was the only one home. When I heard his voice I thought someone was playing a cruel joke on me, pretending to be him. Once he started with the "I'm sorry" and crying, I knew it was really him. I just let him finish what he had to say about how bad he felt about everything and how he had disappointed me and let down his family who loved him and counted on him to be there for them. It was really sad. He is hurting in so many ways. He is very sorry about the choices he made and is now ready to face the consequences and do whatever it takes to get back home with all of us as soon as possible."

The words took a few minutes to sink in. My father, cry? No. It was an act. It was simply an act to get us to feel sorry for him because he is stuck in jail. The concrete wall around my heart was getting bigger. I would NOT feel sorry for him. I would NOT let his phone call play on my heartstrings like it did to my grandma. Who was HE to call here and do this? If I answer the phone and it is him, I will just hang up. I don't want to hear his voice nor his sad story because I am living it as a VICTIM of his actions. I can't get mad at grandma, though. She is always routing for the underdog in a story or a movie. My dad is playing on her emotions. He has known her all his life, so he knows how to worm his way into her heart. What a jerk. Just stay and rot in jail. Leave us alone to start our new life without you.

***

Mom came in later that night. She put a plate of her pizza on my desk and a glass of iced tea. She said nothing. I said nothing. I knew the pizza was a peace offering, but couldn't respond to her yet. The next morning Mom knocked on my door and announced that we were leaving to run errands in 30 minutes. I didn't think anything of it until I was back in my room after a shower. She is supposed to be back at work today. I will question her while we run errands. After a quick bite to eat, we hopped in the car. Grandma was with us. On Saturdays she goes to an assisted living complex to visit a few of her friends. She usually drives herself, but her car is in the shop getting new brakes. I said nothing until we had dropped her off.

"Mom, why aren't you at work? Weren't you supposed to be back today?"
She replied, "Yes, but I was advised by my supervisor to take a leave of absence until the trial is over. I will be meeting with lawyers and having to take time off of work to do that. I also want to be around for you and JC more while this is going on. The police report is going to hit the papers soon. When that happens, everyone will know and there will be questions asked of all of us from the rest of our family and friends. We have enough money saved and with Uncle Vinnie paying part of the rent and grandma's pension, we can manage for a while."
I responded with, "So we won't have to move?"

She smiled, "No, not yet at least. If the rent stays the same and we don't have other issues that cost a lot, we can manage until after the trial. Then I will be able to return to work."

"When will the trial be?" I questioned.

"Probably not for about two or three months." she responded.

"Why does it take so long?" I wondered.

"The police have to do a full investigation and the lawyers have to prepare their arguments to support their clients. This takes time. There are other things going on that they have to attend to as well so we just have to wait our turn." she explained. We went to the post office to get our mail from the PO Box, then to the pharmacy to pick up a prescription. I thought we were headed home, when Mom turned in the opposite direction.

***

"Where are we going now?" I wondered aloud. Mom said nothing. She kept driving. Something wasn't right and she didn't want me knowing what was going on. I pushed further, "Where are you driving us?" Again, she just kept driving. I didn't want to get her mad again, so I just sat quietly and waited. I waited until we pulled into the correctional facility. "NO WAY!!!!" I yelled. I lost it….no control of myself. "You are out of your mind if you think I am going in there!" I screamed.

Mom parked the car. She turned off the motor and faced me. She had this serious look in her eyes. "We are going in to see your father. He can have a visitor for 10 minutes on Saturdays. He needs to see us and know we are alright."

"I am not alright", I choked out, "My dad is in jail

and has deserted his family."

"He has not deserted us. He messed up. Big time. He knows that. I thought I could help his stress by at least being able to see you in person. He told me he wanted to see you and JC to know that you are both OK."

"Well, too bad for him. I am NOT going in and you can't make me. I don't have to do this. I will not do this EVER." I retorted.

"Well, I am going in to see him. He needs us." she stated.

"He made his bed, so now he can lie in it. Alone." I used one of my grandma's sayings, with my part at the end. My mom stepped out of the car, told me she was locking me in while she visited. I knew that if I tried to get out the alarm would go off, so I sat. It was my idea of a compromise. I didn't have to go see him, but I wasn't going to take off on her while she was in there. Off she went...and so I sat. I played a few games on my phone.

During the second game, a text from Jasmine popped up. "What's up? Where are you? I just stopped at your house to see if you wanted to walk to the market with me to pick up chocolate chips then come back to my house to make cookies."

I wasn't about to tell where I was. That would be just plain stupid.

I replied with, "I am running errands with my Mom" (not a lie) I will have her drop me off at your house on our way home." This gave me a chance to be away from Mom for a while. I was not happy about her trying to trick me into seeing Dad. Mom returned about 30 minutes later.

I asked, "If you can only see him for 10 minutes, what took so long?"

Her reply was, "If you came with me, you would know."

A minute later, she explained that there were other people waiting ahead of her, so you have to wait your turn because they only let a few inmates out of their cells at a time. At the word, "inmate" I felt sick. My Dad was an inmate. I told her to pull over. She did just in time. I puked on the side of the road. That one word had such an effect on me. She asked what was wrong. I told her my stomach was upset from the banana I ate this morning. It must have been bad. She bought it. I lied and got away with it. I told her I felt better, so she dropped me off at Jasmine's house. I told her I would be home later but didn't know when, so I would text her. She was happy with that, so off I went.

***

At Jasmine's house we cleared off her island countertop and got busy making the cookies. We had fun and I almost forgot about my problems. Now I was surrounded by them...home with Dad issues and at school with Jessica issues. We had just taken out the last dozen from the oven when the local news interrupted the football game Jasmine's brother was watching. The newsman said, "The clerk from Gossling's Grocery Mart that was shot in the robbery two weeks ago has died. Joseph Gossling, owner of the Mart was robbed at gunpoint, then shot twice after handing over a small amount of cash to three gunmen. The investigation has now changed from armed robbery to a homicide. We'll have more on this story at Newswatch Update at 6pm tonight."
I couldn't believe what I just heard. I ran into

Jasmine's bathroom and started hyperventilating and sobbing.
She heard me and came to the door. "Are you sick?" she questioned.
"Yes. I am texting my mom to come get me. I will be OK." I replied. I texted Mom. She replied immediately and was at Jasmine's house in 5 minutes. I waited outside for her, telling Jasmine I didn't want to get anyone in her house sick with whatever bug I had. She bought it and let me wait on my own on her front porch.

***

As mom pulled up, I ran to the car and jumped in. "Mr. Gossling died. I just heard it on the news. That means Dad is going to jail forever. My father is a murderer." My voice cracked as I forced the words out of my mouth.
"Wait. Don't rush into judgements. I know this is bad, but you don't know all the details of what happened. The news reports what they were told. There is more to this whole situation, based on what the lawyers have explained to me based on what your father told them. Please just try to calm down. We need to have a long talk when we get home. JC is home from track practice and I want you both to hear what I know." mom explained.
"I don't think I am ready for this, Mom. I have so many different feelings about all of this. I don't know if I can handle all the details." I explained between breaths.
"I really think knowing what is going on will help you manage your feelings. Some of it will be hard to accept, but Grandma, Uncle Vinnie and I are here for you and your brother. Just talk to us. Please ask

us the questions that are running through your head and creating all this stress for you. We will work together. We will all be OK." she spoke softly, which comforted me a bit.

Chapter 8

When we went into the house, Mom went to get JC from his room. Grandma and Uncle Vinnie came into the living room from the kitchen. I sat in the rocking chair. The rocking motion always soothed me, ever since I was a baby, according to Mom. Whenever I was upset or sick, she or Grandma would sit me in their laps and rock until I felt better. Dad actually rocked me a few times when I was really sick with the flu when I was in first grade. He worked a lot, so wasn't always around much. Mom and Grandma also took the "night shift" when JC or I were sick so Dad could sleep. He worked construction so he was always tired after work and needed to keep up his strength for his job. Sleep and great food were keys to help him stay healthy.

JC emerged from his room and we were all sitting in the living room together for the first time since Dad left. Mom had brought in a pitcher of iced tea for us to share. We drank it year round and it was homemade with a squeeze of lemon to make it a little sour. I didn't take a glass, even though my throat was dry from the sobbing I had done at Jasmine's and on the way home. Grandma sat very still with a somber look on her face and her hands folded in her lap. Uncle Vinnie sat in the recliner with a look of worry on his face. JC kept looking around the room, avoiding eye contact with all of us. Mom focused on me, cleared her throat, took a sip of the tea and began.

"What I am going to share has to stay within these walls. This is information the lawyers have shared with me that relates to the trial and the fate of your father. Your grandma and Uncle Vinnie already know this but wanted to be here to help me support you and JC. I wasn't planning on sharing all of this with both of you, but with the incident being publicized more, you need to know your dad's side of the story. The news you heard today while at Jasmine's is part of what happened, according to your father's version that he has shared. Yes, Mr. Gossling was shot. Yes, he has died. Yes, there were three men there, but only one had a gun, and it was NOT your father. He didn't know Jake very well. Jake had the gun and shot Mr. Gossling. Your dad did not know he had a gun. He met Jake at work. He didn't know the other guy, someone named Samuel, who was a friend of Jake's. After working a double shift three weeks ago, the supervisor told the crew that next month there were going to be major cutbacks in the company. No overtime, and only 30 hours of work would be the maximum allowed. Some workers were getting laid off. Jake was one of them. Your dad was not losing his job, but with the work time being so restricted, he would not be making enough to afford all our bills, even with my salary included. Jake told him he knew how to make some fast cash. It is something he had done before and gotten away with. Dad agreed to help him if they split the money. He didn't know Samuel was going to be there until they got to the store. They put on masks, went in and demanded the money from the safe and the cash register. Mr. Gossling had been robbed by Jake before, but had cooperated and given him the money. This time was different. Mr. Gossling had a gun. He pulled it out and told them to leave. As your dad was backing out of the store, Jake pulled out his gun, shot Mr. Gossling, opened the cash register and took the money. Your dad was by the entrance, and when he saw what had happened, he ran. He did not take the money or drive away with Jake or Samuel. He ran into the woods and stayed there for hours, listening to the sirens. The police got Jake's license plate on the security camera that Mr. Gossling had installed a week before this happened. The police caught Jake a few hours later and took him to the police station. The camera also saw the two other men involved. The next day, when being questioned, Jake gave Samuel's and your dad's names to the police. He told the investigators that your dad was the one who shot Mr. Gossling. Thankfully the police recovered the gun he threw out the window of his car along the riverbank. Your dad's choice to run is helping his case, because he couldn't possibly have thrown the gun where they found it if he was on foot. It was too many miles away from the crime scene. They just have to prove that he didn't run to an area where there was a vehicle for him to use. That night he got home about 3am. His shift had ended at midnight. When I woke up to him coming through the door, he told me he went out with a friend to a bar after work. I was suspicious about that because he seemed so nervous and had mud and leaves on his work boots. I was planning on speaking with him about this the next day after work. He woke up and told me he was sick and called out of work, but I went to work. That next night before we had a chance to talk….well, you all know what happened then."

I didn't want to think about what happened that night. It was the worst night of my life. I didn't know what to say to Mom. I looked over at JC. He just sat there, straight faced, looking out the side window. The questions started flooding my mind…shouting to be heard from inside my brain. Why did Dad think robbing someplace was a good choice? Did he even think about what could happen? What if Mr. Gossling had shot him? Was he even telling the truth in his story to the lawyers? Could he have been the one with the gun, and the other guy is right? I had more questions coming, but Mom interrupted them by saying, "Your dad is a good, hard working man who loves his family. He did this because he really thought it would help us, at least until he could figure out what to do about getting more work. I know it is hard to process all of this information at once, but you needed to know. The police have been quiet because they haven't finished their investigation, especially because the stories don't match. The news has bits and pieces of this and is sharing only what they know so far. The lawyers told me to expect your dad's name in the police report very soon. At that point many people will know what they read, and may make assumptions of what else happened. The kids at school will only know what their families share with them. Some of it will be true, but there may be a lot of rumors along with the small amount of facts that will be published. You need to prepare yourselves for comments and questions from your friends and classmates that will follow.

I stood up.

Mom said, "Please sit down so we can talk about

this."

I replied, "I don't know what to say. I have so many feelings about so many different parts of this whole situation, I need time to think. Alone." I turned and went to my room. When I got there, I didn't know whether to sit, lie down or put my fist through my wall. I just sort of stood there for a while, replaying the words shared by my Mom as if a movie was playing in my head. Where the characters were actors and the scene was a set of painted plywood objects for the background and the noise was piped in from a machine off to the side of the set with speakers throughout the staging.

Chapter 9

I sat at my desk in my room and pulled out my homework. I wanted a distraction, an escape from all that was happening. I buried myself in my science lab follow up sheet. We had done a cool lab assignment about splitting molecules. I had to respond to what happened during our lab and WHY I thought the result was valid or invalid with an explanation. I spent about forty five minutes finishing it up. I pulled out my laptop and started looking at articles about food insecurity, both locally and internationally. That was the topic both Jessica and I had chosen, bringing us together as partners on the project.

    I chose the topic because Grandma used to tell JC and I stories about how she grew up without a lot of food at home when she was a little girl living in Colombia. She actually fought a stray dog on a city street for a piece of bread the dog had grabbed from someone's sandwich at an outdoor cafe. The dog bit her. She has the scar on her thumb from that battle. She ended up with half the piece, so it was somewhat of a victory. She also used to go through trash cans in alleys behind markets and restaurants. Whatever she found she would bring home for her five younger brothers and sisters. Once she turned 12 years old, she got a few odd jobs sweeping back rooms and organizing storage areas for markets. The owners would either pay her in cash or with food. She usually got enough food or bought enough food so her family had at least two meals each day. Her dad worked at a coffee plantation. It was long hours and didn't pay a lot. Her mom stayed at home and took care of her elderly parents who had health issues. There weren't any rehabilitation centers or assisted living facilities like there are now that help older or disabled people. It was up to families to take care of the elders.

The stories my grandma told me really stuck in my head. I knew that it was important to appreciate the food we had and not be wasteful. Luckily, our town has a food bank and some food pantries that help people who need food and health supplies. Last year I visited a farm that my grandma's friend owns. He donates half of his crops each year to homeless shelters and food pantries. He told me I could work with him next summer if I'd like. It would be really great to do that. Our family now is not lacking food.

***

Two years ago, though, my mom lost her job. The nursing home she worked in lost their licensing because of workers not wearing their masks during COVID. She was compliant and had a good work record, but it took her about 6 months to find another job. Grandma wasn't living with us yet, so with just dad's paycheck we could only afford rent, gas for the car, heat and electricity. We had to give up cable TV and wifi for that time. We also didn't have much food, so we would go to the food bank and food pantry at our church to get food, soap, and other necessities to help us through the bad time. Once mom went back to work and grandma moved in with us and shared some of her money towards our bills, we didn't need to go there anymore. We got back cable TV and broadband.

Every other Wednesday my mom goes after work and spends a few hours helping at the food pantry. She takes turns bringing me or JC with her. It is very rewarding. Some people that come to get food are very talkative and express how grateful they are to you. Others are very quiet and almost seem embarrassed to be needing food. I always want to try to help them understand that they don't need to be embarrassed. I want to encourage them to do the best they can to help themselves and their families but if they need help with some of the important things in life, like a place to live, clothes to wear or food to eat, to stay proud of how hard they are trying and to not give up.

***

I had found a few interesting articles and was halfway through reading the last one when JC knocked and came into my room. He said it was time for dinner. Uncle Vinnie had made chicken marsala. It was his first time making it, so grandma "coached" him. JC had already set the table so we sat right down. I took a small portion, claiming I wasn't very hungry. I actually was, but if it tasted bad, I didn't want to have to eat a lot of it. We didn't throw away food because that was wasteful (another lesson my family lives by because of what happened a few years ago). I took a small bite. It was actually really good. The next few bites confirmed that Uncle Vinnie did a great job making dinner. We all complimented him. He thanked grandma for her help. He said that while he was here with us, as long as grandma was willing, he would like her to help him learn how to be a good cook. He said, since he loves food, he might as well be good at preparing tasty meals. He asked if he could make our dinners every Saturday night.

He doesn't have enough time during the week. He had taken a few days off, but is returning to work at the warehouse (he is a supervisor for shipping), he didn't have time during the week to make a meal unless we liked eating at 9 pm. We all agreed that he could have Saturday nights for his meal making practice. We were willing to be his "guinea pigs", especially if he made meals as good as this one. Nobody talked about Dad during dinner. Probably a good idea, because I know that if I get upset about something, the first thing that happens is my stomach starts to turn and gurgle and I totally lose my appetite. After dinner I cleaned up the kitchen and loaded the dishwasher, then started it.

***

I sat back at the table, looking through the mail that had arrived this afternoon. There was a letter addressed to me. There was no return address...and no stamp, for that matter. Where did this come from? As I opened it, it hit me…..that writing on the front was Dad's! I tore it up and threw it into the garbage. Well, that is what it was to me. His words were garbage, just like his choices.

How did that letter get here? After thinking for a few minutes it hit me....Mom. She went to see Dad today. She must have brought it home. But why did she put it with the mail? There was only one way to find out. I walked into the living room where she was watching TV and stood in front of her. "Did you bring something home for me and put it with the mail today?" I questioned.

"Yes." she calmly replied. "Did you read it?" she wondered.

"Nope, I just threw it away. I'm sure the words are nothing but trash, so that is where it belongs." I stated. "And why was it in with the mail?" I demanded to know.

"I put it on the counter on top of the mail. I was going to give it to you later, but it must have gotten mixed in with the mail. You usually don't pay attention to the pile of mail, so I thought it would be OK there until I was ready to give it to you." she explained.

"Well next time, you'll have to hide it better, I guess." I commented sarcastically.

"I wasn't hiding it. I was waiting for a good time." she said in a serious tone.

"From now on, just save me the trouble and throw it away. Or tell that loser father of mine to stop wasting his time trying to make up for what he did." I responded in my best smart-ass way. Mom stood up, faced me, and slapped me across the face, hard. I stood still, like a statue in front of her, refusing to react, emotionless. Then a smirk grew through my lips.

I found my next response, saying, "Gonna have to

hit harder than that if you want me to react."

As Mom reached her arm back and I braced for a second hit, Uncle Vinnie jumped up and grabbed her arm.

"This isn't the way to handle this", he spoke firmly to Mom. "You are better than this. You are letting her words control you."

I slowly stepped back and turned to leave. I caught Grandma out of the corner of my eye. She was crying softly. What had I just done? I slowly walked to my room and quietly shut and locked my door. Nobody was coming in....until **I** was ready.

All was quiet by about 11pm. I unlocked my door slowly and stepped out of my room. I wasn't hungry or needed to use the bathroom, I was simply sick of looking at the walls of my room. It wasn't until I was at the front door that I realized I had grabbed my jacket and was going out for a walk. My Mom would freak out if she knew. I always had to be home by 10pm and couldn't walk alone on the streets after dark.

***

Our neighborhood had some sketchy characters living in it. We weren't sure why they were sketchy, but you definitely got that vibe from them when you saw them. They hung out on the streets after dark and sometimes got noisy enough that the police were called to settle them down late at night. As I reached the end of my street, I looked back at the house. Something was missing. Mom's car was gone.

Where did she go? I didn't even hear her leave the house. I started thinking about where she could be. I walked four blocks, took a left, then two more

blocks. Nope, she wasn't at our Cousin Carla's house. I walked all the way to school, then past the town hall. As I turned down a side road I spotted a car that looked like Mom's halfway down the street. As I got closer, I was right . What is my Mom doing here? Who lives here? I decided to check it out from the yard. It was a cool night so the windows were closed. I could hear muffled voices from inside where a few lights were on. One of the voices was Mom's. I couldn't recognize the words, but she was talking with another woman. Who was it? I don't know anyone who lives on this street. As I rustled through some leaves, a dog from next door started barking. Luckily it was in a fenced yard. Unfortunately, the dog got the attention of the person who owned it. He came to the front door and saw me in the shadows of the neighbor's house. "Who are you? What are you doing?" he demanded to know. I panicked. I started running through yards. I tripped on a fallen branch and fell. As I picked myself up, I could feel the blood running down my leg. I had skinned my knee. I haven't done that since I was about 7 years old playing tag on the playground at recess.
 I heard a car from the other end of the road. I hid up against a large tree, slowly moving around it to stay out of sight. It was a police car, driving very slowly. The officer looked out the window. What was she looking for? Not me? I am minding my own business. Or am I? I was in someone else's yard late at night. Did that guy call the police on me? How silly. Or was it? I was kind of creeping around someone's house in a neighborhood I don't really know. Once the cruiser had left the street I continued walking. I was going to head home at this

point. It was about 1:30 am, WAY past my curfew. It took me a while to get back home. I went to open the front door. It was locked!

Chapter 10

I didn't have my key. No way was I going to bang on the door and wake anyone up. I would be in more trouble than I've ever been. Think. Think. I jumped. Something just rubbed against my leg! I almost screamed. I scrambled onto the railing of the porch. When I looked down I almost laughed. It was Murray, my neighbor's cat. He was very friendly and loved to be out at night to hunt mice and chipmunks.
 I saw headlights from the end of my road. Mom! Hide! I fell off the railing onto the porch. If I tried to get off the porch I would get caught...there wasn't time to escape. I crawled behind the rocking chair in the dark corner. I wove my way through the spider webs behind it. They stuck to my face and arms. Hopefully the spiders were off hunting somewhere. I am NOT a fan of spiders.
 My breath was quick and noisy. I could hear my heartbeat over my wheeze. I didn't have my inhaler. I hadn't expected to be running, or hiding, for that matter. I was sure my mom would catch me. She would hear me. I had to cough, but fought to keep it in my throat. I could feel it building...swelling inside my neck. I tried to swallow it back down, but couldn't. It was stuck there. I had to hold every muscle in my body totally still while my mind was totally freaking out. Mom came up the steps. She opened the screen door, put her key into the lock and turned. She was in. Or was she? Her key fell on

the porch floor, less than 5 feet away from me. She bent down to pick it up. Success! She stood, pushed the door open and went in. I was safe, for now, but still stuck outside...as she locked the door behind her.

What now? If I sleep on the porch until morning, I am sure to be caught. My window...let me see if I can open one of my windows. I sneak around to my window. There are bushes in front of it. I slide between them and the house. I get the screen pushed up with little effort. Now I try to open the window. It is a big leaded glass that is very heavy. I push up on it. Nothing. My own doing...I always keep it locked when it is closed. I get nervous about someone trying to get into the house through an unlocked window. I am my own burglar. Well, am I really, if I am just trying to break into my own house? I dismiss that thought.

I saw a dim light through JC's window. It is flickering. He is playing video games! Success! I will knock on his window, get his attention and he'll let me in. I knock lightly. No response. I try to peek through the crack where the shades meet. He moves just enough for me to see him. Shoot! He has his ear buds in. Of course he does...if not, he may wake someone up and get in trouble for being up so late playing video games.

No use. I've got to sleep on the porch. As I try to get comfy on the wooden floorboards my mind finally devises a plan. When the newspaper is thrown on the porch I will pick it up and bang against the door. When grandma hears it (she is always up when the paper gets delivered) and comes to investigate, I will explain that I got up early, went to get the paper for her and locked myself out of the house. Perfect! Totally satisfied with my prepared story, I fell asleep.

***

I toss and turn a bit, but am awakened about 5:15 AM when the paper hits the front porch. I jump up, grab it and rattle the front door. As if totally planned, my grandma comes to check out the noise. There I am, holding her newspaper. I give her my story. She smiles, lets me in and then stands in front of me, blocking me from heading to my room.
  "What's wrong, Grandma?" I so innocently ask.
  "Why are you wearing yesterday's clothes and your coat?" she responds.
  Crap....I didn't even think of that. I stand there, silently, trying to come up with another lie. Part two of my deceitful plan. I need more time to think. She isn't buying what I said for a minute.
  I decided to "tattle" on Mom with the hopes it would take the heat off of me. I told her how I went out looking for Mom (only a partial lie, perhaps) and that she was at someone's house we didn't even know and came home really late. I skipped the part about the police and hiding and trying to get in through my window and JC up super late playing video games. I told her I had forgotten my key but didn't want to disturb anyone's sleep, so I waited until morning on the porch.
   She stood in front of me, still, with her arms folded, shaking her head slowly back and forth, letting me know that she disapproves of my actions.
  "Your mother is an adult and can go out if she wants to. There were two other adults here with you and JC. There was no need to follow her or look for

her. You are not her keeper. You need to mind your own business." she lectured. Followed by, "And what you did was very risky. There are parts of this town that are quite dangerous, especially after dark. A young girl wandering around alone is a prime target in many ways. You are VERY lucky you didn't have a problem worse than you ever imagined. I need you to PROMISE me you will never do anything like that again. I will not be able to sleep at night if I can't trust you to stay home all night."

She was right, but I wasn't going to tell her that. My compromise was that I would go out, but let someone know and carry my phone. She didn't agree. In fact, she went and woke up my mom to be part of the conversation. She totally snitched on me. Maybe that is where Dad gets it from.

Mom emerged from her room, rubbing her eyes then tying her bathrobe. She had only gotten a few hours of sleep herself. Grandma looked angrier than before. I didn't like her looking like that, but I wasn't going to give her any reason to soften up. I held my ground with my mother and my "compromise". Then I started questioning her as to where SHE was and who was SHE with.

"It is NONE of your business, but I have nothing to hide. I went to my friend's house. We work together. She is someone I can talk to that isn't personally involved, except through what she knows about our situation. We have always been able to talk about our families and issues that come up that make us worry, make us sad, anger us or give us a reason to be happy."

"Is she a therapist?" I ask, remembering how Mr. Coster explained what a therapist did. This sounded just like it. An outsider listening and helping give different perspectives is NOT necessary.

"No. She is just a friend with a lot of incite and good advice about life situations. She has been through a lot in her life and has learned some valuable lessons, both good and bad. She helps me unscramble my thoughts which takes away some of my stress."

"Oh. I just figured you would talk to me or JC, Uncle Vinnie or Grandma about how you were feeling." I responded.

"I can, sometimes, but I don't want to put my worries and fears on any of you. We all have so much to deal with right now." she replied.

At that point Mom turned to me and said, "You could greatly help us all if you stop doing foolishly dangerous things like walking around town in the middle of the night."

I could see her point. If someone realized I was gone last night there would have been hell to pay today. Much worse than what is happening now.

I responded with, "If you don't slap me, I won't leave at night. Deal?"

"Deal", Mom replied followed by "I'm so sorry. I've never hit you before and will never hit you again."

We sealed our promises to each other with a hug. Grandma's anger had vanished and was replaced with a smile. I headed to my room to get some more sleep. The porch floor was not a favorable place to sleep. I don't think I'll be doing that again anytime soon.

***

I woke up to my stomach rumbling. I was so hungry. I took a quick glance at my phone. It was

1:00pm. All that walking (and attempt at running) along with skipping breakfast left me famished. I strolled into the kitchen and opened the fridge. I grabbed the makings of a good turkey sandwich and sat at the table to assemble it. I had just taken my first bite when JC walked in. He still looked half asleep.
"That's what you get for playing video games all night." I remarked.
"How would you know if I was gaming all night?" he replied.
"Just a guess", I casually answered.
 I didn't want him to know I was looking in his window in the middle of the night. He freaks out over stuff like that. He doesn't need anything more on his mind right now. I may share what happened last night with him someday, but not today. He sits across from me and makes himself a sandwich.
 He looks just like Dad did when he was a boy. Grandma has pictures of Dad on her wall along with his two sisters. My Dad's hair is longer than JC's but his build and face are identical. When JC was little, we used to show him pictures of Dad and he thought it was himself. He can tell now because of the age of the photos and the different hairstyles and clothing. Both of them can eat whatever they want and stay skinny. Not me. I gain weight easily, so I am careful not to eat too much junk food. I probably wouldn't have as much of a problem if I exercised more. Gym class and walking are my forms of exercise. Running last night was a joke. I didn't get 30 feet before I tripped and fell.
 As I thought about that, I realized my knee was stiff. I could feel the dried blood caked on the surface of my skin. I put my dishes in the

dishwasher and told JC to please put away the food because he wasn't finished yet. He had started making a second sandwich. I went into my room to change from my clothes since I didn't change when I went to bed this morning. My knee was all bloody and kind of stuck to my jeans. Ouch. I reopened part of the cut. I reached for a few band aids in my desk drawer to cover it.

When I opened the drawer there was a note. It was Mom's handwriting. I started to read it. She was apologizing again for slapping me. She explained how she is having a difficult time trying to be supportive of Dad when she is so angry with him. She explained to me that her anger is not because of what he did, but the fact that he didn't come to her and talk about how he was feeling and try to work out another solution together. She told me that this is an awful experience for all of us, but she wants me to learn from this situation. She explained that there are going to be lots of ups and downs, but we need to focus on supporting each other, including Dad. That is what families do. She said she understands that it may take a while for me to forgive my Dad, but that I need to focus on trying my best to forgive him so I can help support him as he goes through his trial and jail time. I didn't tear this letter apart. I neatly refolded it and put it back in my drawer.

I walked to my Mom's room. She was folding a basket of towels on her bed. I went up to her and hugged her. " I will try, Mom, but I am not sure if or when anything will happen." I said quietly.

"Obviously you found the letter. I wrote it while you were sleeping this morning and wanted to put it somewhere you would find in the next few days, but not right when you woke up. I wanted to give you more time." she explained.

"I only found it because I was getting band aids for my knee." I replied.

"How did that happen?" she questioned.

"Last night when I was running to hide from the police," I confessed the rest of the story to her. Then before she could say it, I assured her that I wouldn't do that again.

Back in my room my brain finally stopped thinking about my home life. Back to school tomorrow. Jessica. Ugh. I wrote down a quick outline of my ideas for a food insecurity project. I wanted to be prepared to start right away so maybe we could avoid spending extra time together. I hope we were on the same page with how this project could work. If not, more complications in my life. Don't need that right now.

Chapter 11

On my way to Homeroom in the morning, Ms. Lack stopped me in the hall. "I want you to know that I am glad about the partner you chose on Friday. I know you weren't pleased, but you both work very hard in class and always have great incite when it comes to modern day topics and how they relate to history. If you put whatever it is aside that makes you unhappy about her being your partner, I think you will both have fantastic success with your project and also, hopefully have some fun putting it together. I spoke with Jessica and explained the same thing to her on Friday after school when she was leaving cheer practice."

I told her I would do my best to keep drama out of the project work. I then explained how it was going to be difficult to work outside of class because of our schedules.

Ms. Lack replied with, "You may just need to work at each others' homes after dinner, perhaps, or on weekends." I wanted to explain that she couldn't come to my home, but wasn't going to give her the true reason why. I chose to just nod as I walked away towards homeroom.

***

The day went pretty normally through lunch. After lunch was History Class. I sat in my usual seat and waited for Ms. Lack to begin. She came in from the hallway with a big smile on her face. Projects always seemed to make her more happy than usual. She told us that we were going to have the entire class period to get started with planning the projects. We were to use our rubric to drive our decisions as to the components within our project based on the topic we chose. Jessica came over to my desk which surprised me. She started by saying that she had the perfect idea for our project. Well, so did I, but I decided to hear her out. Her idea for a food insecurity project was for us to have a walk a thon and have participants enter the walk a thon by donating two non perishable food items. We could ask a few local stores to donate items we could use as prizes for a raffle held during the event. The food we collect, we could send to Africa. I was glad that she was thinking about it, at least.

But I had my own idea to share. I told her that my idea was to open a food pantry/clothing "closet" for our school. We have a lot of students that would benefit from this. Most of the kids in our school get free lunch because of the financial situation of their family. Jessica was not one of those students. I was one of those students back when my mom had lost her job two years ago. We both really had our minds set on our projects. This was going to be a problem. We decided to let Ms. Lack choose the project she thought was the "best". When she came to check in on our progress, we each explained our ideas and asked her which one was better. Of course, she didn't answer with a set choice. She told us that both ideas were good, so we would have to decide on one and start working on the details. We spent the rest of the period trying to convince each other that our idea was the perfect choice. This wasted the rest of the period for both of us. Neither one of us would budge. Great. We left the class with basically nothing done.

***

On the bus ride home I was sitting with Jasmine. She was talking about the project she and Mark were working on. It sounded really interesting. When she gave me the chance to talk, I expressed my frustration. She was a really good listener….once you got her to stop talking. You could tell she was processing and analyzing all my points I was presenting. When I had finished, she simply said, "Combine them".
 What? I thought. "How?" I asked.
 "Figure out how to have at least part of your good ideas combined to make one fantastic project." she simply stated. I was floored...it seemed easy, yet complicated at the same time. It would take compromise on both our parts, but if each of us could budge, just a little, this may work. I smiled and gave her a hug as I was standing to get off at my

stop.

"Thanks. You just may have saved us from failing History!" I exclaimed. She smiled back and said she'd text me later. I stepped off the bus feeling a lot better than I had since my standstill with Jessica.

As I walked into the house, my Mom was sitting on the couch, waiting for me. I asked her, "What's up?" expecting more news about Dad and what the lawyers had said. I was shocked when she started to cry.

***

It took her a few minutes to compose herself before she could speak. When she did, it changed my thoughts from sarcastic frustration about the whole situation with Dad to shock and worry.

"Grandma had a stroke today after you and JC went to school. She is in the hospital getting treatments to prevent it from getting worse. This morning she was limping and said her arm felt tingly. We both thought it was because she slept wrong on that side during the night. An hour later I went to check on her to see if she felt better and she couldn't speak. I called 911 and an ambulance arrived within a few minutes. At that point she just pointed to her arm and leg that she couldn't move anymore with her good arm. I met the ambulance at the hospital and stayed with her. They are moving her from the Emergency Room to a bed to keep her for a while and hopefully the medications they are giving her will help her symptoms." Mom shared.

I just stood there, dumbfounded. I couldn't believe what I was hearing. Was my mother lying to me? Why would she make this up? If this is true, HOW could this have happened? Grandma was fine this morning. It was a totally normal morning. She was on the couch watching the morning news program she always watches, drinking her coffee. I didn't see her walk, so I couldn't have seen her limping, as my Mom did. I had to know….so quickly replied with, "Is she going to die?" even though I didn't want to know if there were any chances of that happening. Mom said softly, "The doctor's don't think she will get any worse than she was when I left the hospital. The medication they are giving her stops the stroke from getting worse most of the time. It seemed to be working because she had no other complications to show her stroke was getting worse once they gave her the medicine."

"I need to go see her, NOW." I insisted.

Mom smiled slightly. "You cannot go see her. Not at least until she is settled in a regular room in the hospital. Uncle Vinnie went to stay with her so she is not alone in the Emergency Room. I wanted to be here to tell you and JC. I will tell him once he is home from track practice."

I sat on the couch and cried with my mom. I was so scared, for grandma, and for all of us. She was always there for us, even before she lived here. I could always count on her to be there to listen to me and always gave me good advice.

I also loved all her stories she told about when she was little, living in Colombia, when she moved to the United States when she was 20 years old, when her and grandpa got married and had kids, even stories about what my Dad was like growing up. If she can't speak, then the advice and stories end. I don't want her to have to live that way. She loved talking and visiting with her friends. Would she ever be able to do those things again?

Another thought interrupted my sadness, "Does Dad know?" I inquired.

"He should know by now. I called the prison and told the supervisor what was going on. He told me I can call later and speak with Dad, and then he will be allowed to call us for an update at 7pm each evening while Grandma is in the hospital. We can only talk for 5 minutes, but that will be enough time for me to give him an update and him to give me a message for Grandma." she explained.

So they won't let Dad talk to Grandma? He can't call her in the hospital? That didn't seem fair to me. I was still very angry with him, but this is his mother who is so ill. At that point I went into my room. Alone time was necessary. It didn't last very long, though.

***

Just before dinner Jasmine came over to see if I wanted to walk to the basketball courts to watch her brother and his friends play in a town league game. The courts were only a few blocks away. Mom usually let me go as long as I was home by dark and didn't walk alone. JC had let her in, so she entered my room and took me by surprise. She sat on my bed and waited for me to go check with Mom about going. I didn't really want to go, but figured the distraction would help me take my mind off things for a while. It would give my brain a break. Mom said OK, and that she would make a plate for me to heat up when I got back home.

We walked to the courts. It was breezy and cool. I put up my hood and kicked at the orange and yellow leaves that had started falling onto the sidewalk.

Jasmine questioned, "Are you OK? You're being

very quiet."

I replied, "I'm fine. Just in a quiet mood, that's all."

She accepted my response. As we got to the courts, her brother, Malcolm, and his friends were warming up for the game. He was three years older than us. He had his driver's license, so he had driven to the courts. We couldn't drive with him because he can't have anyone in the car with him that is under 18 for the first six months with his license. He is pretty good at following the rules. If someone gets caught with passengers under 18, they would lose their license until they turned 18. He wasn't taking any chances. I don't blame him. Driving is such freedom, in my opinion.

Jasmine wasn't really there to watch her brother, though. She has had a crush on her brother's best friend, who was also playing on his team. His name was Rico. He looked and acted kind of tough, but was really nice. He drove a motorcycle. He was totally not my type. First of all, my Mom would never let me go with anyone on a motorcycle. She said it was too dangerous. She trusted the cyclists, but not most of the other drivers on the road that didn't drive defensively.

We watched the game, then walked back home. When we got to the house, Jasmine wanted to come in and hang out for a while. I told her I had to eat dinner and get my homework done. She gave me one of her "looks", with a raised eyebrow and heavy sigh. She asked me what was going on. Why was I acting so different lately? Why did it seem like I didn't really want to hang out with her? I told her that I had a lot on my mind. My grandma was sick and in the hospital. She said she was sorry.

I decided to let her come back into the house. We passed JC and Uncle Vinnie on the couch watching some game show. They said hello as we went into the kitchen so I could heat up my dinner. I took out some cookies and milk for Jasmine, since she had already had dinner.

I didn't think anything of it until Jasmine asked, "Where's your dad? I haven't seen him in a while."

***

Jasmine loved it when my dad was around. He had nicknamed her "Froggy" because two years ago she had chronic laryngitis, so her voice was raspy for about 4 months. He said she sounded like a frog when she tried to talk. She thought it was so funny and insisted that he continue calling her that, even when her voice returned to normal. He always had some sort of lame frog joke to share with her when she came over. I had forgotten about all of that for the past few weeks.

I just couldn't hold it in anymore...especially with Jasmine. I dumped the rest of my dinner, put away the plate and waved for her to follow me. I was already fighting back tears and had a huge lump in my throat. I couldn't talk yet. She followed me into my room. I closed the door and started sobbing. She sat next to me on my bed. She didn't try to comfort me like when we were at her house right after dad went to jail. She just sat and waited for me to be calm enough to talk.

It took a good 3 minutes before I choked out the words, "My dad is in jail." The look on her face said it all...total shock.

"What are you talking about? Your dad is a great guy. What do the police think he did?" she asked.

"It isn't what he is accused of, mostly; it is what he actually did." I responded. I then told her all I knew about everything my mom had shared with me and JC. I even told her about how mom tried to get me to go visit him right before I went to her house to make cookies, and how the news at her house was talking about Mr. Gossling dying. That was why I all of a sudden felt "sick" and left her house. She just sat there; totally silent, trying to digest all that I was sharing with her.

When I had finished telling her everything, I felt lighter, like a giant weight in my chest and stomach had been lifted out of me. It was the right thing to do, I know it. This was the first time I had talked about it and felt better. I think it was because it was all on my terms...my choice of what to say, how to say it, without any pressure or panicky feelings.

Now it was Jasmine's turn to cry. The tears were flowing down her cheeks and her nose was dripping. I handed her a couple of tissues. It now took her a few minutes to settle down to her reaction to all my information. She started by saying how sorry she was that I was going through all of this…..that all of my family was going through this, including my dad. She, being always so positive, said the police, investigators and lawyers would find out the entire truth of what happened and that my dad would not have to stay in jail for a very long time. She truly believed what my dad had said about him not knowing about the gun or shooting Mr. Gossling. She even made me smile when she offered to be a character witness for him on the stand during his trial. She truly was my best friend. She had my back in this whole mess. I knew she would stand by me and help me through this. I was

lucky to have such a great friend.
 Even though she was so awesome, I still felt the need to say, "Please. Don't tell ANYONE about this. The newspaper will be talking about it once the police have more definitive information to give to the press. The other parts I shared with you are what my mom told me and asked me not to share. But I had to tell someone I trusted. It is you....my best friend."
 Jasmine reassured me by saying that her lips were sealed. She would not say anything to anyone and act surprised when the news hit the papers. I knew I could count on her.
 At that point it was dark, so she called and asked her step dad to come pick her up. She told him that we stopped back at my house on the way home and worked on some school work , not realizing it had gotten dark so quickly. He agreed and picked her up a short time later. Just before he arrived, Mom came home and gave us an update on Grandma. Jasmine listened in as she waited for her step dad.

***

 Grandma's stroke had not gotten any worse. When Mom left, Grandma was alert, but still could not move her right arm or leg, nor could she speak. She tried, but the words came out as garbled sounds, like a baby would make. She did understand what was being said to her and could respond with a yes or no shake of her head. Mom said the doctors couldn't tell her how much mobility and speech Grandma would get back. Tomorrow they would start speech therapy and physical therapy to give her the best possible chances.
 They were going to keep her in the hospital for

another couple of days, then she would need to go to a rehabilitation center to continue therapy and regain as much strength, mobility and speech as possible. This could take a few weeks, a few months, or not happen at all. That last part scared me the most. What if Grandma couldn't regain anything? Would she be in a wheelchair? Could she push herself around with only the use of one arm? How could we talk with her? Her responses would be yes or no. She couldn't even write them because she was right handed. I started to cry. As I did this, Jasmine's ride arrived and she had to leave. She gave me a big hug, told me it would be OK and that Grandma was strong. I didn't get mad at her positivity this time. I needed it to help me keep up hope for Grandma.

 After she left, I went for a snack in the kitchen. There were leftovers from dinner last night that Grandma had made. She was such a great cook. It would crush her if she couldn't cook anymore. She had taught me how to make a few things, but I really wanted to know more. I thought I would have more time to learn all her secrets that made her meals so extra special. Even though I wanted a quick bite, I took out the leftovers and heated them up. JC joined me in the kitchen and we ate them in silence, relishing each bite of the flavorful empanadas and fried plantains.

 We both retreated to our rooms when we finished. I started working on my homework and fell asleep. When I woke up to my alarm I panicked. I hadn't finished the assignment for Spanish Class. Senora Robala was a stickler about getting your homework done on time. I would try to finish it during Homeroom and hope for the best.

Chapter 12

I got off the bus at school and went right into Homeroom, took out my Spanish assignment and worked on it. My Homeroom was usually a bit rowdy, so it was hard to concentrate. I got more than half of it done, when it was time to move on to the first period. I had no time during Science Class to work on finishing it, so I entered Spanish without my completed work. Sometimes Senora Robala just corrected work together with us and didn't collect it nor check it. Unfortunately, today was not that day. She walked around the room while we worked on our partner practice time, conversing with each other in Spanish.
 When she got to my desk, she stopped. " Por que tu tarea no esta terminada?", which means, "Why is your homework not finished?"
 I replied, " Me quede dormido mientras trabajaba en ello." I was hoping answering her in Spanish would lighten up the consequence.
 No such luck. She responded with, "Detencion, manana." and walked away.
 Wait….I couldn't even explain myself further? Now I had to serve a detention? I have NEVER had a detention before. I have never missed an assignment in Spanish Class yet this year. I had heard she was strict, but this was ridiculous. I went up to her and tried to explain more of my situation, without giving too much information, but to hopefully get out of the detention.
 I told her my grandmother was sick and in the hospital. Her response was to ask me if my

grandmother did my homework for me, so that is why it isn't done, because grandma wasn't there to do it? I got mad; really mad. How dare she thinks that I would do something like that….how dare she think my grandma would do anything like that?

I couldn't control my anger at that point. I started yelling at her, telling her she has no idea what she is talking about, and how DARE she speak that way about my grandma, or me! I picked up her textbook and threw it about half way across the classroom, called her a word I would rather not repeat, and walked out of the classroom. I went straight to Mr. Coster's office. Great. The note on the door said he was at a meeting and would be back after lunch. That is two hours away! This couldn't wait.

***

As I was heading to the main office, one of the security officers came up to me. She asked where I was going. I told her. She said she would walk with me. I told her it wasn't necessary, but she just followed me to make sure that is where I was going. I'm sure Senora Robala called the office to report that I had walked out of class. I've seen other kids do this, but I have never done anything like this before. I felt empowered and awful at the same time. When I went into the office I told the secretary that I needed to see Mr. Turbino. He is pretty cool, so I felt comfortable talking to him as my second choice. Great…he was at a meeting too. He was probably at the same one as Mr. Coster.

She offered for me to see the principal, Ms. G. She seemed nice, but I have never had to meet with her. She is usually busy dealing with the kids who are bad. Now I guess I am one of "them". As I entered her office, it was decorated differently than I expected. She had more personal items on the shelves. It looked like she collected giraffes. She had two shelves filled with many versions of giraffe figures. She had some inspirational posters on her wall and a huge calendar on her wall with all of her meetings and school events posted on them. It was packed! She is one busy lady. She had me sit down, gave me a cup of water from her bubbler. I was pretty calm by now.

She asked how I was feeling. I told her better than a few minutes ago. She asked about what happened. I explained my side of the story. She said it was only fair to hear Senora Robala's side too before any consequences could be given. It was only fair. I agreed, even though I was worried that Senora Robala would tell something totally different and Ms. G would side with her. Adults tend to side with other adults instead of kids, unless the kids are their own children, in my opinion. I left her office, went to Spanish to pick up my things I had left behind then went right to History Class. I was only about 5 minutes late, and my pass from the office let me into class without questions from Ms. Lack. Jessica was sitting, waiting for me.

***

Ms. Lack said today we would have the first half of class to finish up our planning and decide how and where we were going to work on the project. We had to hand in our schedule so she would know how each duo was planning their work and if they had enough time to finish a project that would get a good grade if the best effort was put in. Jessica and I still needed to figure out our project, so we had to work quickly. She had started planning out her project idea on the paper that goes with the rubric. When I saw it, I stopped, took a deep breath and told myself to not freak out on her. I sat down and asked her to please listen to a compromise that may make both of us happy. She reluctantly said "OK" and sat back.

  I knew this was crucial. If I didn't explain this so that she would agree, we would still be getting nowhere with this project. We would be wasting more time getting a lot of nothing done. I took the angle of her idea for the project as the first part of the explanation of the "blend" of our two projects. I figured at least she would listen to that part and hopefully agree to the second part, which was my part of the project. It worked. She had a few comments and changes suggested, but it was nothing extreme, so we finally had an agreed upon blend for our project.

 We were almost done writing up the description when Ms. Lack asked for our schedule. We didn't have that yet! Ugh! We could finish it in about 10 minutes, but she wouldn't give us any more time. She wanted it by the end of the day. Our only option was for us to do it during lunchtime. It was the only other time we were together during the school day. We agreed to meet at lunch and finish it up. I would give the schedule to Ms. Lack after lunch because I had Math Class then which was next door to her classroom.

***

  At first it was awkward, not eating lunch with my friends. It probably felt the same for Jessica. We sat down and I took out the scheduling sheet. Ms. Lack wanted us to fill in 15-20 hours of scheduled work times over the next three weeks. The project was due in mid November. She wanted time for each group to share their projects with the class (a 10-15 minute presentation) before Thanksgiving Break. Jessica was the first to announce that she had cheer practice 4 days a week after school. She didn't have it on Wednesdays, so we filled in two hour slots to work together in the library after school on Wednesdays. That was only 6 hours though. She and I agreed that mornings before school were just too early and would only give us an hour to work, so by the time we started, we wouldn't have a big chunk of time to get a lot accomplished. Saturdays and Sundays were all that was left, oh, and Veterans' Day in November. The library was only open on Saturdays from 9am until 1pm. Football games were during that time, so again, Jessica wasn't available to work.

We agreed that Saturday afternoons were good for both of us. We both wanted Sundays off from work. If we worked the first two Saturdays for 3 hours each, that would give us 12 hours, which should be enough time to organize our project based on the rubric so we could get an A or B, which satisfied both of us. Now the major problem was where to work. I did NOT want her at my house. I did NOT want her asking any questions about my family or even talking to them. Our relationship was strictly based on completing a project that got us a good grade. I offered to go to her house so she wouldn't have to walk to mine after cheering all morning. I thought she would be happy about that. She was very hesitant. I didn't give her a chance to say no, or offer to come to my house. I told her that was the easiest way. Also, that meant we could keep all the supplies at her house and not drag them from one house to another. The library had a great selection of supplies to be used for projects, so we only had to bring the papers we would need with the information on them to help us.

  She finally agreed to work at her house. Why didn't she jump at the chance of not having to walk 8 blocks each way to my house after cheering all morning? I knew the area she lived in. It was full of large beautiful homes. The houses had perfectly cut lawns, two car garages and usually a pool in the backyard. I wouldn't mind living in one of those homes.

 My house was nice, but the landlord was letting things "go". The paint on the window sills was peeling on the outside. The porch needed painting and some floorboards to be replaced. We had no garage. The bushes were big and crazy, not manicured and elegant looking. The yard was small and not always kept clean. It was filled with leaves from the trees that often didn't get cleaned up before winter arrived. Inside was clean but old. Dark paneling on the walls and wallpaper that had been there since we moved in 7 years ago made the living room very dim. The kitchen was big. The table took up a lot of the space with the 6 chairs around it. The appliances were older and didn't match. No shiny stainless steel ones. The flooring was old and worn. The cabinets were painted, but chipped over the years of use. My bedroom was the best room for natural light. I had 3 huge windows that faced north. I had a bright cheery quilt and matching curtains. My large rug covered the worn marks on the old wooden floorboards.

I wondered what Jessica's bedroom was like. I felt jealous without even seeing it. That is silly. Why be jealous if I like my own room? My thoughts were interrupted with the bell, sending us to our next class. Jessica seemed preoccupied with thoughts as well. We had spent the whole lunch period together. It wasn't that uncomfortable, but I missed my time with my friends. I'll bet she felt the same. I dropped off the schedule to Ms. Lack who seemed pleased with our arrangements, and headed into Math Class.

Chapter 13

Later on the bus ride home, Jasmine asked how things went with Jessica at lunch. "Fine", I replied. "We were able to finish up our schedule for Ms. Lack. It took a while in class to get our plan for our project all set. She agreed to most of what you suggested about combining our two projects into one. Thanks again for that idea. It helped us get moving on the project itself. When I got off the bus, Mom was at the bus stop waiting for me.
"Is everything OK?" I quickly asked.
"Yes. I am taking you to see Grandma. I think seeing you will be good medicine for her." she responded.

***

I jumped in the passenger seat, buckled up, and off we went. When we got there, my mom told me that Grandma was frustrated this morning because she couldn't do a lot during physical therapy. She needed to be patient and give herself time to recover. She reminded me that Grandma couldn't talk, so to only ask her questions she could answer by nodding yes or no. When we got to Grandma's hospital room, her eyes were closed, but opened as we entered and sat down. I sat right next to her and automatically took her hand. It was her right hand. She did not respond. Shoot, I forgot she couldn't move her right arm or leg. I kept my hand there though. I asked her if she could feel me holding her hand. She nodded yes, so I continued to hold it.

Mom asked if she wanted a snack. There was pudding on the table next to her bed. She nodded yes again. Mom set it up in front of her, taking off the lid and putting the plastic spoon in it for her. Grandma took her left hand and tried to scoop it up and put it into her mouth. Only the left side of her mouth opened so when she tried putting in the spoon, it hit her lips and spilled down her chin. She put the spoon back on the table, grabbed the napkin with her left hand and attempted to wipe up the mess. She was having a difficult time doing this successfully. I offered to help. She shook her head no. Mom bent over to help her and Grandma made a noise...an angry noise and swatted Mom's hand away.

We sat there in silence for quite a while. Finally Mom told me it was time to go home and start on dinner. I asked Grandma if she was hungry. She again shook her head no. She looked upset. I gave her a hug and told her to rest and I would be back tomorrow. Hopefully Mom will bring me again otherwise it is a long walk to get there from school. I wasn't even sure I could get a ride home. I didn't care.

Grandma needed me. She's been there for me all my life, so now it was my turn to be there for her.

Mom and I left and were silent until we were riding home. Mom explained that Grandma has always been so independent that this is really a tough time for her. She needs to focus on being patient with her progress and work hard at her therapy sessions. This morning during her therapy session she refused to try what was being asked of her. The therapist said he would be back tomorrow to try again. He told Mom this morning that this is common, especially in the beginning of recovery therapy after a stroke. He did say, also, that the sooner she begins fighting to gain back her mobility, the better the chances of a full recovery. Grandma needs encouragement and inspiration. I had to devise a plan to help her.

As we walked through the door the phone rang and I went to answer it. As I picked it up and said hello a familiar voice caught me off guard.

"Hi, Nina, How are you doin'?"

I hung up.

"Who was that?" Mom asked.

"Wrong number," I replied.

I didn't consider it a lie because I believed it was wrong for him to call. Also, how dare he act so casual and ask how I am doing? Even if I wanted to answer him, it would take more than his 5 minute limit for me to finish ALL that I was feeling right now…about him, about Grandma, about school, about home, about my crazy life…about how I didn't feel in control of anything. Mom didn't seem to suspect anything. I went into my room and finished my homework.

***

A knock came on my door. "Come in," I called. He stood there….all 6 feet of him, taking up most of the doorway. I smiled ear to ear. He was home. Dad. He was home. He walked over and sat on the edge of my bed. He wore his bright orange work shirt and jeans. They were covered in cement dust from work. His boots left prints on my floor. He had tracked in some type of grime from his job. I didn't care. He was here.

"What….how…" was all I could manage to say.

He smiled. His chipped front tooth made his smile extra special. It gave him character. He didn't always show his teeth when he smiled. He was self conscious about the chipped tooth, but never got it fixed. He got it when he was a kid and a baseball hit him in the mouth. It split open his lip and chipped the tooth. The scar on his lip was almost unnoticeable, but the chip stood out when he fully grinned. His dark hair looked grey from the work dust as well.

"Hi Nina, How are you doin'?" he asked.

I couldn't answer. I was so shocked that he was here. I started to cry tears of joy. I didn't care what he was doing here or how he got home. He was just here, with me. His smile faded slightly.

He said, "I know you are happy to see me, but I have to go now."

"Why? You just got here?" I said, beginning to panic. "Where are you going?" I demanded to know.

"Back where I have to be. You know that. Just be good for Mom until I am back, OK? Be strong. No tears."

I grabbed at his arm, but he was just out of my reach. He slowly backed out of my room. His clothes had changed. How did that happen? He had on a jumpsuit. All the dust was gone. He faded from my vision as he backed away.

"No!" I shouted. "Don't leave me! I love you! I need you!"

"I love you too. Always." he softly spoke as he fully faded away.

"No!" I shouted again.

"Nina...what is wrong?" It was Mom. She was in my room. I opened my eyes. My pillow was wet with tears. It was a dream. In fact, a really good dream. Dad was home. I wasn't angry at him in my dream. I was happy. I loved him. How could I ever think that I hated my Dad? I started crying, really hard. Mom walked over and hugged me.

"You were dreaming, but you yelled out the word 'no'. What were you dreaming about?" she asked.

I just kept sobbing and hugging her. "I love him. I miss him. I am scared for him and for us." I replied in a muffled tone into her shoulder.

Then I confessed, "It wasn't a wrong number earlier, it was Dad. I hung up on him. I am so sorry, Mom. I wasn't ready to talk to him. I was so surprised, I just reacted before thinking. He probably wanted to check on Grandma. Now he doesn't know. He will have to wait until tomorrow. I am an awful daughter." I confessed.

"No. You aren't an awful daughter. You were totally caught off guard. I'm sure he understands." she reassured.

" I just can't hear his voice. It hurts too much right now. I don't know what I would do if I saw him in person. In my dream I wanted to hug him, but didn't get the chance. When, I mean IF I ever decide to visit him, I won't be able to hug him.

Whatever I say to him, other people will hear. I am not sure if I will ever be able to handle that." I explained.

Mom smiled. She had tears running down her face now.

"You need more time. That is OK. People deal with trauma in their lives differently. Give yourself time to accept your feelings...and to talk about your feelings. At some point, probably sooner than you think, you will be able to take steps forward in dealing with your Dad. I didn't really get time to do that. I had to react and deal with everything right away when the police arrived and then with the lawyers needing information. That is probably the only reason I am kind of ahead of you in dealing with all of this. It's a lot to have on your mind. And that is only one part of your life. You have school and friends and now Grandma's situation on your mind also. Just be patient with yourself. Don't beat yourself up about how you are reacting and your emotions about everything. Promise?"

It made sense to me. Hard to accept, but true. I told her I would do my best. She hugged me again and left. It was 11 o'clock. I only had one more math problem to do. I finished it and rechecked my Spanish work to be sure it was complete. I didn't want any more grief from Senora Robala.

I almost forgot. I still had detention with her after school tomorrow. Ms. G said she spoke with Senora Robala and she said that Senora Robala and I needed to talk out the situation so we would totally understand where the other person was coming from in their reaction. I thought she was still wrong in her comments, but would agree that I didn't handle things well. I wasn't going to tell Mom. She would want to know why and I would have to lie to her because I was not going to share my outburst with her.

***

The next morning Mom said she was going to pick me up from school to bring me to see Grandma so I wouldn't have to walk. Now I had to tell her something. I told her I had promised to work with Jessica on the project in the library for an hour, so to pick me up a bit later. She agreed, and off to school I went.
Everything went fine at school. It was a pretty normal day. Then History Class. Jessica came up to me and said we had to switch our work day from Wednesday to today because cheer practice got changed. I told her I couldn't work today. She wanted to know why. I told her my grandma was in the hospital and I was going to see her. She said that wasn't an excuse. I should go later, after we work. I told her I couldn't.
 She made some weird annoying noise, turned abruptly and walked away from me. Whatever…. I already accommodated our work schedule around her cheer practice and games. She can make one adjustment for me. And this was an unexpected change in her schedule. She should be mad at the coach for changing the practice day, not me for not being able to make it today with barely any notice.
The detention was not as bad as I expected. Senora Robala apologized for her comment and I apologized for my outburst and leaving her room. It took about 10 minutes to get through everything, but I needed to serve the entire 60 minutes. She let me work on my homework until the late bell rang

for detention dismissal. As I was walking to meet my Mom, I saw Jessica. She had come out of the library to get a drink. Great timing! Not!

She took one look at me and sarcastically said, "I thought you were going to see your grandma in the hospital?"

I told her that I was going there now. She responded with, "So why couldn't you work with me until now on the project? We could have gotten something done, at least."

I didn't want to tell her I had a detention. To be perfectly honest it was NONE of her business.

I just stated, " I had to do something else first."

She snottily replied, "Sure. You'll do anything to get out of working on this project with me, right?" Then she walked away. What was her problem? That wasn't it at all.

"Why are you doing your homework in the library anyway?" I called after her.

"For some peace and quiet. I don't get much of that at home." she shouted, "As if it is any of your concern."

And she stormed back into the library. I walked out of the building. Mom was waiting. I plopped my book bag into the back and sat in the front seat.

Mom read the look on my face, and questioned, "What's up with you? Are you mad at someone?"

"I just don't get people sometimes. They really complicate things when there is no reason for it." I replied.

Mom told me that it sounds like someone who may need a friend. I told her that this person had lots of friends and was very "popular". Mom said that sometimes the most popular people have problems just like the less popular people. At that point I just turned on the radio. It was Mom's 80's station. I knew a lot of those songs. That is all she listened to….so we sang together all the way to the hospital.

***

Grandma was sitting up in bed. She smiled. It was crooked. Her right side only smiled about half way. I held her hand. Her fingers moved...on her right hand. Yeah! She couldn't grip my hand, fully, but at least she could move part of her hand. Her arm and leg were another story, though. Still there was no movement. She could feel if you touched them, but had no mobility yet. The nurse told us that the finger movement was a good sign though.

The nurse also told us that Grandma would be going to a rehabilitation facility tomorrow to continue her therapy. At least we had something good to celebrate today. She shook her head yes and no as we asked questions. When her dinner arrived, the nursing assistant came in to help her with using her left hand to feed herself. Mom and I both knew this made her uncomfortable, having us watch her do this, so we told her we would see her soon and left. We picked up pizza on the way home.

After dinner I went into JC's room. He had been quiet the past few days. I wanted to check on him. He told me he doesn't want to go see Grandma in the hospital. He said it would scare him to see her that way. I gave him advice like Mom gave me last night about how to deal with my feelings about Dad. He seemed to understand what I meant. I told him that this weekend I would go with him to see Grandma at the rehabilitation center. If he felt uncomfortable he could give me a signal and we could go for a brief walk to give him a break from having to look at her the way she was right now. He agreed to do that. I was glad that I could help him deal with this part of our life, at least.

***

As I worked on my homework, I kept thinking about how this project was going to get done. We still had nothing done based on our blended idea. I started looking up places that we could ask to donate prizes for our raffle and 5K walk a thon. I listed them in my doc on my thumb drive so I could bring it to school and show Jessica that at least I had been thinking about the project and working on setting up a part that we could do together. I hope she will be OK with that. If she wasn't, I don't know what else I could do at this point. Saturday would be our first extended time together to work on it, so hopefully we could get a lot accomplished.

I started thinking about what her bedroom looked like, if that is where we would work. I'll bet it had a huge soft bed with a pink comforter with flowers on it. She probably had all matching furniture that had no nicks or dents in it. Her curtains were probably designer ones and her window shades probably went up and down with the touch of a remote. She probably had a big fluffy white pedigree cat that slept curled up on her bed and purred when you pet it. Her carpet would be thick and warm with no stains on it. Her room probably smelled like fresh wildflowers….no, even better, roses. Maybe even, there would be a crystal vase of them on her dresser. The mirror on her dresser would be framed with pictures of her and all her cheer buddies at games or sleepovers or parties with the football players. She would have a big TV mounted on her wall so she could watch movies with her friends without anyone interrupting them. She may even have her own walk-in closet, perfectly organized with 50 pairs of designer shoes and lots of different outfits displayed in order by color, neatly pressed and ready to wear whenever she needs them. I'd even bet that she had her own bathroom. All white tiles with a pink and purple shower curtain and matching towels. Also she probably has a huge soaker tub for luxurious bubble baths. Why did I agree to go to her house? Oh yeah...to keep her from coming to mine. The less she knows about me, the better.

Chapter 14

The rest of the week was pretty "normal", or at least as normal as it can be. English Class was really interesting. We had finished reading all different types of short stories. We were now going to work on choosing one of the stories that we connected with and start working on a 3 minute speech that explained how the story connected to "us" in some way. We were going to be doing all this in class, so at least it wasn't something extra I had to do at home. Our teachers at school were pretty good at not overloading us with major assignments at the same time. They talked to each other and scheduled when they would assign lengthy assignments that were to be worked on at home. We only would have one at a time so we could focus all our energy on that large assignment and get as good a grade as possible.

***

On Thursday and Friday I went to visit Grandma with Mom. She was now able to move her right arm enough to feed herself. She was still weak and dropped her fork and spoon a few times while she ate, but she is making progress with that. She still couldn't speak and her smile was still crooked. She could bend her leg at the knee but couldn't lift her leg at all. The therapist said within another couple of weeks he would be able to tell what extent of mobility and strength she would probably regain. He said when she had reached her maximum amount of progress that the family would have to determine whether she was going to return home or stay permanently at the rehabilitation home. I didn't even want to consider the fact that she may not be able to come home. I loved having her at home. She was always available to talk or just listen if I had a problem. I know she could still be there for me but it would be more complicated. It would only be when I could get to her place, if she stayed at the facility. And I couldn't talk to her on the phone if she still couldn't speak. At least at home she could answer yes or no when I asked questions. She could also nod when I was talking. I would know by her nod if she was approving or disapproving of my reasoning. It was so much to absorb, losing Dad then possibly losing Grandma at home too.

***

I kept waking up during the night on Friday. Something was racing through my mind each time I woke up, preventing me from falling back to sleep quickly. It was all the "what ifs" I had about going to Jessica's house to work on Saturday afternoon. I was supposed to be there about 2pm and we planned to work until 5pm so I could be home for dinner. All the "what ifs" included: What if I spilled my drink and ruined her carpeting? What if we disagreed on how we were going to do the project and neither one of us would give in? What if she had a mean dog and it bit me? What if she just sat there painting her fingernails and expected me to do all the work? What if she said stuff that got me mad and I just wanted to leave, but we hadn't done enough work yet? "What if…" After thinking about them, I realized that at least most of them were pretty unlikely happenings, but I just couldn't help it.

    I finally slept for a few solid hours, but had weird dreams. Jessica was jumping on her bed and fell off, cracking her head open. Her parents came in and said I must have pushed her because she had perfect balance and would never have fallen on her own. They had me arrested for attempted murder. Jessica could not speak anymore, so she couldn't cheer. She had a huge scar on her head that never healed. She had blood matted in her hair that couldn't wash out. I woke up sweating…. I rationalized the dream of a combination of my anxiousness about going to Jessica's with my dad being arrested and grandma not being able to speak. Oh yeah, the bloody head was just like the one in the horror movie Uncle Vinnie and I watched last night. It is so weird how your thoughts can blend all these pieces of your life together into one weird dream. I decided to get up, shower, eat breakfast then get my other homework done before I went to Jessica's. I hate doing homework on Sundays. I think everyone should get one day off a week from "work", whether it is school work or a regular job.

I got busy with my day. Next thing I knew it was 1:30. It was time to start walking to Jessica's. I had her address and looked up the exact directions to her house. I didn't want to chance getting lost or ringing the wrong doorbell and being embarrassed. I put what I thought we may need in my backpack, reminded my mom where I was going and headed out the door. The skies were grey and the breeze was cool, but not that bad. I had on my heavy sweatshirt and jeans so I was pretty comfortable. It took me an entire half hour to get to her house.

I rang the doorbell right at 2:00. Jessica answered and let me in. As we were walking to her room, her mom stopped her, saying, "Aren't you going to introduce me to your friend?" Jessica mumbled, "Mom, Nina….Nina, Mom." "Hello, nice to meet you", I replied. "So nice that Jessica is having friends over. It's been a long time since we've seen any of them," she commented. I wonder what that meant? So much for the thoughts I had of her having slumber parties with a bunch of her friends in her room. I totally thought of her as the type that always had friends over. That was only the first of many surprises ahead.

Chapter 15

As I stepped into Jessica's room, I was taken aback by all the posters on her light green walls. They were all hard rock bands from the 80s. I knew each band pictured. That is what Mom and I listen to in the car. My favorite band was hanging over the head of Jessica's bed. She must have read my face.

"You know them?" she questioned.

" I know all of the bands on your posters. My mom

is an 80s music freak, so I know a lot of the music from being trapped in the car with her. I am getting to appreciate them more and more lately. My favorite band from then is Queen," I admitted.

"Huh.", she responded, "I guess we do have something in common. They are my favorite too."

All of a sudden a large dog busted through the unlatched door. He ran toward me, filled with excitement and energy. Jessica introduced me to Micro, her Great Dane, who weighs about 100 pounds. He jumped onto her bed and started licking my face. I laughed and started petting him.

"He's a good dog, just a bit energetic. He is still a puppy. He is always like this especially when he gets back from his walk." she explained.

Jessica called for her brother, Will, to come take him out of the room. He whistled and called for Micro to come to him, and off Micro went. The floor shook as he bounded across the floor and out the door. Jessica shut it tightly so he wouldn't return and interrupt us. We took out our papers, compared our ideas based on the agreement to blend our project ideas and started to work. It was pretty quiet for the first hour or so. Jessica's room is upstairs and away from the main living area.

Then I heard voices from downstairs. They slowly grew louder to the point that I could hear every word being said. They weren't happy voices. The man's voice was talking about a credit card bill. The lady's voice was definitely Jessica's Mom. She was yelling back about how it was a great sale and she really needed the clothes. Jessica kept working for a bit, but when we heard something smash and I jumped, Jessica hurried up and started gathering up all the work we had put together.

"Nina, I just remembered that I have a dentist appointment at 3:30. You need to go so I can remind my mom that we have to leave. I don't want to be late." Jessica spoke abruptly.

Before I could even really respond, she had me at her bedroom door, walking me down a different set of stairs that brought us to the kitchen. She let me out the back door and said she'd see me on Monday. Why didn't she just go the way we came in? Whatever.

***

I started walking home. I was about half way home when it started to rain. I didn't have an umbrella in my backpack. I turned around my backpack and zipped it inside my sweatshirt to keep it from getting wet. I had some of the papers we were working on and didn't want them getting ruined. I was hunched over them to protect them even more when a car drove up behind me and slowed down. I kept walking and ignoring it until I heard Malcolm's voice. "Hey...get in, you are getting soaked!" I walked over to the car and told him I can't do that. He could get into trouble because he was only 16. No passengers.

He gave me his impish grin and replied, "You only get in trouble if you get caught. I'm always lucky, so I don't."

He was a responsible driver, right? He did pass the driver's test, right? I was getting wetter and colder by the minute, so I walked across and jumped into the passenger seat and clicked my seat belt into place. He wanted to know why I was in the area, so I explained my project and how I was working with Jessica. He said next time she should come to my house so she can get stuck in the rain instead of me. I laughed, like I agreed with him, but nothing was further from the truth. I would rather get soaking wet and catch pneumonia than have Jessica at my house asking questions about my family. Malcolm drove very responsibly. We even passed a police cruiser and he didn't sweat it. Just acted like he was a law abiding citizen. He pulled up to the house and I got out and thanked him for the ride.

I hadn't thought anything about it until I walked through the door. My Mom and Uncle Vinnie were standing there.

"Who was that?" they questioned.

"Mom, you remember Malcolm, Jasmine's brother. He picked me up when I had gotten about half way home. It was raining hard and I was getting soaked. I thought it was very nice of him to offer me a ride." I responded.

"How old is he?" Uncle Vinnie asked.

"17", I lied.

I didn't want them to call Jasmine's parents and tell on him. He'd get in so much trouble. "Well, even though he can legally drive you, I don't want you in the car with someone we don't know." Mom explained.

"I didn't think it was that big of a deal. He is a really good driver." I commented.

"That isn't the point. What if there was an accident? You need to be safe and make good choices. This was not one of them." Mom explained.

I wasn't going to argue with her. It probably wouldn't happen again, so I just said OK and walked away. Parents...they just get so uptight about things sometimes.

***

    I went into my room to drop off my backpack and take out the papers. I was in luck...the rain hadn't soaked through to the papers. I started thinking about Jessica. It was so weird that she all of a sudden remembered she had a dentist appointment. She hadn't mentioned this at all last week when we were planning our work session. She rushed me out of there so quickly. As I thought about it , I remembered that her parents were arguing. Maybe she was embarrassed because we could hear them. Most parents argue about some things, it is no big deal. My parents argued once in a while. I guess I wouldn't have wanted my friends to hear them, though. Since we didn't work for the entire time, I decided to write ideas I had about the next steps to our project so when we worked together on Wednesday after school, we could hopefully get caught up.
    After dinner we played cards. We used to do that with Mom and Dad. Dad loved to play Pitch, so that is what we usually played. The teams were usually me and Dad against JC and Mom. Uncle Vinnie didn't know how to play so we had to do a few hands showing our cards and explaining what everything meant in the game. He picked it up quickly, then asked me to be his partner. I am very competitive when it comes to games and having a "newbie" was not that exciting for me, but I couldn't tell him no. That would just be rude. He did really well, and we only lost by 2 points. We played two more rounds and won the second one, but lost the third by 5 points. I'll admit that it was my fault. I kept overbidding.

Once the cards were put away, JC asked me to play NBA 2K 21 with him. I am not good at video games, but haven't been spending a lot of time with him, so I said OK, but you need to spot me points. He agreed. When I went into his room I noticed that it was much messier than usual.
"Have you forgotten what your floor looks like?" I joked as I kicked my way through the clothes. He responded with a shoulder shrug, "No biggie. Just haven't felt like picking them up." "What HAVE you been doing lately?" I questioned.
"The usual; school, track and gaming. Isn't that enough?" he replied.
"What about homework?" I asked.
"Sometimes I get to it. If I am bored." he commented.
Wow. He had always been good about doing his work and got better grades than me. Usually he earned all A's on his report card. Last year when at the 5th grade moving up ceremony he got a ton of awards. He had them hanging on his wall; Scholar Athlete Award, Best Writer Award, Math-a -lete Award, Academic Excellence in Physical Education, Science AND in History, as well as the Read-a-holic Award, given for reading the most books out of all the 5th graders. I am shocked by his blase response about homework. I didn't want to annoy him with a bunch of questions, so I just stopped at that point and watched him as he totally kicked my butt in basketball. I wonder if Mom knows he is not doing his work. I wonder when she'd last been in his bedroom? Is he still wearing clean clothes all the time? He doesn't smell bad, but he is kind of wrinkled. I didn't want to get on his back about keeping his room clean and doing his laundry. He

obviously has been choosing to not do either and I didn't feel it was any of my business to bug him about it. I finished, well, lost a few games then retreated to my room.

Chapter 16

Sunday afternoon we went to see Grandma. It was JC's first time seeing her since her stroke. I described what she looked like and what she was able to do, physically. I wanted him to be prepared. Grandma would feel awful if she saw either of us upset about her condition. When we got there, she was in a wheelchair watching TV with a group of other older people. When she saw us she smiled. It was still crooked, but not as bad as two days ago. She struggled, but was able to say, "Hi". We asked if she wanted to visit with us in that room. She shook her head no, so we wheeled her into the hallway. She raised her right arm and pointed the direction for us. I was so happy that she could lift her arm and point. She wasn't strong enough to wheel herself, but I felt very confident that she would regain that strength soon.

    We sat on a small couch in a quiet area set up for group visits. I asked her how she was feeling. She shook her head yes and gave me a thumbs up. I guess "hi" was the extent of her ability to speak right now. At least it was something. We asked her yes and no questions the rest of the time. JC was super quiet. I asked him a few things to get him to share something with Grandma.

    As we were talking, Grandma's physical therapist walked by us. He stopped and introduced himself. He then asked Grandma if she wanted to show us her surprise. She smiled and nodded yes. He moved the leg supports to the side of the wheelchair, supported her with a special belt he carried, and she slowly (and wobbly) stood up. She could stand! We all clapped. She stood for about a minute, then he carefully guided her back down into the wheelchair and put the leg supports back into place. He then proceeded to tell us that this was a good sign in Grandma's progress. They would continue to work on standing for longer periods of time and more steadily. Once she could stand for 5 minutes steadily, they would work on walking. She would start with his belt for support and a walker and progress from there. It was the best news! He excused himself so we could continue our visit.

   Grandma seemed to like it there; all except the food. She nodded "no" when we asked her if the food was good. We reminded her that the faster she got better, the faster she could get home and have our food. Even though she was the primary cook in our house, we all were able to make a few good dishes that we knew she would enjoy. After about an hour, Grandma's eyes started to droop. We had tired her out. She needed her rest. She pointed toward her room, so we took her there and helped her get into bed to take a nap.

   On our way home we talked about how much better Grandma looked and how much her strength had improved. We were all so happy, except for JC. "Why is this taking so long? Shouldn't she be all better by now? How long is this going to take? I want her back at home with us. We can help her get better", he shared with us. Mom explained that right now she needed to be there getting the help she needed. She told JC to be patient. Grandma had to move at her own pace and not feel like we are rushing her. We don't want her to fall and have a setback. That would only delay her getting back home.

He just sighed and said, "I guess you're right, but I still want her home."

***

When we got home I suggested that we give Grandma's room a make-over so when she comes home it will be extra special. Mom said that was a great idea and that JC and I could plan what we would do. We agreed that we should paint her room a bright, cheery color. It was a dull-beige right now. We also discussed putting up a collection of pictures she had on one wall so she would have her own sort of gallery to look at. We would rearrange her furniture so her bed would face the window, so when she woke up she could just look straight ahead to see outside into our backyard at the big oak tree she always admired. She loved watching the squirrels and birds that filled that tree with action. We knew we had time to make these changes, so we could choose paint next weekend after we agreed on a specific color. I also started to sketch how we could arrange her furniture. JC went into her room to take out the box of her favorite pictures and we started going through them and picking the ones we thought she'd like to look at every day as they hung on her wall. We worked through dinner time until I was tired enough to go to sleep.

The next morning when I woke up, as I entered the kitchen, Mom held out the newspaper. Front page article about the police investigation of the robbery and homicide. Dad's name, as well as the two others' were there...in black and white...for everyone to read. Mom made me read the article so I would know if what people said to me was what they read or what they speculated based on what they read. It was hard to re-digest all of the pieces of that terrible night. I asked to stay home from school. Mom said no. It didn't matter when I returned to school because all the information would still be "flying". I might as well go in today and face it. She said she was going to call Mr. Coster and give him advance notice that JC and I may need to see him. She also told me that it was up to me to not show how upset I was, especially when other kids say mean things about Dad, whether they are true or not. If I felt upset or angry, I was to go directly to Mr. Coster's office and she would let him know to call her to come to school if we needed her there.

***

Deep slow breaths….as I step on the bus with JC. Trying not to look nervous, scared, worried. My mind racing on how I will defend myself and my family when someone says something. Middle School is tough in that way. Once one person knows, everyone will know within minutes. They will have comments made, either directly or indirectly that JC and I will hear. JC and I talked at the bus stop before other kids arrived. We will do our best to ignore indirect comments whether they are true or not. We will not try to stop the rumors. Rumors are a beast that cannot be tamed in many middle schools. If asked directly about anything, we will answer based on facts, not feelings, in as quick a process as possible. It is going to be very difficult, but we can't avoid the issue, unless we move far away. And even then, there are no guarantees of anonymity. We sit together on the bus which we usually don't do, but safety in numbers prevails, even though our number is only 2. We've got each others' back. That is family. That is love.

We agree that once we have to split up to go to Homeroom that Mr. Coster will be our "go-to". Mom is calling him first thing this morning, so he should have the updated information about what is happening by the time we leave Homeroom.

Nobody says anything to us about the article on the bus. So far, so good. Their families either don't get the newspaper, or hadn't read and shared the article with their kids before school. Maybe we dodged this...for today. I was also, hoping that for JC's sake that his teammates on the track team will be supportive of him and help shield him from at least some of the cruelty. Me, on the other hand, only have about 4 really close friends who I think would do the same for me. I can picture Jasmine being first in line to tell someone off who is saying anything unkind about me and my family. She'd put her hand on her hip, extend her chin with her "tough" look, step toward them and tell them to mind their own business. I almost smile thinking about her defending me. She's always there for me. A few of my other friends would probably say the same thing, but just not with the gusto that Jasmine has.

***

I make it to Homeroom unscathed by comments. I hope JC had the same luck. Homeroom goes on as usual. First period was normal. Second period was totally routine. As I am walking to Math Class, third period, I notice a cluster of kids in the hallway. Not a good sign. Most of them are cheerleaders. I see a newspaper in hand. Here it comes...ready or not! I put my head down quickly and walk into class. I think I am safe, but then remember that two of those girls are in my Math class. I open my notebook and try to immerse myself into completing the mini task on the front board. The girls walk through the door just as the late bell rings. They slowly walk by my desk, even though their seats aren't near mine. I only see their feet because I refuse to look up from my notebook. They slowly get to their seats, but are not opening their notebooks.

There sat today's newspaper sitting atop one of their desks. I can hear their whispers to those around them. Ms. B asks them to settle down and work on their assignment. They follow her directions, somewhat. As class begins, Ms. B asks if anyone has a question about the "try this" mini assignment. Nobody raises their hand at first. She goes through the steps to correctly answer the problem, with volunteers putting in their adjustments to show multiple ways to find the right answer. I start to relax and focus on the math work. Then, Melissa, one of the cheerleaders, raises her hand. When Ms. B calls on her, she asks Ms. B if she can ask an important question that doesn't relate exactly to what we are doing in math. Ms. B has NO IDEA what is coming. She obviously didn't read the paper this morning. She tells her yes, if it is relevant to this class.

Melissa smiles with a totally deviant look on her face, clears her throat, and calmly asks, "Should people who murder others in cold blood be given the death penalty?"

Ms. B looks confused by this question as to the

relevance it has on this class.

    I am totally losing control...breaths will not help this...going to Mr. Coster will not help this.... punching Melissa in face will .... As I stand up and move toward Melissa's desk, I feel like I am moving in slow motion. I cannot get to her fast enough. Claire, the other cheerleader tries to stand in my way, blocking the path to Melissa. I grab her arms and throw her aside with ease. I surprised myself with how fluid that movement was. I take the last few steps, approaching Melissa. She is trapped in her chair, kind of frozen with fear. I liked seeing her that way. I grab the front of her sweater. Her necklace gets tangled in my fist and breaks. I pull back my other arm, my hand in a tight fist. I think of my family...they don't need more issues...I cannot become another problem that they have to handle.

    I pull Melissa up out of her seat by her sweater...tears are already swelling in her pale blue eyes...her eye liner, starting to leak down her face. I put my face right up to hers and say, "Call this your lucky day. When I stood up, it was to remove teeth from your mouth or break your little nose into 100 pieces, but you aren't worth it. Your only power is your rotten mind and big mouth. Someday you will say the wrong thing to someone and you'll be getting so much more than this!" I push her back down into her seat.

    As I move toward the door, I hear her say, "I guess violence runs in her family."

    She hasn't learned her lesson. I turn on my heels and storm right back up to her, grab her by her long brown ponytail and pull her out of her chair, across the room and into the hall. I throw her onto the floor.

"Someday...you will pay, but it won't be me slamming your face into a wall. I am better than that. I am better than you EVERY day of your existence."

I let her go, and continued to walk to Mr. Coster's office.

Chapter 17

I walked right in. Luckily, he didn't have anyone in his office. He was just hanging up the phone. He took one look at my face and told me to have a seat and get comfortable and do my best to relax. Yea, right...relax. What's that? He went right to his bubbler and got me a cup of water. I took a few sips and set it down on the small table next to me. He asked if I was OK. I shook my head yes...then changed and shook my head no.

I started to cry and punch my right fist into my left opened hand. I was just so angry. I didn't feel in control of myself. His phone rang. There were a lot of "OK's" said on his end. He looked at me as the caller spoke. I knew it was about me. His look changed from empathy to concern and disappointment. I couldn't hear what the caller was saying, so I am sure it was whatever Ms. B or Melissa had told that person.

He finally said to the caller, "Give me some time to speak with her and I will call you back. She is extremely upset and needs to settle down and talk out her side of the story."

At that he hung up. He explained that it was Mr. Turbino on the phone filling him in on what Ms. B had reported to him. His next call was to the school nurse, which is where Melissa was. I rolled my eyes.

I didn't physically hurt her, but she was going to play this up to make herself look like the total victim. Give me a break!

Mr. Coster caught the eye roll and asked, "What was that for?"

"I just know how this is going to go. SHE is playing the victim. That is a bunch of bull. SHE started it. And SHE is lucky not to be missing teeth or dealing with a broken nose." I responded.

Mr. Coster assured me that before anyone is accused of anything, that all sides of the story will be heard. He told me to work on relaxing breaths and have some more sips of water. It took me about ten minutes before I was able to say anything. He waited patiently, and turned away two other kids who wanted to see him during that time. I took a deep breath when I was ready and explained everything from my perspective...of the group of kids in the hallway...the two girls walking out of their way to go right by desk in Math class… the newspaper displayed on top of her desk for me to see...the totally out of line question.

When I was finished, he asked me what I thought was going through Melissa's mind during all of these events. Why are we focusing on her? Who cares what was going through her mind? She is a cruel awful human being. Mr. Coster explained that sometimes you need to look at another person's role in a situation to better understand the entire scene. He then asked how I thought Melissa felt when I grabbed her in Math Class.

I said, "Hopefully she was scared. Hopefully she was sorry about what she asked."

He said based on her remark as I was leaving class may have been because she was embarrassed and wanted to get back at me for embarrassing her. I told him that her question embarrassed me. He reminded me that, from what I had described about the scene, that only her and the other girl from her hallway group seemed to know my issue. I was the one who was making it worse by my reactions.

    I started to understand it more as I thought about it. I **was** the one who made things worse. She just baited me into it so it would become a point of gossip and everyone would want to know WHY I got so upset. That's how this whole thing was going to morph into a huge issue. He said when he and Mom spoke this morning that he had prepared Mom to expect something like this to happen. He actually had predicted that it would be JC in his office because 6th graders tend to speak before they think things out more than 8th graders. I told him I was glad it happened to me rather than JC. I said I thought I could handle it better than him.

    He chuckled and said, "Really? Think about HOW you reacted."

    He was right. I totally jumped the gun on this. Melissa baited me and I fell for it. She was the victim...of me. I didn't feel bad for her though. She should have not asked that question.

    Then I thought about Ms. B and the rest of the kids in the class. They must have been in shock, witnessing this entire scene. Ms. B did come over to me when I grabbed Melissa and told me to stop and step back. That is when I started walking out of class...that's when Melissa made the next comment and I walked around Ms. B to grab Melissa and walk her out of class. I would need to apologize to her and the other kids in the class. They were there to learn, not watch a violent show.

Before Mr. Coster spoke, I told him my intentions of apologizing to them. He seemed happy that I was taking blame for the physical component of the scene. He asked if I needed to apologize to anyone else. I said perhaps, but not yet. I needed some more time.

A knock came to the door. It was Mr. Turbino and Mom. They came in and sat down. Mr. Coster explained our conversation and how he was proud of me for taking accountability for my actions. Mr. Turbino explained that school policy was for me to be suspended for two days. After those days I would be part of a meeting with Mom, Melissa and one of her parents, along with Mr. Coster and Mr. Turbino. At that meeting I was expected to apologize to Melissa and mediate how we could continue to be in class and the hallway together without further incident. I asked, "Will she be expected to apologize to me?"

Mr. Turbino asked why she should apologize. I felt a lump in my throat...she had obviously not mentioned her comment that turned me back around. I reminded everyone there about the newspaper, her question and that final comment. Mr. Turbino explained that the newspaper was nothing...I was being overly sensitive to it being on her desk. Perhaps it was, but I know it was intentionally done to get me going.

"What about the question she asked?" I said.

He said although it was not a math question, that it wasn't directly referring to me, so again, I was being overly sensitive. Mom rolled her eyes at that one. She knew it was a targeted question, too. Mr. Turbino said that was asked in poor taste, but nothing she would be required to apologize for. Her final comment, he felt, was unwarranted and more personal because she was regarding it to me and my family, so she should have chosen a better way to express her feelings.

"I want an apology for that comment." I insisted. "That is the least she should do."

Mom asked if Melissa was going to have consequences. The response was that she would serve an after school detention on Wednesday so it wouldn't interrupt her cheer practice.

I remarked, "Well, we know what the priorities are at this school, then."

Mom silently mouthed the word, "Stop" to me. She wanted me to be quiet at that point.

Mom asked if there was a way that Melissa and I could be put into different math classes. Mr. Coster said if that was possible, that it would be my schedule to be changed, since the request came from my family, and that it would change my entire schedule. I immediately shook my head no. I was very comfortable and happy with all my other classes. I liked the teachers I had and the kids in my other classes. Melissa was the only one I was having a direct issue with. I wasn't going to let her comments create another huge change for me to adjust to in my life. Mr. Turbino excused himself at that point. His radio was calling for him to report to another classroom to assist a teacher with a disruptive student. He told my mom and me that he would see us on Thursday morning at 7:30 for a "re enter" meeting. Then it hit me...another Wednesday of me and Jessica not getting to work on our project together. This time it was all my fault...or was it?

Mr. Coster, Mom and I spoke for about 30 minutes about how I could handle my emotions both at home and at school. I needed to not be so physical and not walk out of class. He brought up the issue with Senora Robala. I hadn't told Mom about that so she was mad because she didn't know about that one. I tried explaining how I was trying to keep her from having extra stress and worries when she had so much on her plate at this time. Her response was not what I expected, "Keeping me from knowing what is happening in school just makes things worse for me, not better. You need to tell me about all your feelings and reactions to incidents that happen when I am not with you. I need to trust you, but right now, I don't." That hurt. Deeply.

What I had done is make things worse, not better for her and our family. I needed to be in control of myself. Mr. Coster gave us the name of a family counselor that he thought would relate very well to my family and our current situations. Mom agreed to call and have us all go as a family to meet with her. Great. Not. Another person involved, that I don't even know, who is going to tell us how to "live our lives". I didn't want to upset Mom any more than I already had, so I decided to tell her later that I have no intentions of going to any family counseling sessions. We don't need it. We just need to stick together and talk to each other. We can solve our own problems. Mr. Coster let Mom walk me to each of my teachers with a slip asking for work I needed to complete through Wednesday. I was so embarrassed! She waited outside the door of each room while I went in and collected the work.

All went well until I was in Mr. Willis's Class. He was getting the work for me and as I looked around, I spotted Melissa glaring at me. She had her wrist bandaged. That wasn't there this morning. I didn't even touch her wrist. She was such a fake! She held it up as she whispered something to Jessica, who sat next to her. Jessica kind of ignored the whisper. When Melissa looked away from Jessica, I swear I saw Jessica give me a thumbs-up. What was that all about? They are cheer buddies. I figured Jessica would be glaring at me or whispering back to Melissa. I wouldn't have the chance to ask her about it until Thursday when I was back in school. At least her action distracted me enough so I didn't look at Melissa again. Mr. Willis gave me the work and I walked out the door.

***

When we got home, Mom told me to head to my room and start on my work. She took my phone, saying I could have it back after school hours. She said that is how each day is going to be until I return to school. I have to get up at my regular time and get ready for "school". She will hold my phone from 7:30am until 2:30 pm, which is school time. If I complete all my assigned work, then I need to come see her.

It only took the rest of Monday and about half of Tuesday to complete all the assignments my teachers gave me. She said that the rest of the time I would be working on "home assignments". These included, scrubbing the kitchen floor, cleaning out and reorganizing the pantry, linen closet and my bedroom closet. Cleaning the bathroom, dusting the entire house, sweeping the front porch, vacuuming the rugs, and dry mopping the wooden floors were also added on to my list as I completed each task.

By Wednesday night the place looked great and I

was totally sick of cleaning and ready to go back to school. Also each night I had to sit with Mom and Uncle Vinnie and strategize how I would react to other possible situations that could arise in school. I was tired of it all, but knew they were trying to help me so this didn't happen again. I got it….believe me, I got it!

Chapter 18

Thursday morning I got up earlier than usual. Mom and I needed to be at school by 7:30am. We drove in silence until we approached the school parking lot.

Mom said to me, "There are people in the world who use the misery in their lives as a catapult to drive other people into miserable states. If you let someone get to you and react to them, all you are doing is fueling their fire and making things worse. If you ignore them, they will either stop because they are not getting the satisfaction of bothering you, or they will continue to the point where THEY characterize themselves as the person with the issue. No matter which of those two things happens, you are no longer involved and brought down by their words or actions. Please remember that, because this is probably the first of many things that will happen related to our family situation. We need to all hold our heads high and ignore people who are trying to bring us down. We did nothing wrong. Dad did. And he is ready to pay the consequences for his actions. That is all he can do at this point. He is being cooperative with whatever is being asked of him by the lawyers. We just need to support him because we are still a family and love him. No relationship would last if you ditched someone who made a mistake, had learned from it, and has agreed to not make that type of mistake again."

I listened carefully to her words and let them soak into my brain. It will be hard at times, but I am tough. I can be the better person.

***

We entered the office and sat down at a long table. Mr. Turbino and Mr. Coster were waiting there already. Two minutes later Melissa and her parents came in. They didn't make eye contact with us. They just stared ahead, looking very serious. As Mr. Turbino started, Melissa's dad interrupted him. He said he wanted to have the police called so I could be arrested for assault. He said that his daughter had done nothing wrong. She had asked a question out of sheer curiosity and was attacked. He claimed that Melissa had NO idea about what my father had done. He told us that Melissa said she had the newspaper with her because she needed an article for current events discussions in History class that day. He said Melissa had read the article but had no idea it was my father. He defended her again by saying that Melissa didn't even know my last name.

It was all a bunch of crap. She had lied to her father and left out a few key things that she did to totally bait me. It took ALL of my energy to not stand up and scream at him about the lies and omissions that Melissa selectively formulated in her story to him. Mr. Turbino let him speak his mind, then asked him to listen to the entire report that included what Ms. B witnessed as well as other students. He said he didn't have time for their stories. His daughter was not a liar. She always told him the truth so he didn't need to hear anyone else's interpretation of what happened because he KNEW it already. He said he just wanted me to apologize and promise to never speak to, nor lay a hand on his precious daughter.

He said if this didn't happen that he would have me arrested and that perhaps I could go spend some time with my father. At that point, my mother turned to look at me with tears streaming down her face, swallowing hard to keep her words to herself. Mr. Turbino was sweating. This was so intense. Mr. Coster suggested that Melissa and I do the talking at this point. He looked at me.

I very quietly said, "Melissa, I am very sorry that I reacted the way I did. I am not a violent person, and will not be reacting that way again towards you."

Mr. Coster turned to Melissa.

She replied with, "Good, I am glad you realized your mistake."

And that was it….no apology. No admittance to her part in all of this.

At that point, Melissa's parents asked Melissa if she felt safe now. She smiled and nodded yes. They then walked out of the room. Mr. Turbino followed them. Mr. Coster asked Melissa if she had anything else to say. I think he was hoping she would apologize now that her parents were gone.

She looked at Mr.Coster and said, "Thank you for letting me get out of that detention. My father insisted that I, being the innocent victim, not have to serve it."

She smirked, stood up and walked out. As soon as the door was closed, it was Mom's turn to speak.

"Mr. Coster, how could you and Mr. Turbino let

MY RUINED LIFE

this meeting go on like this? My daughter was taunted by that girl. I don't condone violence, and Nina knows she cannot react that way towards others, but HOW did you let her get away with NO consequence whatsoever?"

Mr. Coster explained that Melissa's father is a very influential person in the community. He had threatened to sue our family, the school and go to the newspapers about this, saying the school did not have control of it's students. Mr. Coster and Mr. Turbino thought it was a small thing to let go to keep our family out of the press even more. Mom thanked him. I was still mad, but did get that part.

Melissa was the way she was because that is how her father is. Her mother said nothing. She just sat there and let this all happen. I wonder if she agreed or disagreed with her husband. I wonder if she believed Melissa's story or just knew she needed to be quiet. How messed up.

***

Mom and I walked into the hall. As I turned to go to class she told me she was really proud of how I managed myself at the meeting. She said it was hard for her to hold back, so she knew it was hard for me as well. I gave her a quick hug, told her I loved her, and not to worry about anything like this happening again with me at school. I went straight to Homeroom. I didn't look around at all. I didn't want to see Melissa until I had to in Math Class. I didn't have Math until last period today, so that was good. It gave me time to calm down some more and strategize in my head what I would do if she started something again.

Obviously Melissa would get away with anything

that wasn't recorded on camera, and even then, her father would probably accuse the school or the kids of setting her up or dressing like her and making it look like she did something wrong. I wonder what will happen when she gets pulled over by the cops for speeding or running a red light when she can drive. Will "Daddy" come to her rescue so she won't have to pay the ticket?

    The bell rang...off to History Class. I wonder what Jessica thinks of all this. She is probably mad because I couldn't meet with her yesterday to work on the project. Before the bell rang, after I had sat down, Jessica came up to me. I thought she was going to say something about our project.

 She shocked me with, "I want you to know that I had no part of what Melissa did or said to you the other day. She thrives on gossip and targeting other people when they are down. I stay out of those situations of hers. We are friends because we cheer together and have the same group of friends, but I don't agree with what she does to other people. I am sorry you had to go through that."

 She turned and went to her seat. I was totally speechless. She was kind of on my side, but not willing to dump Melissa and join "Team Nina", but at least she knew what Melissa was like and didn't agree with her behavior. I mean, like, we aren't friends, just work partners, but that was a cool thing she just did.

 Once she was at her seat and looked over at me, I mouthed the word "Thanks".

    As I entered Math Class, I had a plan. Anything that upset me, I would cover my mouth, like I was about to throw up and run out of the room. That would get me to Coster's office without having to speak. He would vouch for me, I know it. I didn't look in Melissa's direction at all. I got up to sharpen my pencil. When I returned to my desk there was a small paper in my notebook. I didn't even open it. I knew it would be something terrible. Melissa couldn't have gotten to my seat and back to hers without me noticing, but her cheer buddy sat close enough to do this. I don't know who made it...her or her buddy, but I wasn't going to look at it until later. Melissa sat with her hand raised most of class and Ms. B ignored her.

Finally, Melissa blurted out, "I have a question about slope, but you obviously don't care about your students needing help."

I felt bad for Ms. B. She just didn't want Melissa to say anything to start things up again, I know it. She answered Melissa's question about slope, which didn't really relate to the topic for that class, but it covered her at least as responding to her in class.

As we were getting ready for bus dismissal, I went up to Ms. B and apologized for what happened in class on Monday. I assured her it wouldn't happen again. She seemed genuinely concerned about me and told me that I could come to her at any point during class if I needed to take a break. I thanked her. As I left to go to the bus, I decided to just throw away the piece of paper that was put on my desk. I never looked at it...and never looked back. I was going to be the better person, no matter how hard it was to do that. I would not give Melissa or her buddy the satisfaction of hurting me in any way.

***

I sat with Jasmine on the bus. She knew the whole

story up to this morning. I filled her in on the meeting with Melissa and her parents. She was so mad. She called Melissa some pretty ugly names. We agreed that she was going to have a rough life if she never had to have consequences for her behaviors as a kid or a teenager. I almost felt sorry for her in that respect. She didn't know any better. She just figured that whatever she told Daddy, he would take as truth and defend her forever. Someday she might just lose her teeth when someone punches her and doesn't care what her Daddy would have done to them.

Chapter 19

Grandma continued to get stronger. Her speech was getting better too. Each time we went to visit her that first week she showed us what progress she was making. By the end of the week she was standing for five minutes. Her therapist was going to have her start walking.

JC and I decided on a cheery blue green color for her bedroom walls. We would paint them this weekend. We also would go with mom on Sunday to get a huge pallet from the local bakery. They said we could have it for free. We had leftover white paint from painting our bathroom a few months ago, so we would paint it white. Mom bought clips to attach to the pallet. We would hang it on her wall so she could clip the pictures she wanted to look at, and then be able to easily change them without worrying if they would fit in a frame. Uncle Vinnie said he would put brackets on the back of the pallet so we could hang it safely on the wall in her bedroom. Mom bought pretty fabric and was going to make a cover for her comforter that had a color that matched the walls once they were repainted. It became a family project. Uncle Vinnie also said he would help move the furniture around. It was big and heavy so we would definitely need help with that.

    Our hope was to have Grandma come home in a few weeks. She would miss Halloween, but hopefully be home before Thanksgiving. Thanksgiving was always my favorite holiday. It was about food and being with family. No gifts to worry about buying, no major decorating to do. Just being together was the important part of the holiday. Grandma HAD to be home before then...it would be too much to not have her AND Dad not here this year. We also got together with my cousins to play football the day after Thanksgiving. Usually the adults went shopping and the kids hung out at our house after we played football (I always volunteered to keep score), then we would eat leftovers together.

    Grandma always cooked so much that there was a ton of food left for all of us. This year will be different. We will have to do most, if not all, of the cooking ourselves. If Grandma is home, though, she can coach us through it so it should still taste pretty good. I usually make the pies to help out each year. Pumpkin pie and chocolate cream pie are my specialties. My aunt makes two apple pies and brings one over on "football and leftovers" day, so there is always plenty of dessert for both days. I started getting sad, thinking about the upcoming holidays, and how it would be different without Dad.

    I wonder if he got turkey and all the fixings in jail.

I'll have Mom ask him. No, I'd better not. When I asked her to ask Dad if they let him watch football in jail, she said that I would have to ask him questions myself. Well, I guess I won't know the answers to them then, because I just wasn't ready to have a regular conversation with him yet. The next day after I hung up on him when he called to check on Grandma I had to answer the phone because Mom was outside and nobody else was home. I didn't hang up on him. I said hello.

He asked how I was and I said "fine, I'll get Mom", and called her in.

I kept the phone away from my ear so I wouldn't hear his voice if he was asking me questions or trying to talk to me. It just made me sad to hear his voice.

There were a few "minor" incidents at school related to the story in the paper. Most of them were based on rumors, so I ignored them. The more I kept from reacting aloud, the less I heard people talking about it. A boy in my classes had an older brother get drafted into the NBA, so he was leaving college to play pro basketball. That story took over the gossip in the halls and I was very thankful for that. I knew that each time the paper put another article about my Dad and the trial, once it started, that the rumors and gossip would surface again. For now, I just enjoyed the peace and quiet.

***

On Saturday afternoon I walked to Jessica's again. She greeted me at the door and we went straight to her room. Micro was lying on her bed and wouldn't budge, so we sat on her floor and began working. After about an hour I went to use the bathroom down the hall. I passed her mother, who said hello to me, but kept her head down. I couldn't help noticing that it looked like she had a black eye. Just before I was going to leave Jessica's I asked if her mom was OK. Jessica replied, "Why do you ask?"

I explained that I had seen her mom in the hallway and that she looked like she had a black eye. Jessica quickly explained that her Mom had tripped when she was jogging in the park and hit her face on a bench.

"Wow. That must have hurt. The last time I tried to run I tripped and fell, too," I said, recalling the night I went looking for my mother.

Jessica explained that her mother had tripped on a raised crack in the sidewalk, but that she was OK except for hitting her eye. I admitted to Jessica that I am not all that coordinated, so that is why I usually fall when I run. She told me that surprised her because I walk so gracefully. I said thanks.

Jessica then turned to me and said, "I hope things are OK with you and your family. I was mad at Melissa for bugging you about it. It is none of anyone's business. Family situations should just stay in the family. It must have been really upsetting when your personal situation was put in the newspaper."

"It was," I admitted, "I didn't even want to go to school. My Mom made me. I knew I wasn't ready to handle anything from my classmates. That is why I got so upset with Melissa and exploded."

"Parents just don't understand us most of the time," she replied, "Neither of my parents really care about me or my issues; they are so wrapped up in their own lives. I just come and go as I please and as long as I stay out of trouble, they leave me alone."

I felt bad. My Mom leaves me alone to give me time when I am upset about something, but she is there for me, otherwise. I got the direct feeling that this wasn't the case with Jessica.

I tried to make her feel better by saying, "Well parents who hover over you are no joy either. Sometimes my Mom bugs me when I need some space."

It wasn't the exact truth, but I wanted to try to help Jessica feel better about her situation.

I thought about Jessica and her mom all the way home.

***

Sunday we painted all day. Grandma's bedroom looked bright and cheery. I did two coats of white on the pallet and it looked really good. Mom would put the clips on it this week and Uncle Vinnie would get it ready and hang it up on the wall. Mom also told me that I could have a few friends over on Friday night for Scary Movie Night because it was Halloween. JC was going to trick or treat with a few friends then sleep over his friend's house. Mom said she would make pizza and pop popcorn for my friends. They could come over from 6 until 10pm. It would be the first time I would have friends, besides Jasmine, over, without Dad here. They all knew the situation so I didn't have to hide anything.

I immediately called Jasmine, Danielle, Layla and Maria. They all said yes, except for Danielle. When she asked, I clearly heard her step mom say, "No. I don't want you at her house. With what her father did, I cannot trust that you will be safe there. Who knows what else happens there."

Danielle didn't know that I had heard everything.

She just said that she couldn't come over because her family had plans for Halloween so she needed to stay home. I was crushed. I've known Danielle's family for two years. I've always been polite and respectful when I am at their house. Danielle has come over and even slept over many times. Nothing bad has ever happened. Now am I going to lose her as a friend because of something my Dad did? I had no control over what happened. Nobody did except my Dad. And it isn't like he is even here anymore. So not fair! I called the others who all said yes and got permission right away to come over.

When I was finished with the calls I went into Mom's room. She was sitting in her comfy chair reading a magazine. I sat on her bed across from her. She put down the magazine and asked what was wrong. She read my face. I started to cry as I explained how I heard everything Danielle's step mom said. She asked me if I wanted her to call them and talk with the step mom. I said no because Danielle didn't know that I heard what was said and she gave me a different excuse so I wouldn't feel bad. It wasn't Danielle….it was the step mom's comments. I know that Danielle is still my friend but that she may not be coming over much anymore. Mom hugged me. She said she was sorry and that hopefully things will change as time passes. She said that if I want to hang out with Danielle that she will drive me to the park or the mall so we can meet and hang out there. I said thanks and went to my room.

The next day at lunch all the girls I invited over, including Danielle, were sitting together. We started talking about pulling some funny pranks on Uncle Vinnie. We were all laughing except for Danielle.

She was very quiet with an occasional fake smile as if she was going along with our plans. She didn't tell anyone that she wasn't going to be there. I figured it wasn't my business to tell them, so when she wasn't there on Friday night I would just casually say that she couldn't make it. No need for explanations to everyone else.

Chapter 20

On Wednesday after school Jessica and I finally got together to work in the library. We had two hours before the library closed. Mom was going to pick me up, and Jessica's dad was coming to get her on his way home from work. We got a lot accomplished. We planned on finishing it up on Saturday at Jessica's. When we were leaving the library I said goodbye and went to Mom's car. As we got ready to pull away, I noticed that Jessica's dad wasn't there yet. She was standing alone on the sidewalk. I asked mom to please wait for a couple more minutes. It was starting to get dark and Jessica was the only kid left at that point. I asked her to come wait in our car. At first she said no thanks. Once about 10 minutes had passed and she had texted her dad and mom without any response, Mom offered her a ride home. She looked embarrassed, but said OK.

When we got to her house her dad's car wasn't there, but her mom's was. She thanked my Mom for the ride and went inside. After we pulled away, I said that maybe her dad got stuck in a meeting or something. Mom said perhaps, but he could have at least let her know he would be late, or send her mom to go get her. It was dangerous for a young girl to be hanging out alone at school when everyone else was gone. I didn't think much about it but I could tell that this really bugged my Mom. Later that night Jessica texted me and asked me to thank my Mom again for the ride. I said OK then did something I considered risky.

    I invited Jessica to come over Friday night for Horror Movie Night on Halloween. She said she'd ask her parents and let me know. She didn't text me back that night, so I was figuring on her saying no. I am surprised she didn't already have plans with her friends. It was Halloween, after all. And being on a Friday night made it even better this year!

    The next day she told me that she could come over. I told the rest of the girls coming over while we were eating lunch. Jasmine wanted to know why I invited "her". I explained that I didn't really plan on it, but it just came up as we were texting back and forth last night.

"What were you texting her for?" Jasmine questioned.

I explained that she had texted me and I just replied to her. It was no big deal to me, but I could tell it bothered Jasmine.

"I am surprised that she isn't going out with her cheer buddies for Halloween or to a party with the football players." Jasmine wondered aloud.

"I was surprised by that too," I agreed, "but it will be fun. She is pretty nice once you get to know her."

Jasmine sighed and said, "We'll see about that."

***

    It was finally Friday. Halloween! I've never been a fan of going trick or treating, so having a few friends over for a scary movie night was my way to celebrate not getting a ton of candy and dressing up in a costume. A few practical jokes also made the night special to me. I am not a big practical joker, but for some reason, I was very willing to pull a few pranks on Halloween Night. Usually my Dad was the "victim"...and he loved it. I am hoping that Uncle Vinnie will appreciate them as much as Dad did.

  Jasmine and I decided to choose the 3 best jokes of all time that we've pulled on Dad and repeat them, since Uncle Vinnie didn't know about them. Everyone came over around 6 o'clock. We had pizza with JC then he went to his friend's house. We decided on a double feature with a 10 minute intermission. The first movie featured clowns scaring a town. Clowns are so creepy. Sometimes I wonder why little kids love them and have them entertain at birthday parties.

  We had finished the movie when joke number one took place. Uncle Vinnie said a few inappropriate words when he walked into the giant spider web we set up just outside the back door. Mom helped with that one, asking him to please take out the garbage well after it was pitch-black outside. We all giggled when he came back in with some of the web still stuck in his hair and on his arms. He gave us a hesitant smile and shook his head.

  About half way into the second movie he opened the fridge for a snack. The fishing line attached to the fridge door dropped a fake bat on his head. Again...a few "bad" words slipped out of his mouth. He returned to the living room and we paused the movie long enough for him to ask if there were any more "surprises" for him tonight. We said maybe, trying to keep straight faces.

The third prank happened right before our second movie ended. He went into the bathroom and well, we had JC's remote control spider crawl across his feet while he was brushing his teeth. He yelled and threw his toothbrush, filled with toothpaste, across the room. Jasmine ran back to the couch, pretending to be watching the movie with the remote still in her hand. She ditched it between the cushions as he entered the living room. Uncle Vinnie retreated to JC's room to use his TV, mumbling something loud enough for us to hear about how he wondered how Dad survived us on Halloween Night.

***

After the movies were over, everyone's rides showed up except Jessica's. Finally, after a few texts she sent to her parents that went unanswered, Mom offered to give her a ride home. She seemed very embarrassed, but Mom assured her that it was not a big deal. I had headed into my room, after assuring Uncle Vinnie that there were no more jokes coming his way. About 40 minutes later I heard Mom pull into the driveway. I heard multiple voices. That was weird. Who was with her? As I emerged from my room, Jessica was standing in the living room, talking with Mom. Jessica told me that her parents weren't home yet from the party they had gone to and she hadn't brought her key. Mom offered for her to sleep over, so she texted her parents to let them know.

Here she was. Mom looked upset, but I figured it was because she had driven all the way over to Jessica's for nothing. Jessica and I went into my room and I gave her a pair of sweats and a tee shirt to sleep in. We set up the twin air mattress I kept under my bed for when I had a friend over, gave her my extra bed pillow and comfy blanket at the foot of my bed. We talked for a few minutes about the movies and pranks we pulled on Uncle Vinnie then she said she was tired. I turned off the light and that was it... we fell asleep very quickly.

***

The next morning Mom made us pancakes and bacon. A short time later, Jessica's mom beeped the horn in front of our house and off she went. She thanked Mom and I about ten times for letting her sleep over and making her feel so comfortable and welcome. When she left I went back into the kitchen. Mom was sitting at the table, sipping her coffee and looking upset. When I asked her what was up, she told me we needed to talk. Oh boy...this couldn't be good.

Mom explained that sometimes people who are in a bad situation lie about it to save face. I asked what she meant by that. She said that what she needed to tell me HAD to stay between her and me. I promised.

Mom told me that Jessica's parents were home when they got there last night. When they pulled up, you could hear yelling from inside the house. Her parents were arguing. Mom said she wouldn't let Jessica go into the house. They waited a few minutes to see if it settled down but it did not. Mom heard a crash inside. At that point she called the police. Jessica was very upset.

When the police arrived, they asked if Jessica could stay somewhere else for the night. Mom automatically said yes, she could come back to our house. She drove away after Jessica texted her Mom to tell her she was staying with us. Jessica shared with Mom that her parents fight a lot. Sometimes they throw things around. She even confessed that her Dad has hit her Mom a number of times. She says her Mom won't leave because she feels she had nowhere to go. Her Mom's side of the family lives in Texas and she doesn't want to go there, especially if Jessica and her brother don't want to go with her. Jessica said she and her brother don't want to move far away. They like their schools and their friends. If her mom left, they would choose to stay with her dad. Her father also drinks a lot. Alcohol. He gets drunk, and that is when the fighting usually starts. Dad gets mad at Mom for spending money or not keeping the house perfectly clean, or not cooking what he wants for dinner.

    She said when Dad is sober he is very reasonable and is always sorry after they fight and especially after he hits her mom. When they fight Jessica and her brother stay in their rooms because once they tried to stop him and he hit both of them. They know it is because of his condition when he drinks and that he loves them, so they just don't get involved. She told Mom that the police have come before, but she and her brother just go to her Dad's sister's house (her aunts) and stay there until Dad is sober. Mom then comes and gets them. They both feel helpless. Mom won't do anything to help herself and Dad won't quit drinking.

   I told Mom that I want to help her, but how can I if I am not supposed to tell anyone or discuss this with Jessica? Mom told me to just be a good friend to Jessica. Jessica feels alone. Her brother is the only one who knows about it besides her aunt, and

now Mom. I agreed, but thought that it is weird that she hasn't told any of her cheer friends or the football players. Maybe she is not really close with any of them. She backed me up with the issue with Melissa. I guess I misjudged her.
I walked to Jessica's house a few hours later. It was the final Saturday to finish up our project. Jessica answered the door. We went straight to her room. She was being very quiet and I didn't know what to say to her. I couldn't let her know that I knew her whole story. We worked for about two hours and were almost done. We went to the kitchen for a snack. Her mom was in there, making tea for herself. She had a bandage above her ear. When we walked in, her mom put her hand up to her head saying how much of a mess she looked. She then went on to explain that she slipped on the wet floor in the bathroom last night and hit her head. She had to go to the hospital and get 7 staples. She went on about how she was always careful to wipe up the floor after giving the dog a bath in the tub but had missed a spot. I smiled and nodded as she told me this "story".

***

I walked home with so much running through my brain. How could Jessica's mom live like that? Why did she make up stories about her injuries and cover up for her husband who treated her so badly? How could Jessica and her brother live like this? How could Jessica's dad live with himself, the way he treated his family? I couldn't believe that at that point I considered myself "lucky". I had a loving family. Sure, Dad made a huge mistake and was paying for it, and our family was suffering that way, but he didn't physically hurt anyone.

Jessica always came across as so perfectly put together. She was captain of the cheer team. She hung around with all the "popular" people at school. She had her hair, make-up, clothes....everything so neat and clean. Her home was beautiful. Her parents drove nice vehicles. She had it all....or did she? It was so difficult to imagine her as someone who needed anything. She needed stability in her home life.

Family stability meant so much to me. I knew I could count on Mom, Uncle Vinnie and Grandma to love me and JC and provide what we needed in life. I was never scared to be at home. Sure, I wasn't happy that my Dad wasn't with us. I truly had NO control over that. Jessica must feel like she has no control when it comes to her dad and mom. I wanted to talk to her so badly, but had to keep my promise to Mom. I would get Jessica to talk to me. I would be the friend she could go to and spill her guts about everything....and vent when things got bad. She needed me. I never thought of myself as the friend who had her "you know what" together....but I think I was, at least in this case.

Chapter 21

Monday was a day off. Teachers' had meetings all day. Jessica texted me on Sunday to see if I wanted to come over Monday to finish the project. I went over right after lunch. We worked for about an hour and a half. It was finally finished. We had completed all of the tasks in the rubric so that we SHOULD get at least an A- or better on our project.

When I was about to leave Jessica said something

that caught me off guard. She asked me if my parents ever fought before my Dad went to jail. I told her the truth. They argued sometimes, but it usually only lasted for a short time. Neither of them held grudges with each other. She asked if they ever got mad enough when they argued that they broke things or hit each other.

  I shook my head no, then felt the opportunity to ask , "Why, do your parents do that when they argue?"

 I saw a look of anguish on her face as she debated in her head whether or not confide in me. She started talking so fast that I was glad I had a head's up from my Mom about the situation, otherwise I don't think I could have followed all she was sharing with me. She told me EVERYTHING! Even more information than what my Mom knew. I did my best to look shocked. She was so wrapped up in what she was saying that I think I could have had any look on my face and she wouldn't have noticed. By the time she had finished, she was crying really hard and looked so angry. She told me that she hated her father and thought her mother was a pathetic loser. She didn't side with either one of them. She told me that she wanted to run away and not live with either of them. She said she had a plan to leave, but then started working with me on the project and felt a connection to me. She said we both had broken homes just mine was more obvious than hers. She started watching how I managed my life…at least the parts she could see, and wanted to become better friends. She said I was a strong person. She said she wanted to be more like me.

   I couldn't believe her words. The perfect girl wanted to be like me? I shocked myself at that moment. I hugged her. I told her she was strong and that I could be there to help her stay strong. I assured her that I would tell nobody what she had shared. I said she could text or call me anytime she was upset or scared and wanted someone to talk to. I had her promise me that she wouldn't run away. I had her agree that when her parents fought that she would lock herself in her room or leave the house. I wanted her to be safe. I told her that my Mom would let her stay at our house if she ever needed to get away for a while. I hadn't checked with Mom on this but knew she would be OK with it. By the time we finished talking it was getting dark. Daylight savings time stinks! I called my mom. She was in the middle of making dinner, so Uncle Vinnie came to get me.

***

. As we rode home, he shared good news with me. The physical therapist said Grandma could come home in about a week. Yea! She would be home before Thanksgiving! And her bedroom surprise was all set up and waiting for her. Yesterday when we visited her she was able to walk pretty well with a walker. She had full use of both arms and hands. Her speech was a bit slurred and she spoke a bit more slowly than she used to, but you could understand her. She told us yesterday that her next task for physical therapy was being able to walk up and down three stairs while holding onto a railing. I wondered why she only had to do three stairs. Now it made sense. There were three steps to get onto our front porch from the sidewalk. There were no other stairs except for the two out the back door. As long as she could make those front stairs she was all set for home life. Uncle Vinnie told me the landlord was letting him install a railing on the back steps so Grandma could go into the back yard easily. He said he would get it done this week after work. JC was so happy about Grandma coming home that he offered to help Uncle Vinnie get this done. I was glad to hear this, too. JC spent so much time in his room gaming, that it would give him a break from it while he helped out with this project.

After dinner, Mom and I were cleaning up the kitchen together. I told her about what happened with Jessica and what I had told her about coming over if she needed to get out of her house. Mom agreed that she is welcome any time she needs a break from home. I went into my room just as I got a text. It was Jasmine. She wanted to know why I hadn't texted her back from her first text a few hours ago. I explained that I was finishing up the project with Jessica, then having dinner. She didn't respond. What's her problem? I didn't ignore her, I was just busy. I'll talk to her about it tomorrow on the bus.

***

I saved Jasmine a seat on the bus. She got on, walked past me and sat with someone else. What is going on with her? She always sat with me when she could. I waved at her. Maybe she missed me in the seat. When she saw my wave, she turned to another kid and started talking. Huh….I was clueless as to why she was being this way. When we got off the bus I waited for her and asked her if she was OK.

"I'm fine" she replied, coldly.

Then she just walked away and caught up with Danielle. Something was up with her. She'd let me know. She and I were always open and honest with each other. We'd been "besties" for so long. We didn't argue like most friends do at some points during their friendship.

At lunch I sat with my regular group of friends. Everyone was acting normal toward me except Jasmine.

As we left the lunchroom, I pulled her aside. "What is going on?" I asked.

"Nothing." she replied flatly, then tried to walk away from me...again

. I caught up with her.

"Why are you being like this?" I questioned, beginning to lose my patience.

"Like what?" she snipped

. As she turned away again, I mumbled, "I hate games like this."

Jasmine turned to me and boldly responded, "Just leave me alone. Go hang with your new buddy, Jessica. Are you going to try out for cheerleading soon? Are you dating a football player now?"

She walked away quickly before I could react. She is jealous. She thinks Jessica is my new best friend. Why can't I be friends with both of them? I can't choose. Jessica needs me, but I can't tell Jasmine that without betraying Jessica. I hate complicated relationships! I need to figure out a way to keep things balanced so I don't lose Jasmine. They got along fine at my house on Halloween so I don't know why this is suddenly an issue with her. I decided to give her some space and call her after school to talk.

In History Class, Jessica and I told Ms. Lack we were finished with our project. We had organized the entire event. We had gotten permission from the

Superintendent of Schools to have the walk a thon the first Saturday in December. We knew it would be cold, but didn't want to wait too long to have this event. We wanted to have all the proceeds and donations collected and set before December Break. The food pantry/clothing closet at school would be starting in January. Jessica and I had agreed to help set up the room being used during the school's break after Christmas.

Jasmine sat with Mark on the bus. I didn't expect her to sit with me at that point. I wanted to reassure her that she was still my best friend. I guess that would have to wait.

***

When I got home Mom shared information with me regarding my Dad's trial. The lawyers told her that the trial for Dad is set to begin within the first or second week of December as long as nothing unexpected regarding the case occurs.

I took a deep breath and asked something that has been on my mind since the "horrible" night…"Mom, how long is Dad going to have to stay in jail?"

I had looked up information about sentencing related to crimes like his but there were many different results based on exactly what the person was charged with along with prior arrests among other issues. Mom told me that she didn't know exactly, it would depend on many components.

I also asked if Dad ever committed other crimes. I know that this can affect a sentencing. Mom shared that Dad had been arrested about 15 years ago. He had gone to a protest that turned into a riot. Dad got caught up in the violence and threw a brick through the window of a parked car. He did not hurt anyone, but did damage someone else's property. A police officer had seen him do this and arrested him. He was on probation for a year and paid for the repair of the window to the owner of the vehicle. Mom said other than that, besides a parking ticket and two speeding tickets, he was a law abiding citizen. It had been a long time since he had broken the law so she was hopeful that these incidents wouldn't count against him. She also added that Dad's attorney wasn't sure his arrest 15 years ago would make the sentencing more severe because it had happened so long ago, and he hadn't had any major issues with the law since that time. She said that during the trial she will be going to the courthouse each day to be there in support of Dad. I asked if kids were allowed to go. She was going to check with the attorney. She told me she was surprised I wanted to go because I still refused to go see Dad on Saturdays. She explained that I would not be able to talk to him at all. He would be escorted in by correction officers and be handcuffed and shackled. It may be a lot for me to see, but I wanted to know if I even had the option to go.

   I went to my room to "absorb" all the information then started to work on my homework. It would be a good distraction for my brain. I stopped long enough to have dinner, then cleaned up the kitchen and returned to my room to finish my assignments. When I took a break and looked at my phone it was 9:00.

   Was it too late to call Jasmine? I decided to chance it. She answered. I wanted to start off casually, so I asked her about an assignment even though I had already done it. She gave me a response then asked if that was all I wanted. I said no. I told her I was sorry she was so upset about my friendship with Jessica. I asked her why she didn't like her. She said I didn't understand. I asked her to explain, because they seemed to get along fine at my house the other night. I just felt confused, I explained. She told me again that I just don't understand. She said she had to get off the phone and finish her homework.

I said , "OK, but I hope we can sit together on the bus in the morning."

She just said "bye" and hung up.

At least she knows I care. I called. I am hoping that is enough to at least start us back on the right track. I don't need extra drama. I got ready for bed and fell asleep thinking about my Dad and the upcoming trial.

***

There was a huge crash. I jumped out of bed to see what it was. I heard a lot of voices, most of them I didn't recognize. They were crashing through the living room. Mom started yelling. JC joined her. I stood frozen in the doorway to my bedroom. There were four police officers in my house, telling my mom and JC to move aside. My heart felt like it was going to pound out of my chest. What was happening? I wanted to speak, but couldn't. I wanted to tell them to get out. Why were they here?

They moved quickly throughout the house. A lamp got knocked over and crashed to the floor. One officer pushed the bathroom door open. He had his gun drawn.

He shouted, "Nothing!", and moved toward the

kitchen.

One officer stood at the front door blocking the exit. Two others busted into my parents room. I heard my Grandma scream. The one in the kitchen had gone into her bedroom. She may not have heard them at first. When she takes her hearing aids out she doesn't hear much of anything. I heard the two in my parent's bedroom shout, "Got him!"

I heard my dad yell, as if in pain.

I stepped toward the door and the officer said, "Stop, don't move," to me. I stood in the hall but could see what was happening. The officers were dragging my dad out from under the bed. Why was he there? Why were they grabbing him? Why did they hurt him? All these questions whirled through my head. I felt dizzy. I lowered myself along the wall onto the floor. They have the wrong guy...they must have the wrong address. Man, they are going to be in so much trouble for doing this to my family! They pulled my Dad to his feet. They started reading him his rights as they handcuffed him.

Dad wouldn't look at us. His head stayed down, focused on the floor. Grandma was standing in the kitchen doorway crying. Mom was yelling, "No, no!"

As they were walking my Dad out the front door he said, "I love you all. I am sorry."

What did that mean? Sorry for what? Mom and JC were with Grandma now. They were hugging her and supporting her as she walked to the recliner in the living room. I ran across the living room and out the front door. I picked up a baseball on the front porch, poised to throw it at the cruiser that was taking my Dad away. I stopped myself...I woke up.

I was covered in sweat.
　That was the first time I had dreamt about that horrible night. It was the scariest thing that has ever happened to me and my family. I heard the TV in the living room. I peeked out. Mom was watching the news. I walked out to the couch and sat next to her...really close. I started crying and hugging her. She hugged me back, saying nothing. She just let me do what I had to do. I had to get it all out of my system. All of the emotions from that night came pouring out in my tears. Once I had stopped, I began to tell her about my nightmare. I couldn't breathe. Mom looked me in the eye.
She said, "breathe...slowly....one breath at a time....focus on your breath".
　I followed her directions and started to regain control of my breathing. I fell asleep on the couch, leaning on Mom. She stayed there with me the entire night. I just didn't want to be alone.

***

　The morning brought a sore throat. I get them when I cry hard. Mom could tell by my voice. She asked if I wanted the day off. I had been through so much needed a break. I agreed. A day without school stress would be good. I ate breakfast and then went back to the couch. There was some talk show on. I focused on the conversation about the movie coming out that starred the person being interviewed. After that, the hosts made a dessert for Thanksgiving with a famous chef. It was not very exciting. Daytime TV was definitely boring.
　Mom got a call. Grandma could come home tomorrow or today, if we were ready for her. Mom agreed that today was perfect for her to come home.

She said I could go with her to get Grandma and all her things. We went right after lunch to get her.

We had to stop at the local pharmacy and get the medications that Grandma would need to take from now on to keep her from having another stroke. By the time we got the medications, got all of Grandma's things packed, filled out all the paperwork and had a lesson from the physical therapist showing us the strengthening exercises Grandma should do each day it was mid afternoon. We had to set up home visits with the speech therapist and the physical therapist. Grandma would have one or the other every day for a couple of weeks at least. It took awhile for Grandma to get to the car and into the front seat. She looked tired but happy.

When we arrived home I remembered about Grandma's room being all new to her. I had her sit in the recliner to rest. I didn't want her to see her room until JC and Uncle Vinnie were home. We were all a part of the project so we should all see her reaction together. I took her suitcase into the bedroom for her and told her I unpacked it for her so she wouldn't feel the need to do it herself before we were all home.

About an hour later, JC and Uncle Vinnie arrived home. We told Grandma we had a surprise for her. She walked into her room and started tearing up. Her smile was still a bit crooked, but beautiful. She was so happy. We explained our whole plan and how we worked together to do this for her. She said she felt like the luckiest person in the world to have us as her family. She laid down to rest for a while as Mom and I made dinner. She came out for dinner and looked more rested.

It felt pretty close to normal at dinner. JC told me that I missed a fire drill. Good. I hate them. The alarm startles me and I usually jump out of my seat. I've even thrown my pen into the air when the horn sounds. He also said track practice went well. He has the second fastest time on the team for the 2 mile run. We all told him how great that was. I said that he would definitely have the fastest time by next year if he kept training.

Chapter 22

On the bus the next morning, Jasmine asked where I was yesterday. I told her I didn't feel well, so Mom said I could stay home. She seemed satisfied with the answer. She sat with me, but was pretty quiet after our brief question and answer session. When we arrived at school she saw a kid from her Spanish Class and went over to see her. I just continued to Homeroom.

   On my way there, Jessica stopped me in the hallway. She pulled me into the girls' bathroom. We were the only ones in there. She looked very upset. She started telling me about an issue her parents had last night. After they fought, her Dad left. He took the car, even though he had been drinking. That was such a bad choice. He got arrested with a DUI. Her mom was still so mad that when he called for her to come and get him, she told him she would "sleep on it". Her Mom left her Dad to stay overnight in jail. Wow.

   The bell rang during her explanation, then the late bell rang. We were both late for homeroom. I told her that Mr. Coster was a good listener. She wasn't ready to talk to him. She was afraid he would call and have her and her brother taken from their home. I agreed. Both her parents were having major issues....with each other and with themselves. If they thought the home wasn't safe, Jessica and her brother would not be allowed to stay there for their own safety.

Jessica asked if I could check with my mom and see if she could stay with us for a few days until her parents "figured things out". I knew in my head that they wouldn't. They just keep fighting over and over. I called my mom. As I was calling, the bell rang for the first period. Great. Now we are late and she won't go to Coster and get a late pass. Mom answered. I quickly explained what was happening. She said that Jessica could come over after cheer practice. Uncle Vinnie would pick her up on his way home from work. I told her I would stay after in the library so that I could be with her once cheer was finished. Mom agreed. She did say that she wasn't sure how long Jessica could stay.

Jessica gave her mom's number for me to give my mom so they could talk about this. Man....Mom doesn't need more to deal with. She has always been helpful to others, but she's got Dad's upcoming trial on her mind, Grandma just came back home, and now this situation with Jessica. As we left the bathroom, Jessica said she was going to talk with the cheer coach about some fundraiser they were doing. She said that the coach would give her a pass to get to class without being in trouble. Great...that left me to fend for myself. Think…. I decided to go see Mr. Coster myself.

***

I was feeling overwhelmed about Dad's situation

and now Jessica's. I had to wait until he was done speaking with another student. While I was sitting outside his office, Jasmine walked by to get a drink from the water fountain. She asked why I was there. I told her I needed to talk to Mr. Coster about a private matter. She gave me a look...I usually confided everything with her, so she asked, "What is it about? Stuff with your Dad?" I answered yes and told her I would talk to her about it later. She said she would talk to me on the bus. I then let her know I wasn't taking the bus because I was going to the library after school. She wanted to know why. I told her I wanted quiet work time. I lied and said JC has been playing his video games pretty loud and it broke my focus on my school work. She accepted that and replied that she would come over so we could talk after dinner. I told her she couldn't come over because Grandma just got home and we wanted to not have extra noise and commotion in the house for a while as she adjusted to being back at home. She looked at me weird. It was kind of a lame excuse. She always was able to come over whenever she wanted. She was like extended family.

At that point, Mr. Coster opened his door to let the other person get back to class and let me in. Jasmine just walked away, shaking her head. She knew something was up. I couldn't tell her though. It wouldn't be fair to Jessica.

I headed into his office. Once the door closed I sighed heavily. He gave me some water to sip. I didn't cry. I didn't yell. I just wanted to talk. I told him about my Dad's updated situation. I told him about my dream. I told him about Grandma.

I told him about "a friend of mine", explaining

Jessica's situation. He listened carefully, absorbing all my information. His face changed, though, when I got to Jessica's situation. He asked me if this friend goes to school here. I said yes. He then proceeded to tell me that it was my obligation to tell him who the person is. This is a situation that could lead to a more destructive situation. He needed to keep the student safe. If I was a true friend to this person, I should want to protect her too.

    I explained that I had promised not to tell anyone, but needed to talk about everything and get it off my chest. I told him I couldn't tell him who, but that I did encourage her to come talk to him, but she just isn't ready yet. I explained how we just spent 20 minutes in the bathroom and now were late to class as well. He asked if it was Jasmine. I told him absolutely not. I didn't want him to bring her in here and confuse her and involve her in this situation. He believed me.

    He said this was a police matter. I told him that I have to keep my promise to my friend. He then said something that shocked me. "How would you feel if she, or someone in her family gets seriously hurt or killed and you knew about this issue and didn't tell anyone? Could you live with that guilt?" Wow. That was like a sucker punch to my stomach. I told him I needed time to think about this. He told me to check in with him at the end of the day. I agreed to do so. All day I couldn't focus on my work. What was I going to do? If I gave Jessica's name, she would never forgive me. I would make things worse for her.

    Mr. Coster gave me a pass to class and I left with the certainty that I would not give him any information. I would tell him at the end of the day that I could not betray the trust that was given to me, but would encourage my friend to go see him and talk about what has been happening in her home. Everything seemed back to normal...until. Half way through History Class, Mr. Coster called Ms. Lack and asked to see Jessica. As soon as Ms. Lack gave the pass to Jessica and she saw where she needed to go, she shot me a look of dread. That was followed quickly by a look of hatred. I didn't understand why at first. I asked immediately to get a drink so I could talk to her in the hallway.

Once in the hall I called after her. She spun around on her heel to face me
. "What?" she demanded.
"Where are you going?" I questioned
. "You know perfectly well where I am going. You have a big friggin' mouth. I actually thought we were friends. Now I have much bigger issues to deal with. Coster isn't calling me in to ask how my day is going, right?!"
" I didn't tell him it was you. I don't know how he could have found out. Maybe he is just asking my friends to try to find out for himself." I hoped aloud.
"You'd better be right...because if not, there will be hell to pay. You will have ruined my life." she responded.
I started towards her, "Let me go with you. I want to help." I offered.
"No. Just go back to class and start praying that your hunch is correct." she responded.
I went back to class, but my mind just started racing about how he could have possibly found out. Maybe he called my Mom. Mom may have told him, especially after knowing what happened last night at

Jessica's house. Would Jessica hate me if it was my Mom that blabbed? I hope not. School would become unbearable if she got all her cheer friends and football buddies to target me. I didn't complete any work that period or the next. I was fully absorbed in my own thoughts. At the end of the day I would go see Mr. Coster and he would tell me if he figured out I was trying to protect Jessica.

***

When the dismissal bell rang I shot out the door and straight to his office door. It was closed. I could hear multiple voices inside. I didn't knock. I recognized Jessica's muffled voice through the door. She was STILL in there! That was not good news for me. If he was just checking in with her, she should have been out of there for the last period. I didn't know what to do or where to go. The plan was for me to meet her after cheer practice and go to my house.
    I decided to text Mom. She didn't respond. I walked to the library. As I went by the glass windows in the front of the building there were two police cars out front. I stopped and stared. As my gaze wandered further into the parking lot I spotted Mom's car. I looked into the front office. She wasn't in there. I went in.
    "Is my mom here?" I asked the secretary.
    "I can't tell you", she responded.
    "Her car is in the parking lot. I saw it. I want to know where she is." I demanded.
    "I can't tell you that right now.", she responded, turning back to her work.
    "Look, this is MY MOTHER, I have a right to know where she is in the building." I raised my voice.

"You need to just wait for her, then. If you want to sit in here until she is leaving for her vehicle, go ahead, but I can't tell you where she is." was the response.

So I sat and waited and fidgeted for about ten minutes. Finally I couldn't take it anymore.

"I'm going to get a drink", I announced.

I kept my backpack on and walked out casually. I strode right by the fountain toward Mr. Coster's office. As I approached, Mr. Turbino was waiting outside the door for me. He told me that Mom was inside the office but all he could tell me was this matter didn't involve me anymore. I told him I HAD to go in and see her. He calmly said I would have to wait a few more minutes. I insisted on waiting right there, outside the office door. He warned me that that may not be a good choice, but he wasn't going to stop me.

The voices inside continued. The tones were calm and serious. I didn't hear Mom's voice at all anymore. Actually, I didn't recognize most of the voices at that point. When the door opened the office emptied. There were a number of people inside. Mom came out looking upset. I waited for Jessica. I wasn't sure what I was going to say, but I felt a great need to see her. As she emerged with a woman I didn't recognize, I stepped forward. Jessica stopped in her tracks. Her face was stricken with tear marks.

She looked very angrily at me, pointed a finger at me and remarked, "This is all your fault. You have ruined my life. Don't ever speak to me again."

The person with her just continued to walk with her down the hallway. I wanted to run after her, hug her, explain that I didn't tell on her.

Mom took my hand and softly said, "She needs time to digest everything that is happening. You need to give her time."

I broke away and ran to Jessica. I started rambling to her that I didn't tell on her and that I will do whatever she needs to help her through all of this. She just kept walking, not even glancing in my direction, with a stone faced expression.

The woman with Jessica kept walking alongside her, not responding to my comments. Who was she? It wasn't her Mom. She had a briefcase and was dressed very neatly and in high heels. She didn't seem to be supporting Jessica, just escorting her out of the building. Mom grabbed my hand, a bit more firmly, to hold me back from continuing to follow them. I stopped walking and just stood there.

"Mom, who is that with Jessica?" I demanded to know.

"She is a social worker. She is going to help Jessica and her brother, Will, stay safe for now." she responded.

"But shouldn't Jessica be coming with us instead of going with her, some stranger? We can keep her safe at our house." I responded.

Mom explained quickly to me that this was now a legal matter and the decisions were out of our hands. Mom had offered to have Jessica stay with us, but Jessica was so upset with me that she refused the offer. The social worker said she would contact family members for her and her brother to stay with, or they could go to a foster home until the investigation was completed and more decisions could be made.

At that point I broke free from Mom's grip and turned, walking back toward Mr. Coster. He did this….but how? As I came closer, he began telling me that this was not my fault. I was a good friend to Jessica. That at some point Jessica would realize this, but she needed time to process everything. I asked why he called my Mom. He said that after he watched the hallway cameras to see who came out of the bathroom with me this morning, he saw it was Jessica. He called my Mom to see if she knew any more information than what I had given him. Mom came to school and helped fill in what she knew. He explained that he is a mandated reporter. He could lose his job and be arrested if he didn't report this. He needed to keep Jessica and Will safe. He told me that Jessica and Will would be kept safe now and that I did the right thing by coming to him. Yea, right...I thought. Now my already messed up life would be more messed up because of all this. At that point I just wanted to go home.

Chapter 23

Mom explained that the social worker was going to see if Jessica's aunt would be able to have Will and Jessica stay with her through the investigation. The social worker said they always try to set kids up with relatives, if they are able to keep them safe, so that family remains together. Mom and I knew that they had stayed with their aunt a few times already when things were bad at home. I hoped they could at least stay with her.

   Jessica wasn't in school the rest of the week. I waited a couple of days, hoping she would stop being so mad at me, then tried texting her. I got no response. I called and left voicemails for her. No response as well. I wanted to tell her I was sorry that things went this way, but that I was glad she and Will were in a safe place. I didn't even know where they were.

The next week we had Monday off for Veterans' Day. On Tuesday morning I was really nervous. I had no idea what to expect from Jessica. Would she be mean to me? Would she have her cheer friends be mean to me? I almost asked to stay home from school, but figured I might as well get through whatever was going to happen today and not put it off until tomorrow. I didn't see Jessica on the bus. Then I remembered that she wasn't living at her house right now. I didn't see her until lunchtime. She was sitting with her cheer friends. I was able to catch her eye once. She was emotionless when I waved to her. I hoped it was because she didn't notice I had waved. In History class I walked by her and said "hi". She continued to look away from me as if she didn't hear me. Well, at least her friends weren't being mean to me. I was sure that if Melissa knew what was going on that she would gladly jump in to some type of rotten remarks or actions towards me.

At home that night I told Mom about how she ignored me. Mom said something I hadn't thought about...Jessica would probably not say anything to her cheer friends because they may act weird towards her. Jessica had told me that she wasn't all that close to them, so she may not trust them to stick by her during this hard time in her life. That worked to my benefit, but then I felt bad.

She must feel so alone. She doesn't have anyone to talk to. The one person she trusted totally blew it...me. I didn't do it on purpose, honest. But to be totally truthful, I was glad that she and Will were in a safe place. I hoped her Mom had left the house as well. Mom encouraged me to just keep my distance, but offer a small sign of friendship towards her each day. Perhaps she would realize that I wanted to be there for her and LET me be there for her. It may take time, though. I guess if it were me in her shoes that I would need time to figure things out.

***

A few weeks passed and it was finally Thanksgiving Break. A five- day weekend. Yea! During this time I had been thinking about my Dad...a lot. This was our first major family holiday without him at home. I talked with Grandma about how I really wanted to go see Dad but was afraid. She had gone to see him the week before with Mom. She said he was thinner and had grown a beard, but otherwise looked the same. She said it was hard at first to talk to him knowing she only had a few minutes to speak. She said he seemed so happy to see her. He hadn't seen her since before her stroke. She told me he started crying when he saw her, but they were tears of joy. He asked about JC and me. She told him that we were great kids and explained how we had redone her bedroom for her while she was in the rehabilitation home. He said it made him even more proud of us that we thought of doing that on our own and worked together, as a family, to complete the project. After my talk with Grandma, I told Mom that I was ready to see Dad. We would go on Saturday.

Thanksgiving went great. We worked together to make all our favorite dishes. Grandma helped with some of it while sitting at the kitchen table. She guided us through all the other special recipes she didn't have the energy to make so we wouldn't go without any traditional dish. Then on Friday we had our family football and leftover event. It was so much fun. It helped take my mind off of what was going to happen the next day. Once everyone left Friday evening I started my "what ifs". What if I ran out of things to say to Dad? What if I started to cry? What if he started to cry? What if his time was up and I was only part way through telling him something important?

  Mom looked over at me, and as if she could read my mind, said, "Why don't you write down a few things you want to share with Dad tomorrow, so you won't forget them while you have your visit?" What a great idea. I went into my room and began my list. I ended up with more than enough things to say. I figured whatever we didn't get to discuss, I could talk to him about the next time I visited. The next time. Would I want to go back? I hoped so. Tomorrow's visit would probably determine if there would be a next time for me....for us.

***

  As Mom pulled into the parking lot of the correctional facility, my heart started racing. I started sweating. My mind started with all my "what if's" again. Breathe....relax. This is DAD we are talking to. You've had a million conversations with him during your life, I tell myself. Mom senses my anxiety as soon as we park.

 She reaches over and touches my arm gently, saying, "Try your best not to over-think things. Focus on your time with Dad. The first visit is the most distracting, but you will get through all the disruptions. There will be other voices around you, other people nearby having visits and a guard watching Dad as he talks with you. This is all OK. Nobody is going to judge you. Keep your eyes on Dad and please share that beautiful smile of yours with him, even if it is through tears, which may very well happen. He is still Dad. He loves you and misses you. Remember that he doesn't know you are coming so this will be an emotional surprise for him."

I smiled at Mom. She always knows what to do to help me calm down when I am stressing about things.

As we entered the facility, I had to go through a metal detector. Mom's purse had to be searched. It was weird. We weren't criminals. However, we were visiting one. Gulp. I swallowed the knot that had formed in my throat. I needed a drink. Mom handed me a bottle of water she had in her purse. She was totally prepared...for me.

She put her arm around me as we were guided to the waiting room. There was a TV on the wall. Most people there were watching it. No phones, cameras, tablets or laptops were allowed. Mom had told me this in the car, so I left my phone in the car. I watched the show on TV. It was about renovating a home that was falling apart. Not too interesting, but I didn't want to talk with Mom. I wanted to just focus on keeping my emotions in check when I saw Dad. When the person guarding the door called my name, I stood up.

Mom handed me a disinfecting wipe.

"Here. Be sure to wipe down the phone and cord before you use it. Germs, you know." she warned.

This was something she never stopped doing, even after the COVID epidemic was over. She was kind of a germaphobe now. We had hand sanitizer in every room of our house, attached to JC and my backpacks, in every vehicle's glove box and in Mom's purse....all the time.

***

A guard walked me into a large room. There were booths created by plexiglass with phones attached. The guard told me to go to section 7. I walked to the booth with the 7 marked on the top of the plexiglass. When I looked down through the plexiglass, Dad was sitting in the chair. His face lit up with a huge smile then tears started streaming down his cheeks. He pointed to the phone and I picked up the receiver. I was so focused on him that I forgot to disinfect it. Dad already had his receiver up to his ear.
 I could hear him laugh and say, "Your mom is gonna be mad that you didn't wipe that down first." I started laughing too...and quickly wiped it down. This totally broke the ice.
 "This is the best surprise ever!" he exclaimed.
 "I am glad to see you smiling, Dad. I wasn't sure about doing this. I was so nervous about coming to see you. All those weird feelings I had are gone. You are right here. I am with you, well, as much as I can be. You look different. You are skinnier. Grandma said you were. Is it because you don't eat?" I rambled.
 "No. It is because I am trying to stay healthy. I had a bit of a belly, and that is not good. I run a few miles each day on a treadmill. I actually like running. Maybe that is where JC gets it from." he explained.
 I replied, "Well, that skipped me. You know how

clumsy I am. The last time I ran, I ended up tripping and falling within a few steps."

He laughed again. "How are you?" he questioned. "I am OK. There is some stuff going on with Jessica right now, but my grades are good." I answered.

"Jessica? Who is that? Your best friend is Jasmine." he remarked.

"That's right, Dad. Jasmine and I are still really close, but I have a new friend named Jessica."

As I started explaining in detail everything from the beginning, he sat listening and focusing on my expressions. He was always such a good listener. He wouldn't interrupt whenever I was talking about stuff with him. He'd let me finish everything I had to say before responding. He'd let me get all of it out of my mind. I loved that about him.

Unfortunately we were interrupted by a guard saying, "30 seconds".

I turned and asked if I could have two more minutes; that is all I needed to finish and get Dad's input, but the guard shook her head and said, "Sorry, we have to stick with the set time limits."

I had just enough time to tell Dad that at least now Jessica is safe even though she is mad at me, but he doesn't know the details. He couldn't respond fully. I'd have to remember where the conversation ended so we could pick up where we left off the next time I saw him. He told me he loved me and was thankful that he got to see and talk to me. Told me to stay beautiful, inside and out. That was what he always said to me at the end of our talks... As I went to respond, the phone cut out and he couldn't hear me. His guard was going over to him to escort him.

I mouthed the words "I love you" just in time

through the plexiglass and caught his sad smile as he walked away.

I stood and followed the guard on my side back to the waiting room. Mom stood and hugged me. At that point the tears were coming...she handed me a tissue. We were brought back to the entrance and made our way to the car. Mom didn't start it up and drive away as I expected. She turned and looked at me. The tears had slowed down.

"I didn't get to tell him anything on my list", I stated, "He asked me a question and I just started talking. I talked almost the whole time...he just sat and listened like he always does. I didn't get to hear his voice that much. I wasted my time with him."

"No, you didn't", Mom replied, "You had a normal conversation with him. It was natural. It wasn't forced by your notes you brought to guide your talk. I was hoping that something like this would happen. I am sure your Dad is happy about this too. He missed hearing your voice. He had told me that so many times during our visits."

"Wait, Mom. When is your visit with him?" I asked.

"He is only allowed a visit with one person each week. This was your time with him. I will see him in the weeks that nobody else can go see him. He needs all of us….he's had enough visits with me for a while."

"But that isn't fair. He should get to see us all each week. We are his family." I replied.

"Sorry, honey, but that is not the way things work for someone in prison. He has lost those rights to his family, remember?" she commented.

"Yes. I remember. I just don't like that rule, though. If I ever become a lawyer, I will work to get that rule changed. Even people who make bad mistakes should get to see everyone in their family each week. It helps them have hope for their future and reminds them that they are loved and missed." I explained. Mom said that was a wonderful thought. She commented that this could become a true goal for me. College. Law School. Wow. I never really thought of that. I want to help people. Especially people who have made big mistakes in their lives, but need to know they are still loved.

***

The first weekend in December was the walk a thon that Jessica and I had organized as part of our project for Ms. Lack. It was a bit cold, but we had gotten a lot of kids to sign up for it. A few local restaurants donated snacks and water for the walkers and some had given us gift cards to use as prizes in a small raffle we held at the end of the walk a thon. The local movie theater gave us a "free movie each week" Pass as a prize for the person who donated the most clothing items. The bowling alley gave us 10 free passes for the top 10 people who donated the most packages of non perishable food.

Jessica was still not talking to me, but we got through the entire event without a major blow up. We talked through Ms. Lack, who agreed to help us with the walk a thon. We ended up with over 400 food items and 128 articles of clothing. Some people in the community stopped by to just drop off clothes and food and didn't participate in the walk. The local radio station was there and their DJ covered the event live. He played upbeat music to keep people energized as they circled around the track 12 times to equal a 5K.

At the end of the event, the football team had

agreed to help bring all the donations into the storage room we were going to convert into the pantry. The coach counted this as part of their community service time that all sports teams in our school were required to do during their season. Now all we had to do was wait until Holiday Break at the end of the month to get the room organized and ready to finally execute the final part of our project. It wasn't as much fun as I had hoped it would be, with Jessica not speaking to me, but I hoped it was at least a reminder to her that I still was here for her.

***

The next week flew by. It was parent-teacher conferences. Mom went to both mine and JC's. When she came home, she took each one of us into our rooms to discuss what the teachers had told her. The main complaint from my teachers is that I don't participate in class discussion very often. They said that this began in late September. Well, that was when everything happened with Dad. At first I was mad. They should feel lucky that I even go to school some days. There are plenty of days that I wake up and just want to roll over and go back to sleep. Not because I am tired, but because I just want to escape my life. I am not suicidal, but I just want my life to be like it was before Dad got arrested.

  I never thought of myself as having a pretty good life...just thought of it as average. But now I appreciate all the fun times and love that my family has given me. I know they still love me, but it is just so different now, and I hate it. I think I am dealing with it pretty well. I am still going to counseling and really spill my guts about my anger, my sadness and what makes me happy. I told Mom that many days I have so much running through my mind about what might happen to Dad with the trial and what will happen to the rest of us. She told me she was proud of how I have dealt with most of the turmoil that has happened the past few months. Sure, there have been some pretty intense moments, but overall, she thinks we are all handling things better than she expected when this all began.

   I told her I would try to not focus on all my thoughts about Dad and our family, and now my situation with Jessica too, while class discussion was going on. I would try to participate at least a few times a day in different classes. I like all my teachers and want them to be happy with my progress in all aspects of learning. I want to be successful and learn as much as possible so I can have a secure future.

***

   Mom left me and went into JC's room. I could hear parts of the conversation through the closed door. Mom sounded angry. So did JC. I heard him say something about her not being fair. I heard her saying something about tutoring and summer school. Wow. JC always got good grades and he didn't seem much different from before Dad went to jail. I guess there were some things going on that I didn't notice. At school I didn't see him because we were at opposite sides of the building and had totally different schedules that didn't have our paths cross at all.

   When Mom came out, she was holding a cable for his video game system and JC's cell phone. No wonder he was upset. I waited for Mom to go into the kitchen then went into JC's room. He was lying

on his bed staring at the ceiling.
I asked how he was doing and he said "fine".
I asked about his talk with Mom. He said she wasn't being fair, that she didn't understand, and that his teachers were all jerks. I had a few of the same teachers when I was in 6th grade. They were pretty fun and did lots of hands-on activities with us. It was a lot easier than 8th grade that is for sure.
   He asked me to leave, but I didn't. I told him that I loved him and wanted to help. He told me he didn't need any help and wanted everyone to just get off his back. I've never seen him behave like this. He was always so easy going and kind. He again asked me to leave, so I just said that he could talk with me whenever he felt like it and I would do my best to help him get back his gaming cable and phone.
   He mumbled something that sounded like "sure", and then I left.
   As I came out of his room, Mom was standing there. She asked what happened.
I said, "Not much. He seems pretty mad."
Mom said to give him time to cool off before talking to him again. Hopefully he will come to me and talk at some point. Mom didn't give me any information about what happened at JC's conference. The action of taking things away from him was enough to know it couldn't be good.

***

   The next weekend we spent Saturday decorating the house. We went out in the morning and cut down our Christmas tree. As we were coming home, it started snowing really hard. By the time we got the tree into the house and in the stand there was at least an inch of snow on the ground. It really put us in the holiday mood. Even JC had emerged from his room to be part of the fun.

Mom said that there would be no visiting Dad today because of the road conditions. None of our vehicles had four wheel drive, so when we did go out on snowy roads we slid all over the place even when we were traveling slowly. We had just finished decorating the tree and were getting ready to plug in the lights on it when Mom's cell phone chimed to join Facetime. She picked it up and a huge smile covered her face.

"Wait", she said, "don't turn on the lights yet."

She answered Facetime and we heard Dad's voice. We all started shouting and Mom quickly shushed us so she could hear Dad. He said that they did a lottery drawing of 20 inmates to get to call using Facetime from a prison computer because there were no visitors because of the storm. Dad's name got drawn, so he had 10 minutes to talk. It was perfect timing! Not only did he get to see all of us and talk to us, he got to see us light the tree! It was the next best thing to him being home with us. Even JC smiled a bit as he talked to Dad about the football game on TV. We let Grandma do most of the visiting with him because he hadn't seen her in a very long time.

Just before his time was up, he told us that his trial was starting on Tuesday. He asked us to keep positive and said he had a lot of faith in his lawyer. I had just told him that I loved and missed him then the screen went blank and silent. We all started talking about the trial and what our hopes were for Dad's sentencing. Mom agreed with Dad that his lawyer is good and has a lot of evidence to prove

Dad had nothing to do with the shooting, but he did keep reminding both Dad and Mom that Dad DID attempt to rob the store so he wouldn't get off free and clear. He would have to serve some time, but the lawyer would do his best to make it as minimal as possible. I told Mom that I wanted to go with her on Tuesday. She said she's been thinking about it a lot. She said that she wanted to go alone to get a feel for how things are run during a trial before bringing anyone with her.

Chapter 24

Monday morning brought some bus issues. They were running late because of the icy conditions. Once we finally arrived at school everyone was literally "skating" into the building on the icy sidewalks. I had almost reached the front door when the person in front of me slipped and fell. I bent down to help them up without noticing that it was Jessica who had fallen. She shook her head "no" with tears streaming down her face. She was holding her ankle and her face was very pale.
 "I'll get the nurse", I said and hurried into the building.
 I went right into the office and interrupted a parent speaking to the secretary, "We need the nurse out front. Jessica fell and hurt her ankle and cannot get up. Please hurry." I explained quickly, then went right back to the front where she had fallen.
 A few of the cheerleaders were near her and one of the football players. He was trying to talk her into letting him carry her into the building.
 I again interrupted by saying, "The nurse is on the way. She knows what happened so I am sure she

will bring the wheelchair. If you try to carry her and fall, it would only make things worse."

He looked at me and backed away, heeding my advice. Within a couple of minutes the nurse was there with a wheelchair and her medical bag. Jessica was able to get into the chair with the support of a couple of us holding her steady. Once in the chair, the nurse dismissed all of us and thanked us for our help.

Everyone walked away except me. I walked next to her and carried her book bag for her. The nurse had already called the office on the walkie talkie to call for an ambulance to take her to the hospital for x-rays. The nurse was calling Jessica's aunt to meet her at the emergency room. I put her backpack down and asked Jessica if she wanted some water. She shook her head yes, so I got a cup and filled it for her. As she sipped the water, the nurse told me that I needed to get to class.

Jessica nodded in agreement, saying, "I will be fine. And …....thanks for your help."

She also smiled a bit. I wanted to hug her. This is the first time she has spoken to me since I had tried to speak with her and explain things as she was leaving with the social worker. I had said "hi" to her a number of times, but she ignored me until today. I hope this issue was a small reopening back into a friendship for us. As I left the nurse's office I told her I would get the notes and assignments for her from all her teachers so she wouldn't fall behind. She nodded as I walked out the door. I felt so bad that she got hurt. This may end the cheer season for her. But I was so happy that at least she talked to me and was letting me help in some way.

***

When I got home I went into the kitchen to see what Mom was making for dinner. She had out all the ingredients for lasagna. Grandma was sitting at the table cutting up the onions, peppers and tomatoes that we always added to the sauce. It was great to see Grandma's hands working like they used to before the stroke. The physical therapy had really been helping her recover.

I sat down and told them about what had happened with Jessica that morning. They were both happy that Jessica spoke to me, but Mom warned not to get too excited. She said that it may have been a momentary reaction because she was hurt and needed help. She advised that I don't try to rush back into full "friendship mode". Mom was right.

If I take things slow with small acts of kindness and nice words that maybe Jessica will let me back into her life little by little. I thought of the saying, "Slow and steady wins the race" as hopefully the way to make this work. I would text her the assignments and send attachments with the notes she had missed. Then I could let her decide how much to respond to me. I sent her all she needed.
A few hours later she responded with "Thanks".

It wasn't much, but I'll take it.

***

Mom had on a nice dress the next morning. That's right. Dad's trial starts today. I hugged her on my way to the bus and told her to wink at Dad for me. That is something he always did to let me know he was there for me. It started when I was in third grade and had to give a speech on parent night. I was so scared. When he caught my eye and winked, it made me smile and I relaxed and got through the speech without falling apart on the stage. Since then, every time we needed to reassure each other during a tough time we would wink at each other. He'd know exactly what the message was and who sent it to him without a word being said. Mom promised to wink. To me, it was the next best thing to me being there in person to support Dad.

***

Jessica wasn't in school for the rest of the week, so I continued to get her assignments and gather the notes she missed to help her keep up. Each night I would send them to her along with a quick message hoping she was feeling better or telling her about something funny that happened in school that day. I wasn't pushy, I don't think, but I wanted to keep reaching out to her at least a little bit each day.

The first few days she would just reply with a "Thanks" or an "LOL". On Friday she told me how bored she was at home and couldn't wait for Monday when she planned on coming back to school. Her foot was in a walking boot to support her fractured ankle. She could walk small distances without too much pain. I told her I would meet her outside of school and carry her bag for her. She said no thanks, but that she would see me in class. Little steps….I had to keep reminding myself of that. Don't be too pushy and drive her farther away.

***

Dad's trial was going OK according to Mom. She told me that I could take Tuesday off from school the next week and go with her to support Dad as long as I got all the work I would miss ahead of time from my teachers and have it done before we went to the courthouse. I got all the work on Friday so I could finish it over the weekend. The math was quite difficult because it was based on what we were going to learn on Monday. I had to read ahead in my math book and check with Uncle Vinnie about some of the steps. He was a math genius in my opinion. Math was always his favorite subject and he got a lot of math awards when he was in school. I was done with all the work by Sunday around lunchtime.

In the afternoon Jasmine came over and we decorated the outside of the house with Uncle Vinnie and JC. Mom and Grandma stayed inside watching a movie, but took a break from it long enough to make us hot chocolate and serve us outside on the front porch when we were about halfway finished. Grandma put just a bit of cinnamon in the cocoa. It was so delicious.

We did a "grand-lighting" ceremony as soon as the sun had set. The colorful lights danced against the grey background of the house. I started to tear up. This was always Dad's favorite thing to do in preparation for Christmas. Even though we decorated the same way as last year, it just didn't seem as perfect as when Dad does it. I did make sure to hug and thank Uncle Vinnie, though. He really worked hard trying to make everything look the same as last year.

***

Jessica said hi to me when I came into History Class on Monday. She beat me there because she got out of each class a few minutes early so she could get to her next class without having to deal with the busy hallways between class periods. During class Ms. Lack offered to have Jessica and me stay in her room for lunch to avoid the crowded cafeteria. I looked at Jessica and she shook her head yes, so I agreed. At lunch I went to the cafeteria and got her lunch and mine and brought it back to Ms. Lack's room.

I kept quiet at lunch. I didn't want to annoy Jessica and harm the progress I was hoping was happening with repairing our friendship. Ms. Lack did most of the talking. Jessica talked a little bit about how bored she was at her aunt's last week. I wondered if being away from her home during the holidays made her feel worse, but I wasn't about to ask. We both had big changes from last year at this time.

At the end of lunch I reminded Ms. Lack that I wouldn't see her until Wednesday. As we walked out of the classroom, Jessica asked why I wasn't going to be in school. I told her the truth about going to my Dad's trial. She just said, "Oh."

As she was going into her next class, she turned around and said, "Good luck tomorrow."

I was so happy that she offered a nice comment, I replied with, "Thanks a lot. That really means so much to me", and smiled as I continued to my next class.

***

That night after I had finished my homework it started again. All the "what ifs". " What if Dad wouldn't look at me and I couldn't give him a wink? What if someone said something bad about my Dad that wasn't true...I couldn't respond to them. What if someone there realized I was his daughter and said something mean to me? What if Mr. Gossling's family was there? How could I face them? Should I say something to them, like how sorry I am that he died?" I knew that if I didn't talk about these thoughts that I wouldn't sleep. When I went into the living room the TV was on, but Mom was in the shower. The light was still on in Grandma's room so I knocked lightly on her door, in case she had fallen asleep.

"Come in" she called softly.

She was sitting in her comfy rocking chair, knitting what looked like a winter hat. She put the needles and yarn in her lap and motioned to the edge of her bed.

"Have a seat. Be comfortable." she offered.

I did just that, then started fidgeting and biting my nails.

"What is on your mind? You always bite your nails when you have something bothering your mind." she commented.

"I am worried about tomorrow." I admitted.

"What about tomorrow worries you?" she questioned.

I went through all my "what ifs". She listened to them all before responding then finally replied, "You know it isn't going to be easy. You will probably hear things you either don't agree with or just don't want to hear. You need to trust that the lawyer will do the best job he can to defend your Dad. The Gossling's may be there. If they are, it is not a time for you to say anything to them. They will be emotional, whether it is with joy, sadness or anger. You need to let them have their feelings without interruption. If they say anything to you it would probably be best for you to just look straight ahead as if they weren't speaking to you. A reaction from you would be a reflection on your Dad, especially an angry or hurtful response. Check with your Mom, but I think Uncle Vinnie has tomorrow off. If you get there and things are too intense for you, have her call Uncle Vinnie to come pick you up. Your Dad will understand if you need to leave."

At that point Mom poked her head into Grandma's room. "Everything OK?" she asked.

"Yes" I answered, "Grandma was just helping me through my 'what ifs' about tomorrow."

Mom smiled softly and stated, "We are so lucky to have such a wise woman living with us, aren't we?"

"We sure are", I agreed.

Grandma just smiled and went back to her knitting. I felt pretty tired at that point, so I said goodnight to them both and went to bed." I had no trouble falling asleep.

Chapter 25

I woke to bright sunshine streaming through the windows. It was so crisp and clear outside. I showered and put on a nice dress with my high boots. My stomach was nervous, but I knew I needed to eat something. I didn't want my stomach grumbling in the courtroom. As I entered the kitchen, Grandma was making homemade waffles. This was the first time she had made us breakfast since her stroke. She knew her waffles were my favorite breakfast food. She had cut up fresh strawberries and was warming the maple syrup on the stove. She heated it just enough to keep the waffles warm and gooey through the last bite. I poured myself some apple juice and sat down. JC had already left for school.

The courtroom didn't open until 9am so I had slept a bit later than usual for a school day. Mom came in right after me, poured herself a cup of coffee and took a seat across from me. She had a skirt and blouse on with high heels. She looked so professional. She could walk perfectly in high heels. I tried her heels on once and almost broke my neck just trying to stay balanced as I walked. I'll stick with flat shoes or very low chunky heels. No spiked heels for me.

I had two waffles and they totally filled me up. I would be good until lunchtime for sure. Mom put a couple of granola bars and bottles of water into her large purse. She said that sometimes there is a break in the morning so we will have a snack ready if we want one. I brushed my teeth, hugged Grandma and off we went. As we were leaving, Grandma reminded me to be someone who would make Dad proud today. I knew exactly what she meant. Don't let my emotions run out of my mouth and create more problems. I knew I could handle this...well, I hoped I could.

***

As we entered the courthouse I could feel my heart starting to race.

I mumbled to myself, "Stay calm".

Mom heard my mumbling and asked, "You OK?"

I shook my head yes and started focusing on other things around me. I needed distractions from the reality that was settling into my brain. Most of the people hanging out in the hallway were seated on benches. Nobody looked happy to be there. Maybe they were waiting to go into another courtroom.

  I know there are a few in there because of a field trip I went on in sixth grade while we were studying how laws work. We got to do a mock trial in one of the smaller courtrooms. It was pretty cool. We worked with a lawyer that visited our classroom every Friday for about two months. He helped our teacher arrange a fake trial and gave us the information about roles in a courtroom. We then were assigned roles and practiced for a couple of weeks before our tour and mock trial. I was a witness for the defendant, so I had to answer questions after swearing to tell the truth or be in contempt and get into a lot of trouble.

  I had pictured my Dad's trial as looking like the mock one I was involved with, but got a quick dose of reality in the courtroom as soon as we walked through the door. First, the trial was in the huge main courtroom. There were already a number of people seated and there were cameras from local news stations set up in a few different places in the room. As I looked around at the other people who were seated, I wondered who they were and WHY they were there to watch part of my Dad's trial? A few of the people looked pretty young and had notebooks. Maybe they were in college and taking a class about law so they had to attend trials to learn about them in real life situations.

  As I glanced over to the side, there seemed to be a group of people of various ages sitting together. Maybe they were a family. It didn't hit me at first, but after a few minutes I looked over again and two of the younger people in the group were staring at me and Mom. They didn't look happy or curious about who we were...they looked sad and perhaps angry. I'll bet they were Mr. Gossling's family. I avoided eye contact with them.

I leaned over to Mom and asked if she knew who they were. She said no, but she recognized many of them from being in the courtroom on other days during the trial. She agreed with me that they were probably Mr. Gossling's family members. I whispered to her if she thought that they blamed Dad for Mr. Gossling's death? She said maybe they did. I wanted to go over to them and explain what I had been told about that night, but I couldn't. First, Mom would never let me just walk over there and start talking to them, and second, the judge was walking in so we needed to stand and start paying attention.

I was so wrapped up in the other family that I didn't see Dad walk in. He was at a large table in the front of the room with a guy in a suit and a guy in a corrections uniform. I figured the guy in the suit was his lawyer. Dad's lawyer asked for a witness.

A man in the same outfit as Dad's was walked into the courtroom, escorted by two corrections' officers. He was brought to the stand and promised to tell the truth. Dad's lawyer started asking him to explain what happened. The man started telling the story that I was familiar with, until he got to the part about the gun. He said that Dad took out the gun and shot Mr. Gossling. I started to stand up and Mom put her arm across my body to keep me seated.

She whispered, "You have to listen and hold back your words and actions in the courtroom, otherwise we will be kicked out and could get into trouble. Trust the lawyer and let him do his job."

Dad's lawyer did just that. He started asking

specific questions and the man on the stand started slipping up and showing that he obviously wasn't telling the truth in the beginning. Mom sat calmly and I saw a small smile on her face when the lawyer had the man testifying so befuddled that he just stopped talking and took a long drink of water. The lawyer finally got him to admit that he wasn't sure who fired the gun. Then the lawyer explained this to the judge, giving him papers from the investigation, that stated that Dad's fingerprints were not on the gun, nor was there any evidence of him being in the vehicle that left the store after the shooting. Also he had more information that Dad's boot print was in the wooded area he claimed to have hidden in after he left the store. They actually had pictures of the print in the mud and Dad's actual boots. The lawyer continued with more evidence to defend Dad's innocence when it came to the accusation of him shooting Mr. Gossling.

***

I was so immersed in the information that before I knew it, the judge broke for a 45 minute lunch. Mom had me stay seated until almost everyone else cleared the courtroom. In the hallway I saw the group from the courtroom. They were slowly making their way out the front door.

As Mom and I walked behind them, one girl, probably a year or two older than me turned around and mouthed the words, " I hate you" to me.

I pushed away from Mom and headed in her direction. Mom caught my arm and pulled me back. "What are you doing?" she asked.

"Mom, that girl just said she hated me. I just wanted to talk to her and ask why she hated me. I didn't do anything wrong. AND Dad didn't kill Mr. Gossling. She has got to believe that."

Mom walked me a few buildings down to a small diner. We sat in a booth in the corner. I was crying at that point. She reminded me that I cannot react to what other people say to me regarding the trial or my Dad or our family. We KNOW who we are and that we are good people. It is hard when one person in a family makes a big mistake. It reflects on the family and people say and sometimes do things to members of the family to "get back" at the person who caused all the trouble for their family. I didn't want to order anything.

I had no appetite. Mom ordered for herself, then ordered grilled cheese and fries for me. She knew that was one of my favorites. By the time we talked some more and I had settled down, I realized how hungry I was. When my food arrived I ate every bit of it.

As we walked back to the courthouse Mom reminded me again about keeping control of my actions. If I did or said anything, no matter what, it would only make things worse for Dad. I promised to be good. The afternoon flew by. There was more questioning of witnesses. The man who lived across the street from the store said he only saw one person jump into the car and drive off after he heard the gunshots. That helped Dad.

The police officer that pulled over the car verified that the driver wasn't Dad and that the gun that was found had the same prints and DNA on it as the inside of the car. He also said there was none of Dad's DNA or prints in the car at all, so he had not been in that vehicle the night of the robbery and shooting. I noticed that even though Dad still remained very serious, he held his head a bit higher as all this evidence and information was being shared with the judge.

After the judge had told the lawyers that tomorrow they should be prepared to make their closing remarks on the case regarding Dad, everyone stood as the judge left the room. I remained standing as Dad was escorted out of the courtroom. He walked near me and it took all my energy to keep from reaching out and touching him. As he caught my eye, we both winked at each other, which made me smile.

***

As Mom and I walked outside the courthouse a reporter from the local TV station approached us with a large microphone and asked, "Is Ricardo Moreno innocent for the murder of Joseph Gossling?"

Mom kept on walking.

I wanted to shout, "Yes, he is not a killer", but knew that would only create more drama in our family and perhaps hurt Dad's case.

The newsperson continued to follow us, asking the same question.

Mom stopped, turned to face her and the camera and replied, "The courtroom is the place where that decision will be determined. My family's thoughts on this was not of concern to anyone else."

Wow. The reporter had no more questions at that point.

I am glad that Mom responded instead of me. She did a great job in shutting down the nosy reporter. When we got into the car I told her how awesome her comment was. She admitted that she broke her own rule of not saying anything, but that this reporter had been in her face every day of the trial and she always said "no comment" or just ignored her, but today she figured if she responded with something besides her regular reactions that maybe the reporter would leave her alone now.

We got home, had dinner and turned on the news. Sure enough, Mom and I were on TV and Mom's comment made the segment as well. After that we turned off the TV. Mom had not been letting us watch the news because she didn't want us more upset by other people's comments.

I hadn't told her, but I had been watching the news on my phone in my room. I wanted to know what was happening with my Dad, besides the information I was getting from Mom. Some of the comments were unkind and some didn't make any sense at all. I couldn't show Mom when I got upset about the nasty remarks because she would have taken away my phone and laptop.

Mom offered to take JC to the trial the next day, but he said he had a test and didn't want to have to make it up. He hadn't even asked to go to any of it since this all began. I wanted to go again, but knew Mom wouldn't let me miss two days of school in a row.

The next day a few kids commented that they saw me on the news. They didn't say anything about what my Mom had said. Jasmine, however, said Mom's comments were great. She told me when it was just the two of us walking to lunch that she had been reading everything about the trial in the newspaper and watching the news every night. She said she never believed that Dad could shoot someone anyway and was glad it seemed to be going that way in the trial.

Danielle, on the other hand, had been avoiding me totally since the trial began. When I asked our lunch group what was up with her they said that her step mother told her to not be around me because it would make her look bad. I wanted to talk to her and see if she was avoiding me because she was afraid of what her step mom would do if she got caught hanging out with me, or if she believed my Dad and my family were bad people. It bothered me so much. Her step mom was always the type that jumped to conclusions about people and gossiped a lot. Danielle always seemed embarrassed by her, but then sometimes she was a lot like her.

Chapter 26

Dad was found guilty of robbery. We were all trying to prepare ourselves for the worst, but the evidence collected through the investigation worked in his favor....big time! We were all so grateful. Now we had to wait for the sentencing. We were hopeful that it would be for a matter of years rather than if he had been charged with murder or manslaughter...life in prison.
That is what Dad's "buddy" from work, Jeff, was facing. He had been found guilty of manslaughter.

I hadn't thought about how this would affect his family because I had been so focused on how everything was affecting my family's life. I didn't know if he was married or had kids. The dynamics of my family had changed and would stay changed at least while Dad was in prison, but at some point, he would be back with us. I know things would never be the same, but at least at that point I could hug him. Jeff's family may never be able to have that again. Jeff's friend that my Dad didn't know, who was part of the robbery was charged with the same as my Dad. I guess he left the scene and was no part of the shooting or fleeing the scene with Jeff.

***

At dinner the next night, we got the news that Mom was now able to return to work. Even though we loved having her at home more, we all knew she needed to go back to her job that she loved. Her boss had told her she could return on Monday, only three days away. Uncle Vinnie was going to move back to his old apartment with his friends. He had really come through for us, helping with the bills for a few months while we waited to see what Dad's fate would be in the courts.

Mom was very open in telling us that money would be tight, but she would get a second job and work one day on the weekend and a few part time shifts during the week. I felt bad. She worked so hard as it was. I told her that our neighbor had asked me a few days ago if I knew anyone who would be willing to babysit for her two little boys every Saturday while she worked. She was a single Mom and her work week was being changed, making her have to work on Saturdays.

I told the neighbor I would check with some of my friends who babysat. I hadn't thought about doing it myself until now. I told Mom that I would take the job and give her the money I made babysitting every Saturday. It would stink because I would be giving up one day of fun every weekend, but that is what family does. They help out. They work together to keep life as happy and stable as possible. At least

that is what I think families should do.
 Some people can help out more than others. Grandma also offered to put up a notice at the Senior Center and the local stores to do clothing alterations. She was a great seamstress. She made a lot of clothes for me and JC when we were younger. We used to get compliments on them all the time. We are lucky that she got back full use of her arm and hand from her stroke so she could still do this to help out. JC looked at the floor. He seemed embarrassed that he couldn't offer anything. Then I thought of it. He did a great job raking leaves and mowing lawns and shoveling snow at our place. Why couldn't he offer those services to our neighbors? I know it isn't a weekly commitment, year round, but it is something. When I suggested it, he seemed happy that there was a way for him to help out. He said that he would put the money he made into an account and use it to pay for his clothes, shoes and "fun" money, that Mom usually gave him when he would go somewhere with his friends. He hadn't done that in a very long time, but now at least it wouldn't be money spent that Mom needed to pay the bills.

   Uncle Vinnie offered to take care of our car so that we wouldn't have to worry about an unexpected bill if it broke down or needed an oil-change. He loved working on cars. He said that was at least something he could do to help out even though he wouldn't be living here with us.

   Together we would be supporting our life as a family. When Dad hears about all of this he will be sad that he isn't able to help out, but I know he will be proud of all of us and how we are sticking together and making this work. It was getting late,

so I went into my room to get ready for bed. Just as I laid down, JC knocked then came into my room. He sat on my bed and had tears in his eyes. "I need your help", he stated.
"With what? I replied.
"School work. Especially Language Arts." he responded.
I was shocked. I knew he was having some school issues but didn't know the details.
He confessed, "I am close to failing that class and am really confused about some of the content I missed not paying attention. If I don't get my act together I will either have to go to summer school or repeat 6th grade next year."
Wow. I didn't see that coming.
"What happened? You always did well in school." I responded.
"I've messed up. With everything that has happened with Dad I have escaped reality through video games. I used to just play for fun, but it has gone way beyond that. I just didn't want to think about anything in my life, including school. I didn't want to admit anything either, but a few weeks ago I started talking with Mr. Coster at school. He brought me in and told me about summer school or repeating 6th grade. After I was done making excuses to him about why this was happening, he offered to meet with me a couple days a week to help me figure out what direction I was going in, school wise, and if I wanted to fix things. I finally decided I will try to get my grades up but not by staying after school. I want you to help me, if you are willing to. School is not my favorite place right now. I know I need to be there and work hard, and I am now ready to make a true attempt at doing the

work but I have a lot to catch up on. I have to read two books and write two essays and a poem by the end of the upcoming Holiday Break or I will fail."
I didn't hesitate.
"Of course I can help you, but you need to be willing to do the work. While we are on break I need to work on my History Project at school for a few hours each day so you will need to do work while I am there. When I get home, I can help you with anything you are stuck on." I offered.
He thanked me, hugged me, and went to bed.

Chapter 27

The next week started Holiday Break. Our Christmas Celebration was small, just "us" at home. We do a Secret Santa and pick names to give one gift. Mom always gets something for both me and JC though. Mom got me a beautiful angel necklace. She said it was a sign of how much she appreciated me and my dedication to our family. My other gift was from Grandma. She had chosen my name. She replaced my broken ear pods.
"How did you know I needed new ones?" I questioned.
She responded with, "You always used them until a couple of months ago then when everything was first happening with your Dad, I noticed they weren't around anymore. I figured something happened, so I took and chance that they were broken or lost and decided you needed new ones." I hugged her and thanked her.
"You are very observant", I replied.

***

The weekdays of vacation went by quickly. Each morning Mom would take me and Jessica to school. Mom had called Jessica's aunt and made arrangements for her to take both of us to school and for Jessica's aunt to pick us up from school and bring us back home when we were done for the day. It was totally awkward the first day when all Jessica said was "thank you for the ride" to my Mom when she dropped us at school.

Ms. Lack helped the conversation flow on the start of the first day. We were painting the walls. The custodians had washed the white walls and moved all the clothes and food to the middle of the room so we could paint easily. We had decided as part of our original project plan to paint each wall a different color. We chose sunny yellow, royal blue, lime green and black. We figured to put the clothing on the blue and black walls and the food along the green and yellow walls. The tile floor was grey with black flecks so it blended well with our bold color choices. It took us the entire first day to paint the first coat on the walls.

We agreed on Christmas music to play because all three of us celebrated Christmas. We ended up singing along to the ones we knew and the overall feeling in the room grew happier as we worked. When we stopped to have our lunch, Jessica commented about how she loved tuna sandwiches, but her aunt had packed her ham instead. I had tuna so I offered to switch with her. She smiled at me as she suggested, "halves". We exchanged ½ of our sandwiches with a smile. I opened my bag of chips and put them in the middle of the table to share. Ms. Lack brought some cookies she had made for us to share as well. Things weren't back to normal, but

I definitely liked the direction Jessica and I were going in, friendship wise.

We finished the first coat of paint at about 2 pm and Jessica's aunt picked us up and dropped me at home. I was tempted to text Jessica later that night. I didn't want to be pushy though.

I ended up giving in to my temptation, but just texted, "See you at 7:45 tomorrow".

She responded, "See you then."

At least she responded.

***

Day 2 was similar….we finished painting and cleaned it all up. Lunch conversation was good. Ms. Lack shared that she was going to visit her cousin in a few days. He had broken his leg skiing the week before Christmas.

"That stinks", Jessica replied. "I hated being on crutches. They are so annoying. I was lucky to have help when I got hurt."

She looked directly at me and smiled. More of the "ice" from our chilly relationship was melting.

I smiled back, replying, "That is what friends do."

She accepted my comment without further response.

Day 3 we spent setting up the racks for the clothing and the food items. We had gotten clothing racks from a store in the city that had gotten new, larger ones for their store. We didn't have shelving for the food items when we brought everything in after the walk a thon. I asked Ms. Lack where they came from. She sent Jessica to the office to get a few supplies from the secretary.

She sat down and motioned for me to sit too. She then explained that the shelves had been donated by the Gosslings. They were not going to reopen the store and wanted to empty it before they sold it. I started to cry. Their world was shattered more than anyone else involved in this situation. And yet they are willing to donate to get the pantry set up.

"Do they know that I am one of the people setting this up?" I asked.

"Yes", she replied. "They are glad that you are doing such a great thing for our school community. Mrs. Gossling even commented that you must be a very thoughtful person."

It floored me. How could she not hate me? My Dad tried to rob her family's store. Her husband was dead because of that incident. I kept wiping away the tears. I felt so appreciative of the comment as well as the donation. Mrs. Gossing wasn't holding anything against me. She must be an amazing lady.

Jessica appeared with the supplies. She saw my face and asked what was going on. I shared the information Ms. Lack had just given me. She walked over and hugged me. This was the best gift I could have gotten. Ms. Lack walked out of the room and gave us time to talk. After about a half hour of Jessica apologizing for blaming me with what happened after she told me about her family and me reassuring her that I wanted to be there for her, Ms. Lack returned. We spent the next two hours setting up the rest of the shelving.

***

That night Jessica called me after dinner and we talked for an hour. She told me that her parents were getting divorced. She and her brother would be moving back home with her Mom in a couple of weeks. Her dad was going to move to Ohio to live with his brother and continue with his daily AA meetings. He was able to get a job set up for when he moved there. She is sad he will be so far away, but is glad he is getting help.

Her mom and she and her brother have been going to Al Anon Meetings to help them deal with the aftermath of what they have been living through for so many years. They are also going to counseling together. Her Dad has agreed to send enough money to keep them living in the house until Jessica goes to college in four years. Then they will sell the house and Mom will get something smaller that she can afford on her own.

***

The next day was spent organizing all the clothing, categorizing it by size and type and getting it all put on hangers and a couple of shelving units. Labeling the shelving and racks for sizes was how we finished that day's work. Ms. Lack was going away for New Years' so she only had two days left to work with us.

Our fifth day was setting up all the food on the shelving. It was on this day that I shared an idea I had with Jessica and Ms. Lack.

"I know that many people have helped with donations, but the Gosslings gave us most of the shelving we needed. Can we name the pantry, 'Get it at Gosslings'? That will keep the memory of the generous family in our community that suffered a terrible loss, both a family member and their business, somewhat "alive"?"

Ms. Lack reached out and touched my arm. "That is a beautiful sentiment."

Jessica just shook her head yes with a huge grin on her face. Ms. Lack said she would have to get it approved by the school and check with the Gosslings to be sure they would be OK with this as well.

The last day of setting up I was really tired. I had been helping JC out after dinner almost every night for a few hours to help him be caught up with his work so he would not fail 6th grade.

Ms. Lack ordered pizza for lunch to celebrate our final day with set up for the pantry. We got the room all cleaned up and ready to open the second week in January. We wanted to have a grand opening ceremony over the morning video announcements. Ms. Lack was helping arrange that with us as well. As we were leaving that day Ms. Lack wished us a Happy New Year and said, hopefully we would have the name for the pantry approved and grand opening set up the first few days back at school.

On the way home I asked Jessica if she wanted to spend New Year's Eve at my house and sleep over with Jasmine and me. She smiled and asked her aunt who said yes. The next night was New Year's Eve!

Chapter 28

I had forgotten that Dad's sentencing was New Year's Eve. When I woke up that morning, Mom had already headed to the courthouse to be there in support of Dad. The lawyers had told Mom that the length of his sentence would be somewhere between 3-10 years. This was longer than we had hoped. Because Mr. Gossling had died as a result of the robbery, even though Dad did not shoot him, it

heightened the severity of the sentencing. Damn Jeff….if he had just taken off when Mr. Gossling took out his gun; this would have all been better. Not perfect, but better.
The morning dragged on and I kept texting Mom to see what was going on. She only answered the first text, telling me that she would let me know when she knew the result.

I went into JC's room. He was working on finishing up an original poem. He had read all the poetry books already. Mom had his phone and gaming system so he wouldn't be tempted to wander from his assignments. She had agreed to give them back when he had finished ALL the work. His goal was to celebrate New Year's Eve by gaming with his buddies all night. I had discussed with him the poems he had to read and interpret, because I had read them when I was in 6th grade. He understood the themes and various forms in poetry. He was proving that he was still a great student, just had been lazy and dealing with other issues instead of getting his work done.

He waved me out of his room, saying, "I've got to finish this, so please just leave for a while. I will let you read it when I am done."

He was lucky…he had a great distraction from what was going on while Dad's sentencing was happening. I tried to watch TV with Grandma. I could tell she was distracted. She kept changing the channels, not committing to any specific program. At noon she went into the kitchen to make lunch. I went in to be there with her. We ate grilled cheese sandwiches and had tomato soup which was one of my favorite lunches. JC emerged long enough to eat and then went right back to his room to work.

When we finished, Grandma suggested we make chili, cornbread and cookies for tonight's New Year's fun. We worked for about an hour when the home phone rang. I jumped to answer it. It was Mom.

The sentencing was over. The judge had sentenced Dad to four years in prison. It was a punch in the gut. I had secretly hoped that the judge would have the kindness of the Christmas Season in his heart and go easy on Dad. Maybe he'd only get a year in prison? Not the case. I guess he had to do his job, even though I didn't like the result. Mom was calm as she explained how everything went. She said Dad seemed sad, but that was expected. It would be silly for him to be happy about having to be without his family for four years, except through visits we would make to him. Mom then said she was going to stop at the store to get some soda and popcorn for my sleepover tonight then she would be home.

When I hung up, I explained what Mom had just told me to Grandma. She started to cry. She had been very hopeful that his sentence would be less. She commented, " I am worried that I will not live long enough to hug my son again." I hugged her, tightly. I started crying too. I told her that she is a strong person and that she can make any goal she sets her mind to. I had never thought of that. She is worried about time. That she wouldn't get more time with her son before she has none left. I focused on what Dad would miss while he was gone, but never anything that serious.

I didn't want to disrupt JC, so I didn't go tell him.

Mom walked through the door and sat down on the couch as JC exited his room claiming,

"FINALLY FINISHED!"

Mom then filled him in with the information.

His first comment was, "He will be able to be at some of my high school track meets. I just need to keep up my grades so I can be on the track team. He can also be here to help me learn to drive. I will be almost 16 when he gets out."

I was glad that JC was sounding positive about all of this. I guess the talks with Mr. Coster and the therapist were helping him. I know it wasn't going to be an easy four years, but it could have been so much worse. I will have to talk to Mom about how we can help Grandma stay positive as well. She needs to be here to welcome him home. She needs to go visit him the next four years. With there being four of us at home, we could each take a Saturday to visit with him so he could see each of us once a month. Oh, wait....Mom and I would be working on Saturdays.

Chapter 29

Jasmine and Jessica came over around dinner time. We had chili and cornbread. It was delicious. As soon as we finished, JC practically ran to his room to start his all night gaming excursion with his friends. Grandma shooed us out of the kitchen, saying she would clean up. Mom was on the phone calling family and friends to share the results of Dad's sentencing. Uncle Vinnie was finishing packing up his vehicle. He was returning to his apartment tonight with his friends. I was sad to see him go, but he promised to have dinner with us at least once or twice a week. He even asked Grandma if she could continue to help him with cooking lessons so he could prepare delicious meals each week for us. She seemed very happy that he wanted to continue this weekly event. I am sure it made her feel appreciated and valued.

  Having my friends there really helped with all the emotions rushing through my head. My Dad...My Mom...JC...Grandma...Uncle Vinnie.... All of us moving in different directions, at different points of our lives and trying to keep our family somewhat cohesive. I had told Jessica and Jasmine about my Dad's results today. They were both so great. They hugged me and promised to be there for me.

  I am so lucky to have two such great friends. We've been through our share of ups and downs but always have managed to come back together and let go of our anger and frustrations that can happen in any relationship. It makes our relationship stronger. Many people I know brag about having so many friends. It isn't the number of friends you have, but the type of friends you have that matters to me. I plan on sticking with these two friends for life. Even if we go in different directions with school, careers, family, I just know deep inside that we will always be close.

  As the ball dropped and we counted down; Mom in the recliner and Jessica and Jasmine on the couch with me, filled with soda, cookies and popcorn, I decided my resolution for the new year would be a lifelong one; To be there for the people in my life that need me....and to let them be there for me.

END NOTES: (Nina's Story)

1. The opening of "Get it at Gossling's" was a huge hit. The Gossling's agreed to come to the grand opening. They were very appreciative of our school wanting a place that helps youth and their families in our community, our school, be named in honor of their family.

2. I was able to visit Dad one Saturday each month. Jasmine agreed to babysit on that day for the time I needed off in order to see my Dad.

3. Mom's second job let her work evening shifts on Saturdays so she could spend time with her husband and get her family back and forth to the prison so they could visit him as well.

4. I graduated from middle school with honors. I am attending a magnet high school that focuses on political science, history and law. It will hopefully be a gateway to a future as a lawyer, or even maybe someday, a judge.

5. JC turned 16 just before Dad came back home. He waited for Dad to be home so that HE could teach him how to drive. He is a top contender on the varsity high school track team. He is studying electrical engineering at a technical high school in our town.

6. Grandma. She had another stroke, but fought back again. Although she now needs a cane to help her keep balanced when she walks, she is happy to

stay living with us...all of us, including her son who learned a very big lesson in life and is determined to make good choices the rest of his life so as not to hurt anyone, especially his family.

7. Dad served his four years. While in prison he was allowed to take college classes. He received his Associate's Degree in Engineering and Design. This will help him get a good job through the post prison job opportunity programs offered for inmates that have completed their sentence with good behavior.

This wasn't an easy four years. There were lots of ups and downs for all of us. That is life though. Life is not all good or all bad. It is what you make of it. I've decided that when life seems bad to me that I shouldn't give up on things and shut people out who care about me. I choose to work hard and love the people in my life, even when they don't agree with me about things happening around us. I need to be true to myself and the people in my life.

JC's Story –

Chapter 1

My brain starts to spin….it must be going a million miles per second. I feel the pulse in my temples as the blood tries to break through the veins. My heart...I know it is going to explode, spilling my blood throughout my body, yet my skin will hold it inside of me. I've got to do something. The energy is so intense! The adrenalin is pushing my entire body into action. I know the only thing I can do that MIGHT help. Run. Run as fast as I can and as long as I can until I collapse.

I throw on my sneakers and jump off my bed. I don't even know if the sneakers are tied or even on the correct feet. I don't care. I've got to save myself from this eruption inside. I push open my bedroom door and aim straight to the front door. Mom tries to stop me, but I pull my arm from her attempted grip.

"Just leave me alone!" I shout and burst through the front door into the fresh air.

It is late afternoon. The Sun is starting to set and the air is crisp and dry. It stings my throat as I gulp for fresh air to fill my lungs as I start a full sprint. Where? I don't know. I just need to be moving. Somewhere. Anywhere. Away. But away from what? Away from who?

Right now my mind just isn't clear. I run across streets without looking for cars. Luckily I am running the side roads near my house that aren't very busy. I don't have any answers as to where I am going, or what path I will follow as I run.

Damn. I got a rock in my sneaker. Each time my left foot hits the ground it wedges into the ball of my foot, right under my big toe. I focus on the pain. I let my brain have a break from the spinning and the blurring images around me. If I run long enough without removing the sharp pebble I will get a blister. Maybe it will pop and bleed. Yes! That will be enough to release all my emotions....or will it? How can such a small object cause such discomfort? How can such a small object break through skin and create pain that lasts for days?

 I just keep going. I am about three miles from home when I start to actually think logically. Whenever I decide to head back home, it will be the same number or miles, or close to it at least. I can turn back toward home and just continue running closer to home. Nope. I don't want to be home. There I will have to talk...and I am not doing that. Not today, not ever. I have nothing to say...only feelings to have. I keep running. Two more miles down the road and it is now practically dark.

 Mom must be worried. She doesn't even know where to start looking for me, IF she is even looking. Who knows what is happening in that crazy home of mine. It wasn't always crazy. In fact, I considered it a pretty normal home until a couple of days ago. It only took one action...one choice....and my world is messed up, forever.

 The shadows are long and kind of creepy. I used to be afraid of shadows when I was little. I had nightmares about them coming to life and trying to hurt me. I would wake up screaming. Dad usually came in to calm me down and help me fall back asleep. I push those memories from my mind.

 As I look around I realize that I am only a block

away from Uncle Vinnie's apartment. I create a reason for stopping by to see him as I run the last block. I knock on the door. He answers. I tell him I went for a run and lost track of time. Not a lie...really. He nods and asks if I want a ride home. I may as well take it. I can lock myself up in my room and at least play some video games to get my mind focused on something that makes me happy. As I am using the bathroom, I hear Uncle Vinnie talking on his phone to Mom. She better not be mad at me. I can hear her now..."What were you thinking?" "That was so irresponsible" and of course, "You're grounded". Hey...as long as she doesn't take away my game system, I can deal with all the rest.

Mom comes out of the house to talk with Uncle Vinnie and I escape to my room and lock my door. I ignore Grandma, who is sitting in the recliner sewing. A few minutes later I hear the front door close. Mom doesn't come to my door. Good. I need my space. I stare at the paper lying on my desk. I walk over and crumple it up...shot...two points ...into my garbage can. That is where that belongs. It is all a bunch of trash...the words...the apology...all just a bunch of garbage.

***

I game until about 2am, then crashed on my bed. No shower...no changing....just crash in the clothes I had worn all day. I might stink from sweating on my run, but so what. I toss and turn the rest of the night. I finally decided to get up at about 4am. I am just so very thirsty. I head to the kitchen for a glass of water. Uncle Vinnie is on the couch. How did he get there? I thought he had left when he dropped me off. Whatever. I don't know what to think of anything anymore.

Back to sleep, well, more like toss and turn again. I finally fall asleep around 6 am. Not a restful sleep, my weird dreams keep my mind active.

Mom wakes me at 7. My covers are all over the place. I must have been moving in my bed while all those weird dreams were happening. Shoot. Bus is coming in 10 minutes. Brush my teeth, grab my book bag and a protein bar along with a bottle of water and head out the door. No goodbyes, just a fast exit. I'm at the bus stop before realizing that my sister isn't there. Maybe she isn't going to school today. Oh well.

Chapter 2

I nap on the ride to school. Nobody sits with me. Good. I stink. I can actually smell how badly too. I don't really care, though.

I step off the bus and head to Homeroom. I sit at my desk, put my head down and nap again until the bell rings. I walk alone in the hall. Nod to a few kids who say hi to me. Not ready for conversation yet. Reading Class is first period. We just finished up a cool book. Hoping the next one will be just as interesting. The new one we are starting is about the Holocaust. It could be good or maybe lame. We'll see.

My buddy Marvin sits next to me. After a few minutes he comments that someone stinks. I nod and wait for him to realize it is me. Mr. Noll, my Reading teacher is rambling on about all the stories of the Holocaust and how we are going to be working in small groups and reading different stories all on this topic. We will have discussions and debates over topics within the stories based on the main theme. Yippee....I usually like to debate, but just not looking forward to it at this point.

In Math Class Marvin sits next to me again. We sit in alphabetical order by last name. At that point he realizes that the stink is back. He connects it to me.

"Dude...what is up with you?" he whispers.

"Nothing, why?" I respond.

"It is you. You smell bad. And didn't you wear that shirt yesterday? Did the city shut off your water or something?" he questions.

"No. I just got up late. That's all." I respond.

Marvin shrugs off my comment and goes back to his work. I look at the numbers in front of me and they mean nothing. I try to reread the directions and look at the few notes I wrote down. I am clueless. No idea what to do or how to do it. When I look back at the notes on the board, I realize I only have about half of them written down. So what? I've got other things on my mind much more important than the order of operations.

I raise my hand, ask to use the bathroom. I head out the door. In the bathroom I decide I will just hang out for a while. Not the best atmosphere, but better than trying to do math you just don't want to do right now. I know if I ask for help I will understand what to do; that is if I can concentrate on what is being explained. Not too sure if that is happening today. There is a small window in the bathroom. I sit on the heater and look out. The leaves are really starting to turn. Soon the landscapes will be so colorfully brilliant...not just shades of green and brown.

My mind wanders until someone comes into the

bathroom. A kid I don't know. He just looks at me, uses the bathroom and leaves. I start to wonder about whom he is and what his life is like. Is his world falling apart like mine? Does he hate one of his parents? I've got to do something to get my brain working right again. It is a jumble of thoughts that don't make any sense to me. Maybe if I tell someone at least part of what happened it will help me figure out what to do next. But who; who can I trust? The person I thought I trusted the most is not there for me. Who knows if or when I will see him again?

My anger starts up...I breathe deeply and try to calm down. It's not working. I kick at the cinder block wall. Now my toe is throbbing...great. Last night the pebble, now this. Can't blame this one on anyone else but me...or can I? My anger is not about me...it is about HIM. It is HIS fault I am so messed up right now. The bell rings. NO! I never went back to Math Class. I've been gone for at least twenty minutes. I ran back into class to grab my stuff. I tell my teacher, Mr. Waters, that I had a stomach issue but it is better now. He buys my excuse and off I go to PE.

***

A brain break at last! PE is definitely one of my favorite classes. Being on the move is my thing. Sports that have constant movement are my favorites. They help me get out my stored up energy and I always seem to think more clearly. In the fall our options for PE include soccer, track, archery and badminton. The rotation group I am in is currently doing track, which is perfect.

As soon as attendance is called, I head towards a

designated trail that loops two miles around our school grounds and through the little neighborhood behind the school. We are allowed to run the path under two conditions: first we run with a partner, and second, we have to be a student in good standing...which basically means we follow the rules of the school. I grab my friend, Ryan, who runs on the cross country team with me, to be my running partner. Off we go. I take the lead...I have so much energy and emotion to burn. He follows closely then begins to lag behind.

"What's with you today?" he asks.

"Funny, I was going to say the same to you, slowpoke", I replied.

"No" he comments, You just seem, well, 'different'. Are you OK?"

"Yes, I am fine. Just have a lot of energy. Keep up the pace. We need to stay together so we don't lose this privilege." I remark.

"Well let me set the pace WITH you so we can both be happy with our run today. It isn't a meet. There is no winner here in gym class." he responds.

"Just remember that second place is the first place loser!" I call behind as I pick up the tempo of my steps even more.

I couldn't slow down. My mind and my body wouldn't allow it. Not today, at least. As I run, my mind clearly processes what my next move is going to be. Perhaps I'll talk about it. Tell someone...but whom? Not any of my friends. Not ready for that yet. What adult can I confide in? Who can I trust?

I chose Mr. Christian, my Art teacher. He is the teacher I first felt a connection with when I started school this year. He made it a point to talk to each student individually during the first two weeks of school while the other students were working on their art assignments. He wasn't the kind of teacher that just circulates and nods at your work, or just comments that everything you do is good because it is how YOU look at it. He really gives you constructive feedback and asks for your personal connections to whatever piece you are working on in class. He just seems to "get" us.

***

Art Class was last period. I waited until everyone seemed to be engrossed in their work. I asked Mr. Christian if I would speak with him for a minute, privately. We stood off to the side, away from the other kids. He always had upbeat music playing, so our words would not be heard by the other students.

It was hard to start...I wasn't sure where to begin. I ended up being general with the details of the initial incident that started all of this chaos in my life. I focused on what was going on now and how upset I was after reading the letter...and all the emotions that flooded my body and mind. How I ran...and ran....and ran. My retreat to my room and how I just let myself be absorbed in my video games. This is the tactic that lets me forget the turmoil of my life.

My questions...What was going to happen now? How can I deal with all that is coming into my life....all the changes that are taking place? My anger....my full blown, deep set anger that pulses through my body when I think of what is happening.

Mr. Christian listened without interrupting. One kid came up to ask him a question and he silently held up a hand, letting the student know that she needed to wait a bit for her answer. She walked back to her seat to wait for him. When I had finished and was hopeful for some magical words to leave his lips and fix my world, I was so disappointed. He told me that my feelings were totally justifiable. How I was feeling was OK. It was not bad or weird or unexpected. He also let me know that he needed to share this information with one of the counselors or social workers at our school.

I told him I wanted this to be just between him and me. He said he couldn't do that. It is his job to get the help kids may need when having tough issues whether inside or outside of school. I didn't like this, but I understood that he needed to do his job and not get in trouble. I just added that I would like to be the one to go see someone else, not get called out of class and be forced to "talk about my feelings" with whoever called for me. I needed to do this when I was ready. We agreed that he would tell Mr. Coster and Mr. Turbino. I said I would go to either one when I was ready to talk to them. As I left class at the end of the day, ready for a good long run, I thanked Mr. Christian and headed to Track Practice.

Chapter 3

It felt good to run. We just did time trials for our upcoming meet qualifications. It was a quick practice. Ryan's dad brought me home as usual. Grandma was starting dinner so I decided to help her. I felt kinda bad about ignoring her yesterday. None of this mess is her fault. I know she likes help when she is cooking, so I figured that helping her was a way to make up for yesterday without having to get into a discussion about what was going on.

She asked about my day and I gave her the normal, "school was good" comment. She started talking about how she was trying a new tomato sauce recipe one of her friends at the Senior Center gave to her. It smelled great. My stomach started rumbling. I had not eaten much at lunch and hunger was catching up with me.

My sister, Nina, walked in the back door. She usually beats me home from school, so she must have gone somewhere after. She looked upset. Her eyes were red and swollen. She probably was crying. The doorbell rang and Grandma went to answer it. It was the FedEx guy. She usually talked with him for a few minutes. They were both from Santa Marta, Colombia, so they usually shared a story or two from when they were living there.

Nina asked me about school then asked if I told anyone about what was going on with our family. I acted like it was not a big deal that I told Mr. Christian. It wasn't like it was a secret or anything. I did tell her that I wasn't going to let my friends know about it. Not yet at least. Some of them are immature and judgemental. I don't need them being jerks towards me or making up rumors based on their assumptions from the information I would share with them. Just going to lay low...not get noticed...fly under the radar. As long as I keep acting normal, then things will stay normal, right? I hoped so.

Mom and Uncle Vinnie came in and told us about what happened at the police station and with the lawyers involved in Dad's case. I just listened as if they were telling me about a movie they had watched. My sister, on the other hand, was kinda emotional. She left the table without finishing her meal. It's her loss. I just took in the words without letting them really process into my brain. Shut it all out...that is the key to survival for me in this situation.

After clearing my plate I went into my room. Didn't feel like doing any school work so I just picked up my controller and let myself be led into the game unfolding on the screen in front of me. Escape...at last! I had to pause when Uncle Vinnie came in to check in on how I was doing.

Why was he doing this? Mom should be checking on us, not him. He did help out when I needed a ride last night, but now he was going to be fully involved? I'm not going to tick him off, but I just want to be left alone. I nodded and "umm hummed" until he got the hint that I was not going to have a true conversation with him. Then back to my game...my world.

***

About eleven o'clock I went into the kitchen for a snack. I had the peanut butter, marshmallow cream and graham crackers out, building my mini sandwiches when Mom came in. She pulled out the milk and joined me at the table. She sighed as she sat down.

Her hair was messy...and there were grey hairs woven through the straight brown strands. I never noticed that before. Were those there a few days ago? It must have been. Grey hairs don't grow that fast, do they? She looked so tired. Not sleepy tired, but weary. She has to deal with a lot now too. Not just Dad stuff, but how it is affecting all our lives.

Mom is always the glue that holds us together when there is a crisis. Like when the apartment next to ours at our old place caught fire in the middle of the night. She made sure we all got out safely and when we couldn't return to that place, she found the home we are in now. It is all ours. We don't have to worry about anyone else leaving papers next to a space heater to catch fire and mess up everyone's home. The home we rent now has a decent yard and front porch. We all have our own bedrooms, too. You can have the privacy you need by just shutting your door.

I wanted to say something to help her know she is appreciated, without getting all mushy. I am not the "I love you" and huggy- type. I like to keep a semi tough image. I am a bit small for my age, so I don't want anyone thinking I am wimpy or weak. I tend to tread between "cool" and "tough" with an occasional smile. I finally found the words to share with Mom.

"Thanks for taking care of us when we had the fire a few years ago. You knew just what to do to keep us safe and help us get back on our feet. I really like this house. It is perfect for us." I share.

She smiles, touches my hand and responds with, "It's my job as your Mom to be there for you, to protect you, and to love you. It is the best job I could ever have with two of the greatest kids in the world." Then she adds on, "Oh, by the way, I love you too."

I smile. She knows what I mean. She knows how I am feeling. She is letting me process everything at my pace and on my terms. I am very lucky.

I crashed about midnight, but actually remembered

to set the alarm on my phone. Hit snooze four times the next morning, then it was too late to shower. Stinky boy heads to school...day two. Nina was not on the bus again. Is she even going to school? I don't want to be there right now, but even I know if you miss a few days it just brings attention to you. People want to know why you were out. It is none of their business, but as long as I can be there, less questions will be asked.

Chapter 4

I am doing well with playing "normal". I say enough to my friends so they don't suspect anything is up. I had a can of deodorant in my locker, so before homeroom I went into the boys' room and sprayed myself so I wouldn't attract any attention with my stench. It seemed to help at least a little bit. I was glad not to be a girl and worrying about not having makeup on or my clothes perfectly matched. This morning I grabbed clothes off my floor that looked decent and ran a comb through my hair. Luckily messy hair is in style. I forgot to brush my teeth, but had some gum in my backpack and chewed it on the bus on the way in.

    I jot down enough notes and do my best to look attentive in class. When the teachers start asking questions I just pretend to be busy finishing up notes or reading part of the assignment we are working on. I have no clue what is being discussed in class or how to do any of the assignments. I just fake it.

    During discussion groups I nod and choose someone to agree with so I don't have to form my own ideas and opinions. Just keep blending. I wonder how long I can keep this up. At some point I am going to be called on this behavior and my lack of work, but I am not going to worry about it now. I've got bigger things on my mind. More important than any article we are reading or math problem we are solving. I know school is important, but only when everything else in your life is going well. Crisis excuses you from work, right?

Half way through the day I get called to Mr. Coster's office. I know what is going to happen. He will "blah blah blah" about the information Mr. Christian shared with him and ask how he can help me. Well...he can't. Nobody can. I just need to figure everything out on my own.
Sure enough, he tries to get me to talk about how I am feeling. I tell him I am fine and to please just leave me be. Not that easy, he says. It is his job to help students. I let him know that I don't need help. He makes me promise to come see him if I ever want to talk. I oblige so he will just let me get back to class.

Sure enough, I walk back into class and Marvin wants to know why I got called to Coster's Cave. That is what the 6th graders call it. He keeps his office dimly lit and the cement walls resemble that of a cave. I tell Marvin he called for me by accident. He got me messed up with another kid that needed to see him. Marvin buys the lie and drops the conversation.
It starts to rain and track practice is canceled.

***

I put in my ear buds and sit in the back seat of the bus listening to music from my phone. I tune out everything else and everyone on the ride home.

When I get off the bus, Nina seems annoyed but won't tell me what her problem is. Sisters...8th graders...so dramatic. As I step onto the porch she asks if Coster talked to me today.
"Yes, but I didn't really talk to him," I replied.
 "Good. The less involved he is the better. And don't forget...this is a private matter. No blabbing about it to your goofy little friends," she instructs.
 "I've got it under control. Just keep it to yourself too," I remind her.
 As I step inside, the rain stops. Great. I could've been running right now. What is stopping me? I put my book bag in my room, throw on shorts and a sweatshirt and head out the door.
I am free! Running makes me free! I pace myself so I can run for quite a while hoping to get in at least 3 miles today. I have a pattern that I run for a short run, mid run, and long run. I start on my long run route.
 I totally forget, until I am approaching it. Gossling's Grocery Mart. No cars are in the lot. The door and windows are boarded up. There are remnants of yellow police tape near the entrance. I pick up my pace and try to focus on everything else around it...the purple house that looks haunted, the white house with the orange jeep in the driveway, the beagle running in the yard with two little kids. None of those things keep my attention for more than a few seconds. My eyes are drawn back to the mart. My brain starts the racing feeling again, like the other night.
I pick up my pace to keep up with my heartbeat. I start to picture a scene inside my head...inside the Mart.
 I look around to distract myself, but it doesn't

work. I hear yelling. Dad's voice in my ears...I hear a loud pop and I jump. A car at the corner had backfired. My brain goes right back to the thoughts... a body...blood...the bell ringing as the door swings open...the sound of boots slamming against the asphalt in the parking lot. Sirens in the distance are now coming closer. The sound winds down like a wild cat screeching in pain.

A horn beeps. I am at a corner and the driver wants me to cross safely. Can he tell that I am distracted? I start to hum to the music playing in my ear buds...drown out the thoughts. It helps. My stomach hurts. I feel like throwing up. That is my typical reaction when I get really upset about something. Running usually helps, but not this time.

When I get home I go straight to the bathroom to shower. The hot water stings but relaxes me at the same time. I stare at the pattern in the tile on the walls. If I squint through the water dripping down my face it looks like it is moving. I had never noticed that before. My stomach settles a little. I dry off and head to my room until dinnertime. Just need more space to think, or truthfully, to avoid thinking about everything.

Chapter 5

I am quiet at dinner. Mom asks what is up. I tell her I have a stomach ache so that is why I am not eating my usual two platefuls of food. Grandma looks concerned. She will not bug me about anything unless I come to her. She is pretty cool that way.

After dinner Nina came into my room to "check" on me. She just wanted to know how I was dealing with everything. And she also warned me again to keep our family issues private. I gave her the answers that would get her out of my room the fastest and off she went. I can be pretty convincing about things when I focus on it.

   A couple hours into my gaming, Mom knocked. I let her in, planning on giving her the same type of responses I gave Nina after dinner. She sat on my bed. Great...she was in for a full conversation, not just a quick check in. She proceeded to tell me that Uncle Vinnie was going to move in with us for a while to help out. I shrugged. She then continued by telling me that he was going to be sleeping in MY room!!!!

That was enough to make me pause my game and look her in the face with a serious, "No way."

She told me it wasn't an option at this point. Tomorrow he would be bringing his bed into my room so I needed to make space for it.

   "Forget it." I retorted.

No way was I going to give up my privacy because Uncle Vinnie thought he needed to help out in some way. Mom told me that if I didn't move stuff around that she would while I was at school tomorrow. Fine. She can do it. Then it hit me...why wasn't she going to be at work? I asked her flat out. She told me that she took some time off from work. Uncle Vinnie staying with us would mean he also helps with the bills. I hadn't thought about that.

   We don't have Dad's paycheck anymore. My mind started with all the questions...Will we have to move? Will Uncle Vinnie stay with us until Dad is out of jail? When will that be? Instead of asking her, I just turned back to my video game and pressed continue. She got the hint and left the room.

***

I stayed absorbed in my games until my phone buzzed. It was Deacon. He and I have been friends since kindergarten. It sucked because this year we had no classes together. We had totally different schedules so we didn't even get to sit together at lunch. We tried to talk a few times a week and spend time together on the weekend, but my track schedule and his soccer schedule didn't make it easy to do.
"Hey", I answered.
"What's up?" was his response.
"Nothing. I was just gaming. Been busy with chores and homework", I lied.
"Oh. Do you want to get together on Saturday afternoon? I have a soccer game in the morning, but it is a home game so I will be done by noon." he informed me.
"Sure," I replied.
I surprised myself. I didn't feel like being around anyone. What would we do? What would we talk about? That's stupid...we always had stuff to talk about and do, why would that be different?
I stayed quiet, so he quickly said he had to go finish his homework and hung up. That was fine with me. I didn't have anything else to say to him anyway.

***

My mind started rushing with questions about how things would be with Uncle Vinnie here on a more permanent basis. I went into the kitchen for a snack. He was in there helping himself to a glass of apple juice.
"Why are you here?" I inquired.
"I'm here to help out. I love you guys and know

that everyone is hurting. I want to be here for all of you." he remarked.

"You don't have to live here to do that, you know. You can just give us money each month to help with the bills." I suggested.

"I can't pay my rent somewhere else and help pay bills here too. I am not made of money." he retorted.

"I guess that makes sense. But why can't you just sleep on the couch so I can have my room to myself?" I questioned.

"There aren't enough rooms for each of us to have our own bedroom, so the most logical thing is for me to share with you. And the couch isn't a place to get a good night's rest. It is fine for a few nights, but that is about all." he commented.

I guess he is right. I don't like it, and will still try to figure out something else, but he is right. His final words to me were, "I am here for you. I know you are hurting. We all are in some way. I want you to come talk to me. We can go for a run together or get some ice cream and have our own conversation without anyone else knowing. Also, know that I am upset about this. I have always looked up to your Dad. He has known me since I was eight years old. That is when he started dating my sister...your mom. I could always talk to him like a brother. He has helped me out with many issues I have had growing up. Remember that your Grandpa Chico died when I was five, so I didn't have a father figure until your Dad came around. He always let me tag along with him and his friends. I miss him too. I am angry too. I just want to help because I know he would help someone in this situation."

I got mad at Dad. I blurted out, "Well HE is the

one who has put us all in this rotten situation. HE is the reason we are all mad and messed up."

Uncle Vinnie did something totally unexpected. He hugged me. And I let him...but just for a few seconds. Then I broke away and went into my room.

Chapter 6

My alarm went off. Friday! It's my favorite school day. Usually the teachers are worn out from the week so they do something more "fun" or they give us something independently to do so the room is quiet and they can have their peace and quiet to end their work week. I am actually OK with either.... If we do something fun then I don't have to try to focus on learning new things and can just blend in with an occasional smile or laugh. I can get into a group with kids who will do the activity while I basically watch and pretend to pay attention. If we work independently, then nobody bothers me and I can just be alone with my thoughts and fake the work.

I scoff down a plate of bacon, eggs and English muffin that Grandma had made for whoever was hungry. Nina came in and grabbed a piece of fruit and went back into her room until it was time to go to the bus. I return to my room, put my books in my backpack, throw my comforter over my bed so it looks like some attempt to tidy my room and off I go. Nina joins me at the bus stop and just stands there and waits quietly. Both of us are pretending to be engrossed in our phones. On the bus, she sits in the middle, while I head to the back.

***

    I sit in an empty seat across from a kid, Derek, who is in seventh grade. I've heard he can be a jerk and he doesn't seem to have many friends. I always say hi, but that is it. I do so, and take my seat. All is fine until I hear him saying things under his breath. Nobody else hears him but me. I suddenly realize he is singing a made up song. I hear bits and pieces of it. It is about a guy who robs a store and kills someone. I know it is made up because it is terrible. The lyrics don't flow and there is no real beat to the music. He keeps looking at his phone as he continues until we are almost at school. Then I catch him looking at me...actually staring at me….then he smirks.

  I can't help myself, once the bus stops and is almost cleared of passengers, I say to him, "Who sings that song?" trying to stay cool.

  He responds, I just did, Dummy."

I ask for clarification with, "No. Who wrote the song? What famous singer sings it?"

He smirks again and replies, "I just made it up. Don't you like it?"

  I am not sure if it is just a really weird coincidence or if he is truly messing with me. The bus driver tells us to get off the bus and head into school. We exit through the door and on the sidewalk that is basically cleared of students at this point.

I cannot help myself but ask him, "Do you write and sing a lot?" hoping he will not sense my growing anger.

  "No", he replies, "just when I hear about things and think they need to be shared with others in song."

  I say "oh" and move on, pretending to not care.

I head to Homeroom, but he is right behind me. He keeps singing about someone who is innocent getting killed by thugs, by criminals who don't care about other people, just about money and themselves. Why is he following me? The seventh grade wing isn't anywhere near ours. He keeps going on and on. He won't stop. Finally I turn around and ask what his problem is.

His response is, "I don't have a problem. Why? Do you?"

That smirk leaks onto his face again. That's it. I no longer have control over my emotions, nor my muscles. I swing and hit him in the face with my clenched fist. I hear his nose crack and as the blood starts pouring out of his nose, he jumps on me and tackles me to the floor. He punches the side of my head. My ear starts ringing. I hear lots of noise around us. I grab the collar of his shirt and punch with my free hand again. He blocks it and spits on my face.

He's got me pinned down. I wiggle and fight to move out from under his body weight. I get part of myself freed up to swing again and connect with his throat. He, in turn, grabs my throat and begins choking me. I gasp for air and try to break free of his grasp. I throw my arms up against his and the motion is enough to give me time to take a breath.

At that point two teachers have broken through the crowd that circled around us. One teacher grabs him and the other grabs me. I gasp for another breath as I am pulled to my feet and away from my new enemy. I was brought to Mr. Turbino's office. The other kid is brought somewhere else. Good. I don't want to look at his face. He needs to stay clear of me.

***

Mr. Turbino, of course, wants to know "why" this happened. I can't tell him. I just said that the kid, Derek, started singing on the bus and it was aggravating me. He wouldn't stop. He followed me and kept doing it. Mr. Turbino wanted to know why I was so agitated by his singing? I told him that I just didn't like it. So why, he asked, didn't I just keep going to Homeroom and ignore him? I didn't have an answer...well, I couldn't answer him. Not without giving more information to him than I wanted to share at this point. I wasn't sure how much he knew about my situation. He didn't need to know any of it, in my opinion. This was my business. I should never have told Mr. Christian. Maybe he told both Mr. Coster and Mr. Turbino, but I didn't know, so I wasn't willing to chance telling him if he didn't already know.

School policy...physical altercations mean automatic suspension. I was given three days of In School Suspension. Derek only got one day because he didn't throw the first punch. In my opinion, he did, it just wasn't a physical punch. We were both now given assigned seats on the bus for a few weeks. His seat was closer to the front and mine was still near the back. Only the driver knew about this, so as long as I didn't say anything to Nina, she wouldn't notice. I don't want her to lecture me about behavior. I also don't want her to feel bad about what Derek had done. It would make her so sad and angry. I had to protect her.

Mom had to come to school and meet about my altercation. She waited for a better explanation than I had given Mr. Turbino. She didn't get it though. I just gave her the same story. I didn't want her to be sad about it either.

***

After Mom left, I was escorted to my locker to get whatever I would need for the day to get all my work done. The teachers had already sent assignments for me to do for today. I couldn't even go to lunch. The cafeteria would have a meal sent for me to eat in the room. I had never been to the ISS room before. It was in the lower part of the school building. It had no windows except the one in the door that looked out into the hallway. It was like a cell...a prison cell.

Guess I have something in common with Dad now. IF I ever choose to speak to him again, we can compare our rooms. No way. That will never happen. Also, my issue is so small it is like comparing an amoeba in the ocean with a blue whale. They both live in the ocean, but that is about all they have in common. Dad and I both live on Earth, but that is all we have in common at this point in our lives.

I finish some of the work assigned. It actually was a distraction from my anger. Also, the fact that Derek was sitting on the other side of the room from me kept me from looking up to make eye contact with him. It was very quiet and I started to calm down and settle in for the long haul when Derek started humming ever so softly. Barely audible, but I could hear it. He was humming the same "tune" that he put words to on the bus...and in the hallway. He didn't make eye contact with me, but I could see that he was smirking as he "fake read" his book.

"Shut up", I said aloud.

"What?" Ms. Ahmey replied. She was the ISS monitor.

"Sorry. Not you Ms. Ahmey, HIM!" I pointed to Derek.

He looked up and responded with, "What? What am I doing? Just doing my work. That is all I am doing. What is your problem?" He was playing the innocent victim quite well. It just got me madder.

"Stop the humming...NOW!" I exclaimed.

"Since when is it illegal to hum? It helps me concentrate while I read. You've got some major issues there, my man", he stated.

I stood up. Ms. Ahmey stood up between the two of us. She motioned for me to sit back down. I complied. She turned to Derek and asked him to please stop because he was disrupting others. He asked her if she even heard it. She said no, but that I did, so to please stop. He said OK. Things were quiet and mellow for about twenty minutes.

Then he started again. I slammed my math book on my desk and chucked my pencil across the room in his direction. Ms. Ahmey called Mr. Coster. He came downstairs immediately and took me to finish my day in ISS in his office. That is just fine with me. I got away from that jerk, Derek. Why was Derek doing this? He didn't even know me. HOW did he know about what was happening with my family?

***

Once I was in Mr. Coster's office, he wanted to talk...or give me the option of talking things out with him. He told me he knew the situation through his conversation with Mr. Christian. He asked why I was so angry with Derek. I figured I may as well tell him. I got part way through the explanation and had to stop. I was reliving it to the point of getting angry again. I was so angry that I started yelling about it. Mr. Coster stopped me by reminding me that quiet classrooms around us would hear me and could make things worse, especially if I wanted to keep things private.

I had to stop for a while until I felt under control again. It took about an hour. I had eaten my lunch. Mr. Coster and I had gone for a walk outside on the part of the building that had no windows, so none of the students would see me with him and possibly question me about it. He was good about that. He kept things low key so nobody else would become involved. I was starting to trust him. Maybe at some point I could really talk to him about how I was truly feeling. Right now, though, I just couldn't share my thoughts, my fears, my anger.

My anger consumed me at times and didn't allow my brain to function reasonably. Sometimes my anger scared me. How can I control it? Am I like my father? Maybe he did things out of anger. Did he kill Mr. Gossling? Was he angry with him? Is this anger genetic? Is my future going to be like my Dad's? Will I end up where he is? If so, why am I wasting my time in school? I had so many questions.

Mr. Coster interrupted my thoughts, "Hey...where are you? What is consuming your mind right now?"

I wasn't ready to share all of this with him, so I just replied that I had a lot of things on my mind and was trying to sort them out. He told me that he would be very happy to help me sort them and perhaps answer some of them, or at least help me be able to manage my emotions a bit better than I did this morning.

    We returned to his office. I ended up telling him about this morning. Rehashing it cleared up some of my thoughts. I let Derek control me. He knew he was getting to me, so that fueled his fiery attempt to torment me about my awful life. It was awful. My Dad meant everything to me. He was my best friend as well. Now he was gone and I didn't have answers...any answers. I didn't go into any other details about my life with Mr. Coster. Not ready for that, just ready to deal with the issue with Derek.

    Once I explained my situation Mr. Coster did share with me that my story did not match Derek's explanation. That didn't surprise me. Why would he admit to what he had done? Mr. Coster thanked me for sharing what I did with him. He also said he was going to try to get my ISS down to two days instead of three. I begged him not to share the information with anyone else. He said he would only share it with Mr. Turbino because he is the one who could change the original punishment. I didn't like the idea of that, but agreed. ISS is not fun. I didn't have as many distractions from my home thoughts.

    When I was done talking with Mr. Coster and had finished my assignments I had two hours left of the school day. Two hours of thinking about my ruined life. I drew for a while and that helped pass the time. Tomorrow I will be back in the ISS room. Derek would be back in class. He only got one day of suspension because he was the "victim" based on the original story he told and the limited story I originally told.

    Right before dismissal, I asked Mr. Coster how he

thought Derek might have gotten the information to "sing about". Mr. Coster showed me today's newspaper. There was a small article with a few minor details about the robbery and Mr.Gossling getting shot. It was vague, but included the names of the men involved. My Dad's name was there….in black and white….for the world to read. Either he read the article or someone in his home did and then discussed it before he left for school. I still don't know why he targeted and tormented me about it. I may never know why. I just know that this is not the end, but the beginning of the public knowing more and more about what my Dad did. Everyone will know about how he ruined my life.

Chapter 7

Mr. Coster walked me to the front of the building so I could get right on the bus at dismissal and he could let the bus driver know of my assigned seating that had to happen to help avoid more issues between me and Derek. I sat, slouched down in my assigned seat, hoping Derek wouldn't be on the bus. Luckily I would only have to deal with him on the ride home on days I didn't have track practice; well, once my ISS was done. Derek got on the bus and ignored me until we started moving. He then glared at me. I could see him out of the corner of my eye but didn't want to make direct contact. I just wanted this to be over. I don't think he was ready for it to be over yet, though. When the bus got to my stop, I stood and walked down the aisle. As I passed by him, he had his head down, but was humming the same tune as this morning.

I was enraged and wanted to just jump on him

and beat him to a pulp, but truly, what would that solve? Nothing. I was letting him control me. Why was I going to give him any power over me? The answer...I wasn't. I couldn't. If I reacted with violence, I would look like the person with the issue, not him. If I let him control me, I would be just like a puppet...no brain of my own, no choices of my own, just allowing myself to be influenced by someone who meant nothing to me.

Derek wasn't my friend, so I wouldn't be losing a friend. I only knew his name because the bus driver had spoken to him a few times about his behavior on the bus ride in the past month. Now that I thought about it, his behavior usually involved him bugging someone else on the bus. He was a bully. He targeted people for different reasons and attempted to torture them with his words and actions. I guess I was just his next "victim". Well, hopefully he would move on to someone else next week and just leave me alone. At least he knew that I was willing to fight him and he could get hurt. His nose was still swollen from my punch this morning and one of his eyes was turning black and blue. Let those be reminders of me not tolerating his harassment.

Nina interrupted my thoughts when we got off the bus by asking how my day was. I told her it was fine. If she didn't know about what happened, then let it be my secret. I don't want her bugging me about how to behave or feeling bad for me. She refocused on her texting and left me alone as we walked home.

As we walked up the sidewalk, Nina asked if I minded Uncle Vinnie staying with us. I said it was OK, even though I was still mad about him being in my room. Today was the day he was supposed to put his bed and dresser in my room. When I went inside, I could smell the pizza that Mom was making. I dumped my book bag in my room. There was another dresser in my room, but not a bed. As I went into the kitchen for my after school snack, I spotted a bed in the back corner of the living room. Usually there was a desk, chair and stand with plants on it there. As I passed Mom's room, I saw the desk was in her room now. Not sure what happened with the plants, but, so what....Uncle Vinnie would not be sleeping in my room. Yea! At least I would have some privacy at night. He'd need to come in to get his clothes, but that should be all. No biggie compared to what I thought it would be like. As I sat with an apple and jar of peanut butter to spread on the apple slices, Mom called Nina into the kitchen. She said she had information about Dad to share with us.

***

Mom explained that she met with the lawyers representing Dad. She said that Dad had agreed to a plea bargain because he was going to give all the details of the incident that got him into this situation with the police. There were no eyewitnesses and each man was giving information that didn't match each others'. Based on the evidence gathered in the investigation, it looked like Dad's story seemed to match up better than the other guys. By giving his story and if it fit with all the collected evidence and details the detectives had gathered, this may help him not serve as long a sentence in jail. Holy crap!

Dad....going to jail....going to trial...he has messed up so badly this time. This isn't like when he got arrested for speeding and had to go to court and paid a fine. This was the "Big Time". He is such a loser. He didn't learn from his previous minor experience, so he went on to do something much worse. He did something so bad that it took him away from his family. For how long would he be gone? Actually, that didn't matter to me anymore. He was not going to be a part of my life anyway. I don't need a father...or a best friend. I just need to act cool, especially around family and friends so they don't know how much anger, sadness and frustration are pent up in my body, all the way through my soul.

    I will never be the same again. This "event" has changed my life forever. Dad's bad choices will imprint in my mind and develop me into a different kind of adult, with a different kind of life that I ever imagined for myself. I won't be a star athlete...or get a college scholarship...or heck, get a good job once everyone knows everything about my Dad. He is a bad person, so that makes me one, too. We're blood...so what is in him is in me. My rotten future is inevitable.

    I asked a few basic questions so that Mom would think that I was listening and that I cared. It was so untrue. My sister got upset and left the room. I stayed until Mom was done "informing" us about all she knew about Dad.

    I wanted to blurt out, "Can he stay in jail until I am old enough to be on my own?", "Mom, you are crazy to want to stay with him. Divorce his ass and let him rot in jail. He obviously doesn't care about us, so why should we care about him?"

    What kept me from sharing these thoughts was Grandma. She is Dad's mother. I know that no matter what I did in life that Mom would love me and defend me. If I was bad, it would hurt her as much as it would hurt me. That is a Mom's love. She would forever have my back. I am sure Grandma feels the same way about Dad. This might be hurting her even more than it is hurting me. I never thought about it that way. I need to keep my thoughts and emotions to myself so I don't hurt Grandma, no matter how awful I feel. She is always there for us, cooking, sewing, cheering me on at track meets and award ceremonies. She never asks for anything in return. My love for her has to stay strong. I can't do or say anything that would hurt her.

Mom is tougher...she can handle some of my tough times, like earlier today with Derek. I just need to limit my problems that she has to be aware of. I know she must be having a rough time. Dad has broken all of us. Nina isn't afraid to show her emotions. I am not afraid either, but just am choosing to hold it inside or run it off until I feel better.

***

Just before dinnertime I emerged from my room. Uncle Vinnie was on the couch reading a car magazine. I sat next to him.
"Thanks", I offered.
"For what?" he replied.
"For not putting your bed in my room. I really appreciate the privacy. Sometimes I like to game until late at night and I wouldn't be able to if you were trying to sleep in the same room." I explained.
He responded with, "Well, I thought back to when I was your age. I had to share a room with your

Mom. It was torture for me. I didn't have any time to myself, or a space to call my own. I figured you probably felt the same way. Just promise that you won't game too late into the night. Don't need you getting 'video game brain'", and he laughed.

I smiled back as Mom called us to dinner. Nina didn't join us...she was still upset about the talk after school.

I gamed until about midnight then fell asleep. I tossed and turned all night, though. I kept thinking about what it would be like if Dad hadn't made such a bad choice. It would be "normal" around here. Mom and Dad would be going to work. Grandma would be helping with meal prep and spending time with her friends at the Senior Center. Nina and I would be going to school during the week and hanging out at least one night on the weekend with Mom, Dad and Grandma either watching a movie and eating popcorn or having a family game night...usually playing cards.

We always ate dinner together whenever we were all home. We would clean up the kitchen together afterwards so it got done quickly. We also watched a few game shows or sitcoms together at least a few days during the week unless Nina and I had a lot of homework to finish. It is just so different. Everyone is living together, but we aren't "together" anymore. Mom isn't working right now. She spends time during the day with lawyers and most evenings she stays in her bedroom. I am not sure what she is doing there, but she seems lonely and sad, too. Uncle Vinnie is here and just seems to read magazines or watch TV when he is not working.

Grandma just seems sad as well, but tries to put on a "happy" face so we won't feel bad for her. She can't hide that from me, though. We have a special bond. Ever since she took care of me after I had my appendix out when I was in second grade. She made me whatever I wanted to eat, played any game I wanted to play and watched whatever I wanted to on TV while I was recovering. She also told me lots of stories about when my Dad was little. He was a lot like me, or rather, I am a lot like he was as a kid. I hope this doesn't mean I am going to grow up and do what he did and end up in jail. Can I grow up to be totally different from my parents? Is it in the genes?

***

The next morning I "faked" going to track practice. I was told that I couldn't go until I was done with my suspension. It usually lasted about an hour or two. I timed it so that I ran to the park that was near school. There were a bunch of guys a few years older playing basketball. I sat to watch them for a while. One of them had to leave early, so they asked me if I wanted to play to fill in and keep the teams even. I said OK, but warned them that running is more my thing. They didn't care, though.

We played for about a half hour. I sunk a few baskets, but my strength on the court was definitely out running the other's across the court. I was fed the ball a few times and that was when I made a few baskets. I only was successful if nobody was in my face trying to steal the ball from me. As the game was breaking up, one of the kids was walking towards his Mom's car as she pulled up to take him home. As he jumped in, the tinted side window rolled down and Derek glared out the window at me. As they pulled away he spit out the window in my direction and then flipped me off. I wanted to shout at him or make some inappropriate gesture back at him, but instead I turned away and ignored. I considered that a point for me. I didn't let myself get sucked into his nastiness.

One of the other kids noticed and said to me, "Hey...do you and Derek have a problem?"

I told him we had a fight, but that Derek had started it. The kid said that didn't surprise him. He said Derek's brother told them that Derek is miserable and nasty at home, ever since his dad died last year. He told me that Derek doesn't have any friends because he is just so mean to everyone. He said that Derek wasn't like that when he was younger. He said that when David (the boy I had played basketball with) and Derek's Dad died that they went through a really tough time for a while. He said David still gets upset once in a while, but Derek has just been awful ever since it happened. Wow.

I thought I had it bad. I was mad at my Dad, but he wasn't gone forever, like Derek's Dad. Maybe I would be like him if that had happened to my Dad. It really bothered me, now, that I had punched him. I know he was being a jerk to me, but now I felt bad for him. I promised myself not to hit him anymore. Hopefully, I will be able to keep that promise. I am usually good at sticking to my promises, whether they are to other people or too myself.

I ran home with a lot on my mind. I had questions. I wanted to know what happened to Derek's Dad. Was he sick? Was he in an accident? Did Derek consider his Dad his best friend as well? I decided to try to find out information, but that may be complicated. I did not know Derek's last name.

When I got home, Mom asked why I hadn't gotten dropped off, like I usually do. I told her I had gotten dropped off at the corner because Ryan's dad had to be at an appointment somewhere and was running late, so I told him to just leave me at the corner to save him a minute or two. She bought my lie. I headed to the shower. Once I was clean and not smelly anymore, I headed to my room to do some investigating about Derek.

Chapter 8

Later that day, Mom and Nina came into the house. Mom must have picked her up from somewhere. I had just opened my laptop to do some more investigating about Derek's Dad, when Mom came to my door and called me into the living room.

Nina was in the rocking chair. Share was pale and didn't look good. She had tear marks down her face and her nose was running like crazy. Grandma looked upset and worried. Uncle Vinnie just looked mad. What now? Are there more complications? I didn't want to hear the news. After quickly glancing at everyone's faces, I knew it couldn't be good. I would avoid direct eye contact with everyone at this point.

If I didn't like what was being said I would focus on something in the room...an object that meant nothing to me, like the curtains or a cobweb in the corner of the room. I would try to find something about them that I had never noticed before. Was the cobweb there the last time I looked? Like the pattern in the curtains, or the colors within the pattern. Had I ever noticed one of the colors? Did the pattern repeat, or was it random? What colored stripes were thinner than the others? I just focused on stupid things to think about to keep my mind off of the reality being spoken that I was supposed to be absorbing and accepting into my brain. Well...if I don't really hear all of it, then I don't have to react or dwell on it and get myself angry.

My mind needed a break from all the racing thoughts it has dealt with lately. I truly believe that brains need to rest...and not just when you are asleep. Mine hasn't even been resting while I sleep. I haven't had much sleep and when I do, I have crazy dreams that wake me up, my heart pounding in reaction to my dream.

Even though I am focusing on "not focusing" on the words my mother is sharing, I do catch the basic parts of the information. TV News...Mr. Gossling died. Now a homicide charge will be given to at least one of the men, if not all of them. Sure Dad...great job...you've really messed up your life and ours, but to be involved in TAKING someone else's life away from them....and taking someone else away from their family FOREVER. Who the hell do you think you are to be a part of that? What possibly gave you the right to be a part of this? If you were the one who killed Mr. Gossling, you will be losing too. Not just spending your life, or at least most of it, in jail, but you will lose your son.

I will not be any part of his life. He will have lost me forever. When someone asks about my Dad who doesn't know about what you did, I will simply tell them that you are dead. It will not be a lie. You will be dead to me. I cannot connect myself in any way with someone who would do that to another human being. If it were a matter of self defense, it would be a different story, but you chose all of this.

You chose to rob the store with the other two guys. You knew what you were doing. And if you had a gun...where did you get it? Why did you even have a gun? Our family is not one who likes hunting or shooting for sport at targets, so why...why.

Mom said something about it not being Dad who shot Mr. Gossling. Why does she believe him? I don't know what to believe anymore. Why do the lawyers believe him? I just stared out the side window...trying to find a new focus to take my thoughts away to some other place. I couldn't do it...my mind was reeling...Mom. She was a sucker to believe all that was being shared.

Mom then said something that hit another chord of reality....the newspapers. There would be more in the papers and on the evening news perhaps. Great. Now my secret was going to be written in the sky for everyone to read. I would have no more privacy on this issue. Derek would have a field day with the information and continue to torment me. I would take it without fighting him though. From what I learned about him this morning, he has it worse than me...or does he? His Dad is gone forever, yes, but he didn't kill anyone or wasn't part of a robbery...a criminal. I don't know which situation was worse. I do know that neither life of ours was happy right now.

***

The saying, "Misery loves company" came to my mind. My grandma used to use it when either me or Nina were upset and then annoyed each other until we were both upset. Grandma explained to us that when someone is truly unhappy, what often makes them have a false sense of happiness is done by making someone else worse off than they are. Like when I used to get in trouble for having a messy room. I would go into Nina's room when she wasn't home and mess it up. I was pretty good at doing it without being caught. She would come home and be so mad. I would act all innocent, pretending not to have any idea of what she was talking about. She would get in trouble and have to clean her room. I know it was a rotten thing to do, but I was mad and wanted someone else to be in trouble like me. Nina was the closest and easiest target. I only did it a few times before Grandma pulled me aside and told me a story that was based on the "Misery loves company" concept. She knew it was me, but didn't rat me out to Mom and Dad. After our talk, I stopped doing it. I waited a whole year to admit to Nina why I did it and apologize. She wasn't all that mad because a lot of time had gone by and I had stopped doing it.

  Derek was living the "Misery loves company" through his behavior of bullying other kids who were having problems or just seemed weaker than him. Maybe if I focus on helping him in some way it will distract me from my life. That will be very hard though, especially if he chooses to keep harassing me with all the news that is out now about my Dad. I've got to figure out how I can help him. It will be a great distraction from my crappy life. And, to be honest, I like helping people. As I decide to truly take on this challenge, I remember that I have to figure out a few things before I put "Operation Derek" into full swing. I need to know his last name...I need to figure out what happened to his Dad so I know how to plan my mission.

  I step into Nina's room. She is still upset and doesn't want to talk. I tell her I just have one question she may know the answer to. I ask her what Derek's last name is. She doesn't even know who he is. We do go to a large middle school, so you really only get to know some of the kids at school. I tell her that he has a brother named David. She says that she knows who David is. He is in 8th grade like her, but they only share Computer Science Class. She says he sits near the back of the room in the corner where the kids whose last names start with letters towards the end of the alphabet sit. That is all she can tell me. I say thanks and head out of the room quickly before she can ask me why I want to know.

   I continue my search. I figure that if Derek's Dad died about a year ago, I can look through all the obituaries listed in the local newspaper online. I will look for a guy who would be between 35-50 years old to start. I will begin in September of last year and go from there to December. If I don't have luck, I will back track to August. I will read the obituary and see if they mention sons named Derek and David. I worked on it for about an hour.

***

   My stomach started to growl, I hadn't eaten much at lunch, so I went into the kitchen. Nobody is in there. Nobody is in the living room. I hear Mom's TV on in her bedroom. I peek in and see Grandma working on a quilt in her room. Uncle Vinnie must have gone out. I look in the fridge. Some leftovers from last night are sitting there, waiting to be consumed. I heat up the meatloaf, mashed potatoes and carrots in the microwave. I grab a soda to drink. We usually drink juice or milk, but hey, nobody is here to stop me, so what the heck. I sit at

the table and eat while playing a game on my phone.
  When I look at my phone, I see that Deacon had texted me about coming over...three hours ago. Shoot! I forgot we were supposed to hang out this afternoon. I had to think about what excuse I was going to give Deacon. I decided not to lie. Chances are, he's already heard about my Dad. It was in the newspaper and on the local TV news channel. I texted him a message. I told him that my family was meeting about what was happening with my Dad. Within two minutes he called and told me that he wanted to know what was happening. I asked him what he knew. He only knew that my Dad got in trouble with the police for robbing Mr. Gossling's store. His step mom and dad hadn't told him anything else. He hadn't read the paper or seen the news on TV. I guess his parents didn't want him to know.
  Deacon was so mad. He said his parents didn't want him at my house. They said I could come to their home. I knew why, and it made me mad too. They were judging my entire family based on what my Dad did. Just another way that Dad was wrecking my life. Deacon said that tonight we could game together and not let anyone else join our game so that we could talk if I wanted to. He said he had questions, but would not get mad if I didn't want to answer them. I agreed.
  I did something I had never done before....I locked my bedroom door. Our family never locked doors except the doors to our home. We just always respected privacy and didn't enter a bedroom or bathroom without knocking and being invited into the room. I couldn't take the chance of Mom, especially, coming in to talk with me after our family

meeting this afternoon. I had heard her going into Nina's room, so I figured that I was next. I just wanted her to know that I wasn't ready to have a conversation with her about all of this, and I didn't want her to hear me talking with Deacon. He was my best friend, and I was ready to spill my guts and tell him everything I knew. Even the information I was told not to share...I know I could tell him and that he would keep it secret. He had never told anyone any of the secrets we shared throughout all the years we had been friends. I had always kept his secrets as well. I think that is why I considered him my best friend. I had a lot of friends, but he was the one I could trust in any situation. I told him we could talk while we gamed against each other. He agreed. We hung up then logged into our favorite soccer game.

So it began. We started playing. After about ten minutes I decided to tell him all that I knew about that night, based on what Mom had shared with us. As I was telling him, I realized that I did hear more of the details about what Mom just told us as I sat in the living room, trying to distract myself from the reality that was being shared in Dad's situation.

Dad did not shoot Mr. Gossling. He said he left as soon as that guy Jake took out the gun and shot Mr. Gossling who was holding his gun, pointed at them. Based on what he told, it matched up with what the police had found through their investigation. They even found Dad's boot prints in the mud in the wooded area that he said he hid in when he left the store. The surveillance camera on the store showed only one person getting into the car after the shooting. The police caught Jake and arrested him. The next day, he told the police that my Dad was the one who shot Mr. Gossling. My Dad's prints weren't on anything...the vehicle, the gun the cops recovered miles away from the crime scene. Just the video showed it was him going in with Jake and some guy named Sam.

  Dad did this because his hours at work were being cut and that would not give him enough to pay all the bills. I guess he thought it was a quick way to get some money. What an idiot he is, thinking he could do this and get away with it. And to just think this was OK to do. To take someone else's hard earned money that was not his. I can't even believe he considered doing this at all. I thought I knew him, but I guess I don't.

  Deacon was totally quiet, listening to every word, absorbing the entire situation involving my Dad and all of us on the home front. When I had finished spilling my guts, I felt a huge relief. I swear I was ten pounds lighter. The weight that was pushing on my shoulders and filling my stomach with huge knots had almost disappeared. I heard Deacon sigh. I could picture him shaking his head side to side, looking at the floor. He did that whenever he was processing serious information. When we would get into trouble in elementary school, which wasn't often, but we had some "intense moments" a few times in the cafeteria and on the playground, as we were being reprimanded, he would hang his head and shake it slowly back and forth. I, on the other hand, would keep eye contact with the adult addressing us about the issue. I know that it was part of Deacon's culture to not make eye contact with someone disciplining him. It was considered disrespectful.

  Once he had absorbed the information and had

recovered from the shock of the story, it was my turn to listen. He first told me he was glad I had told him everything. He said that he was sorry that me and my family were going through such a hard time. He then shared that he would be there for me, no matter what happened with my Dad. He explained that his parents' reluctance to have him come to my house is because they didn't know the whole story. He then promised NOT to tell them, but to still hang out with me. He said I could come over his house whenever I wanted to, or needed to. He also said if I didn't feel comfortable doing that, that we could meet at the tennis court that was half way between our homes.

 Deacon admitted that he didn't have any answers for me, but that he agreed with me that this situation just sucks. He did say one thing though, that made me kinda mad. He told me to not be mad at my father. He reminded me of what a great guy he was and all the awesome things he had done for me and with me throughout my life. He understood that I was mad at him for putting our family in this situation, but not to be mad at him for making a mistake. He agreed that there was no way Dad could have shot Mr. Gossling. He said that he believed what my Dad had said about leaving the scene as soon as the gun came out of Jake's pocket. I sat in shock. I was still mad, but Deacon was really helping me with my feelings...with my anger. It was less. It was still there, but some of it left with the weights leaving my body as I talked about it with someone.

 As we hung up, we agreed to meet tomorrow at the tennis courts. I didn't feel comfortable being at his house if his parents weren't happy with me or my family. I wouldn't know what to do or say if they mentioned anything about this to me based on what they heard on the news or from the newspaper. Would I defend my Dad? Would I agree with their opinion of him? I wasn't at the point that I could say anything to anyone else about what was going on, so it was definitely safer to just avoid Deacon's family for now. Hopefully, at some point, I could go to his house and feel comfortable, but I am just not sure when, or if, that would ever happen.

***

I heard Mom knock, and decided to let her in. She heard me unlock the door.

"Why did you lock your door?" she questioned.

"I needed my privacy. I needed to know that I had control over who came into my room, and that I would be ready to talk to them." I explained.

She didn't lecture me about it. She just said OK and sat on the edge of my bed.

"Can we talk?" she inquired.

"Sure. About what?" I responded, somewhat sarcastically.

"I need to know that you are alright. I need to know how you are dealing with and processing all the information you are hearing. You and your sister are my number one priority. If you aren't dealing with this situation well, then we need to do something about it." she explained. "Like what?" I wondered aloud.

"I think we need to go to family counseling. I think having someone sit and listen to how we are all thinking about everything going on with your Dad and how it is affecting our lives directly and indirectly would be beneficial to all of us." she suggested.

"No. I'm fine." I stated in a serious tone of voice.

"Then please just go to support me and your sister. That way you can hear how we are processing this all. You may realize that you aren't the only one with some of the feelings you are having. I know you are angry. Ever since everything happened, you've been angry and shut off from us." she said.

Wow. She is more perceptive than I thought. She should know me that well, though...she is my Mom. She usually knows what I am thinking even before I realize I am thinking it. She calls it "mother's intuition". I just shook my head back and forth.

"I don't want to talk to someone else about this. The less people that know, the better our lives will be." I reasoned.

"Well, you have no control over that at this point. The press and the news programs have access to all of the information the police are required to give them. Reporting it is their right. Freedom of the press is what it is called. By law, they have a right to certain things that happen in society. They report on whatever they choose to be most important and most interesting. We have no say in what information they share with the public." she informed me.

I didn't like what she was telling me, but it was the truth. I learned about it in my history class last year when we studied the Constitution. I ended up telling her that I would go to the counselor, but that I wasn't going to speak. I was just there as support for her and Nina. I could tell by her face that she wasn't happy with some of what I said, but she accepted it without further argument.

Mom then asked me how I was feeling about Dad

based on what she just told us. I decided to lay it out to her by telling her that I hated Dad for not only what he had done to our family by his actions, but that I hated him for being part of ending someone's life. He ruined another family more permanently than ours. IF he was telling the truth and didn't shoot Mr. Gossling, he was still part of the reason he was dead. If he hadn't agreed to the robbery, then maybe Jake and Sam wouldn't have done it. Or maybe there would have been something else that was different that would have resulted in nobody getting killed. I told her that I wasn't happy about her going to the lawyers and supporting Dad through all of this. I think he should rot in jail alone. He should go through all of this alone. He didn't ask us what we thought about his decision to be a part of this awful crime, so why should we be there for him.

I got a bit out of control. I threw my controller across the room into my closet door. I told her that when Dad came home, or rather, **if** Dad comes home, that I would be moving out. I would find another place to stay. I would not live in the same house as his ever again.

Mom started to cry. I didn't soften. I just stood there seething with my anger that I thought was better after talking to Deacon. Nope...it all came back with a vengeance. I told her to leave. I told her to get out of my room and leave me alone. I had agreed to what she wanted, but that was it. Don't expect me to ever love Dad again. He had done too much to ever go back to the way things used to be.

I walked toward her to kind of "help" her leave. She got the hint and kind of ran out of the room in tears. Well, too bad for her. She needed to toughen up and respect my feelings. I then went to my controller. I put in the batteries that had fallen out. No luck...it was broken. I took out my second controller that I never use, and put in the batteries. Yup...back in action...ready to reabsorb my life into the video screen before me.

Chapter 9

Uncle Vinnie came in to tell me it was time for dinner and to let Nina know. I went into her room to tell her. She was working on schoolwork. Not me. I haven't done any homework since the night Dad left. I try to do some work in school, when I can focus. I actually did the most work while in ISS yesterday. Even though I was upset, I used the work to help my brain escape what was going on around me. I need to get better at doing that. I know my grades will slip if I don't get my act together.
    We sat down at dinner. Uncle Vinnie had cooked chicken marsala. Grandma was helping him learn to cook so when he was on his own, or living with his friends again, that he could cook something besides the basics, like spaghetti, hot dogs, burgers, and other easy meals. He loved food and appreciated good meals, so he figured that the best way to know you are going to get a good meal is to know how to make it yourself. Dinner was delicious. He did a great job.
    Grandma was a great coach. She had been cooking since she was ten years old. Her family grew up in Colombia. They were very poor. She had to help them in many ways. She had odd jobs as a child that earned her money or food to take home. Her mother took care of her elderly parents who

lived with them. Since her mom was busy doing that, she also had to do many chores at home as well. Cooking was one of them. She told me that she used to try all different creations based on the food that was available at home. When they had the ingredients to make good, hearty meals, her mother would cook and she would watch so that next time they had the ingredients she could cook it herself. There weren't too many things that Grandma didn't know how to cook.

My favorite was her empanadas. I have tried empanadas at many different places...friend's homes, restaurants, holidays where other family members made them for the celebration. Never have I tasted any that were better than Grandmas. Uncle Vinnie was definitely benefitting from her being there to suggest what to cook and how to cook it. I figured that once I hit high school that maybe I will start paying attention to how she cooks. That way, once I am out on my own I can still eat good food. Uncle Vinnie is smart to think that way.

While we ate, the conversation was sparse. After the food compliments were over, there wasn't much to say. Everyone still seemed upset and nobody wanted to talk about our family meeting this afternoon. If so, we would all lose our appetites quickly. Mom reminded me that next week was my turn to go with her to the food pantry. She goes every Wednesday and Nina and I take turns going with her.

Mom does this because when she lost her job a few years ago during the COVID Pandemic, we got food from the pantry because we didn't have enough money to pay all the bills and put food on the table. Grandma didn't live with us yet, so we didn't have some of her retirement to help us. Dad worked a lot at that time, taking overtime shifts whenever he could. It took about 6 months for Mom to find another job at a rehabilitation center, doing what she loved...taking care of the elderly and disabled patients. She made sure that they ate well, exercised and laughed every day.

Mom always believed in the power of laughing. She said that laughter set off chemicals in your body that helped you heal faster, be stronger and live a good life. I wish she could work that power here at home right now. I could use a good laugh. I would enjoy anything that would boost my mood and help me to be happy again. I wondered when that will happen?

When would I feel true happiness again? Sure, I have smiled or chuckled at something for a minute or two, but then the gloom and doom of my life would resettle, weighing me down. I wonder who has noticed the change in me. I used to be upbeat and happy almost all the time. I was the type of kid that cheered up others all the time. I always had a joke or funny story to share to pick up people's spirits. Those had disappeared. I really miss being like that. It is something you can't force. It has to come naturally from your inner spirit. I kind of feel like the character Eeyore from Winnie the Pooh. He is always so glum. Even when he tries to express happiness, it just doesn't come out the right way.

***

After dinner, I help with the dishes then retreat to my room. Mom slips an envelope under my closed door. I recognize the writing...it is Dad's. It has my name on the front and is sealed with paper inside.

Instead of picking it up I stomp on it. I slide it under my foot, along my floor and kick it under my bed. That is where it belongs. Under my bed with all the dust bunnies, lost dirty socks and whatever else has rolled under there. That is how much value it has to me at this point. But where did Mom get it from? I DID want to know that. I stepped out of my room and decided to ask.

Mom was in the kitchen. She was sitting at the table with the bills in front of her. I didn't waste any time beating around the bush.

"Where did that envelope come from?" I inquired.

"Didn't you recognize the writing on it?" she counter questioned.

"Yes, it is Dad's writing, but HOW did you get it? Have you had it for a while?" I continued. "No. Dad gave it to me today when I visited him." she answered.

What? How did she see Dad? Why did she go see him? Why would she want to go see him? The questions swirled through my head.

As if she could read my mind, she continued her response, "On Saturdays Dad can have a visit with a family member who lives at this house for 10 minutes. I know that you and your sister and Grandma are not ready to go see him. I don't know how ready I am to see him, but I didn't want him to not have anyone show up. He needs to know that we are here for him. He needs to know that we love him and miss him."

"Well I hope you didn't include me in any of your delusional thoughts about how we feel about Dad. I don't miss him. I don't love him. I don't want to be there for him. What he has done is beyond what I can call something that is 'forgivable', if there is such a word. He doesn't deserve my time, even a lousy 10 minutes on a Saturday. I hope you don't expect me to ever go see him. That is not gonna happen....not in this lifetime, at least." I explained.

Mom just looked down at the floor. I thought I saw a tear drop from her face into her lap. Why is she being such a sucker? She should just leave him there to think...and rot away. Think about what his life could have been like if he hadn't betrayed all of us. All those lies he told us about the importance of honoring yourself and your family. How family is the key to happiness. How family supports each other, no matter what happens in life. Nope. He is not the person I thought he was. The person I counted on him to be. The person I trusted to be there for me...always. He is garbage. He is a liar. He is a joke.

At that point I just walked away. I didn't want to make Mom cry, but I couldn't be all loving and forgiving and understanding at this point. I just gave her space...and time to absorb what I had said. Now she knows a little better what is going on in my head. How I am reasoning this whole situation out in my world. Mom cannot seriously expect me to be OK with any of this? Why is she pushing Dad on us? Why did she even give me some stupid note from him when she knew I wasn't ready for it. Who knew when, or even if, I would ever be ready to hear his words...or his laugh.

***

I loved Dad's laugh. It would boom across the house when we were home. You could be in the shower with tunes blaring and still hear it clearly. Along with that laugh came his smile. He had a chipped front tooth from when he, as he would say, "caught a baseball with his mouth" when he was about 8 years old. His family never got it fixed. I asked him once why. He said they didn't have dental insurance so they couldn't afford it. He said once he was in high school and his family had the insurance that he went to the dentist. The dentist wanted to fix it, but he was used to it. He actually said that it gave him "character". It made him unique. He liked standing out in a crowd.

Dad also would always wear a baseball hat with a unique team logo on it. He didn't wear the typical pro teams on it. He would wear some college team logo that was different than any others. He said he liked it because sometimes it brought up questions from strangers. They would comment on it, or ask if that is where he went to college. He'd say "no" and strike up a conversation with them.

Dad loved people. He loved talking with people and meeting new people. Learning about their lives and sharing funny stories about his life. This would happen everywhere we went. It could be at the park, in the checkout line at the grocery store. Heck, it even happened when we were in the middle of Grand Central Station in New York City trying to figure out what train to take on our vacation two summers ago. Some guy commented on it because the guy had gone to that college. He and dad talked for twenty minutes, like they were old friends. When they walked away, we realized that we had missed the train we needed to take. Nobody got mad. Dad laughed and asked what Plan B was.

We always had a Plan B set when we went places together as a family. Plan B simply meant what was our back-up plan if the original plan wasn't going to happen for some reason. It helped us save time from trying to rethink what we were going to do. Dad said that wasted time. We needed to be prepared for the unexpected. Well...Dad being in jail was definitely unexpected...and I had no Plan B.

Chapter 10

Something was bugging me. I wasn't able to focus on my video games. They had truly become a great escape from reality for me, but for some reason, my mind couldn't focus on the action and navigate me through strategies to get the upper hand over my opponents. I hit pause and began to pace...back and forth in my room. What was it? There was some reason for this. It took me a good 10 minutes of pacing before I looked under my bed. It was like my body knew what to do even though my mind hadn't thought of it yet.

It sat there...among a few empty soda cans from the times I broke the house rule and brought soda into my room. Mom only allowed water in our rooms, so if it spilled, it wouldn't stain or be a sticky mess to clean. There was lots of dust that included some pretty large "dust bunnies" as Grandma called them, piling up on the wide planked wooden floor beneath my bed. I only clean underneath my bed twice a year, when my Mom has us to a big room clean and supervises us to be sure it gets done effectively.

If I lied flat and fully reached out with my arm, I know I could retrieve it. But did I really want to know what was written in there? My mind kept saying no, yet I reached and slowly guided it out, into the broad opening of my bedroom. Clear as day, through the dust it had gathered, I could read my name. Yup, it was Dad's handwriting. It was sealed shut. I wonder if Dad sealed it or if Mom read it first then sealed it. Either way it didn't matter. I fixed my hands into position to rip it into pieces. Small pieces that would make it impossible to reconstruct and read. My hands froze in that position. Why? Why couldn't I just do it and get it over with? Why was my brain and my body not working in sync with each other? I put the envelope down on my nightstand. I wouldn't destroy it...yet.

***

I opened my laptop and started looking through more obituaries, trying to find out about Derek's Dad and what had happened. My mind allowed me to focus on this task. I was looking through our little local newspaper and the regional paper as well. I flipped back and forth, one date at a time, day by day.

After about an hour and a half I found it! The obituary was for Maury Royal. He was 40 years old and had two sons, Derek and David and a daughter Shannon. It didn't say, though, how he died. It just said "unexpectedly". Well, at least that meant that he wasn't sick for a long time. Now I need to see if there are any news articles that aren't obituaries that may lead me to what happened.

Another thirty minutes later, I read an article that would end up giving me nightmares. It was about Mr. Royal. He was killed in a car accident. He had his daughter, Shannon with him in the car. She was seriously injured, but was expected to survive. From what the article said, their car slid on wet leaves that had fallen onto the road during a bad rainstorm. Oh man! That must have been so awful for that family to go through. Sure, I've read plenty of stories and articles like this, but I have never actually known someone in the family. I had a new perspective on how I looked at Derek...and how I was going to be kind to him...and perhaps try to be his friend. I know this task was not going to be easy, especially if he kept taunting me with what was happening in my family. I will be strong. I will not retaliate in any way except through kindness. I will not let him know that I know about his Dad and his sister's accident last year. I will wait until HE is ready to tell me about it, **if** that ever happens.

I tried to go back to gaming. I am still not able to focus. Why? I had been able to focus on finding the news article and information about Derek's father. I wonder if my brain just wanted me to read the letter and get it over and done with, then allow me to go back to my "life" of gaming. I opened the envelope slowly and sat down in my desk chair. The letter was written on a plain piece of white paper. It was unlined with no fancy heading on the top of the paper. What did I expect; that he would get personalized stationary in jail? I almost laughed out loud at that ludicrous thought. It started with "Hey Bud". Really; he thought he could still call me Bud? I am not his buddy, his friend, his pal. I am his son, and only because blood tests could prove it. That is the only relation we have with each other at this point.

***

The first words of the body of the letter were, "I'm so sorry. Please forgive me." Give me a break...too late for apologies. You did the crime, you do the time...and lose at least part of your family, too. I am usually someone who is quick to forgive and get over issues that arise with me and other people. I am one that cannot stay mad for too long. But then again, nobody has ever ruined my family before. This goes way beyond any of the other incidents when I thought I was so mad that I would never get over it. Usually by the next day or two I would be ready to talk to the other person who I was mad at, and settle things so our lives could get back to how they always were.

The letter explained what had happened the night of the robbery, in my father's opinion. It also explained his reasoning for making the decision to be part of the robbery. I knew all of this already because of what Mom had shared with us earlier. As I read through it I started to shed a few tears. I didn't know if they were tears of sadness, anger, frustration, or a combination of those emotions. I was mad that I had any emotion. It was like, yea, Dad won...he got me to have feelings about all of this that made me cry.

I stopped reading about half way through. I put the paper back into the envelope. This time, though, I put the envelope in the top drawer of my desk. It would be safe there until I was ready to read the rest of the letter...IF I would ever be ready for that.

***

I went into the kitchen to get a snack. It was so quiet in the rest of the house. Weird. It was only nine o'clock. As I was popping the popcorn in the microwave, Uncle Vinnie appeared. He sat down after getting a ginger ale for himself and a root beer for me. He knew it was my favorite kind of soda.

He had grabbed a small bag of pretzels, some M and Ms, a can of peanuts and some raisins.

"What are you doing?" I wondered aloud.

"Making my own trail mix. And hoping you are willing to give me some of your popcorn to add to it." he replied.

I filled a big cup with the popcorn and handed it to him. "Thanks. Want some trail mix?" he offered.

"No thanks. I'll stick with my popcorn." I responded.

He went on to tell me about trail mixes. He explained that he loved the different tastes as they combined and complemented each other as one form of a snack food. He said he didn't like raisins or peanuts alone. They were too boring for his taste buds, but he loved them in trail mix. I could tell he was getting at something, but I didn't know what.

Finally I asked him, "Why the lesson on trail mix and its components?"

He smiled. He knew I had figured out that he was talking about more than just trail mix.

He chuckled a bit then began, "Trail mix is like a family. Each person is a different part of the combination, like in a family. Each food can stand on its own and be appreciated, but together they work to create a whole new taste. Each person in a family is important. When they are together, there is a unity...a bond that nobody else outside of the family ever really understands. It is different with each family. If one of the components of trail mix, or of a family, is not *present*, then the taste changes. It is not ruined or inedible, just different. The trail mix is still OK. If a person is not present in a family, that doesn't ruin the rest of the family, it just changes the dynamics. It is not broken...just different. Do you get what I am saying?"

I did. He was comparing our family to trail mix. I understood what he was saying, but didn't agree with all of it.

"But what if the reason you eat trail mix is because you love popcorn and all of a sudden the popcorn isn't there?" I questioned.

He answered by saying, "Even if your favorite component is missing, you can still appreciate the other flavors and the new overall blend of them without the popcorn being present."

I got it. Dad was the "popcorn" missing from our trail mix/family. I had given up trail mix/family because one ingredient was missing. So I was missing out on enjoying all the other ingredients/people in my trail mix-family.

I had to comment with, "Sometimes it is hard to accept the change in your trail mix. Sometimes the popcorn goes away, and is substituted with another ingredient, like cheesy crackers. It takes time for your taste buds to decide if they like the new combination."

I then proceeded to tell him that his trail mix metaphor was quite unique. I then took a handful of his trail mix. He smiled and we ate the rest of both snacks silently. When I got up to head back to my room, he put his hand up and I high fived him.

He responded by stating, "I know I cannot fix things for you, but I want to be here to help you as well as everyone else while they deal with their feelings and adjust to this new situation. I am here for you. When you need me, you know where I am. I will stay here as long as necessary, but not overstay when I am no longer needed to be here."

I thanked him and did something I hadn't done in

a long time. I walked over to him and hugged him. It was just a quick hug then I retreated back to my room. I started thinking about how much Uncle Vinnie is sacrificing for us all. I need to appreciate that and let him know in my own way.

***

Back in my room I was finally ready to game. Deacon was already in another game with another group. I joined a group that my friend, Shaun was just starting up. I didn't know the other two kids in the game, but was partnered up with one of them who went by the name DR King. We actually worked well together and ended up winning the first game. We continued gaming until well after midnight. It must have gotten windy outside at one point because I heard something hitting my bedroom window. When it gets windy there is a tree branch that sometimes scrapes my window. It freaks me out. I barely heard it, though, because I had my ear buds in so I wouldn't make a lot of noise and wake anyone up. If I did that, I would have gotten in trouble and would have had to stop playing.

After a few games, Shaun wanted to change partners so he and I could be on the same team. We changed it around so that could happen, and then Shaun and I got our behinds whooped by DR King and his partner. I was finally able to just relax and laugh (quietly). I guess that the talk with Uncle Vinnie helped me to realize that my family isn't broken...it is just different.

I know so many kids with so many different types of families. Some kids are adopted, some live with aunts and uncles, some have two moms or dads, some only have one parent. One kid I know lives with his older sister. It is just the two of them. She goes to college and works a full time job. They have a tiny apartment, but he likes it there. He is on my bus. He lives with his sister because his parents are both in the military and are stationed overseas for this year. Since his sister is 19, he was allowed to stay with her so he wouldn't have to leave his friends and school for a year and live in another country, which he didn't want to do. All those are just different varieties of trail mix. None are better than the other...just different. Some of the families I know have gone through changes. My friend, Shaun's parents are divorced. He had to go through having a parent move out. He lives sometimes with his mom and other times with his dad. When I go to his house, I always have to ask which place he is at because he considers both places as home. We only have one middle school in our town, so he can take one bus to and from dads when he is with him, and another bus to and from moms when he is with her.

***

The next morning I slept in. When I got up at 10 to have breakfast only Grandma and Uncle Vinnie were up. Huh. Usually Mom and Nina are up way before me. Grandma offered to make me homemade waffles. Yum. I love them, especially with strawberries and whipped cream. I was eating my fourth waffle when Mom came into the kitchen. She looked really tired.
"Are you OK Mom?" I asked.
She smiled and responded with, "Yes. I am fine. But thanks for asking."

It was the first time I had shown care and compassion for anyone in the house since Dad was gone. It felt pretty good. And it was a start…

Chapter 11

At school the next day, things were pretty normal, well, for the first few classes. Coach called me to his room right before lunch. He told me that he looked at progress report grades. Mine were not good.
The comments the teachers had made were all pretty much the same. "Lacks effort and work completion in the classroom setting. Does not complete homework. Does not participate in class." Coach seemed confused. He said that he looked at my grades from last year that were on file and knew I had straight A's back then. He asked if I was having trouble adjusting to middle school. I told him no. He asked if the work was too difficult for me. I told him no again.
Coach looked confused. He wanted to know what was going on then. He knew about my fight, but since I got along with everyone at track, and even showed some leadership toward the other 6th graders, that there wasn't a serious social issue going on. I took a deep breath and decided to let him know a little bit.
"I am having some family issues at home. I figured you already knew about my Dad." I offered.
He looked truly concerned. "No. What about your Dad?" he inquired.
I told him that Dad was in jail and waiting for his trial. Coach just shook his head and looked very concerned.

He commented, "Gee, JC, I had no idea. I live a few towns away and don't get the local paper, so sometimes I am the last to find out about things going on around here. I am really sorry your family is going through such a hard time. I am here for you to talk to, if you ever want to."

He continued explaining, "Unfortunately, the rules for the team are very strict. If an athlete on any team from school gets more than one D on a progress report or report card, they are on probation. If they get an F, they are suspended from the team. You have both an F and two D's on your progress report, you cannot attend track practice nor compete in track meets until you bring these grades up to at least a C. What I usually do is have a player tutored, but that isn't the case for you. This is all on you…you are a very capable student. I'd bet that if you worked for a couple of weeks to complete what you are missing, and you do your homework and classwork as expected, that you'd be ready to rejoin us and help us win some of our upcoming meets. We only have 4 meets left. You will miss two of them, but hopefully you can join our last two of the season."

I had forgotten all about the athletic contract we had to sign the beginning of the season. We had to agree to get C's or better in all our classes or face exactly what the Coach just explained to me. I told him I would do my best…or at least try. I asked him to please not tell my Mom. She didn't need to have this on her plate right now. He agreed. I asked if I could attend practice today at the start of the session so that I could tell Ryan.

I would ask Ryan if I could still get a ride home from "practice" each day, but if he could pick me up from the library on his way out to his Dad's car. That way I could work on what I needed to make up during that time to improve my grades. Luckily Coach said yes, I could do that. I thanked him and went to lunch.

Shaun had saved me a seat at lunch. I went over to him and took my food from my bag. Didn't like the lunch choices for today, so this morning I made myself good ole' PB and J. Usually I will eat the hot lunch, but today it is a fish sandwich. Not for me. One of the few things I won't eat. I think it is because of what happened a few years ago. I got a fish sandwich and bit into it, but there was a bone in it. It totally creeped me out. Since then I have avoided them altogether.

Shaun wondered why I was late. I told him I had to talk to Coach about something for track. Not a lie, right? I just left out the details and the fact that Coach wanted to talk to me, not me just stopping by to ask him a question.

***

Anyway, we started talking about our weekend. I didn't have much to share. I haven't told any of the guys I was sitting with about my Dad. None of them have said anything directly to me, so I figured that they don't know. To be honest, I don't think boys tend to care about the personal lives of their friends unless it affects their friendship in some way. I do my best to act as normal as possible, so I don't draw attention to myself. The fight with Derek was just blown off. They asked and I told them that he was aggravating me and wouldn't stop. He bugged me to the point of physical reaction. No big deal. They accepted my story, and went on with another totally different conversation.

As we were talking about the weekend, Shaun mentioned a kid he befriended through gaming. I asked him who it was. He said it was the kid DR King. He asked if I knew someone by that name. I told him no. He said that the kid had told him that he went to our school, but didn't share any more information with him. I agreed with Shaun that DR was very good at gaming. I said we should figure out who he was and maybe hang out with him at the basketball courts.

He said he would try to get more information about who he was when they gamed together tonight. Shaun was on the school newspaper as an editor for the 6th grade reporters, so he had access to the school roster. He said he couldn't find anyone with the last name King at our school. He said maybe he is new to the school and not on the roster yet. Since they updated the roster every other week, he said he would check again next week, after the update, if he hadn't gotten any more information about him.

After lunch, as I was walking to History Class, I reminded myself that I had to do my work and pay attention in class. This was the class that I had an F in on my progress report. It wasn't a boring class. The teacher was nice, too. I just wasn't that into History. I preferred Math and Science. As I sat in class I made sure to take notes on what was talked about. I also raised my hand and asked a question that pertained to the topic we were talking about. My teacher looked pleasantly surprised. Some definite effort was shown. Now I've just got to keep it up. This will be my hardest class for that, but I know I can do it.

My Mom is gonna flip when she sees my progress report. I am going to get grounded. Hopefully, I can have my teachers tell her that I am already showing improvement by the time the grades get mailed home so my consequences won't be that bad. I will check with Nina when I get home today to see how she is doing with her classes. Maybe if she is not doing well then Mom will just chalk it up to our situation and not be too harsh on us. Nina is a good student. She usually gets As and Bs, but has to work hard. School comes easy to me...learning is very natural to my brain, I guess. I just need to stay focused and do my work and the rest will fall into place. I hope.

***

In the Library after school it is pretty calm. Most students are there because they have a project to work on or are in a program called "Homework Club". It isn't really a club. It is a time where kids can stay after school and have a few kids from the high school there to help them with their homework if they get stuck. I know that if I don't improve my grades that I will end up being required to join. It isn't some fun club where you sit around and talk about things you have in common and make stuff. It is more of a help-line for kids who are struggling students.

The high schoolers who help with Homework Club, do it as part of their Service-learning requirement. At the public high school, each student has to do 4 hours service work each month. There is a rotating schedule of kids who come to our school to help out and count it as their service hours. The librarian, Ms. Shon signs off on their hours. I know about this program because my cousin told me about this during our family picnic on the 4th of July last summer.

I worked for a while next to the "group work" room. That is where kids can go to work on projects that involve multiple people. It can get a bit noisy, so they put them in a back room so as not to disrupt the kids who need a quiet atmosphere to focus on their work. I am OK with noise in the background. I usually do my work with music playing through my ear buds. I had to promise my Mom that I would listen to instrumental music only. I actually like most of it.

As I start to work, my mind wanders and I have to keep stopping and getting back on track. I am trying to tackle the pile of History assignments I haven't completed. It isn't working, so maybe I should work on a subject that interests me more. I switch to Science assignments and complete 4 assignments that are past due before Ryan shows up to tell me we need to meet his dad in the parking lot to go home. Cool. If I complete 4 each day, I will be caught up soon. I've just got to stay focused. It is easier said than done, though.

The ride home was pretty quiet. Ryan started to tell me about track practice. What a big mistake. If his father was listening, he would know I wasn't there and might start asking questions.

I gave Ryan a look and then said, "Oh. That must have happened while I was running that errand for Coach."

Luckily, Ryan caught on to why I said that and stopped discussing track practice. His dad didn't seem to catch on, so I was saved….for now. When we reached my house, I thanked Ryan's Dad for the ride and headed inside.

***

As soon as I stepped in the door, I knew something was up. Mom was sitting on the couch and the TV was off. She wasn't reading a book or magazine. She wasn't working on her latest cross-stitch. I dropped my bag and went to sit next to her.

"What is wrong? Something happened. What? Is it about Dad?" I spurted out sarcastically.

I quickly thought about why I would care if it was about Dad, but dismissed the reasoning as Mom began speaking.

"It is Grandma. She had a stroke today after you left for school. She is in the hospital. The nurses and doctors are giving her the medicine she needs to keep it from getting worse," she explained as tears inched their way down her light brown cheeks.

I hugged her. She was so scared and sad. To be honest, so was I. I had questions.

"How did this happen? Is she going to be OK?" I blurted through my sniffling.

"Grandma was having some trouble walking this morning. She had some issues with the right side of her body. At first we thought it was because of her sleeping on that side, but then she couldn't talk. At that point, I called an ambulance and they took her to the hospital", she explained.

I had to know..."So she can talk now, right?"

"No. When I left to come home to tell you and Nina, she still couldn't talk. She is not able to walk on her own at this point either. Her right side is paralyzed. The doctors gave her medication to stop the stroke from getting worse and so far, it seems to be working. They have no idea about her recovery. That will have to be taken day by day. Some people recover fully and others don't improve at all. Let's just keep positive thoughts. Grandma is a strong woman. She will fight to get better with all her might," Mom responded.

Then she added, "I called and let them know at the jail so Dad is aware of what is going on."

I got mad. Why did Dad have to know? He wasn't here to help her...to help us, get through this. He could just sit back and relax in jail while everyone else worried and worked to help HIS mother!

I got up and started walking away from Mom. She stopped me and asked if I was OK.

"Yup", I quickly responded, then went into my room.

I didn't know what to do...I couldn't handle another serious issue with my family. I wanted to scream...to throw things....to escape. I knew the answer. I put on my running shoes and headed out the door. Mom let me go without trying to stop me. She knew that this was how I blew off stress and worry.

***

She just called as I got to the front door, "Please be careful. Call me if you get to the point that you want to stop running and need me to come get you."

I took off. I ran down the road at a full sprint. That lasted about a quarter mile before I settled into my quick pace. Another mile later, I stopped at the basketball courts. I recognized some of the kids playing. I also saw Derek. He was watching his brother and friends play. I don't need any more issues, especially right now. I was about to turn around when Derek spotted me.

"Hey loser" he called.

I pretended to ignore him, as if I didn't hear what he just said.

He yelled louder, "Hey...did your Dad get out of jail yet? Oh, that's right...he is gonna be there forever."

It took ALL of my energy to not go over to him and attack him. I kept thinking in my head that he isn't attacking me personally, he is just throwing his words at me to help HIS pain. I then heard his brother, who had stopped the game to speak to Derek. He told him to shut up and stop causing trouble. Derek swore at his brother, but then stopped yelling at me.

I was already back to my fast pace when I heard the ball start bouncing and the guys restarting their game. I was still seething from Derek's words. The saying "sticks and stones may break my bones, but words can never hurt me" is a bunch of garbage. Derek's words hurt. They just poured hot vinegar into my open wound; the one left by my Dad in my heart. In fact, my heart started to pound faster than it usually does.

At first I ran faster, trying to keep up the motions of my body with my heartbeat. I couldn't do it. I stopped running and tried to catch my breath. My chest felt tight, like someone had a huge belt around it and just kept tightening in, one notch at a time. It got tighter and tighter. I took out my phone, so glad that I brought it and dialed Mom's number. When she answered, I had a hard time telling her where I was. She got enough of it to say she'd be right there. I sat on the curb, focusing on my breath; stretching my chest; reaching my arms out from my sides. I was trying to break free of this tightness that was crushing my lungs. I focused on my breathing until Mom arrived.

She took one look at me and said, "I am bringing you to the hospital. Something must be wrong. You are pale and sweating much more than you usually do."

I shook my head no. She doesn't need any more to deal with! She complied, but only with the promise that I would tell her if the feelings continued. I told her I was feeling a bit better already. I continued to focus on my breathing. I kept it steady and slow.

***

I closed my eyes and thought of things that made me happy and calm. Things like my dog, Brutus. Even though he died last year, whenever I hugged him or petted him, I couldn't help but be happy and calm. It used to upset me to think about him, but a few months ago when I was upset about losing a race in the summer fun run competition, I pictured him jumping on me, practically knocking me over. I swear I heard his deep rough bark, as I saw drooling jowls and huge block shaped head. He was the biggest black lab I had ever seen. He was boxy shaped and weighed over 110 pounds.

Brutus looked scary, especially if you didn't know him. The mailman and delivery people wouldn't even ring the bell after doing it once...he would run to the door barking. What they didn't know was that if he ever got to personally meet them that they would be covered with drool-filled kisses. He was the biggest love there was.

We had had Brutus since I was one years old. I had never known my life without him. If anyone tried to wrestle with me, or if my parents were mad at me and yelled at me, he would step between me and them. He was my protector. He loved everyone in our home, especially Grandma when she cooked. She'd slip him little treats every chance she got. But when it came to protection, he was there for me and Nina. My parents would let us out to play in the yard when we were younger, but only if Brutus was with us. He would never leave the yard. He kept me and Nina in his sight at all times until we were safely back in the house.

Brutus slept in my bed. It stunk like a dog and was full of his black fur, but I didn't care. Each night when I was headed to bed, he'd jump up, take up half the bed, and stay there until I got up in the morning. Nina used to get mad and want him with her. She would make him go into her room and onto her bed. He would stay there for a while, but then get off the bed and scratch at the door to be let out. As soon as that happened, he would go straight to my door and cry to be let into my room. Now just the thought of him makes me smile and relax. I miss him, but know he was in pain with cancer, so at least now he isn't hurting anymore. We gave him a good long life.

***

By the time we were in the driveway I felt better. I thanked mom for coming to get me. I sat on the couch and watched a game show with Uncle Vinnie for a while to get my mind off of everything. I went to the kitchen for a snack. I had just finished my second glass of milk when Uncle Vinnie came in to talk with me. He told me that Grandma was stable. She wasn't any worse. She was upset about not being able to talk. The nurse had given her a white board, marker and washcloth. Since she was left handed she could write down what she wanted for others to read. Uncle Vinnie said she was sorry she had made such a mess in our already crazy lives. He told her it wasn't her fault and that we would all be OK and make sure that someone visited her every day. He said that made her happy. She smiled a crooked smile, because of her stroke, and her eyes lit up with that promise of visits.

I didn't know if I could go see her like this. If I got upset then she would be upset and feel guilty all over again. Later that evening when Mom came in to check on how I was feeling, I told her about my worry of seeing her. She told me it was OK. She said that she would go see her every day and that when I was ready then I could go with her. She suggested that I write her a note so at least she would know that I was thinking about her. I agreed to do just that.

Chapter 12

Dear Grandma,

I hope you are feeling better. I hate to think you are in pain and can't tell anyone. I want you to know that I want to be there for you. I am having such a difficult time thinking about how I will react when I see you. I love you so much and want you to just be "you". I know you are really still "you", but you cannot tell me in your own words. I want to help you, but I don't know how.

I want you to get better soon and come back home. Home just isn't home if you are not here.
We have all been through a lot and having you here makes me feel safe. I know you couldn't beat up an intruder, but that isn't the safety I am talking about. I am talking about

keeping my heart safe.
When Dad had to leave, he hurt all of us. I thought I was going to go crazy. I was so sad and angry and confused. You were the first one to talk to me and help me settle down. You stayed with me in my room and hummed our favorite song from when I was little until I was able to fall asleep. You were upset and sad about Dad, too, but you focused on helping all of us and put your feelings to the side until we were all OK. Mom told Dad about you and he is allowed to check in with her each night while you are in the hospital. I hope you will not be there very long. Hospitals scare me. To me, they are a place for people who are very sick and might die. Please don't die. I couldn't handle that. I need you to be home. Even if you aren't all better, I will help you. I promise. I can cook and clean and do your laundry for you. You may have to explain how to do things, even if you have to write them down, I will follow the directions.
I am very scared to come see you. I don't know how I am going to react when I see you. I might not be able to look at you. This would be because I wouldn't be good at handling you not looking like who I am used to seeing. I don't want to see you struggle. I don't want to see you in pain, or sad. You have always been what some people call a "rock", the one who keeps things stable in a family.
I will come see you as soon as I feel that I can handle it. Please don't be mad at me if it takes a little while for that to happen. If I can't do it by next week, I will write you another letter. I promise.

Love,
JC
(Your favorite grandson) xxoo

 I folded the paper and put it in an envelope. I put Grandma's name on it. I didn't seal it. She would need someone to open it for her if I did that. I hoped she could just open it and hold it and read it on her own. I didn't want anyone else to see it. I didn't have control over that, though. I had to take that chance, though. She needed to know how I felt and what I was thinking about everything.

I went to Uncle Vinnie first. I handed him the envelope. He smiled, then shook his head and gave it back to me.

"Sorry, bud, but I won't get to see your Grandma for a couple of days. I have to work and then have class the next couple of nights.

I had forgotten that he was taking college classes. He usually did the classes online but I guess he had to physically go to classes this week.

I went to Mom. I handed her the envelope.

"Please don't read this, it is for Grandma. I want you to give it to her when you go see her tomorrow." I asked.

"Why don't you come with me and give it to her yourself?" she suggested.

"I can't. I have track practice and then need to get my homework done." I responded.

It was partly true...the homework part.

Mom gave me a look...then said, "What's up? Why don't you want to go see Grandma?"

She knew me. She knew it was too much for me, so why was she pushing me to do something I wasn't comfortable with...something that I may not be able to handle well? I decided to be honest with Mom about how I felt about seeing Grandma. I explained my worry...my stress. The look on her face turned to one showing true concern. She understood my reasons for not going to see Grandma. She agreed to give Grandma the letter.

She was going to the hospital in the morning to bring her robe, comfy clothes and her hairbrush, toothbrush and stuff like that. She said that she figured Grandma would be in the hospital for a while.

    The doctors and therapists would be determining what kind of care Grandma would need for the best possible recovery. Once the plan was made, then she would go to wherever she could get this help. I asked if Grandma would have to live there forever. Mom said she didn't know. She hoped it would only be for a while until she could manage getting around at home safely. I promised Mom that I would help Grandma when she came home. Mom smiled. She loved the fact that I was willing to give up my free time and fun with my friends to help Grandma.

    As I returned to my room, I realized that I hadn't done my regular homework. I looked at my TV...no gaming? I needed to game. I needed that break from reality. But I HAD to do my homework. I HAD to improve my grades. I decided to work on homework for a half hour, then game for half an hour and go back and forth like that until the homework was done. It worked for the first round of homework then gaming, but then I was in the middle of a great game and just kept going. I only finished about half my homework. When I stopped gaming it was almost midnight. I pulled out my English assignment. I started to work on it, but fell asleep. I woke up to my alarm in the morning. Shoot. I couldn't go to school without it done.

***

    I got up and went into Mom's room. I told her I didn't sleep well and had a stomach ache. It wasn't a lie...I did go to bed much later than I was supposed to, so that is kind of like not sleeping well. And my stomach hurt over the fact that I hadn't done all my homework. Since I never ask to stay home from school, Mom decided I could miss today. She said she would call school and let them know I wasn't feeling well. I asked who she would call. She gave me a suspicious look.

"Why does it matter who I call about this?" she inquired.

"Just wondering." I replied as casually as possible. She still seemed suspicious, but let the conversation end by saying, "I usually just call the secretary. Do you need to give a message for your teachers? I am going to ask them to email you with the work you have to do, so please keep checking your computer today so you can work on what you have to do when you are feeling better. Is that a deal?"

"Deal", I agreed.

Wow. That could have gone bad if she called Mr. Coster. He may have told her about my grades or the fact that progress reports are being mailed this week.

After Mom left for the hospital, I finished my homework from last night. Then I had an idea. Since none of my friends were home to game with me, I would work on the assignments that I needed to make up. I finished the English ones first that I had started yesterday in the library after school. Then I needed a break. I went into the kitchen for a snack. It was about 11 o'clock. It was too soon for lunch.

When I looked in the cupboard I spotted a box in the back. It was an unopened box of frosted fudge brownies. Those are my Dad's favorites. Mom would always bug him about eating junk food so he would stash a box way in the back of the cabinet so she wouldn't notice. I smiled at those memories. It is the first time that I smiled about anything that involved Dad in the past few weeks.

   I decided it was safe to put the box in my room and hide them from Mom. I was the only other person in the house who liked these anyway...and Dad wouldn't be able to eat them before they went bad. Or would he? When people visit someone in jail, can they bring them a snack...or a book to read? I wonder. Not like I was going to do that, but just was wondering.

   I've seen old movies where someone bakes a cake with a nail file in it and the criminal uses it to break out of jail. I always thought that was so lame, but it made me laugh. I am sure it is much harder to break out of jail nowadays anyway. All the doors are probably locked. There are a lot of people who guard them now, I think. And if they escaped, where would they go? If it was Dad and he came to our door, I wouldn't let him in. If I did, then I would be a criminal, too.

   Dad needs to serve his time. What he did was awful. I still cannot believe that he justified taking someone else's money. How selfish. If he said he did it for us, then he would be lying. I wouldn't accept anything bought with money he had stolen. Even if it was food and I was starving, I wouldn't do it. And the thing is...we weren't starving.

   I know that my parents wouldn't have told me and Nina if our family was having money issues. They wanted us to just focus on being kids...enjoying our friends, getting our work done in school and having some extra- curricular activities, like me having track. I just can't imagine not being able to pay bills and get food. We managed when my Mom was out of work for a while. Grandma helped us, and still does.

Then my mind went to Grandma. What if she doesn't get better enough to come back home and live with us? Her money will go to whatever place she is living in. Without her money and without Dad's money, how will we manage? Mom makes OK money, I guess. Uncle Vinnie isn't going to want to stay here forever. Will we have to move? Will Nina and I have to change to another school? My somewhat happy mood from finding the frosted brownies disappeared.

I grabbed the box and went back into my room. I hid the box in the bottom drawer of my desk. It is filled with extra pencils, pens, art supplies for working on projects at home. I had just enough room for the box in the back of the drawer. Before I placed it there, I opened it and took one pack of brownies out and enjoyed the sweet treat.

I worked on math I owed for about an hour, but then fell asleep. I woke up to Mom coming into my room to check on me. She startled me then questioned me. "How are you feeling? Do you have a fever?" I told her I was better, just tired. She saw I was working on math, so she complimented me on remembering to check my email from my teachers. Little did she know I had totally forgotten about it. She didn't know the work in front of me was past due assignments. Once she left the room, I finished the old math work I had to do. Before I started on the Science and History work I had to make up, I checked my email. Sure enough there were assignments from ALL my classes, including

Spanish. Yikes. I had a lot to do.

I decided that I needed lunch first. I went and heated up some canned soup. Grandma wouldn't have been happy. We only have that soup if it is an emergency. Grandma makes her own soup from scratch. It is so much better than the canned soup, but Grandma isn't here to make it...so canned it is. Mom walked into the kitchen as I was eating,

Mom said Grandma will be staying in the hospital for a few days. They need to figure out a plan for her to go to a rehabilitation center for physical, speech and occupational therapy. She cannot move her right leg or arm. She also could not speak in words that could be understood. She would have speech therapy to make that improve. Mom said there were no guarantees of how much improvement Grandma would make. Time would tell. She did say that Grandma was very determined to do things on her own, and that was a good sign.

When Mom gave Grandma the letter from me, Grandma worked with her left hand to get it open on her own and read it. Mom told me that Grandma smiled, but cried a few tears as well as she read it. Mom did have to help her refold and put it back in the envelope. Grandma then wrote on her board to put it in her drawer next to her bed. It was fortunate that she was left- handed, so her writing wasn't affected.

Chapter 13

I went back to my room and actually got all of my assignments done that the teachers sent today. It actually felt pretty good. I was sure that the two weeks of working in the library after school, instead of going to track practice, would be enough time to finish all that I owed. I just needed to keep up with my daily assignments, too. Then once I was caught up, I would promise myself to finish my homework before gaming or going onto my laptop (unless it was for homework purposes).

  I am going to be ready for the last two meets of the season. Even though I can't practice with the team, I will run a few days a week to stay competitive. Mom won't question me if I run on the day's I don't usually have practice. I will tell her I just want to be in extra good condition for the meets.

  I actually talked Mom into letting me go running that afternoon. I told her I had finished all my work and felt great. As I started my run, I decided to stay away from the basketball courts. No use in getting upset by Derek if he was there again. A few of my friends ran around the outskirts of a big housing project. They said the outer road all the way around the loop was exactly one mile. Perfect. I would warm up by running the quarter mile to the entrance of the housing project, then run two laps for my two miles, then the quarter mile slow jog home to cool down.

***

  There was a long, large hill to get up to the one mile loop. I was pretty winded because I kept my regular pace all the way up the hill. I refused to slow down. I started the loop. It was pretty flat with a few small inclines that were declined on the back half of the loop. As I ran past a house I thought I recognized a car in the driveway, but I couldn't remember where I had seen it. On my second loop,

I picked my head up to look at it again.

Derek was taking out the trash from the side door of the house. It was the car Derek was in the other day, picking up his brother, David from the basketball courts. I put my head down, hoping Derek wouldn't realize it was me. Unfortunately he did.

"Hey...what are you doing in MY neighborhood?" he shouted to me.

I slowed down, and responded, "Just going for a run.", hoping that would end the talk.
No such luck.

"Why weren't you in school today?" he asked, "Skipping?"

"No. Didn't feel good this morning, but I am OK now. I just wanted to get outside for a while." I explained.

Why did he care? Wow. He noticed that I wasn't in school. That was weird. I was going to ask him about it, but just kept going. He left the conversation, returning inside the house. I finished my second lap and headed home. Maybe if I just answer his questions directly and mind my own business otherwise, this could help things be better between us.

I decided to strike up a conversation with him on the bus in the morning. It would be just a general one. No major details, just a quick exchange of words without getting mad. If he started being a jerk to me, then I would just ignore him. But what would I talk to him about? I had to think about that.

I went home, followed my normal after school routine, shower, dinner, and instead of homework time, since it was already done, I got in a couple hours of gaming. I would stop in time to get to bed at a decent time. I also had to figure out what to say to Derek to start a conversation without getting him mad.

As I started gaming, I noticed DR King needed another person to make a foursome in the game he was starting. I offered to join and he accepted my offer. We were partners again and dominated the duo playing against us. After we had beaten them four games simultaneously, they decided to stop playing against us. I told DR thanks for letting me join and I turned off my console. I was pretty tired, so I fell asleep pretty fast.

***

The next morning I got up a few minutes before my alarm went off. I packed my book bag with my work from yesterday, including my past due assignments. I would hand them in today to my English and Math teachers. I hoped to see Mr. Coster to let him know I was making good progress. I wouldn't go to his office and bug him, I'd just let him know quietly if I saw him in the halls today. One thing I forgot to do yesterday...laundry. I put on a semi clean pair of jeans and my last clean t-shirt. I threw on my favorite black sweatshirt with the hood lined in bright blue, and went into the kitchen for breakfast.

No scrambled eggs, hash browns, waffles...all my favorite breakfast foods. Grandma wasn't here to spoil me by making them for me on school days. I grabbed the cereal and almond milk from the fridge, along with the orange juice. I was done in 7 minutes flat then cleaned up my stuff and headed to the bathroom. Teeth brushed, face washed, hair combed and off I went. I had totally forgotten about talking to Derek until I got to the bus stop. Derek was on the bus, but sitting in his assigned seat near the front. I couldn't really talk to him from my assigned seat in the middle of the bus, so I decided to catch him as soon as we got off the bus as we were walking into school. As we unloaded at school, Derek was headed into the building. I called for him to wait up. And he did. That truly surprised me, but I was leery of his intentions.

He just said, "What? Decided to come to school today?"

Instead of getting mad and being sarcastic back to him, I responded with a smile and, "Yea. Home gets boring when there is nobody to game with. Everyone else was in school, so I had to keep busy until after 3pm."

His response was, "Really? What's your best game?"

I told him and he chuckled and said, "That is my favorite too. We should compete sometime. I would crush you."

I told him that maybe we *should* play sometime.

At that point we had to separate to go to Homeroom. We both said bye and headed in our different directions. Wow. We actually had some sort of civilized conversation. It was short, but since I didn't react badly to his sarcasm, it was somewhat productive. I'd have to look him up and game against him. Maybe he is as good as he says. We can compete against each other that way, and maybe talk a bit too while we are gaming.

***

I headed into Homeroom feeling somewhat productive about my day already. Things went

pretty normal throughout the day. I remembered to hand in my English and Math assignments that were past due. My teachers seemed surprised to get them so soon. After school I went to the library. I started working on more of my past due Science work.
There was a lab sheet that I never handed in and was struggling to remember what happened in that lab so I could answer the questions to get full credit for the assignment. I asked one of the high school kids that was there to help with Homework Club. I was explaining what I remembered about the lab and he was telling me that he really couldn't help me because he didn't know all the details of the lab.

Then I heard a voice behind me, say, "I did that lab last year. I remember it was weird because the result wasn't what anyone expected it to be."
I looked up. It was Derek.
The high schooler that was trying to help suggested that Derek help me since he remembered what happened in the lab. I thought for sure that Derek would laugh and walk away, wishing me "good luck" in his sarcastic tone. He didn't though. He said he had a couple of minutes before Gamer's Club started. He sat and explained his experience with the lab last year in about three minutes. It was enough information to help me complete my lab sheet with some confidence. As he was walking away, I thanked him.

He responded with, "You owe me one."
Not sure what that meant, but I said ok to him.

***

That night AFTER I finished my regular homework and had dinner, the phone rang. I answered it.

"Hey there Jace. How's it goin'?" It was Dad. I didn't know what to say. Should I tell him that things suck because of what he did? Or did he know that already? I almost hung up.

Mom grabbed the phone from me quickly. She knew it was him, looking for an update on Grandma. As Mom started telling him about Grandma's progress, which was pretty good, and the fact that she would go into a rehabilitation facility in a few days to continue recovering, I went into my room.

I just sat for a couple of minutes...thinking. Was Dad as surprised to hear my voice as I was to hear his? He acted so casual. He called me Jace, same as always. Did he expect me to just strike up a conversation with him? I hope not. That isn't going to happen...ever. I have nothing to say to him. Well...nothing that he would want to hear, I'm sure. My usual escape would be to run, but it was pouring out, and pretty cold. I wasn't that desperate for a run.

My next choice of escape was to play video games. Then I remembered...I was going to see if I could find Derek to play against. I wasn't in the mood to really talk to him, but we could just play against each other quietly. At least I could see if he was as good as he claimed to be. Nowhere could I find Derek that matched up with the last name Royal. There were not even Derek R's that fit who I was looking for. Maybe he went on through his brother, David. I checked. Nope. No David's that matched with the last name Royal or even R for a last name. I'd make it a point to check with him tomorrow on the bus and ask him if he went by a different username when he games. I jumped into another game being set up by my friend Mario from Math Class. It was fun, but not as challenging. When I am not challenged, my mind wanders away from the game and back to my personal issues at home. Like Grandma and Dad. I needed to talk to Derek so we could connect and challenge each other through our favorite game.

    Guess who wasn't on the bus the next morning? You've got it...Derek. I suppose he was out sick or something. I was wrong. I saw him later that day from a distance in the hall on my way back from lunch. He was with a couple other kids so I didn't want to run up to him and start talking to him like we were good friends or anything like that. I wonder why he wasn't on the bus? Maybe he overslept or had an appointment in the morning.

    Track practice was canceled because Coach had a meeting to attend so I took the bus home since Ryan's Dad wouldn't be picking us up. Derek was on it, but we weren't sitting close enough to talk. Next week will be better when we can choose our seats again. I got home and had a snack...just some jello. Don't want too much in my gut when I run. I changed and was headed out the door. It was cool at first, but once I built up my speed I was comfortable.

***

    By the time I got to Derek's street I started thinking. What if he came out and saw me running by his house again? He'd think I was being creepy. How can I do this without him noticing? The quickest answer in my head was to run the loop in the opposite direction. I know it sounds lame, but it was something different. As I approached his house

I moved to the opposite side of the street as well. Not sure why I thought that would make a difference. There was no car in the driveway. Maybe his Mom is at work or shopping.

As I passed by Derek's house I realized that there weren't stairs to the front and side door. There were ramps. Huh. That was weird. Maybe the person who lived there before needed them and they just never took them down. By the time I had thought about that, I had passed the house and forgotten to look for the number. The street was Oak Street, so at least I knew that. I did another loop...no number on the house, but then next house down had 37 on the mailbox. There number should be 39 or 41 if the lots were considered double sized lots. Also, I lucked out. Nobody came out. And the car was home at this point.

That night after dinner, Nina came in to check on me. She wanted to know why I hadn't gone to see Grandma. I was honest. I told her that I didn't want to see her looking "different". I wouldn't know how to act. What if it really upset me and I couldn't handle it? If Grandma thought that she upset me in any way, she would feel awful. I told her that I needed more time. I needed to have Grandma be able to do more things like she used to. I could probably handle her being in a wheelchair, but to not be able to talk at all was just awful to me. Nina told me that Grandma was already showing some improvements so hopefully she would be talking soon. Nina talked me into going with her to the rehabilitation home this weekend to see Grandma. She said I could give her a signal if I couldn't handle seeing Grandma and we would go for a walk to give me a break so I wouldn't get upset in front of her. I agreed. I missed Grandma terribly and really did want to see her.

By the time I had finished my homework, it was getting late. I looked up the address on my laptop. It said that the property belonged to Melinda Royal. Maybe that is Derek's mom. Or it could be the landlord's name, if they rent the house. I looked for Derek Royal in the gaming index and there was none. I looked up David Royal. He wasn't there either. I guess the mystery continues. I tried one last thing. I texted Shaun. I asked him to see if Derek or David's last name was Royal in the school roster. He said he would check on Monday and let me know.

I ended up playing soccer against Deacon for about an hour before I felt tired. We talked about maybe getting together over the weekend. I told him about Grandma and not wanting to go visit her. He wished me luck and told me to call him when I got home so we could meet at the tennis courts.

Chapter 14

I dribbled and shot...swish! Dad clapped his hands and let out a booming laugh. "Lucky shot", he said. It was his turn. He stood in the same spot as me and took a shot. It hit the rim, bounced off the backboard and then dropped onto the pavement. I started jumping around like I had won the NBA Championship. It was only a game of HORSE. I lost most of the time. Ever since Dad decided that it was time for me to live in reality and learn how to deal with losing games. He also wanted me to be prepared to go up against people taller than me.

I was a bit short for my age. I must have gotten

my height from my Mom's side of the family. Dad was six foot two and built like a football player. He had broad shoulders and muscular arms. If you didn't know him, he might seem intimidating when he wasn't smiling, but that wasn't very common to see.

    We both loved sports. We would watch all types of sports of TV together on the weekends. The season would determine what we would watch...football, soccer, baseball, even golf. I thought golf was boring, but when Dad started explaining the technique involved and the mindset the players needed to be successful, I became much more interested. As that thought popped into my mind while we were taking a break and getting a drink of water before our next "match", I asked Dad when he was going to actually take me out on the golf course and let me swing the clubs he had. His face suddenly turned serious. I asked what was wrong.

He responded with, "Well Jace, I have to go somewhere for a while. I will not be able to take you golfing. There is something I have to do that I cannot avoid. Hopefully when I am back, we can golf together. If you want to learn from someone else, I totally understand. When I am back at home, we'll golf, I promise."

I was shocked at his response.

  I came back with, "Where do you have to go? When are you going? How long will you be gone?" I started to worry. Panic set in. Dad hugged me. He was sweaty. When he let go, he wasn't in his t-shirt and sweats anymore. He had on a jumpsuit.

"Dad, where are you going?" I asked again.

"I have a commitment that I have to fulfill right

now. Just promise me you will be good. I'll see you again. Always remember that I love you. Nothing will ever change that." he spoke as he slowly backed away from me.

My legs couldn't move. I don't know what is wrong with them. I reached out for him as he turned away from me and walked to a large van parked on the street.

"Dad!" I shouted after him, "When will I see you again? When will you be back home?"

He just hung his head down and shook it from side to side as he got into the van and it drove off. I watched it until it turned at the corner and was out of sight. At that point my legs moved. In fact, they collapsed and I fell onto the dirt at the edge of the court and began sobbing.

I woke up. My pillow was damp from my tears. The crying from my dream had pushed through to the reality of my bedroom in the middle of the night. My blankets were all over the place. I must have been moving around a lot in my sleep while I dreamt. The house was dark and quiet. My throat hurt. It usually did after I cried hard, which wasn't too often.

***

I got up and went to the kitchen for a drink of water. The door to Grandma's room was ajar. I could see that her night light was on. It had a sensor that turned it on when the room got dark. It worked whether she was in the room or not. I walked to the door and slowly pushed it fully open.

The room smelled like Grandma. Her powder, perfume and hair products all blended into this wonderful aroma. I walked in. Of course, she wasn't there. I really needed her right now. She was the one I always went to after having a bad dream. She would let me sleep on the floor with my blanket and pillow next to her bed until morning. She would hum softly until I went back to sleep.

I took a pillow from her bed and the quilt from the back of her rocking chair and laid on the floor. Even though she wasn't there, I was comforted by the thought of her, the smell of her. I did something I hadn't done in about three years. I not only laid down on her floor, but fell asleep humming to myself.

I woke up to someone walking around in the kitchen. Shoot! What time was it? I looked at the clock on Grandma's nightstand. 6:00am. Must be Uncle Vinnie getting ready for work. He is usually gone before I get up in the morning. The heavy boots hitting the floor verified my thought. I waited for him to go into the bathroom, then folded the quilt, put back the pillow and stepped into the kitchen.

I wasn't tired, so instead of going back to bed, I grabbed some juice from the fridge and popped a bagel into the toaster. Mom walked in and was surprised to see me up so early. I told her I just couldn't sleep anymore and was hungry. That ended the curiosity and the questions. When I was done eating, I went into my room and got ready for school. Then I remembered...today was Saturday. No school. And now I was wide awake at 6:30 am. I've got nothing to do now. Great.

Chapter 15

I decided to go for a run. It was sunny and cool outside. Hopefully the run would motivate me to get other things done today. I told Mom I was headed out. She told me that she got a text message a few minutes ago from the charge nurse at the hospital. Grandma was going to be moved to a rehabilitation home today. She was out of danger from her stroke and now just needed to strengthen her weakened side as much as possible. Mom said she was going to meet the ambulance at the home for when Grandma arrived and help her get settled.

I was off the hook for going to have to see her today. Mom said she'd like the three of us to go visit Grandma tomorrow. I agreed. I missed Grandma so much. I would conquer my fear of seeing her weak and unable to do things she was able to do at the beginning of this week.

I headed out the door. The run would help me work out how I was going to manage my reaction to Grandma. It would help me prepare myself so I wouldn't embarrass myself or make Grandma feel bad about me seeing her in that condition. I started running my "new route" over by Derek's house.

I really liked this new course I followed. There were a few hills to challenge me. There were sidewalks most of the way, so I didn't have to run on the side of the road. Some drivers come so close to you, you'd think they were going to hit you. I always wore a brightly colored shirt or my reflective vest so I would be visible. I used to think this was lame to do, but one of my teammates from track actually broke his elbow running because a driver didn't see him and the side mirror on the car hit his elbow. He had to have surgery and lots of physical therapy. The driver told him it wasn't his fault because my friend was wearing a black shirt and wasn't easily visible. Both of them were really at fault.

As I ran I imagined going to see Grandma. Hopefully the place didn't have a weird smell. Some places where there are sick people have an odd smell to them. Maybe it is the cleaner they use combined with the smells of the people living there. I blocked that thought...I had no control over that.

So what could I control? I could control my reaction to seeing her. I would hug her gently so as not to hurt her, but to let her know I was glad to see her. I would only ask yes and no questions so she wouldn't be embarrassed by not being able to answer my questions. I would check with Nina about that too. If anyone asked Grandma a question and she tried to answer, and I didn't understand what she had said, it would upset me. Grandma is good at reading my face, so even if I tried to hide being upset, she would know.

I would look around her room at the place and see if there was anything I could bring from home to help her feel more comfortable while she was there. Maybe I could bring her something like a picture from her room...or our family photo from the past summer. Maybe not. Dad is in the picture. Maybe seeing that would make her sad. Maybe it would make her happy. Either way, I would skip bringing her that since I couldn't be sure how it would affect her feelings.

I could bring her favorite vase and get a few flowers to put in it. I'd get daisies. Those are her favorite flowers. She loves them because they grow both in the wild and in gardens...and they are hearty.

They last a long time and don't need a lot of care. They can survive a lot of rain and a bit of drought too. They are so much like Grandma. She can handle all kinds of situations. The stories she told me about growing up proved how tough she was, and how dedicated she was to her family.

***

    I was right near Derek's house. I was sure he was still sleeping. Someone was coming out of the door. It was his Mom. She had on a uniform. She must be going to work. By what she was wearing, it looked like she worked at the Casino.
    I wondered what she did for work. Early morning...maybe she worked the game tables for the early risers. Maybe she worked the breakfast shift in one of the restaurants. Perhaps she worked in the hotel. That would mean Derek was stuck at home unless he got a ride somewhere. Hopefully there were other kids in this neighborhood he could hang out with. Maybe he and his brother spent time together. Oh yea, he had a sister too. I wonder if she is little and they need to take care of her while his mom is at work? That would stink. Having to babysit on one of your days off from school is not my idea of fun. What if his Mom worked Sunday's too? Then he'd have to watch her both days. I am glad I am the youngest. No little ones to have to entertain or feed or just be stuck at home with.
    I waved to his Mom as I passed the house. She waved back and smiled, with a "Good Morning" for me. She seemed really pleasant. On my second lap, the car was gone from his house. The lights were on in what was probably the living room. I could see the flicker of the TV light as well. Someone was up.

I wonder if he is lying on the couch trying to go back to sleep while the sister watches some little kid cartoons.

Curiosity got the best of me. I slowed down; then stopped. I wanted a closer look. No. I couldn't. Well....no. I just needed to keep going. I finished my second loop of his block. I saw someone up ahead at his house, walking to the newspaper box at the end of their sidewalk. It was David. I picked up the pace and caught him just before he was going inside.

"Hi", I shouted.

He looked surprised to see me. "What are you doing around here?" he questioned.

"What does it look like? Running." I replied.

"Why so early? I am only awake because I have to watch my sister." he admitted.

I stopped running to talk with him. I told him I woke up early and was going to get ready for school, forgetting it was Saturday. Since I was wide awake, I figured I would go for a run. "That's right. You are on the track team. My friend Joe is Captain." he commented.

"I know Joe. He is a good Captain. He really helped me a lot when our season first started." I informed him.

At that point, Derek stuck his head out the door. He told his brother that breakfast was ready so he needed to come in before it got cold. Then he realized it was me who David was talking to.

"What are you doing here?" he questioned.

As I started to explain, David interrupted me and told me he'd explain it to Derek over breakfast so I could finish my run. I nodded, waved, and off I went.

Huh...Derek cooks. That surprised me. I don't cook unless it is with Grandma. He cooks because his Mom isn't there to cook. I guess he doesn't like cold cereal. I wonder what he made. Pancakes? Eggs? Waffles? Maybe I could ask him about that when I get a chance to talk to him. Kinda break the ice by talking about food when I get a chance to have another conversation with him.

I finished my run and flopped on the couch for a few minutes. Mom asked why it took me longer than usual. I told her I ran into someone on my run from school and we talked for a couple of minutes. And I forgot...but I did run an extra lap around that neighborhood. My phone buzzed. It was Deacon. He wanted to know if we were going to hang out today or tomorrow. I told him I'd meet him at the tennis courts in an hour. That would give me time to shower and have breakfast.

***

When I got to the tennis courts Deacon seemed different. He usually had a big smile and lots to say. He was quiet. Something was on his mind. I didn't want to pry, but I did want him to know I was willing to listen. We played "hand tennis" with the tennis ball he brought. Neither of us had rackets, so we just used our hands as the rackets. After about ten minutes Deacon made some general comment about how, "it's not fair".

"What isn't fair?" I asked.

He sat down in the middle of the court. I went and sat down next to him. I was ready to pry... "Are you gonna tell me what is going on?" I blurted out.

He then went on to tell me that his Dad got a new job in Millsville. That town is about an hour from here, I thought.

As if reading my mind, he said, "Since that is about an hour away, my Dad doesn't want that long of a commute. We are moving to Rouse.

"But that is a half hour away. You will have to change schools. We won't be able to see each other anymore." I choked out.

Deacon was my best friend...and had been for what seemed like forever. Now what? He understood me. He listened. He really cared about me AND my family. This sucked. It just really sucked! Deacon told me that he got really upset when his parents told him about this move. He actually told them that he was going to ask if he could come live with me and my family. His parents didn't like that at all.

Deacon's parents did promise, however, that at least once a month, I could come spend the weekend at their new house. AND they said that they would let Deacon stay at my house at least once a month as well, as long as my mother was OK with it. I was glad that at least he could come to my house now, but it wouldn't be the same. It would be all totally planned out. Sometimes the best times we had were ones that were totally last minute meets at the tennis courts. No more of them.

I asked him when they were moving. He said they weren't going anywhere until Holiday Break. Good. At least I still had him here for a few months. We still had Halloween together. We always went trick or treating together in his neighborhood. There were usually four or five of us together. This was the year that all parents agreed that we could go without one of them chaperoning us. I was happy to get that time with him before he left.

Chapter 16

Ready or not, it was time to go see Grandma. Nina had described what she looked like...what she was not able to do at this point. I did my best to prepare myself. When we walked in, the place seemed nice. Almost like a hotel lobby. There was no odd smell. The residents were friendly, saying hello as we passed by them. When we got to Grandma, it was hard for me to look at her, sitting in a wheelchair. She looked frail...and old. I never thought of her as "old". This is probably because she was always busy cooking, sewing, going out with her friends. Heck, she didn't even need a hearing aid yet. I know most of her friends had them. She had always had glasses, so that was no difference.

   She said "hi" to us. I was surprised. Nina said she couldn't speak. I guess it was a true shock to Mom and Nina as well. They began clapping their hands, so I did too. That was all for her talking, though. She then pointed to where she wanted to go and answered all of our "yes/no" questions with a nod. I just kept telling my mind that this was temporary, so to play along as if it were a game, not reality. It worked. Her physical therapist showed us how she could stand. But she was so wobbly. That bothered me more than the speech issue. Grandma was always so steady on her feet. She had great balance a week ago.

   On the way home from our visit, I lost it. I thought she should be better than she was by now. Why was it taking so long? The stroke took away so much from her in such a short amount of time.

Why can't she get everything back just as quickly? I think being home would help her, too. She loved living with us. Isn't that part of healing...being happy where you are so you can focus your strength on recovering? Can't the therapists come to the house and work with her while we are at school? When we get home from school, we can help her with her strengthening exercises. We can keep doing the cooking, but she can sit at the table and guide us by nodding as we ask her questions about what to do. That would make her feel more valuable...not just sitting in a wheelchair looking out windows or watching TV between therapy sessions.

Mom was kind, but firm in telling me that Grandma was in the best possible place for the help she needed and for safety reasons. If she falls at home then she may lose all the progress she is making and have to start all over again with her recovery. I got it. I didn't like it, but I got it.

Nina suggested that we redo Grandma's bedroom to surprise her when she got back home. Mom agreed, but said she truly had no idea how long it may be before Grandma came back to live with us; if ever. Focusing on doing something for Grandma was going to help me keep positive about her returning back home. I told Nina I would help.

When we got home I went into Grandma's room to get her box of pictures. She loved looking at them, so I thought it would be great if we could display them on the wall somehow so she could see them easily without having to lug out a box from her closet, and then put them away when she was finished. I wasn't sure how we would display them, but we would figure out some way. Maybe even a display that allowed her to interchange the pictures so she wouldn't have to be stuck with just some of her favorites. The pictures could take turns being a focal point in her room.

  I also sketched an arrangement of how her furniture could be moved that gave her a better view of the backyard and more space to move around. She may have a walker or cane when she came home, so she would need clear and open pathways to move smoothly within her bedroom. After doing this, I went into my room. Nina came in and made some comments about my bedroom...and the mess it was. I just blew off the comments. I didn't need to argue with her.

  The next morning, Mom shared a newspaper article with me. It told all about Dad and his "escapade" with the two other losers. Mom got mad when I referred to all three of them as losers. I asked her if "winners" do things like this. She shrugged my sarcasm off. She said she was going to let Mr. Coster know about this first thing this morning so if Nina or I needed him, he would know what is currently going on with the situation.

  My stomach was in knots, but I refused to act upset. That is a weakness. I am not a wimp. Nina was upset and nervous about what other people may say. We had a conversation while waiting for our bus at the stop that morning. We agreed to leave the rumors to just that...rumors. Don't get involved with what other people are saying.

  At that point I started thinking about Derek. Was he going to have a "field day" with this article? I was hoping that our last few brief conversations were enough of a positive connection that he would leave me alone. Nina was so nervous, and it clearly showed through her behavior. I decided to sit with her on the bus so that I could block her….protect her, at least for the ride to school. Once we were there and separated…it was open season on us without the support of each other. Hopefully Mom did call Mr. Coster to warn him. The bus driver didn't notice that I wasn't in my assigned seat…oh yea…I don't have an assigned seat anymore…as long as I stay out of trouble. Derek was already in a seat near the back, and since we were in the middle of the bus I wouldn't hear comments from him unless he clearly yelled them to me, so I was safe…for now.

***

I went directly to Homeroom. I was safe, so far. All seemed good until PE. A kid I don't really know came up and asked me if my Dad's favorite color was orange…or if he preferred stripes. At first I thought he had mixed me up with someone else. Then as the words processed through my brain I understood what he meant. He was referring to the colors and pattern typically worn by inmates. By the time I realized what he meant, he had moved to a small group of boys in a corner of the gym. One of them raised his hand and asked the teacher if we could play tag today. He said, like the way they played in elementary school, where if you got tagged, you went to "jail". All the kids in their group started laughing and one pointed at me.

My first instinct was to go in swinging…I may not be able to beat them all up, but I could bloody a few noses. But where would that get me? Suspended again? If I reacted with violence then others may say I am like my father, which is the last person I want to be connected with. I walked away. My fists were clenched and my face was red. I was gritting my teeth with my tongue in between them to keep from saying something to them. My PE teacher, Ms. Harland, came over to me. She commended me for staying in control of myself. She told me to head to Mr. Coster's office to cool down and give myself space from the boys that were harassing me. She knew exactly what they were doing. She promised me that they would be spoken to by the principal.

  I followed her directions and headed to Mr. Coster's office. He had two other kids in there, so I waited in what he calls the "Chill Chair" outside his door. I heard Ms. G being paged to the gym. If there is a problem in a classroom, they try to get the adult to come deal with the kids instead of letting the kids get out of class and possibly cause trouble in the halls as they travel to the office. I was hoping that call was for her to speak with the boys. I am hoping they get the message and leave me alone. I've done NOTHING wrong! I hate kids who target other kids about something they have no control over. As I waited, Deacon walked by. "Hey, what is going on?" he inquired.

 Since he knew about everything except this morning's paper displaying the information for everyone to read about, I told him what had happened. He was so mad. He wanted to go fight the boys. I told him it wasn't the answer, but totally appreciated his backing me up. My anger turned to tears as I was talking to him.

  When Mr. Coster opened the door to let the other two kids go back to class, he pulled me AND Deacon into his office. Deacon explained what had happened while I calmed myself down. Mr. Coster asked why Deacon had to escort me. He explained that he just saw me in the hallway and listened to me while I waited for Mr. Coster to let me in. Mr. Coster complimented Deacon on his great listening skills and true example of a good friend. That made me even sadder.

"And now he is moving away", I whined. "My best friend all through elementary school is leaving me when I need him the most."

Deacon put his hand on my shoulder, saying, "The timing is awful, but I am just a phone call away. We can even face time if you need to see me when you are upset. I will still be there for you. You can't get rid of me that easily" he said, laughing at the final comment.

I cracked a smile and thanked him for helping me "vent" while waiting in the hallway. Deacon went back to class. I sat down, ready to hear Mr. Coster's words of wisdom. He surprised me by saying something I already knew, "Mean kids suck". I agreed. I shared with him how I felt abandoned by so many people lately, that some things that usually don't bother me are bugging me worse than the itch after a bee sting. He liked that simile.

Between my father, my grandma and now Deacon...I just kept losing. I kept losing people who I really counted on. Mr. Coster agreed that the timing of these things was lousy, but that there was no control over it. Dad made a choice...that started the chain of abandonment, but Grandma and Deacon had NO control over what was going on that was taking them away from me. He reminded me that Grandma's situation is most likely temporary, so I need to just hang in there in that situation. Deacon, he said, was still going to be there for me, just in a different way. Dad...well, Dad's issue has not come to a solid conclusion. Nothing will be known for sure until the end of his trial and the sentencing. I had to be patient. I know that isn't easy, and just shutting him out of my life will just stop the hurting he has caused...or will it?

By the time I left his office I felt better. **I** was in control of my life, no matter what happens. **I** call the shots. **I** will NOT let anyone determine how I think or what I feel or who I am. That is all up to me. I felt empowered. I was not nervous about the next PE class with those jerks. They will not have control over me. I am nobody's puppet. I just hope this feeling sticks inside of me and doesn't weaken over time.

I will fight....not with my fists, but with my will; my will to be a good person; my will to have a good life. My will to not let other people, including family, dictate my future. I need to remind myself this EVERY DAY...maybe multiple times a day. Mr. Coster said I should write this inside my planner, so that it is always with me in school. I should read and reread it as often as I need throughout the day. First, read it during Homeroom to start my day strong. Then reread it to "recharge" my strength as I need to. He said some days I may read it once and other days I may read it 10 times. It doesn't matter, as long as it gives me the strength I need to be who **I** want to be.

Chapter 17

I knew the right words to say with Mr. Coster. I knew what I should be doing...how I should be reacting to other people's words and actions. It was much easier said than done. That same afternoon, only a couple hours after I seemed to have it all together...it all fell apart. I was heading to the bus. There was no track practice, so I didn't have a ride home from the library. I would have to work on what I needed to do at home. That was my plan, at least. Nina wasn't on the bus. She must have something going on at school and is getting picked up later. If Nina was there, I am sure it would have made a huge difference.

    I said hi to Derek. He was sitting with a kid I didn't know. The kid was a known trouble maker. I'd heard him target kids on the bus, steal their stuff from their lunch bags and backpacks. Most of the kids on the bus were scared of him. He was big and tough. He was an eighth grader who wasn't very mature. He would buddy up with someone to be his partner in crime when he was going to target someone. Well, today, he had chosen Derek to be his buddy. I'd bet he wouldn't have chosen him if David was on the bus, but unfortunately, he wasn't there today.

    Anyway, I was his chosen victim today. He must know about what was going on because he started as soon as the bus was moving away from the school. He quietly got my attention, like he had something cool to share with me. Then he asked me if I had helped my dad kill Mr. Gossling. What!? That is crazy! I told him no. He said that I was probably lying because they won't put minors' names in the paper. You have to be 16 to get your name in print for any crimes you commit. He said that I looked like a criminal, and that I acted like one too.

    I tried to keep my head down and stay unnoticed. At that point I ignored him. But of course, that didn't stop him. He then asked me if that was the first person I had ever helped my dad kill. He went on to ask if my dad was a serial killer and I was his right hand man. He asked if my dad and I ever dressed up like Bonnie and Clyde for Halloween when I was smaller...you know, to get me in the right mindset for murder. He wouldn't stop saying things. He was so quiet about it that the general noise of the bus drowned out his comments and questions. Only I heard them...well, and Derek. Derek just sat there and smiled, saying, "Yeah...Yeah...", whenever the other kid looked at him.

Derek wasn't saying things like that, but he was going along with the kid who was. He would laugh when the kid asked me if I had helped my dad plan the entire robbery and murder, or if he just told me he was taking me for some candy with his buddies so it would be a cool surprise to be a part of the whole crime. I just kept looking out the window...then suddenly the kid was sitting next to me in the seat. The bus driver didn't even notice, or ignored it.

The kid started poking me with his finger and actually spitting in the side of my face. I was totally trapped and seething with anger. There was no escape. Derek just kept laughing quietly, but nervous-like. When it was my stop, I couldn't get off. The driver had to ask me why I wasn't getting off. I told him I had spaced out during the ride. I stood up and the kid let me out, but followed me.

The kid told the driver that he was coming over to my house to hang out. The driver let him get off...at my stop! Home was only 6 houses away. I was hoping to outrun him, but he caught my backpack and pulled me backwards and I fell. He jumped on me and pinned me to the ground. He asked if I ever wondered what it felt like to be shot. I panicked.

Did he have a gun? No, he didn't. But he did have a huge size advantage and I was trapped beneath his body.

I wiggled to get myself loose from him, but he sat on top of me. He kept spitting in my face. I freed one of my hands and pushed it against his face. He grabbed my wrist and pinned it down. As he leaned closer to my face, I had one last opportunity. I threw my head forward and head butted him in the face. I missed his nose, but my forehead hit his mouth. He was bleeding. That wasn't stopping him, though. He was now spitting his blood onto me. When he opened his mouth wide enough, I saw that one of his front teeth was missing. That HAD to have hurt! He punched me on the side of my head. I thought my brain was going to explode! All of a sudden his weight was off of me.

As I squinted into the sun to look up, a large shadow loomed over me, holding the kid who was on top of me by the back of his jacket. The kid was squirming to be released from the grip.

A deep voice said to him, "If you keep it up, I'll have to cuff you".

Oh shoot...it was a cop! I didn't even hear a siren or anything so I was very surprised. There was no noise of a vehicle either. When I sat up and looked around, trying to regain my bearings, I saw there was no police cruiser in sight. There was a bike, though. It was one of the police officers who rode a mountain bike on their route. They were usually closer to the downtown area, but not today. Man, did I luck out.

Once I took a few minutes to put my brains back together, at least that is what it felt like, I saw the officer talking on his radio that was clipped to his uniform. He had requested two cruisers. Oh man, I didn't do anything! I was the one who got jumped. The kid followed me off the bus and attacked me! I am innocent! I had to stop and focus on my breath. I needed to calm down before trying to speak to the officer. If my Mom got a call from the cops that I was in trouble; that would totally break her. I can't let that happen.

As I tried to get up, the officer asked me to stay where I was. The other kid was still giving him trouble. Maybe if I listen well at this point, he won't have me brought to the station. I will follow ALL his directions. I stayed put.

I listened to the "story" the other kid was telling. It was all lies….he said I had been harassing him on the bus and he got off at my stop because he wanted to try to talk things out. He continued by saying that I was the one who jumped him and tackled him to the ground and that he was just trying to hold me still so he could talk and we could settle our issue peacefully.

At that point I shouted, "What a total lie!"

The officer asked me to stay quiet and that he would hear me out when the other kid was finished. I tried to stand again. The cop told me to sit and wait, or be charged with "evading arrest". What?! I was getting arrested? For what?!!!! My head was spinning. I don't think at this point that I could have run without losing my balance and falling.

The two other cruisers pulled up. A few of the neighbors had come from their houses to see what the commotion was all about. The officers blocked me, so they didn't see me at first. When one of the other officers helped me up, I heard Ms. Miller gasp.

I looked over and she shook her head and said to Mr. Nicholas, another neighbor, "I guess he is learning behaviors from his father."

I wanted to shout to her that I am NOTHING like my father. I am the victim and only defended myself, but it just didn't matter. They are going to think what they want to and say what they want to about me and probably my whole family. I cannot stop that. They are just jerks for labeling me because of what my father did. I wish they would just mind their own business and go home.

I actually did shout to them, "Why don't you go home and take care of your business? And be careful jumping to conclusions, you could get hurt."

My sarcasm flooded through my words. It just gave them more to talk about, not budging from their front row view of the scene.

The officer moved me to the side and started asking me my version of the story. I told him everything...starting with what happened on the bus. He said he believed me because the reason the first officer arrived was because the bus driver called the police with the thought that there was a problem between me and Kirk (the name of the kid who did all this to me). I admitted that I didn't think the bus driver was even paying attention to what the kid was doing to me on the bus. The officer said that it seemed like the driver saw some things, but not everything. And the driver hadn't heard what Kirk was saying to me, either.

The officer went to his cruiser and got out an instant ice pack. I asked what it was for. He said I had a huge bump on my forehead. I told him it must have been from when I head butted the kid because he had me pinned down and was spitting in my face and not letting me up.

I looked over, and "Kirk" had an ice pack held up to this mouth. Good...hope it hurts. The officer asked me to focus on our conversation, but I could hear Kirk raising his voice to the officer, telling him that he wanted me arrested for assault. Great...just what I needed...to have a criminal record at my age. Hey, if I had started it and got arrested, I'd take my consequences and hopefully learn from it. But this was totally different....I was the victim. I was just defending myself against someone older, bigger and meaner than me.

I had a request that was a risky one. I told the officer that all the stuff that happened on the bus was witnessed by another kid. Could that kid be questioned so that they could see if the stories matched up with what I said, or with what Kirk was saying? He said that definitely would help. I only hoped that Derek would tell the truth with Kirk not being there....and a cop asking for the truth.

I gave the police officer Derek's address. He said he would have Derek get questioned by one of them as soon as possible. He told me to get into the cruiser so he could take me to the station to get picked up by my parents. I begged him to not do this. Mom would be so upset getting that call. It would be better if I just walked 4 more houses down the road to get home. He agreed to that, but only if he escorted me home. That was fine with me. As we walked onto the porch, Mom came running out.

"What is going on? JC, how did you get that large knot on your head? Why do you have blood splattered all over you?" she questioned.

The officer was trying to calm her down, but she ignored him.

"I want answers from my son first. Then I will listen to whatever you have to say." she insisted. I explained everything, exactly as I did to the officer. Mom was angry, I could tell, but not angry with me. She waited after I had finished and listened to the officer.

All he said at first was, "Your son shared everything with you, just as he did with me. The other boy involved wants your son arrested, but I don't think that is going to happen. I am going to head to the home of a witness from the bus and get his story. I will call you with the information in the report that will be filed. If for some reason, Jeancarlos is going to be arrested, we will let you know so you can bring him to the police station to go through the process together, since he is a minor. I wouldn't concern myself with that right now, though. I'd just have him get cleaned up and try to relax. He seems like a good kid. I believe him, but unfortunately, it has to go beyond that since there may be charges being pressed."

My Mom responded with, "If they charge him with assault, then we can charge the other boy with it too, right?"

The officer said that is our right, but to please wait until all the information has been processed. Mom agreed to wait.

Now was the hard part. Waiting. I kept wondering if Derek will tell the truth to the cops. Will he be afraid of Kirk's wrath if he speaks out against him? Even if they ask him and he makes something up to shield Kirk, it won't match what Kirk said, so they will know he is lying....I hope.

I took a shower, then an ibuprofen. I now had an awful headache where the bump was; So much for getting extra work done today. I did my best to just get my regular homework done. It was so hard to concentrate. I was waiting for the phone to ring with information.

***

   When Uncle Vinnie came home, he spoke with Mom, then came into my room. He told me that he wanted to help me avoid this happening again. He said he could teach me some pressure point moves that would help me control someone bigger than me, should things get physical again with someone. Man, did they hurt....I never knew about pressure points, but just one touch in a certain area could bring anyone to their knees in pain. And it didn't take a lot of strength to do it. Uncle Vinnie let me practice on him until I was confident enough to effectively hit four different points on someone. I thanked him.

   He has not been very vocal about things going on with my Dad, but he really does seem to want to help us out. This definitely helped me. I promised to not use them joking around with my friends or on NIna when she bothered me. I was to only use them if I couldn't escape a physical confrontation. I asked Uncle Vinnie if I could practice on him a few more times over the next week to be sure I had the moves down. He chuckled and said as long as I promised to stop when he said, "Give". I agreed.

Chapter 18

The next morning I had to get on the bus without Nina. Mom was bringing her in later for some reason. Anyway, as I got on the bus, the driver told me to sit up front. I asked if I was in trouble. He said no, but that he could see me better if anything was going on. I agreed, but really wanted to talk to Derek and see what he said to the cops. They never called last night, so they may not have finished all the paperwork and investigating they said they needed to do.

Derek was sitting with his brother, David on the bus. Kirk wasn't on the bus at all. Thank goodness.

I waited for Derek after getting off the bus. David stayed with him as we talked. I asked him if the cops were at his house last night. He said yes. I asked if he told them the truth about what happened on the bus. He again said yes. Then he said something that shocked me. He said that when Kirk followed me off the bus, that he told the driver to call the cops because he knew that Kirk was up to no good. I smiled and said thanks.

I asked him why he didn't say anything to Kirk when he was bugging me on the bus. David explained that Kirk lives near them. They have known him for years. Kirk picks on other people and always has. He told me that Kirk had informed him that he has anger issues. When he gets mad, he can't control himself. He has been in different programs that are supposed to help and even though he is better, sometimes he just can't control it. David said Kirk used to pick on Derek all the time, so Derek wants to stay on his good side.

At that point, Derek chimed in saying, "I wanted to stand up for you, but I couldn't. If I did, Kirk would have turned on me. The best thing I could have done was tell the bus driver to call the cops so you would be safe. I am sorry they didn't get there before he hit you."

I smiled.

Wow.

Derek was on my side. I understood where he was coming from. I probably would have done the same thing. At that point I shared with them what had happened. I explained that the huge lump on my head was my doing. And that Kirk was missing a tooth, or at least part of one. They both smiled and said they were glad I didn't just let him get away with this without him having any pain. I admitted that I hate fighting.

I am going through stuff about my Dad, as they know. I sometimes lose control, as Derek knows, when someone bugs me about my Dad. I told them that I am nothing like my Dad. I told them that I hated him.

David spoke up saying, "You shouldn't hate your Dad. He's your Dad no matter what. You should feel lucky that you have a Dad around, even if he can't be there all the time with you." Then I remembered that their Dad was gone...forever.

I put my head down and shook it, saying, "I guess I have to think about it differently. I am not sure that I can, but I will try."

We parted ways and headed to our Homerooms.

***

During Science Class I got called to the office. When I walked through the door, a police officer, my Mom, Mr. Coster, and two other people I didn't know, were standing in a circle, talking. I nervously went next to my Mom and stood, listening. The man I didn't know seemed OK, but the lady glared at me.

The officer introduced me to Kirk's parents. I offered my hand and Kirk's Dad shook it, but his Mom just huffed towards me and then turned and looked away. The officer explained that based on the investigation that my story had the most truth to what happened based on other witnesses from the bus, who remained nameless. The Dad said that he didn't want me arrested. He agreed that my headbutt was in self defense. Kirk's Mom disagreed and said that I should have found another way to escape Kirk's grasp. His Mom was insisting on me being arrested. At that point, my Mom grabbed my arms and pulled up the sleeves of my shirt. Both my wrists were black and blue.

She held them out toward Kirk's mom, saying, "So you think your son had a weak grip that could have allowed my son to escape? Take a look at this!" She continued by saying, "I am sorry your son's tooth was knocked out, but it wouldn't have happened if your son didn't target mine and harass him, then physically harm him."

Way to go Mom! You tell her!

Kirk's Mom finally sighed loudly then agreed that she'd let it go THIS time, but any more issues would result in my arrest.

She then commented, "I hope that you are doing your best to teach your son right from wrong. I'm sure you don't want him to end up like his father."

I watched Mom's face turn purple. She took slow deep breaths to keep her cool. She wanted to compose herself before replying.

Her response gave me something to think about, "JC's father is a very good man and an excellent Dad. He, being a human that isn't perfect, made a few choices that have hurt other people, both directly and indirectly. He is ready and willing to pay the consequences for his actions, but that is not up to **any** of us to decide at this point. Just remember that nobody is perfect and those that learn from their mistakes should do their best to forgive themselves and to be forgiven by others. People who continue poor choices need help and support from their family and friends. I hope that **both** our families rally and thrive through all the good and bad that life hands us."

  Nobody knew what to say to that. I just beamed with pride. My Mom had it together....her thoughts, feelings and the words to express it so well. I hugged her right in front of everyone. She had given us ALL some things to think about. At that point, Kirk's parents left with the officer. Mr. Coster gave both me and Mom a high five after they were out of sight. Mom totally understood what our family was going through...not just what she had to deal with, but what all of us were dealing with. At that point I knew that I had to talk to her more. I also was ready to go and participate in family counseling sessions so our family could not just deal with issues as they arose, but deal with our future, no matter what that brings.

Chapter 19

Grandma was doing better every day. I only went to see her a couple of days her first week in the rehabilitation center. She could stand for longer periods of time, and was ready to start walking. We were hopeful to have her back home before Thanksgiving. Her speech was improving also. When we spoke with her, she only gave us short answers, and some of her words were tough to understand. She still had issues with some letters and blends. Like the blend "th" sounded like T, so words like "thought" sounded like "taught". Also r's sounded like w's. The letter s was not always clear, too. But she was definitely doing much better and working really hard to get back to where she was with her speech and movement before the stroke.

Grandma knew how to push herself. She used to talk to me about running and doing my best, not just for my team, but for myself. She would help me with ways to think and how to focus on my breathing and speed of my pacing while I ran. When I followed her advice, I always did better than I expected. The funniest thing was that she was never a runner. Not at least competitively. What she did was apply what she taught herself about success with physical work and adjusted it to fit with running.

She would even watch running events on TV and take notes, then share what she observed with me. At first I thought it was funny and didn't take her seriously. But when I tried her suggestions from her notes, just for "fun", they worked! She also read articles from Dad's Sports Illustrated Magazines that were stories about runners and athletes who needed to be able to run fast as part of their sport, like soccer players and running backs and receivers in football. She read articles about endurance from tennis players and basketball players. It was always funny when we would have dinner together and she would talk about a football player, like she was a big fan. Dad would laugh and start asking her questions about the "stats" of the player or the team. She would tell him that that information wasn't important to a runner, so she didn't know the answers. She would tell Dad that the other information he was interested in was just "extra junk". He would laugh so hard. I really miss his laugh. It boomed. It came from deep inside his heart. If you didn't expect it, you could get startled by it. But when he laughed, I always ended up laughing with him. It was infectious.

***

We started working on Grandma's room makeover. We agreed on a cheery bluish color. Uncle Vinnie and Mom agreed to help with some of the tasks that Nina and I may not be able to do well, like sewing and attaching hardware to hang things. I was willing to help with the hardware, and Nina with the sewing, but we weren't confident and experienced enough to do this on our own. Mom and Uncle Vinnie said they wanted to help anyway, so now the true family project began. We even recycled a pallet from a local bakery and painted it, attached clips on the front and brackets on the back. We hung it on the wall with some of Grandma's favorite pictures set in the clips. This way she could exchange the pictures and have a different variety of them to look at from her large box of family and friend pictures she had collected since she was a young girl.

***

I had managed to finish up most of the past due work that I owed. When our progress reports arrived in the mail, Mom got to them before I was home from school. I knew as soon as I walked in that she was not happy with me. I asked her if I could explain and give her good news. She looked confused at first. What good news comes out of this kind of progress report? I told her that I had all the work I was missing made up already. I confessed that I was suspended from the track team for a few weeks until I showed improvement. I explained how I spent the track practice time in the library working to get everything made up. I let her know that I have been taking notes and paying attention in class more too. I did admit that some days are better than others, but at least I am really trying to do better.

I showed her some of my notebooks. We always have to date our notes, so she saw the difference between the beginning of the month and now. She said she was ready to take away everything from me...my phone, video games, computer, and TV, but seeing as I took responsibility for my neglect of work and effort and showed true improvement that she would let me keep all of it under one condition. I had to get a note from each teacher (they could write it in my notebook) saying that I was participating more in class and my grade had improved to at least a C and was still able to become a B or higher by report card time. I sighed...really? I had to do this? How embarrassing! But if it is the only way to keep all my electronics, then I would do it. Mom said I had two days to get this all set, otherwise it would be only a light bulb in my room that used up electricity for the next month.

***

The next day at school I asked my teachers to write the note to my mom. They all agreed, except for my history teacher. He said that even though I had made up the work, that my F was now only a D. It was some improvement, but not enough. I asked him how I could raise my grade. His response was for me to do a community service project.

Our town is really big on community service. There would be multiple projects going on for me to choose from. The local group called "Community Cares" does small to large projects throughout the town to help it keep looking like a nice place to live. The real estate agents help with funding because all these projects draw new people into town to buy homes or rent places to live. Since the agent's main job is selling a home or helping people buy a home, or rent one, they really know the importance of keeping a town and its structures looking good. The more the appeal, the more likely someone is to move into our town.

I chose a mini project...just a two day project. In one weekend, I can move my grade from a D to at least a C. Mr. Juong, my history teacher, showed me the website with the list of upcoming mini projects on the Community Cares website. I chose one for the upcoming weekend. I wanted to get this over and done with. It is close enough to home so that I can just walk there. I didn't pay attention to the details, just the area of town it was happening in. I could manage anything for a couple of days, so I would just "suck it up" and get it done. Mr. Juong said he would send the details to my email so I would know exactly where this was taking place after he had registered my name as a student volunteer.

That afternoon at home, I showed Mom the notes from all my teachers. Then I explained how I was going to volunteer this weekend to help my History grade get to at least a C for now. Mom agreed that she would take away my electronics IF I did not go to the project this weekend. She said it was a great opportunity for me to take pride in our town and help others in need.

That night I read my email from Mr. Juong. The project was rebuilding two ramps and rebuilding a carport that had been destroyed at the end of last summer when we had a hurricane. As I read the address, I began to panic….it was Derek's house! I was going to spend the weekend at his house. What would he say to me? If he acted like a jerk to me, what would I do? I wasn't going to be in school where adults would intervene. Would the workers there even care if he said awful things to me or just irritated me to my breaking point? Maybe I could ask Mr. Juong for another project instead. But why? It would be like I was running away, or scared of Derek. I wasn't. I knew his story. I had to be the bigger person. If he was a jerk, I had to just let him be a jerk and not retaliate in any way.

I could do this. I would be helping his family. I don't know why they just don't take down the ramps and put in stairs. That just seemed so weird to me. Maybe I would suggest that to the workers when we got there to begin working.

The rest of the week went by quickly. I was back to track practice and had two meets to prepare for within the next few weeks. I was doing my best with keeping up with homework. I made myself work on some of it before turning on video games. Some days it was awful because I wouldn't get to gaming until about 8pm some nights.

A lot of my friends could only game until 8:30 or 9, so I ended up playing in a group with DR King most nights because he didn't have a gaming curfew. When we were partners, we totally destroyed our opponents. When we gamed against each other, it was always a good match. He won most of the time, but I always gave him a good challenge. Whenever I won, he would get very quiet until he beat me again.

***

The weekend had arrived. On Saturday morning I had to get up at 8am to be at Derek's by 9am. I had to bring lunch and food and drink for breaks. We would work until 3pm on Saturday, then pick up where we left off on Sunday at 9am and work until the project was done, or 3pm, whichever came first. I packed a cooler, ate breakfast, grabbed an extra sweatshirt and off I went.

When I got there, about 10 other people were there already, unloading tools and wooden boards. The head of Community Cares greeted me and explained exactly what the plan was. He said the two boys who lived in the house were going to take turns working with us because one of them had to stay in the house with their younger sister and care for her since Mrs. Royal was at work. David was the first to join the group . They let me work with David and two other men on the project of disassembling the ramp to the side door of the house. It didn't take long. We wore thick work gloves and used hammers to break apart the ramp so the new one could be built. As we started working, I asked why we were rebuilding ramps instead of just putting in stairs. David had just stepped away to get a few tools off the truck. The two men working with us said that they just follow the directions given, so a ramp it is. Then I thought that maybe their Mom had a bad knee or something, so a ramp would make it easier for her to get in and out of the house. That must be it.

    We worked until lunch break at noon. We had finished the side ramp. It looked great. There was a lot more to it than just putting up triangular sides with boards across them. We had to measure accurately and determine the correct slope of the ramp to meet the legal standards set for safe use. We had to cut the boards that were made from a composite material instead of plain wood. This material didn't warp like wood does. Also it doesn't need to be painted or stained and sealed to protect it from the weather.

    David told me as he went inside that Derek was taking the afternoon work shift with my group. He thanked me for coming to help today. He didn't know that I kind of had to do this for a better grade in school. I had just told him that I chose this project through Community Cares and it happened to be at his house. I said I was glad that I chose this project because I got to know David a little better. He was really nice. He acted more mature than other 8th graders I know. I would have guessed him to be mid high school age or even older based on how he spoke and how he worked on this project. He blended right in with the men and knew how to do most of the math work without help. He must be really good at math, then.

    After David went inside I started to wonder. Did he tell Derek that I was out here working? If so, was Derek mad that I was here? Was he embarrassed that his family needed help and had Community Cares here working on their home? I ate my lunch with a knot in my stomach waiting for what was to come when Derek joined us for the afternoon shift.

Chapter 20

I only ate about half of my lunch. The knot was taking up the other half of my stomach. One of the guys I was working with had brought cupcakes that his wife had made. I did manage to squeeze it into my stomach. It was great, a lemon cupcake with strawberry frosting. I'll have to let Grandma know about that combination. I'll bet she can make them even better, once she is able to bake again. I am more than willing to help her make these!

Derek came out of the house as we were starting to put all the tools and boards near the front steps. He and I carried the portable saw table from the side to the front of the house too. He was kind of quiet at first. Once the two guys we were working with started telling each other really lame jokes, but always laughing together at the ridiculous punch lines, Derek and I started looking at each other and laughing too. We weren't laughing at the jokes, we were laughing at how the guys thought these jokes were actually funny. So we were sort of laughing at them, but not in a mean way. Even lame jokes can be funny sometimes. One of the guys had a very unique laugh that included snorting, you know, like a pig.

***

The other guy's laugh was like my Dads. It made me happy and sad at the same time when I heard it. I was lost in thought, thinking about my Dad and remembering the time that he had offered to clean the bathroom when Mom had sprained her ankle and was on the couch for a couple of days. He used furniture polish instead of a bathroom cleaner on the toilet seat. When Grandma went to sit on it, she slipped right off onto the floor. She swore really loud. After we realized she hadn't been hurt, Dad started laughing about it. He said he had never heard his Mom swear before and didn't even know she "had it in her" to use that kind of language.

Grandma said there were lots of things about her that none of us knew about that would make us laugh. Dad said something like maybe she was a professional wrestler when she lived in Colombia. When we tried picturing it, we all started laughing. Grandma was so sweet and gentle, we couldn't even imagine her wrestling someone to the ground unless they had stolen her purse when she walked down the sidewalk in the city. He said she would run after them and wrestle them down to the cement, grab her purse and start hitting them over the head until the police came to save the purse snatcher from Grandma. I started smiling, thinking about that story and how we teased Grandma about being extra careful each time she headed into the bathroom for the next week.

***

Derek broke into my thoughts. He snapped his fingers near my face, asking me what planet I had gone to. I started laughing, telling him Saturn. He asked why I picked Saturn. I told him because I had a lot of rings of dirt on my arms from working, just like the rings around Saturn. He chuckled and we went back to work. Derek was pretty handy with the tools. He said he used to build things and help make repairs around the house. He told me about a loft bunk that he helped build a few years ago. He explained that his bedroom is kinda small, so the bunk left more room on the floor for him to construct building block projects. He said he has a special table for building with drawers underneath the table to hold all the block pieces for that project. When he finishes a model, he has shelving on his walls to display them.

His latest model he is working on has over 10,000 pieces. I was impressed. He said that he hasn't worked on it for a couple of years though. He just lost interest in it. I asked why and he told me that it was a personal reason, so I didn't bother him about it anymore. As I thought about it, I figured that he probably stopped building when his Dad died. Maybe his Dad had been working with him on it when the accident happened. Maybe someday he would tell me more about it, but most likely, not today.

During the break in the afternoon, Derek went inside to grab a snack and some more water. We were almost done with the front ramp. It took a lot of energy to keep up with the two men who were very confident in what they were doing. I asked one of them and he explained that he was a carpenter. He worked all week building homes, putting additions on homes and remodeling. That is why he busted on the other guy who mismeasured the board earlier. The other guy is an x-ray technician. He knows medical terms, but admitted that working with his hands on construction isn't his forte. He said that he volunteers with building projects to help himself get better at this type of work. He wants to remodel some things in his house, but wants to do it right. He said he loves giving back to his community as well as learning important skills in the process. The carpenter then shared that when he was young there was a fire where he lived. He said he watched the carpenters work to rebuild the damaged part of his home and was fascinated with the work. He said that helped him decide to become a carpenter so he could do that type of work. He said it also made him aware of the importance of helping other people, even those you don't know, when they are in need.

That brought him to be an active volunteer for Community Cares. He said that was the group that helped to fix his burned home. I will admit that I never thought about helping other people in need, especially if I didn't even know them. Listening to both their stories made me more curious about different projects with Community Cares and that maybe I can help them with other projects, just because I want to...not because I will get a C in History, or anything else out of it except the satisfaction that I did something nice for someone in need.

Just before quitting time, both ramps were finished and the other workers had set the supports and built the frame for the car port. Tomorrow we will finish the car port. Only four of the workers could make it back tomorrow, including me. As some people started to leave, the supervisor went to the door and asked David if the ramps could be tested. He said sure. A couple minutes later he opened the door and pushed a young girl from inside down the side ramp in her wheelchair.

***

I was in shock. Was this his sister? Was this Derek's little sister? The girl seemed happy with the smooth transition from inside to outside. They then went to the front ramp and up, back into the house. It HAD to be the sister. Who else could it be? Why was she in a wheelchair? Now at least I knew why the ramps weren't being replaced with stairs. But I had so many other questions. But I can't just start asking questions that aren't really any of my business. I was so curious though!

   As I walked home I just kept thinking about Derek and his family. Man, to lose your Dad AND have your little sister in a wheelchair. That is a lot for any family to handle. At least the sister looked happy when she was wheeled around for the ramp testing. I hope she isn't in the wheelchair because she has something that will just get worse. As I think about it, last year at my elementary school, I remember seeing a girl who was in second grade in a wheelchair. I bet that was her. She wasn't on my bus. But then again, neither was Derek. The routes were different in elementary school. I remember that there was one bus that just picked up kids from one large neighborhood. There were enough of them that it filled the bus. I'll bet that was Derek's neighborhood. Then I figured that his sister was probably on a bus with a lift or a ramp, not one of the buses that we ride. Now I understand more of why Derek may be angry or resent kids with families that seem to have no issues. So why did he pick on me earlier? My family is NOT a family without issues. You'd think he would choose a kid that seemed to have no problems. But then, what would he pick on him about, right?

***

   The next day I got to Derek's ten minutes early. I ran there with work boots, which were required to work on this project, in my backpack along with my lunch and water. I was going to run a lap around since I was there early, but David was outside already. His Mom was there too, getting into the car, headed to work. I waved to her as she pulled away. Then I went over to David to talk for a couple of minutes before we started working. He said he and Derek were switching shifts today, so he would be back out after lunch.

The other three workers arrived and I was told that because I am under 16 years of age that I cannot climb ladders or work on roofs. That is the policy of Community Cares. So I was stuck being the errand boy all morning, along with Derek. We would get whatever supplies the three workers on the roof or ladders needed. There was some down time, so I asked Derek what name he used when gaming.

"Why do you want to know?" he questioned.

"I remember you told me how good you were, so I figured that we could play against each other sometime. I looked for your name and couldn't find it," I admitted.

"Well, I use my initials and then another name so that most people can't figure out it is me that they are playing against." he commented.

"Why does that have to be a secret?" I wondered aloud.

"I am a private person. I don't want a lot of people knowing me and bugging me about things." he replied.

"What kind of things?" I asked.

" If I told you, then I would be divulging top secret information," he replied, smiling.

At that point I wouldn't give up. I knew he was just messing with me. Maybe he was trying to get me mad so I would just leave him alone. Since I did know a few things about him that he wasn't aware of, I figured that I would keep talking with him until he told me something personal about himself. I think that would break the ice from our "rough" beginning back at school a couple of weeks ago.

We just started talking about gaming and some of our not so secret strategies. I kept the conversation going between running tools and boards and roofing tiles to the three workers. At one point he commented that he considered himself the "king" of gaming.

I looked right at him and shouted, "That's who you are! DR King! I've been playing against you AND as your partner in some cases. You are really good. You are the best challenge I have when we face off in a game."

Derek laughed. He admitted that is who he was. Then he told me that he knew it was me all along that he was playing against because I used my first name and first letter of my last name.

At that point it was almost lunch time. David would be coming out to help finish up the project. We probably only had an hour of work left. I was kinda bummed. Derek and I were connecting and, I think, enjoying hanging out together. I decided to go out on a limb. I asked Derek if he wanted to join me and some of my friends on Friday night as we trick or treated in Deacon's neighborhood. He looked happily surprised by the offer, then his face slowly saddened.

"I can't. I have to take my sister out around our neighborhood with David. We go together every year. Mom stays home and passes out the candy while we go." he explained.

Then he totally shocked me by saying, "Hey, but you could come here and trick or treat with us. We get a ton of candy. Everyone gives out the good stuff, too."

I said, "Sure. That would be great!"

I was so excited by Derek finally wanting me to be part of something in his life...even if it was just trick or treating together. As he was going in, he told me that we'd work out the details on the bus this week. I told him that sounded perfect. David then came out and within an hour, we were all finished with the project. The supervisor gave me the official letter for me to bring to Mr. Juong to let him know that I participated both days and helped complete the project. Great! Now I at least had a C in History and could work on improving the grade to at least a B, I hoped, before report cards were sent home.

Chapter 21

As I ran home, I started thinking. What was I going to do? I now had two totally different commitments for trick or treating. I was finally making progress with Derek, who I really thought needed a friend. It also was my last chance to trick or treat with Deacon before he moved away. We had trick or treated together for the last 6 years. It was a tradition. How could I break tradition? But how could I back out of Derek's offer without messing up our newly developing friendship? By the time I got home my head hurt from thinking so hard about all of this. I had to figure out a way to keep everyone happy. But how could I make that happen?

I went right into my room, but not to jump into my video games and forget about my problem. I had to think...really think about how I was going to "fix" this. When I had problems and went to Grandma, my go-to person, she always told me to write about them. I could write a paragraph or an essay, if my problem had a lot of parts to it. She also encouraged me to write a pros and cons list. That is what usually brought the best answer to me. So that is exactly what I did. I sat at my desk with a clean crisp piece of lined paper and a sharpened pencil with a good eraser. I used pencil so if my thoughts changed as I listed things, I could easily erase them instead of having a bunch of cross outs. If I changed my mind again, I could easily rewrite my thoughts and keep everything neat and organized on my paper. It helped keep my mind focused on the problem instead of being frustrated by a messy paper. Here is what I started with:

Deacon/Halloween

<u>Pros:</u> We always have fun.
    I get along with most of his friends.
    I know his neighborhood (from past Halloweens).
    Mom already said I could go with him.
    We get lots of candy.

<u>Cons</u>: I need a ride to get to his house (can't just walk).
    When I sleep over (like this year) I sleep on the floor and it's uncomfortable.
    One of his friends is annoying and tries to hog all of Deacon's attention.
    I know his parents aren't happy with my family and think bad of my father (not sure why that

bothers me...I think bad of my father).
   Sometimes they make fun of my costume because it is always homemade (they get props and costume parts from the local Halloween shop).
   I may lose the opportunity to become friends with Derek.

<u>Derek/ Halloween</u>

<u>Pros:</u> It is a new adventure.
   I can walk to his house and not depend on a ride.
   His brother is cool and will be with us.
   Derek said the neighbors give out all good candy, and lots of it.
   This will help Derek want to be my friend.

<u>Cons:</u> Deacon will hate me because I am skipping out on him after saying I would go with him.

   After I finished my list, I went through and starred the most important pros and cons. Grandma always told me to pick just ONE pro and ONE con from each that meant the most to me. So now my final starred list included:

<u>Deacon/ Halloween</u>

<u>Pro:</u> We have fun (well, except for his annoying friend).

<u>Con:</u> Derek will probably not want to be my friend .

Derek/ Halloween

<u>Pro:</u> Derek will start being my friend.

<u>Con:</u> Deacon will hate me.

So, do I lose a friend I have had for many years, but is moving away soon? Do I make a new friend with someone who really seems to need a friend, and seems pretty cool to hang out with?
 I HATE making decisions like this. I couldn't ask Derek to come with us because he has to help his brother with his sister. Maybe I could ask Deacon if he wants to join us? Would Derek be OK with that? Would Deacon be willing to come with us and not go with his regular group of friends? I don't think Deacon would do that, but it is worth a shot. But I had to be sure that Derek would be OK with him possibly joining us.
 I was pretty tired at that point. I finished up the last part of my homework, ate dinner, took a shower and went to bed. I was more tired than I thought. Construction work was harder than it looks.

***

 The next morning I stepped on the bus with my mind on talking to Derek. He was sitting with David. I looked at the seat next to him and realized why. Kirk. He was on the bus. He looked angry. I was going to steer clear of him so I just sat near the front. The bus driver breathed a sigh of relief when I did. No issues, hopefully.
 We got off the bus without a problem arising. David went over to ask Kirk a question about PE Class. This gave me a chance to talk to Derek.

"Hey Derek, is it OK if I invite my friend Deacon to trick or treat with us in your neighborhood?" I asked.
"Why do you want him to go, too? If we get too big a group, the neighbors pull out the lame, cheap candy when we get to the door." he replied.
"If it was just ONE more person, that shouldn't matter, would it?" I inquired.
"Why can't you just go with me, David and my sister? If you want to back out, go ahead, whatever." he said in a rough tone.
"No. That isn't it. See, I have been going with him and his friends for years so he kind of expects me to go with them this year." I admitted.
"Then just go with them." he replied and started to walk away.
I had to think fast...I was going to lose a potential friend.
"Wait, Derek. I just thought that you would like Deacon. He is a nice guy. Can't I at least ask him to join us?" I semi-pleaded.
"I guess so, but nobody else. Like I said, big groups get cheap treats." he said.
I smiled. Success! Now I've just got to get Deacon to agree to come with us. Then I will be able to have my cake and eat it too! This was another one of Grandma's sayings for tough decisions.
The school day flew by, as did track practice. As soon as Ryan's dad dropped me off, I went straight to my room.

***

I texted Deacon. I asked him if he wanted to change up our Halloween routine this year. He asked how, so I asked if he wanted to trick or treat in a new neighborhood. My phone rang. It was Deacon. He started asking, "What is going on? Why do you want to change things? This was the year we were all allowed to go without a parent. It is going to be a blast! What neighborhood are you talking about?"

I took a slow breath to give me a few seconds of think-time.

"I've been running through this neighborhood that is kinda near my house. It is really big and the people who live there seem nice. I know a kid, Derek, who is in 7th grade who lives there. He said we could go with him, his brother and sister. He said they always get great candy."

"Is this the Derek who you got into a fight with? Now you are buddies with him?" Deacon asked.

"Our fight was just a misunderstanding." I explained, "He is a pretty nice kid. His brother, David is in 8th grade. He is nice too."

"Well, if you want to go with them, then that is your choice. I want to spend my last Halloween here trick or treating with my buddies in my neighborhood." he stated.

I had to take this chance, since he wasn't going for the change in his plans.

"Well I hope you won't be mad if I go with Derek, then. This way, next year, when you are away, I will have a place to go for Halloween that is closer to home. I won't want to go with your friends in your neighborhood. I am not really friends with them even though we get along OK." I said, waiting for him to be mad and hang up on me.

He didn't though. He sounded kind of mad, but not mad enough to ruin our friendship.

"I guess that makes sense. I was just hoping to

hang out with you. This last Halloween we are together, but if you want to try this other place with Derek, then we will just trick or treat with different groups." he conceded.

***

So I ended up trick or treating with Derek, David and Shannon. Shannon explained to me that she is in a wheelchair because she was in a car accident. She didn't seem upset by telling me that. David was OK, but Derek was pretty quiet after she had told me. Maybe being reminded of what happened still affected him alot. We got a lot of candy, as Derek had promised. All three of their costumes were homemade like mine. I didn't feel out of place. Derek had offered for me to sleep at his house. He has an air mattress. It was comfortable. His Mom had to go to work the next morning, so after David made us chocolate chip pancakes for breakfast, Uncle Vinnie came and picked me up so I wouldn't have to walk home in the cold rain that started early that day. I was tired from staying up late watching a movie with Derek and David. I went to my room to take a quick power-nap.

***

The front door flew open and the lamp next to the door was knocked over. I jumped out of bed and met up with Mom. We were both yelling at the intruders. Wait...they weren't intruders, they were police officers. There were four of them.
I started yelling again, "What do you want?" "Why are you here?" "Get out. You are in the wrong house!", but they ignored me.
They pushed my mom and I aside and two of them

went into my parents' bedroom with guns drawn. Another officer was in the bathroom. Nina was standing there, frozen in place. Grandma started screaming. A cop was in her room after checking out the kitchen.
 "What is happening?" I asked Mom.
 "Just stand here and stay quiet." she commanded.
 I heard a loud thump and Dad yell.
 The officers shouted, "We've got him in here!"
 I went to help Dad. What were they doing to him? They had to have the wrong house?
 As I moved, Mom grabbed my arm and said, "No." What!? What do you mean, "no"? I can't go help my father? Mom pushed me back and stood in front of me, blocking me from coming out of my room. The cops had Dad handcuffed and were reading him his rights. One was in front of him, one behind and two escorted him out, roughly, from each side of his body.
 As they left, Dad said fairly loudly, "I love you all. I'm sorry."
 I pushed Mom and ran to the door. I watched the officers put my father into a police cruiser. One of them saw me in the doorway and warned me to stay inside. I followed his direction. I was too stunned to move any further. I shouted through the screen door, "Dad! No!" as the officer shut the cruiser door and pulled away.
 The others followed in another cruiser and an SUV. I shouted once again, "Dad! No!"
 As I turned around, Grandma started to collapse. Mom and I caught her before she hit the floor. We guided her to the recliner. Nina had run out onto the porch. I went out to check on her. My head was spinning...everything was blurry. I was sweating and

felt like throwing up.

***

My sheets were damp. I had sweated from my nightmare to reality. My room was quiet. The sun was setting outside my window. The shadows were long and dark. As I laid there I could hear someone in the kitchen rumbling around getting dinner ready. What a nightmare...or a daymare, since it was during a nap. I had tried my best to block that night...the worst night of my life, from my memories. Even when Mom wanted to talk about what happened that night, I ran into my room and locked my door. I needed to be away from it all. I needed to be away from the reality of what had happened. Dad. What have you done, Dad?

After dinner I called Deacon and asked how trick or treating went with his crew. He said it was kind of lame. The kid that always hogs Deacon was annoying the whole night. Deacon said he was dressed up as a werewolf and just kept howling. He even scared some little kids. I told Deacon that didn't surprise me. I admitted that his friend kinda bugged me all the times we went out for Halloween together. He asked me why I never told him that before. I explained that I didn't want to be excluded from the group so I just kept my mouth shut and dealt with it. Deacon laughed and said that I must be more mature than them because I noticed the annoying behavior years before they did.

"It just wasn't the same without you there," Deacon admitted.

"I had fun, but it wasn't the same without you, either." I agreed.

I looked at next year's calendar.

"Hey, Halloween is on a Saturday night next year. Let's agree to go to my new trick or treat spot with Derek. Then maybe you can both sleep over." I suggested.

Deacon seemed happy with that idea. I know in reality that he may have new friends in his new neighborhood and want to go with them. If that happens, then I'll just go with Derek, David and Shannon again. They are so funny.

Before Shannon told me about the accident, the three of them were telling stories about how their Mom used to dress them as a popular three-some for Halloween. One year she made them the 3 Little Pigs. Derek was mad because he had to be the one with the straw, which he called, "the stupidest pig". David said his Dad even dressed up as the big bad wolf that year and walked them around the neighborhood because they were too young to go alone. The Dad kept saying, "I'll huff and I'll puff" instead of "trick or treat" when people came to their door to hand out the candy. That made all three of them laugh. It was good to see Derek laugh. He is a pretty serious kid, but I know he has the potential to let loose and have fun. That was the first true sign of it.

***

The next week Grandma came home. It was a surprise. Mom and Nina went to get her while I was at track practice and Uncle Vinnie was working. When we got home it was celebration time! Mom and Nina waited for us to be home to show Grandma her room. She loved it. She started crying and saying how beautiful it was. She especially loved her picture display. We showed her how the clips just release the pictures so she can interchange them whenever she wants. She said she was a bit tired, so she laid down for a rest while dinner was being made.

We talked at dinner about our day. We had a fire drill, so I got out of Science Class for about 15 minutes. It was cool, but sunny outside so we were happy for the academic break. Nina was happy. She hates fire drills. The alarm freaks her out. I also shared that as of the time trials we had today at track practice, that I am the second fastest runner on the team for the 2 mile. Now I have a new goal...not to just beat my own time for running, but to beat the kid who has the fastest time. He is a seventh grader, so he will still be on the team next year. As long as a super fast sixth grader doesn't enter our school next year, I KNOW I can keep training and take over the number one spot for next years' season.

Chapter 22

The following weekend was a track meet. When it was my group's turn the butterflies in my stomach turned into bats. I was so nervous. One of the kids in my group was the number one runner for his school. I wanted to beat him. I had to beat him. My competitive thoughts were controlling my brain. Then I heard my coach's voice telling me, "Just focus on beating YOUR best time and let the rest fall into place."
I shook my head to rattle those words out. I know they made sense, but they didn't mean a win for me.

Bang! The starting gun fired. I took off at a quick clip. Pace yourself...pace yourself, I had to keep reminding myself. I slid into a pretty fast pace. There were two others near me; the kid who was best at his school and Ryan, my track friend. Ryan was number three on the team for the fastest two mile, so he was going to be someone who would push me to move faster as well.

We stayed very close until the last quarter mile. The other kid and I pushed ahead of Ryan by about 20 paces. Not much, but enough for the winning edge. With about 100 yards left I picked up the speed to full throttle. So did the other kid. He beat me by one second. One second! I was so bummed. I hung my head as Coach walked over, beaming. Why? Coach congratulated me on beating my fastest time-trial from practice by 12 seconds.

I shook my head and said, "but it wasn't enough".

Coach told me to look him in the eyes.

When I did, he responded with, "You just beat your own time and now have the fastest time for the 2 mile on the school team. You are now ranked first. The kid you just lost to by one second is first overall, and you are second overall for BOTH teams. You should be proud of yourself, not kicking yourself! And the kid you just lost to is an 8th grader. You still have two years left of middle school track to become even faster and stronger than you are right now. Adjust your outlook. The glass is half full...not half empty in this case. Stay positive and keep up with your training, even in the off season. And even more importantly....keep your grades up. That is always number one priority for school."

I got it. I know what I have to do. I walked over to Mom who was standing off to the side from the other parents. She hugged me and told me how proud she was of me. A few minutes later, we left the meet. As we started on the road she told me that she needed to stop somewhere on the way home. That was fine only until we pulled into the correctional facility.

***

"Mom, what are you doing?" I asked.

She explained that the meet ran a bit later than she expected, so if she brought me home first then came back to see Dad, she wouldn't make it back during visitor's hours. She asked me to come in and sit in the waiting room with her. That way we could talk until it was her turn to go see Dad. I agreed.

It was weird. We had to be searched and go through a metal detector. I took off my running shoes and my hoodie. Mom's purse had to be checked thoroughly. Her shoes and jacket had to come off as well. I just kept telling myself that I was doing this for Mom. I needed to be there for Mom. I know she has gone alone a few times already, but that must have been hard for her to do. I know I wouldn't want to come here voluntarily, alone.

I asked her while we were in the waiting room what it was like.

"What do you mean?" she responded.

"Do you get to sit and talk to him face to face, privately? Can you hold his hand or give him a kiss goodbye when you are leaving?" I inquired.

"Well, we do see each other, but through plexiglass. It is not private. You are in a room with up to 8 other people visiting other inmates." she explained.

Wow. She called my Dad an inmate. I didn't like thinking of him like that.

Then she said, "Why don't you go see him this week

instead of me? Tell him about your track meet today. You know if he wasn't in here that he would have been cheering you on at the finish line."

This took me by surprise. I didn't expect her to ask me to do this. Should I? Was I ready to see him...face him? What if he didn't want to see me? Questions swirled through my head. The motion was interrupted by a guard opening the door and saying our last name. Mom stood, then looked at me. Her eyebrows asked the question...well? I stood.

I don't know why.…I didn't want to go, but yet I did. I am still very angry with him. I don't think that will ever stop. But should I still go see him? I guess it is happening. Mom sat back down. "Aren't you coming with me?" I wondered aloud.

"Only one visitor for 10 minutes each week." the guard explained.

Mom shooed me with her hands. I followed the guard down the cinder block hallway, painted a boring tan. I noticed that some of the paint was peeling off the walls. Not a very welcoming place, but then again, it IS jail.

As we approached the room, there was a dark green metal door with a tiny window. The guard signaled and the door popped open. They must be locked. But who opened it? I looked up quickly to see there were cameras...everywhere. As I entered the room I automatically looked all around the place. There were cubbies made of plexiglass. The petitions between each cubby were some type of metal. A phone hung on the right side of each cubby.

"Number 2." the guard instructed.

I saw the numbers atop each cubby. I walked over

to the one with the 2. Dad was sitting on the other side. I wanted to run. Run right out of there. My heart was racing a million miles an hour. I was about to turn around and leave when Dad waved with a huge surprised expression. He was smiling ear to ear. I numbly sat down in the chair across from him.

"Hi" I said.

He pointed to the phone...oh, I get it, we need to talk through that so we don't have to shout. That way our conversation isn't heard by everyone around us. I picked up the receiver and held it to my ear. I was at a loss for words. Dad wasn't.

Dad started by telling me how happy he was to see me. How much he missed me. He asked what I was up to. He wanted to know about Halloween. OK. That gave me some talking points. I explained about Halloween with Derek. He thought I was going with Deacon, like always. I explained Derek was a new friend. Deacon was moving away, I told him. He shook his head saying how sorry he was about that. He knew what a good friend Deacon was to me. I agreed, but explained we have a plan to still see each other. He was happy about that.

I told him Grandma was home now and doing better. He smiled as tears pooled in his eyes. As I examined his face more closely, I noticed he had wrinkles forming around his eyes. He looked older. He looked tired...at least his eyes did.

I asked him how he was doing and he just said "fine".

He asked about Track. As I started to explain the details of the meet today, the guard told me that time was up in one minute. I didn't get to tell him everything before I had to leave. Just before I hung up, Dad said something...the receiver had already cut out so I glanced up at him. He mouthed the words, "Love you, Bud".

I smiled and turned away. I couldn't say anything back to him, I know I still love him, but I am not ready to say it to him. I don't know if I will ever say that to him again.

By the time I got to Mom I was tearing up myself. She hugged me and told me she loved me and that what I did today was the bravest thing she's ever seen me do. I had gone to see Dad in jail. I was silent on the ride home. I just kept replaying the whole conversation with Dad. He seemed casual as he spoke. Maybe he has adapted well to prison-life. I started thinking questions I should have asked him. No. I pushed those thoughts aside. If I have questions then I would need to see him again. That won't happen for quite a while...if ever.

I just felt so uncomfortable about everything. The whole situation was just so weird. I felt like I had just visited another planet, another world. I did NOT want to talk about any of it. Just before we got into the driveway I asked Mom for a huge favor. I asked her not to tell anyone that I was the one who saw Dad today. I am not ready to talk about it, with anyone. Mom agreed, but made me promise to come to her with any questions about the visit, whether it was about what I saw or what I heard while talking with Dad.

It was a great surprise when we walked into the house. Grandma was in the kitchen, seated at the table, coaching Uncle Vinnie as he started to make dinner. Her speech was much better, but if she started getting tired, her words would slur. She was quite clear with what she expected Uncle Vinnie to be doing as he started making bandeja paisa. I needed some time alone, even though I was curious to see how Uncle Vinnie would manage with making this dish for the first time. I headed to my room. I didn't even share anything about my track meet with them. I just said I was tired and going to "chill" for a while.

***

I kept everything bottled in for a few days. When I came home from school the next week, Grandma was watching TV. Nobody else was home. She motioned for me to come sit with her. I plopped down next to her and let out a big sigh.

"What is going on with you, Jeancarlos?" she asked.

"Nothing, Grandma. Just got a lot going on in my head. You know...a lot of thinking to do." I replied.

"Thinking about what? School? Friends? Track? Dad?" she inquired.

As soon as she said "Dad", my face fell.

"Ah ha...Dad." she concluded.

At that point, I looked at her light brown eyes. They were sad. The sad eyes and her worry lines on her forehead broke me. I told her all about seeing Dad. How I felt. All the questions I still had to ask him, but didn't want to go back and see him. Her response shocked me.

"You are lucky. You got to see him and talk to him."

I responded, "Grandma, why don't you go see him?"

Her eyes started welling up with tears. She told me that Dad had told Mom not to bring Grandma to see him. He felt that he had no right to see his mother. He was a disgrace to her and her family. He was an embarrassment. He didn't want her to see him locked up. He felt it would break her heart even more than he already had.

"Wow, Grandma. I had no idea. Dad should want to see his mother. You have always been there for him since he was born! It is stupid and selfish of him to not want to see you...and to have you see him." I responded.

Grandma's reply was simply, "Then why don't you tell him that when you see him again? He won't listen to your Mother. Maybe coming from you or Nina will make more of an impact on him."

That would mean that I would have to go there again. I didn't know if I could do it. Not for a while, at least. It was funny in a weird way...Grandma wanted to go see Dad, but he wouldn't let her, and I didn't want to see Dad, but he wanted to see me. I started thinking about this whole situation. I guess Dad realized that he messed up big-time. Not just messed up on his end, but our family's end.

***

Dad's actions have put a scar on his family tree. I wonder why he is willing to see Mom, me and Nina, but not his own mother? Has he shamed her so severely that there is no recovery? Maybe he thinks that Grandma wonders what she did wrong in raising him to be an adult to think...to justify in some way, his actions...his reasoning that it was OK to steal from someone else...to take what was never his...and to be a part of something that ended someone else's life. Some innocent man who was just doing his job and working hard. Someone with a family. Being a part of something that many people consider an unforgivable crime? Will he ever be able to forgive himself? Does it take that for him to be willing to see his own mother? Can he ever look at his reflection and validate that he is a good man?

In prison, he has a lot of time to think. Does he replay the whole situation over and over again? Does he have nightmares about it? He has said, "I'm sorry" about this whole situation. Is he sorry that it all happened or is he sorry that he got caught? Those are two totally different concepts. As my family continues to do their best to cope with all of his actions and poor choices, is HE also coping? Is HE truly regretful? Is HE ever going to be the same again? Are any of us? My answer is no.

We are all changed forever. We are all broken in some way. Us at home...we are incomplete. A piece of our home is missing; A key piece; The piece that was the cornerstone to our family structure. It is like our family is a jigsaw puzzle, and someone has taken a piece and altered it. Even if that piece gets returned to our puzzle, it will never "fit" back in to make it truly whole, truly complete.

I wonder if I will become like my Dad when I am a man. Will I make one decision that will ruin my family? Just one conscience, deliberate, intentional action, that will bore a deep, gaping hole in the life of my family? No...I will NOT become my father. But how can I guarantee that it won't happen? Mom is doing a great job raising me. Grandma and Uncle Vinnie now, too, are key influences in my life. Dad was doing a great job, too, I thought...until.

I was afraid. I was afraid of what my future held. I can say right now that I will never let anything like this happen to me and my family when I am an adult. But what surety is there? That freaks me right out.

I am sure that my Dad NEVER planned as a kid that he would commit ANY type of crime, especially one that involved the end of another human's life. Even if he didn't know that Jake had a gun and was willing to shoot Mr. Gossling, Dad was still a part of it. He was part of the original plan. He had to own up to his involvement. He has to live the rest of his life knowing that his ONE decision to be involved with what he thought was just a robbery, had turned into so much more.

It is all out of his control right now. He can never go back and "redo" that one decision...that one day...that one moment. It scares me to think that I have those genes in me. Sure, I am not perfect. Nobody is. But to alter your integrity for what? What would he have gotten if Mr. Gossling didn't have a gun? What if the three of the men just robbed him and left? Dad would have gotten some money. Even then...would it have been worth it? Being a criminal for some money? Taking what is legally not yours...that you didn't earn...from someone who worked hard to earn that money.

I would beg on the streets before I would steal from someone else. I would swallow my pride and get help from local agencies that help families in need. Even if it meant we lost the house we rented and had to live in a one bedroom shack somewhere. We would all be together...we would have made it work...we would have worked together to get back on our feet, financially.

Chapter 23

The next week, Grandma surprised all of us. She told Mom that it was about time that she gets to see her son. She knew that Dad had told Mom that he didn't want to see her, more like face her, but she said he needed to know that she still loved him and was sticking by his side throughout this whole situation. Mom was hesitant but agreed. She thought it would be good for Dad to see all of us, especially with Thanksgiving coming up. She said he needed to remain thankful for his family and know that we still love him. I rolled my eyes at that one. I do love him, but am not willing to admit it because I still have so much anger towards Dad.

While Mom and Grandma went to see Dad, I went to see Derek. I ran to his house so he and David and I could shoot baskets in their driveway. Their hoop was a bit bent, but it worked for just shooting around. Shannon watched us and even brought out her pom poms to cheer for us when we made baskets. After taking turns playing one on one games and a few rounds of HORSE, we went into the kitchen for a snack and drink.

Their Mom had baked cupcakes with Shannon the night before. They were pumpkin cakes with cream cheese frosting. Shannon explained how she was in charge of the measuring, mixing and frosting the cupcakes. She even sprinkled orange colored sugar on top of each cupcake. They looked great and tasted really good, too. When we had finished our snack, David said he was going to work on a project he had to finish for English Class that was due on Monday. Shannon wanted to watch a movie about mermaids.

***

Derek asked if I wanted to play video games. We went into his room, but before he had the TV on, I asked about the lego model that sat, partially completed, on a table in the corner of his room.
"Want to work on this instead of game?" I asked.
"Nope." he replied.
"Why not?" I questioned.
"It is fine the way it is now." he said.
"But it isn't done. Let's see how much more we can get done in the next hour, before I have to leave." I suggested.
"I can't. I had promised to work on it with someone else. I can't break that promise." he informed me.
"Oh, sorry, I don't want to mess up that promise. Maybe next time I'm here I can see how much more you guys got done." I commented.
"Well, you won't see any progress. The project is as done as it is going to be." he replied with a defensive tone.
"Well, can't you just let me help until your friend can get here to do more with you? I am sure we won't even come close to finishing it today. We can just kind of help the progress move forward a bit." I encouraged.
"No. We are not working on this. It will never be finished." Derek retorted.
"Why? Did your friend move away? My friend, Deacon is…" I started explaining.
 Derek interrupted me, quite angrily. "No. Don't you get it? I was working on this with my Dad! He was my partner. I had promised him that we would do this together. That is impossible now, so just drop the offer!"

I didn't know what to say. I stood there stunned. This was the first time he had even mentioned his Dad to me. I could tell he was hurting, but didn't know what to do.

Luckily, David entered the room and asked us to check out his project so far. We went into his room to check it out. It was a medieval castle made of cardboard. He used paper towel rolls to form the rounded towers. He explained that he needed to finish all the construction on it today so he could spray paint it grey tomorrow morning, then draw the details for the blocks on the exterior tomorrow afternoon, once the paint dried.

As we started back to Derek's room, David asked me to wait a minute. Once Derek was out of ear shot, he said he heard what I was trying to do in helping Derek with the model. He thanked me and explained that Derek hasn't touched it since their Dad died. David asked me to please not give up on Derek.

David said Derek needed a true friend, and believed that I would be a good friend to him. He said that I am patient and kind. He said Derek pushed away all of his friends after the accident. Derek had shut them out of his life and hasn't had a true friendship since. David told me to keep encouraging, keep nudging him to do things, like work on the project. He said that would help Derek get back to being "himself" again. He said that just the fact that Derek had asked me over and had me trick or treat with them was a huge step in helping him cope with his Dad's death and get back to enjoying life.

I told David that I would try my best. I really liked hanging out with both of them and wanted to keep our friendship, and hopefully make it even stronger. At that point I walked into Derek's room and we played video games until I had to go home.

***

As I walked home I tried to come up with ways to help Derek. The counselor my Mom, Nina and I were seeing had talked about the importance of friendships. Family is important, though, too. As far as I could see, Derek had a great family. Shannon and David were great siblings. They were easy going and liked to laugh. All three of them seemed really close. Their mom had to work a full time job and even a couple of nights a week at a part time job. David had told me that while we were working on rebuilding the ramps a couple of weeks ago.

Not having their Mom around a lot must bum them out. But it seems like she does things with them when she is able to be home. She made the cupcakes with Shannon and helped David start his castle project. What about Derek, though? What kind of relationship did he have with his Mom? Had he pushed her away as well as his friends?

Anyway, back to friendships. So right now it seemed that I was Derek's only friend. He had let me into his life, but it hasn't been easy. He gets angry quickly and I have to back off and do my best to change the subject. This distracts him from his anger...so far. I need to be patient with him letting me know more about his life...his family...his Dad. David and Shannon seem to be happier than Derek. Why have they been able to move on more easily than him? Even Shannon, now in a wheelchair because of an accident, is making the best of her life. There is something more to all of this. But what is it? How can I help Derek heal from the tragedy of losing his father? Do I know enough about life and feelings at my age to help Derek? Is just being his friend enough? Time would tell. I wasn't going to abandon him. He seemed to have a lot to offer as a friend, but just wasn't going to let people into his life...into his heart, that easily.

***

The next few weeks I focused on training for my last track meet of the season. It was actually the Junior State Track Meet. I would be competing against sixth through eighth graders who ranked in the top three in the two mile run from each middle school in our state. There were about 40 middle schools in our state, so that was 120 kids! They broke it up into 12 runs with 10 kids in each group. The times would determine the overall placements. Even if I won for my group race, I may not even place in the top 10. It was all about my time...like Coach kept telling me.
"Forget about everyone else around you and focus on your breath and your pacing. Shut out all the noise around you and just run." was his daily guidance for all of us on the team.
I would run after dinner, even though I had run at practice. I'd run through Derek's neighborhood most of the time. If I told Derek when I was going, he would join me at his house and run one lap with me...but then he was done. He wasn't a big long distance runner. On nice days, Shannon would bring her pompoms outside with her and cheer us on as we passed. One day she even brought out David's phone and blasted upbeat music through his blue tooth speaker.

I'd run on the weekends too, sometimes once in the morning and then again after dinner. The rest of the time I spent either at Deacon's house or the tennis courts with him, or at Derek's house. I had invited Derek to my house a few times, but he felt guilty leaving David to watch Shannon, and he would have to walk because his Mom worked weekends.

My grades were slipping again. I was paying attention in class and taking notes, but I wasn't getting my homework done. I was busy training. Then I was too tired to do the work. I was hoping that my grades wouldn't be too bad because I was getting class work done. I know that Coach wouldn't check grades again. Report cards weren't coming out until the week after our last meet. That would get me through Thanksgiving before Mom knew that I wasn't being diligent about getting all my work done for school. I'd deal with it then. I will try my best to get some of my homework done at least.

***

The State Meet was about 30 minutes away. We had followed Coach's directions and ate pasta meals the night before. Pasta was supposed to give us the endurance boost we need to do our best. Even though only three of us qualified, the bus was filled with the whole team and the cheerleaders too. The team all wanted to be there to support the three of us that were running. The cheerleaders had even created a special cheer to do at the finish line when each group was completing their 2 mile run.

Deacon's Dad agreed to bring him there to cheer me on. Deacon's Dad went to college on a full scholarship for track, so he loved the fact that I was into running. Deacon ran, too, but only for training for soccer. He was pretty fast. I tried talking him into joining track with me this year, but he said running is boring except when you have a ball to kick or person to block while you are running. Mom wasn't going to make it. She would miss her time with Dad. She offered to skip it this week, but I told her that I could tell her all the details when I got home. She only got to see Dad for 10 minutes a week and I knew how much she missed him. I didn't want her to sacrifice that to stand around in the cold for a few hours to just see me finish one race that only took less than one minutes view of the finish line once the runners were nearing the end of the race.

When we got there, we were told that the groups were based on ranking. Four groups of the 3rd place ranked runners, four groups of the 2nd place runners from each school and then finally the last four races were all the 1st place runners. I was in the third of those four groups. There was only one group to race after me, so I had a long wait until it was my group's turn. I kept jogging in place and jumping around to keep warm after I had stretched. My heart was racing way before my legs began running.

As I began running I was in the middle of the pack. I had to keep reminding myself that this was a group of runners ranked first for their schools. They were all fast. I set my pace with the plan to burst into full speed about 120 yards before the finish line.

I started to get a cramp in my side. NOOOOO! I had to breathe...breathe through the stitch in my side. I hadn't drunk enough water this morning, I'll bet. I focused on my running, doing my best to ignore the pain. About a half mile later, it subsided. Thank goodness!

I started my sprint and pulled ahead. I was hoping that 20 extra yards of sprinting would give me the boost I needed to win. It worked! I won for my group. I had to contain my excitement because I would look foolish celebrating, but then not placing when all the times were posted from all the races. AND there was one more group to run.

The wait time was agonizing! I kept looking over at Deacon. He and his Dad gave me a "thumbs up" for confidence and encouragement. Finally!! The results came. They announced the top ten for the state. I waited patiently. Ryan placed 9th in the State. The 8th grader who I beat in the last race was 5th in the State.

Now it was time for the ribbons and medals for the top 3. Number 3 in the State was ...ME! I was really happy. Out of 120 runners to rank Number 3 as a sixth grader was a great accomplishment. I stayed focused for the top two. Number 2 was an 8th grader from the other side of the state. Cool...He would be in high school next year, so he wouldn't be competing next year with us. First place went to a 7th grader in the town to the east of ours. He was the one I would focus on beating next year. I would watch his times in the newspaper next year to give me a set time to focus on beating.

After the medal ceremony, Deacon and his Dad came over to congratulate me. Deacon said that I would outrun everyone on the soccer team in a race. I thanked both of them for coming. Deacon's Dad told me to keep it up and that I looked like college scholarship material to him. Geez, I never thought of that. Going to college for free! That would be a relief to Mom. No extra payments to make. I know college is expensive. Now I heard Coach's voice in my head...grades first! Too late to fix for this report card, though.

***

Thanksgiving was different, yet the same. Of course Dad wasn't with us, and Grandma had to guide us through the prep of some of our favorite dishes that we weren't willing to give up just because Grandma didn't have the strength and energy to make them. Luckily she was willing to talk us through preparing them. Each of us took one of our favorites as our responsibility to make. Mom knew how to make the turkey, so that was her job. She also agreed to make the potatoes. That left the green bean casserole, one of my favorites, for me to make. Nina was making the cornbread stuffing and Uncle Vinnie was preparing the corn pudding as well as the candied yam casserole. The day before Thanksgiving, Nina and Mom had made a few pies, so dessert was all set.

When we sat down at the table, Grandma insisted on saying a prayer, then we were each to tell one thing we were thankful for. When it was my turn, I said that I was thankful for Uncle Vinnie. It had been on my mind lately, how much he had adjusted his life to help us. I wanted him to know that all his sacrifices hadn't gone unnoticed. He seemed surprised and grateful for the comments I made about him. He really was doing a great job at helping all of us through this tough time. He knew how to be a part of our family without trying to be "Dad" to me and Nina. I mean, even with

Grandma...he wasn't even related to her, but helped with her room redecoration project and gave her rides to places if he wasn't working and Mom was busy. He'd gone running with me a couple of times. He slowed me down because of his bum knee, but it was nice to have someone to run with once in a while.

    Thanksgiving night I was talking to Derek while we gamed against each other. I invited him to come play football with all my cousins the next day. He could actually make it. His mom had the day off, so he didn't feel as much responsibility to watch Shannon.

***

    The next day was so much fun. We met up with all my cousins while the adults went shopping. We played touch football for a couple hours, then came back to my house to have the leftover pies and any other foods that we didn't devour on Thanksgiving Day. Derek fit right in. He laughed and joked around. He was like a different kid.

    I was glad I helped him get a break from home. I think school is his only break away from his family. Not that families aren't great, but everyone needs time to do other things away from home. I think it helps get your mind off of your troubles. Once the adults came back from their shopping expedition, Uncle Vinnie and I drove Derek back home.

    On our way back to our house, I unloaded all about Derek to Uncle Vinnie. It still bothered me about him not wanting to finish the model he had started with his Dad before the accident. Uncle Vinnie agreed that I shouldn't pressure him to work on it, but I shouldn't give up suggesting that we work on it either. He told me that even though Dad isn't with us, we can still see and talk to him sometimes, so I should feel fortunate compared to Derek. I agreed. Even though my situation sucked...Derek's sucked worse than mine.

***

The next weekend was a walk a thon that Nina and her friend, Jessica, organized as part of a History Class project. All our family went. David, Derek and Shannon went too. Their neighbor offered to drive them. It was fun. It was the first time that all three of them were with me and my family. Grandma sat and watched aside the track. She helped with selling raffle tickets. Deacon walked with us. This is the first time he has hung out with me, Derek, David and Shannon. We took turns pushing Shannon's wheelchair.

She was so happy to be a part of this. She liked talking with all of us. She was asking a lot of questions about our favorite TV shows, movies, music, foods. At the end of the event the neighbor was getting ready to take them home, she looked tired. David said she'd probably nap on the ride home. He said she is stuck in the house so much that an outing like this takes a lot of energy from her. Nina told us later that a lot of donations were made for the school pantry that she and Jessica were organizing as the second part of their project.

The week after the walk a thon was parent teacher conferences. We had half day sessions all week so the teachers had time to meet with all the parents. Mom went to see Nina's teachers then my teachers all in one afternoon. Mom took Nina into her room to discuss the conversations she had with her teachers. They were in there for about 15 minutes. Then it was my turn. I had really hoped that the teachers would focus on what a great job I had done catching up after progress reports rather than how I had not done most of the homework assignments and projects the last three weeks. No such luck.

***

My teachers told Mom how much potential I had, but how I was definitely not doing what I should be. They specifically mentioned assignments to be done outside of class. Mom was pretty mad. She even was raising her voice, which she rarely does. I raised my voice back to her, which was another big mistake. She told me that she agreed with my teachers that I would attend summer school if I stayed working to this capacity. She also said that they mentioned tutoring after school. I told her no way. I don't do the work because I choose not to, not because I don't know how to do it. She said she doesn't know what to believe anymore. That hurt. I wasn't lying to her. I don't lie. Well, I rarely lie. But I totally was being truthful to her now.

Mom took the wire to my gaming system, so it wasn't connected to my TV. She also took my phone. She said I could have it once I had shown her my completed assignments each day. I also had to finish all the past due assignments as well. That wasn't fair! Gaming was still my escape. Homework wouldn't be my escape. I would lose my mind without an escape. Why did the teachers rat me out?

Nina came into my room to "talk". I didn't need that right now. She seemed concerned about me. I just listened to her words and replied with "fine" and "sure" to just get her to leave. When I get mad, the last thing I want to do is talk….or be talked to. I just want to be left alone. I have to figure out how to motivate myself to get my work done at home. I just hate being home. It just reminds me of my family. I still love them, but it is too different. And Dad's trial will be coming up soon, so that will be even more stress on me.

Chapter 24

   Our bus was late for school. The roads were super icy. I sat with Derek on the bus. He seemed really nervous. I thought it was because the roads were bad and our bus had slid a bit. He kept looking at his phone. Each time he did, he seemed more on edge. When we got off, he got mixed in with a crowd of kids and I lost sight of him. David was behind me. I turned and asked him what was up with Derek. He hadn't noticed his behavior on the bus. When I explained what he was doing he shook his head.
   "He is waiting for my Mom's text", he said.
   "Why? Is he in trouble? Is something wrong with your Mom?" I inquired.
   "No. Derek gets really upset when the roads are bad. He worries that our Mom will be in an accident. He has been that way since Dad's accident." he explained.
   "Man. That has got to be awful, to be waiting for a text to know that your Mom is OK." I said. "My mom is a good, safe driver. Her work is not that far from our house. She will be OK. Derek just overreacts and worries so much. He doesn't want to lose another parent. He talks about it with me

sometimes. He worries that if anything happens to Mom that we will be put into different foster homes and he will lose all of his family." David shared.

"Why would you guys go into a foster home? Don't you have family that would take you all to live with them?" I questioned.

"No. Not really. Our grandparents on both sides have health issues and are just too old to take all of us. We wouldn't want to do that to them anyway. Taking on three kids is a tough deal. My Mom is an only child, so we have no aunts and uncles on her side. My Dad has a sister that lives about 300 miles away. She has two kids and is a single parent. She has a tiny house that could not fit even one of us in it." he shared.

I nodded and walked away. All this information was clouding my concentration. I went through the first two periods, unfocused and not completing my work. I had to know that both Derek and his Mom were OK.

***

At the beginning of third period, I couldn't wait any longer. I asked to go to the bathroom. Instead of going there, I went to the seventh grade wing. I know what team he is on, but didn't know what class he was in. I had to peek into the windows of the classrooms until I saw him. He was sitting with his head down. I needed to get his attention. I finally caught the eye of the kid sitting in front of Derek. I motioned for him to get Derek's attention. He turned around to Derek and then pointed at the door. Derek looked confused at first, but then raised his hand and asked to use the bathroom or get a drink. Some reason to leave the room. When he got out in the hall he seemed agitated.

"What do you want? What are you doing?" he whispered.

"I need to know that you are OK. That your mom is OK." I replied.

"Why are you asking about my Mom?" he responded, sounding annoyed.

I didn't want to lie to him. David didn't tell me not to say anything to Derek about me knowing how he feels.

So I told him, "Your brother told me why you were acting differently than usual this morning. Did your Mom text you?"

"No. I haven't heard from her yet. I have my phone on silent, so I just sneak a look at it to check whenever I get a chance." he said.

"Why don't you just text her or call her?" I asked.

"We get detention if we are caught with our phones, so I wasn't going to spend any length of time on it and chance that." he explained.

I then had an idea. I told him he should go see Mr. Coster. He would let him call his Mom if Derek would tell him why. He was hesitant at first, but then agreed to go ask his teacher for a pass to see him. As I turned around to go back to class the school security officer stopped me. She said I was in the wrong hallway. Why? I couldn't tell on Derek, so I told her I just needed a break from class so I went for a quick walk. She saw that I had a bathroom pass. She said she'd leave my fate up to my teacher.

She walked me back to class and told Mr. Juong that I was in the seventh grade hallway instead of the bathroom. He told her he'd take care of that. Since I told him I needed a break and a walk, he gave me a detention. Great. He said I needed to spend as much time in class as possible to get my grade up. It had not budged from the C that I earned by doing the Community Cares Project. Great….just great. How was I going to explain staying after school with Mom? She knows that track is over.

***

It wasn't until the bus ride home that Derek thanked me for suggesting he go to Mr. Coster. He said that Mr. Coster let him call his Mom after he told him about how worried he gets when the roads are bad. I am sure that Mr. Coster knows what happened to Derek's father. David was in sixth grade when the accident happened, so Mr. Coster may have helped him through that terrible time, or at least knew about the accident causing Mr. Royal's death and Shannon's injuries.

I told Derek about me getting a detention. He felt bad. He said it was rotten that I got a consequence because I was being a good friend and trying to help someone. I told him the only thing I worried about was my Mom getting mad. I explained to him about my grades going back down and how I had lost my phone and cable for my gaming system. Derek said he was wondering why I hadn't been playing.

Derek said he could help me. He had a plan for me to serve my detention without Mom knowing. He said that I could tell my Mom that I needed to work in the library after school. I could say that Derek was going to help me with some work I had to do. He said that he would stay after in the library and wait for me, then we could walk out together when Mom could pick us up. She could drop him off at home. He would tell David that he needed to stay after for a work reason as well and that my Mom would drop him off after.

I didn't like lying to Mom, but wanted to spare her any more reasons to be mad at me. She bought my excuse without an issue. One "hook" though. She wanted to know WHAT work Derek and I were doing together. She wanted proof of it. The next morning on the bus I told Derek that I had to show my Mom some proof that we worked together. He said that I could give him the assignment after school. It was a math assignment, because I ALWAYS had Math homework during the week. He said he would do the work so it would be in his writing. He said then when I show my Mom, I can tell her that I did work on a scrap paper and Derek wrote in the other part on my homework paper. That sounded good to me.

***

We met after the last bell of the day. I hurriedly gave him my assignment for that night and headed to detention. I served detention with Mr. Juong. He had me write an essay about the importance of staying in class and not wandering the halls. I was finished in about half an hour. That left me with the other half hour to work on other homework I had. I had just finished the Spanish homework when he dismissed me from detention. I told him I had learned my lesson and would stay in class unless I really had to use the bathroom or get a drink.

I met up with Derek. He handed me the homework. I shoved it into my bag and we headed out to Mom's car. After we dropped Derek off and got home, Mom asked to see the work we did. I handed it to her. As she looked at it, I explained that Derek wrote on the page based on the work I did on scrap paper.

Her head started to shake back and forth...there was something up with the paper. She asked me to explain how to solve an algebraic inequality. I was able to give her the answers and explain how I used a number line to help. She showed me the example. It was wrong! So if this is the wrong answer, but you just gave me the correct one, how could you have gotten it wrong an hour ago? I didn't know what to say. As I tried to backpedal with reasons, she just told me to stop talking. She told me to go to my room and when I could come out and tell her the truth that she would be ready to listen to me.

I went to my room. I couldn't believe it! I know that Derek had mentioned that he had some trouble with math, but I figured 6th grade math should be OK for him. I had totally messed up. And Mom knew. She caught my lie. I don't think it was a terrible lie, but still it was wrong. After about 15 minutes, I went into the kitchen. She was working on dinner. Grandma was taking a nap, so Mom was alone.

I spilled everything to her. About Derek and his worry, and WHY he worried so much about his Mom. Then I told her about how he and I schemed up this whole thing so I wouldn't get her upset with being in trouble and getting a detention. She listened very patiently until I was all done.

Then she said, "You need to decide what your consequence is for lying to me. That is what I am most upset about. I know you aren't perfect. I actually understand your concern for Derek and am GLAD you wanted to help him. I cannot let the lying go, though. You need to decide what a fair consequence would be. You aren't in trouble for getting detention or skipping a part of a class to do something YOU thought was what a good friend would do. Head back to your room and let me know what your decision is by the time dinner is ready, which will be in 30 minutes."

I agreed to her suggestion and went into my room.

***

After I thought for a while, I had an idea. Our front porch was messy and dirty. We kind of use it like a dumping ground for things as we come and go from the house. We haven't touched it in about two months, so things have piled up and it has leaves that have blown from the yard and the trees, all jammed in the corners and beneath the railings. The floorboards needed to be swept and then washed too. It would probably take me about three hours to get everything cleaned and neatly arranged so we could decorate it for winter.

We string white lights around the posts and hang bows off of the front that complement the wreath we hang on our front door. I told Mom that I would spend Saturday morning cleaning the front porch. She agreed that it was an appropriate consequence, and that the porch did need a good cleaning. She also made me promise to be truthful with her. She said it is hard to be a good parent and raise good kids if the kids are not honest.

On the bus the next morning I told Derek what happened. He apologized for messing up the math work. He just has issues with math...especially algebra. He said when he does this work at home that David checks it and helps him when he is unsure of what to do. He felt bad that I got caught.

I told him about my consequence. He said that on Saturday his mom doesn't have to go to work until 1pm. He offered to come over and help me, since he was part of the whole situation. I told him I'd ask and let him know.

Mom agreed that Derek can help me with the porch. We actually got it done in two hours AND got to sample the cookies that Grandma was baking. She finally had enough energy and strength to do some baking. She would work for about an hour, then rest for a while. It was just enough time to bake a large batch of her butterscotch chocolate chip cookies. About noon, Derek's mom came and picked him up.

***

My family spent the afternoon decorating the house for Christmas. I really felt upbeat, with Grandma baking and Derek helping me out with the porch cleaning. I was originally going to just hang in my room, but I quickly changed my mind and joined all of them. We unpacked the decorations and put up the tree. The snow had just begun falling. I had forgotten that we were supposed to get about 8 inches of snow this afternoon and tonight. I didn't pay that much attention to the forecast because it wouldn't give us a snow day from school.

As we were about to plug in the lights to the tree, Mom's phone chimed. It was for a face time. Who could that be? As soon as she answered, she told us to wait a minute to turn on the lights. The face time was Dad. Since the storm was going to get bad quickly, they had some drawing for some of the inmates to face time their families. Out of the 20 names drawn, one was Dad's.

It was cool that we got to all talk to him for a couple minutes. I hadn't seen him since my one and only visit with him a few weeks ago. He and I talked about football for about a minute or so, then we turned on the lights so he got to see our tree all decorated and lit up. He had a beaming smile on his face and tears in his eyes. He was with us, but not really. It just wasn't the same. Right before he had to hang up, he told us that his trial was starting and to stay positive. He said his lawyer was tough and really ready to fight for him. Just before he got off the phone he told us he missed us and loved us.

It was good and bad to see Dad. It made me feel good when I was with him, but afterwards, I feel awful. It just reopens the wound of him being gone...with no timeline for him coming back home. I keep jumping between missing him and hating him. How can you love and hate someone at the same time?

Mom had asked Nina and me if we wanted to go to watch some of the trial. She said she'd go first so she could prep us before entering the courtroom. Nina wants to go. I told her I am not sure. Too many emotions are running through my body at different times. I don't want to be there, near him, when some of them are hitting me.

Chapter 25

When it was Nina's day going to the trial, I rode the bus to school with her on my mind. I wondered how she would deal with it all. I just wasn't comfortable being around all those people as they judged my Dad. There would be people there who hated him. I am the only one who can hate him right now...well, maybe Nina, too. But she doesn't seem to hate him like I do. I feel alone. I feel like I am the only one who has these emotions...deep hatred AND love for Dad at the same time.

I am so torn. Torn between wanting to defend him, but then having the fact that he did commit a crime, and someone lost their life due to the crime he was a part of. If he was the one that had killed Mr. Gossling, I would only feel hatred toward him. But knowing the story we have been given, it really seems like he knew nothing about the gun and left the scene without any money and being any part of the murder. That is the part that allows my soul to hold onto love for him. He made a bad choice to commit a crime, but got into a much worse situation he was totally unaware of until it was unfolding before his eyes.

I felt like my brain was on a see-saw. Some of the time I just missed him and forgave him, while other times I just saw red and wanted to hit him and yell at him about how much I hated him for thinking this was OK to do to another human being and their family...and ours. If he loved us that much, why didn't he let that love guide his brain to make the right decision? The lawful decision, the decision that wouldn't have ruined the lives of his family? Did he even consider those that loved him and supported him in his day to day life?

"Hey", Derek said, snapping his fingers in front of me, "Where are you? Where is your brain at?"

I blinked and my brain refocused on the bus scene. On the general noise of the kids who were awake enough to be conversing, and Derek, sitting next to me.

"I'm sorry", I replied, "Nina is going to the

courthouse today to watch some of my Dad's trial. I was just thinking about it all."

"Are you going to go to any of it?" Derek inquired.

"No. I am not sure I could handle being around all those people saying things about him. I don't think I could stay quiet. I would want my thoughts about my Dad heard." I replied.

"You're lucky", Derek commented

"Why?" I wondered.

"You have a Dad to be mad at, or be happy with." he retorted.

I just looked at him and so wanted to ask him about his Dad. I couldn't do this while on the bus, though. There were too many people around. I don't want him to get mad at me and have an issue that the school gets involved with.

"Can I come over after school today?" I asked.

"Sure. What do you want to do?" he replied.

I told him I just didn't want to wait at home after school for Mom and Nina to come home. I wasn't sure I wanted to know how things went, or hear a description of Nina's day at the courthouse.

***

After school I got off my stop. I dropped my book bag on the floor of my room, told Grandma I was going to Derek's and headed out the door. I was going to run, but decided to take it easy today and just walk. It took about 20 minutes to get there.

I went through how I would get Derek to talk more about his Dad and his feelings. I just wanted to know what was going on in his mind about things….things involving his Dad. He gets so angry and quiet. He shuts people out, whether it is me or his brother, or other kids at school. I am his only friend. Well, at least I am the only friend who spends time with him. Like David told me earlier, after their Dad's accident, Derek shut out all of his friends. He only spent time at school or at home with his Mom, David and Shannon. Why? Why didn't he lean on his friends for support? Or at least let his friends help as a distraction from the rotten situation going on in his home life?

Derek rarely spoke about his Dad. When he did, that was when he would usually shut me out of his life for a while, usually just a day or two. It was like he needed time to deal with losing his dad all over again. I know a parent can never be replaced, but David and Shannon seemed to be doing OK. They had friends and seemed happy most of the time.

Why was Derek acting differently than them? People handle tragedy in different ways and heal at different times, but it has been two years. The bitterness and sadness in Derek's heart was still so fresh. I decided to "push" the issue about working on the building block model with Derek. I don't want him to explode, but I do want to know better about HOW I can help him start to heal.

When I got to Derek's house, he and David had just gotten Shannon off her bus and they were getting ready to have a snack. I joined them and listened to each share how their day at school went. David talked about a math test on slope. He said it was easy. They were allowed to have one page of notes to help them. He said the page he wrote to prepare for the test had ALL the information he needed on it to get him a good grade. Derek shared a lunch story about a kid who found a bug in his pudding. Luckily it wasn't from a school lunch, or else nobody would be taking a hot lunch for a long time. He then explained that it was a fake bug that his friends put in the pudding when he went to get a napkin. He thought that was a pretty good practical joke.

   The boys quickly explained that they have Shannon go last because she always has a lot to share. She waited patiently, listening to her brothers. She then asked if I wanted to share something. I shared with them that my Science teacher announced that she was pregnant. She was going to have a baby at the end of April. She would be out from April Vacation through the end of the school year. I told them that I hope we get a good substitute teacher. Science can be torture if you have someone teaching it that doesn't really like Science. They all agreed that good subs are important.

   Then Shannon took a deep breath and began. She told about a boy in her class who snuck his pet lizard into his backpack and took it out to show his friends at snack time. The teacher started screaming and stood on a chair. She was terrified of reptiles. The kids all laughed. The boy had to bring the lizard in the box he had, to the office until his parents could come get it. He had to return to the room and apologize for disrupting the class and scaring his teacher. She said everyone kept laughing about it the rest of the day.

   She then told us about gym class. She said today they played volleyball. She said it was fun. They used a beach ball. She then explained to me that she was the score keeper because she couldn't play in a wheelchair. I felt bad. She was part of the activity, but not as a participant on the court. I wonder if she liked gym class better when she wasn't in the wheelchair, or if she didn't like the physical activity. After Shannon was done taking, Derek got very quiet. Here we go again! He is shutting down. This time will be different...this time I will get him to talk. I was determined to help him.

***

I followed Derek into his room. I sat in his desk chair. He turned on the TV, ready to game. I suggested that we do something different today. He thought I would want to game, because I still couldn't at home. I would get back my cable and phone by New Years', as long as I kept showing Mom my completed assignments each day and completed any past due work I still owed. Derek asked what I wanted to do instead. I looked at the model. Derek's face grew angry.
"I already told you that I am not working on that," he said sternly.
I decided to take a chance.
"So let's take it apart and put it away. All it is doing is gathering dust and taking up space in your room." I suggested.
"No, leave it alone. It is fine where it is." he replied, red faced.
"Why?" I asked, "Why can't you either put it away or finish it? I know you were working on this with your Dad. Don't you think he would want you to do SOMETHING with it, even if he can't be here with you to help?"
Derek started crying. His body shook...his shoulders slumped. I panicked. I had pushed Derek too far from his comfort zone. He took a deep breath and sat in his game chair.
"It was my fault", he said quietly.

I didn't know what he meant.

"What is your fault?" I spoke softly.

"My Dad died because of ME. My sister is in a wheelchair for the rest of her life because of ME." he shared.

I was so shocked. It took me a minute to respond. "You were with them in the car?" I asked.

"No, but it is still MY fault." he repeated.

"I don't understand how this could be your fault. You weren't even there with them." I reminded him.

He took a minute to breathe and relax. He regained his composure.

Then he looked me in the eye and said, "I have never told anyone what I am about to tell you." he said sullenly.

"I just want to be here for you, Derek. You just are so sad and angry. Tell me what will help you." I replied.

"Just listen. And please don't judge me. Please don't hate me. The afternoon of the accident I was at my friend Eddie's house. He lives about four blocks from here. I had walked to his house and didn't want to walk back home. It had started raining and was cold. I didn't want to get wet and cold. When I went to Eddie's it was with the agreement that I would walk home. David was at basketball practice, and Mom was going to get him on her way home from work. Dad was home with Shannon. I called Dad and begged him to come get me so I wouldn't have to walk home in the rain. At first he said no, that I could walk. That was the understanding we had when I left for Eddie's house. I called again a few minutes later and begged him to come get me. He finally agreed and said he'd be there in a few minutes. He never came. His last words to me of 'I'll be there in a few minutes' were said out of frustration because I had annoyed him to the point that he gave in to me. He had Shannon with him because she was little and couldn't stay home alone." he confessed.

He then went on, "He was going around a corner that had lots of wet leaves on the road. His car slid and went down an embankment. He was killed instantly. Shannon almost died too. Every time I look at Shannon, I think to myself, "I did this to her. I am the reason she cannot walk anymore."

"And I am the one who took Dad away from all of us...me, David, Shannon and Mom. Now Mom has to work so much to keep us financially stable. She doesn't want us to have to move from our home. She has no time to do things she used to do, like classes at the gym and scrapbook weekends with her friends. She doesn't have the time or the money to do any of this. All she does is work and take care of the house and us. She has no fun in her life.

David had to quit the basketball team because he has to come home from school and watch Shannon with me. Once in a while he can go to the courts to play with his friends on Mom's day off, but that is it. And Shannon...everything has changed for her. She can't even ride the regular bus to school with her friends. She can't go to dance class or gymnastics anymore.

I even saw a bill from Shannon's hospital stay. Mom pays a lot towards it each month. I don't even know how long it will take to pay this off. All of this is ALL MY FAULT".

Derek hung his head. He looked like a deflated balloon. All of the air, all of the pressure on him was finally let out. But I didn't know what to say right then. I didn't know what to do. I went and sat next to him. I put my hand on his shoulder. He didn't shrug it off.

Chapter 26

The trial for my Dad was over in less than two weeks. He was convicted of robbery. The guy Jeff that did shoot Mr. Gossling was found guilty of manslaughter. The other guy with them was convicted of robbery like my Dad. I wasn't sure about how I felt at this point. I know I was glad that Dad wouldn't have a life sentence, or, like 60 years in jail, but I was still angry.

 I thought my anger was focused just on Dad and the crime he committed. It was more than that. It was anger about change in my life. I was angrier about my Dad not being there for me than I was of him committing robbery. I don't know if that is normal or not, but it is how I feel. I didn't go to the trial at all. I felt kind of guilty about it.

 One evening I told Grandma how I felt when it was just the two of us. She said that she didn't blame me for not wanting to go. She didn't want to go either. She thought that Mom and Nina were brave for going and listening to others' criticisms of Dad. She then told me that I am not a wimp for not going, though. She said it is just as brave to do what you know is best for yourself in this situation. There was pressure to go to the trial, but both of us didn't cave to the pressure. We stood our ground and did what was best for us, whether it was the right thing to do or not. Nobody can judge us on that. And if they try, we agree to have each others' backs and defend their choice.

Now our time was spent waiting for the sentencing hearing. This would happen sometime around New Years' Day. Christmas Day was torture without Dad. I made my secret Christmas Wish, like I do each year. I write it on a piece of paper and leave it in the tree on Christmas Eve. The wish is supposed to be for something that is not an item...like a few years ago when Nina and I fought all the time, I wished that Nina and I would get along better. I hate fighting with other people. Nina is my sister and I know we were supposed to be kinder to each other. Anyway, on New Years' Eve Mom and Dad would sit with us and we would discuss our wishes and how Nina and I could make them come true. If the wish didn't involve each other, we talked about how we could support the person with the wish to help them make it come true.

My wish this year was for my family to be able to stick by each other while Dad was in jail. We needed to help each other out. I haven't been good at that so far, so I know that I need to change. I need to be there for my family. I never talked to Nina when she looked sad or upset. I was so focused on how I felt that I almost forgot that she is going through this rollercoaster of emotions. I am sure that Mom is,too, but just hides it better from us.

***

Mom was able to return to work now. Uncle Vinnie was moving back in with his friends. He promised me that he would stop by at least a couple times a week and spend time with us. He asked Grandma to still help him with cooking lessons on Saturdays. She agreed. So at least on Saturdays he would be here to make dinner.

    Mom also explained that money would be tight, and she would need to work a part time job a few evenings during the week and at least one day on the weekends. That would take her away from us alot. Now we wouldn't have Dad around at all and Mom only here some of the time, when she wasn't at work. Nina offered to babysit on Saturdays and give her pay to Mom to help out. Grandma offered to do sewing jobs for people and contribute her earnings to our bills as well.

    I had nothing to offer. I felt like such a loser. Then Nina came up with an idea for me to mow lawns, rake leaves and shovel snow for our neighbors when they needed it. It may not be much, or steady work, but at least it is something. I told her I would use the money for my own spending money so I wouldn't have to ask for money when I go places or want new clothes. Mom said we could give it a try and see if we could make things work.

    Mom was going to sell Dad's car, so that money would help. Dad had told her to do that at her last visit with him. Uncle Vinnie loves working on cars, so he said he would maintain Mom's car. All she would have to do is fill it with gasoline when it was low. Uncle Vinnie would take care of everything else.

    As I thought of all the offers and how we were going to make things work, I realized this was part of my wish from Christmas already coming true. We were being there for each other by working together as a family. Each of us had something to contribute that would help us manage our life together while Dad was not here.

***

I also decided to go to Nina and ask for her help. I was still struggling with some of my assignments and was still behind. I asked her to help me, especially with English work. It was always a subject that I had to really work hard at to get good grades. This year, because I slacked off, I really didn't understand a lot of what I needed to do to get a good grade in this class. This was the first time I had asked anything of Nina since Dad was gone.

I didn't want to look "weak" or "needy" in any way. I wasn't weak, but I was "needy". I needed her to help me get back on track with my schoolwork. I had tried on my own and had minimal success. It was time to make a true commitment. One that I wasn't going to back out of. One that I would not allow to fail. But I needed help to get myself together. I needed someone to hold me accountable for my work until I truly was on the right path. I couldn't ask Mom to do that. She had enough to do. Grandma would try to help me, but sometimes she just didn't understand how to do the work the way we are expected to at school. Nina had to be the one.

When I asked Nina, she seemed happy that I was at least reaching out to her in some way. She put on her "I'm taking charge" face and told me what her expectations were of me, if she was going to help make this happen. I agreed to what she had said. It was going to be a long Christmas Break...with lots of work to be done, but I had time to do it. This was the only way I was going to be able to get back my phone and cord for my video game system.

My friends were also busy, so they wouldn't be distracting me over the break. Deacon was leaving in a couple of days and had to help with packing. I wasn't as upset about him moving as I originally was. Sure, we would stay friends and spend time with each other, but we would both spend time with our other friends too. Derek was spending most of this week at his cousin's house that was about two hours away. David and Shannon were with him. Their Mom went with them from Christmas, but then came back home to work. She'd go get them in a few days.

Chapter 27

I worked through the vacation on my assignments. When I needed a break I went running. Nina was working at school during the days, setting up the school food and clothing pantry as part of her History Project. I worked on what I needed to complete while she was gone, then after dinner she would go over what I did and help me prepare for what I would do the next day.

She was really good in English. She helped me truly understand the assignments and get caught up with my classmates for when we returned to school. I made sure to thank her each time she helped. I wanted her to know how much I appreciated her. One of my assignments in English Class was to write a poem about a time in our life that we were either really happy , really angry or really sad. At first I didn't think I could do it...I wanted to write about my feelings related to my Dad, especially the past few months. I was scared to do it. I put that assignment off to last. I had to work on keeping my emotions in check while working on it. It took me the entire day to finish it. I kept writing and rewriting. Erasing and changing the wording. At one point, I put it down and went for a run to clear my head so I could start again with a fresh mind. My thoughts changed, my words changed, my mood changed as I wrote. When I finally finished after a few agonizing hours, I had this:

The Unthinkable Life

A rock, stable and strong
Loosened by the waves
Attacked by the current
Moved helplessly by nature
Caught up in a storm
Tossed in all directions
Falling, falling
Landing in a new place
Soft, warm, secure
Until the tide returns
Jolted in all directions
Nowhere to turn
No wedge of security
Rough edges, Sharp points
Cutting its surroundings
Damaging, chipping away
The surf attempts
To heal the wounds
To smooth the surface
As the tide returns
Constant pressure
Exterior rounds
The same rock
Yet unrecognized

**Until it accepts the change
And learns the forces
Of life**

Not a lot of words, but a powerful message of change and acceptance. I am hoping that if anyone reads this, that they can apply it to some big life event of their own. Wondering if those that read it and know it is written by me, will understand how I have felt the past few months. I was exhausted when I finished. So much emotion drained me, physically. I took a break to eat dinner, then went back and finished it so I could show Nina. Mom had agreed to give me back my cable and phone once everything was done. I had planned on gaming with Derek all night for New Years' Eve, which was the next day.

Chapter 28

When I got up the next morning, Mom had already left. I thought she had gone to work, but Nina reminded me that Dad's sentencing was today. I had totally forgotten about it. I was so wrapped up with getting my work done before New Year's Eve, when Derek would be back home that it totally slipped my mind. I started to think about Dad and what may happen today. I know we had said that maybe the judge will go easy on him and it will be a three year sentence. That would be the best possible scenario.

Dad's lawyer told Mom that the worst scenario would be about 10 years. Yikes. That would be awful. Dad wouldn't be back home until I was 21 years old! He'd miss everything! He'd miss all my track meets, both my graduations, teaching me how to drive, and all the other day to day things that happen in middle school and high school. He'd even miss me starting college. Could I go to college? Would Mom have enough money to help me pay for it? I spent the day trying to keep busy.

I went into my room and looked over the poem I had written and did some last minute editing that Nina had suggested to ensure that I would get a good grade. I helped Grandma make some snacks for tonight. Nina was having a couple of her friends over to count down for the New Year. I then went into my room and looked over the poem. It was good. It came from my heart.

I was so busy with the small drawings I was putting in the margins of the poem, and had my ear pods in, that I didn't hear Mom come home.
I came out of my room yelling, "Finally finished!" and waving my poem in the air.
I handed it to Nina as Mom explained all that had happened today. Nina had hoped that the judge would have the spirit of the season in his heart and go super easy on Dad. She had it in her mind that he'd only get one year of jail time, then probation. She looked pretty disappointed.

***

Mom explained that Dad and the other man who wasn't involved with the shooting, each got sentenced to 4 years in jail. This means he'll miss out on some important events. He'll miss both my 8th grade graduation and Nina's. Four more Christmas's without him? I asked Mom. She said that usually the time served begins when he was first arrested. If that is the case, then there will be only three more Christmas's without him. Still sucks, but not as badly.

I tell myself to focus on positives...Dad will be here to teach me to drive. Dad will be at some of my high school track meets. Dad will be here for my high school graduation...and Nina's. I start to really reflect on how I feel about my Dad. My love for him is in the lead of the "emotional race" that my mind is experiencing. My frustration and hatred and disappointment are still there, but they are not in the forefront. I need to keep them there.

When I felt those negative emotions and let them overwhelm me I was just miserable. I was unable to focus on my life. I was unable to love my family that is here for me, right now. I was selfish. I was alone.

When I let love lead me and forgiveness guide my feelings towards Dad, I won. And so did everyone else I care about. I know it won't be easy. I am sure there will be times of anger, sadness and overall negative attitude, but I will fight it. I will admit to my feelings and move on.

That is what the counselor has told all of us. Don't battle with yourself. Recognize your emotions...allow yourself to feel them, but don't let them dwell inside your body. Negativity breeds trouble...physically, mentally, socially. It breaks down all the good things you want in life. "Recognize it, then release it so it leaves you to enjoy all the good things life has to offer." is what he reminds us.

I need to just keep his voice saying this in my head. And believe in all the good that is to come in my life. I just need to allow the wonderful things in.

Chapter 29

Even though I spent most of the night gaming with Derek, I decided to go to Derek's house on New Year's Day. We haven't spoken about the day he broke down in his room. I hope he has at least talked to David about his feelings. I walked into his room and he was finishing up a game. He turned it off.

He showed me a couple of things he had gotten for Christmas. One was a new building block model. He said he was going to work on it, but not yet. I figured he needed more time. I was in total shock when he said that it was always a rule to not start a new model until you finished the one you were working on. He walked over to the dusty model on the table in his room and asked me if I'd like to work on it with him. I told him I would be honored to help him. We both smiled.

Derek was healing. It was a step in the right direction. He wasn't standing still, living in the shadow of blaming himself. He was moving on to begin living again. As we started working, I told him about my Dad's sentencing. He'd be gone for a while. I told Derek that I couldn't wait for him to meet my Dad. I explained that he was really a fun guy to hang around with. He always had a joke to tell or was eager to play a game, kick a ball around, shoot hoops, whatever I wanted to do.

Derek was quiet for a minute. I thought maybe I made him feel bad about not having a Dad.

Then he said softly, "I'm sorry".

"For what?" I asked.

"For being mean to you. I was not a good person. I let my sadness and anger take over the type of person I want to be. I want to be known as a good, nice person. One who can be a true friend." he explained.

I told him that he **was** a good friend. I knew he would be one long before this time. That is why I've stuck around and wanted to spend time with you. I need good friends. I need people who won't judge me because of what my Dad did.

I am glad we got into the fight a few months ago. It put me in your life. It started out rough, but just got better each day. Each time we were together, on the bus, building ramps, gaming.

We worked for hours on the model. Most of the time we were both quiet. My mind jumped from what each member of my family was thinking about Dad's sentencing and how they were going to cope until he could be with us again. Mom, without her husband, working extra hours each week. She also had to deal with raising two middle school, then high school kids. We weren't always that easy on her.

***

What about Grandma? I hoped she would stay well. Maybe this would help her to work hard at being well so she could be with her son when he returned home. All the help she offers at home. The cooking, or coaching us to cook and sewing whatever we need. Her sewing for others and making money when most of her friends are just relaxing and enjoying their golden years.

Nina would be going through most of high school with no Dad around. Who would intimidate any boys she brought home? What about the Father-Daughter Dance that happened in April of this year? Would Uncle Vinnie take her? Would it be too weird for her and she would decide not to go?

How about Uncle Vinnie? He did his best, trying to be there for us...all of us. He really tried to help without intruding on us, trying to be a "father figure" on a temporary basis. Then having to back off when Dad returns.

How will this all happen? Only the future knows.

***

Derek broke into my thoughts by saying, "I told my Mom and David about what happened the last time you were over. I told them what I said. I let it all out. It helped me...a lot. It was like I was keeping a secret that was so painful. I was hurting myself, and other people around me because of my behavior. I felt like a brick wall I had imagined around me had come crashing down. A wrecking ball had shattered all the built up emotions and set them free. Mom is going to set her schedule at work so that we can all go to counseling. All of us have things to set free as we deal with something that happened two years ago. Mom said it is time for us all to heal. I guess they have all had issues too. I was just so wrapped up on how I was feeling that I didn't notice that they are all hurting too. Mom made me promise to work on not blaming myself for the accident. She said that is the first thing I need to do. She said it was just that...an accident. It was nobody's fault, just a terrible thing that happened."

At that point I told Derek that we should promise to be there for each other. Friendships can be just as strong as family bonds. True friends become family, without the blood relation, but just as important in life to have. We agreed to spend time talking about our Dads...and our family...and what we wanted for our futures. We even joked that if either of our families decided to move away that whoever was moving would stay and live with the family not moving so we wouldn't have to deal with a long distance friendship. We laughed at that agreement, joking about where the "newcomer" to the family would sleep and the chores they would have to do.

I finally felt at peace. At peace with my family, my Dad, my friendships, school...my life.

END NOTES: (JC's Story)

1. I will turn 16 just before Dad comes home. I'll have him teach me how to drive. I chose to attend the technical high school in our town. I am studying electrical engineering. I am a state- ranked competitor for the track team. Derek and I started our own little landscaping business. We have about 8 yards that we maintain for people. We mow, garden, clear leaves, and shovel snow in the winter.

2. Derek goes to the same high school as me. He is studying computer technology/graphic design. He is hoping to work in the gaming industry some day. His brother is in college studying business and finance. His sister is on the cheerleading squad at the middle school. She wheels around and cheers on the team always showing her huge bright smile.

Derek's Mom got a management position. She still works a lot, but makes enough money to help David pay for college.

3. Grandma had another stroke while Dad was still in prison. She fought back. Even though she now needs a cane to support and stabilize her when she walks, she still makes the best empanadas and fried plantains!

4. Nina goes to a magnet high school that focuses on political science. When she graduates, she wants to go to college, then law school. I know she can do it! She'll help a lot of people as a lawyer someday.

5. Mom worked her second job, but managed to have her Saturday shift be evenings so she could bring us to see Dad, and so that she could see Dad. She is looking forward to him being with us, full time, after he pays his "dues".

6. Dad got an Associate's Degree while in prison. He will be in a program that helps former prisoners get a good job based on the degree they earned while incarcerated. The last time I saw him, Dad told me how excited he will be to be back at home with us and making a decent living so Mom can quit her second job and he can help pay for Nina and me to go to college. That is exactly what he did after he served his four year sentence.

The four years of Dad being in prison were tough times. We faced financial hardships and went without some things. Our family grew closer than ever. We supported each other through our words and our actions. Sure, it wasn't perfect, but it was a time in my life that I will never forget. I learned so much about who I want to be as a positive contributor in friendships, family and society. Life is a roller coaster. If you take the good times and treasure them, and take the bad times and learn from them, it all balances out. Just keep faith in yourself and not only recognize what is good in your life, but treasure it as well.

ABOUT THE AUTHOR

Beth lives in Connecticut with her husband, Phil. She has two adult sons, Matthew and Connor, as well as a cat, Critter, and dog, Flynn. She currently teaches middle school math. She has been a teacher for 30 years. In her spare time she enjoys spending time with her family and friends. Her favorite activities include golfing, hiking and scrapbooking.

The illustrator of the cover design, Christopher Ramos, agreed to illustrate this for Beth when they were in high school 35 years ago! He is retired from the U.S. Army and currently lives in North Carolina with his wife and family.

This is Beth and Christopher at their 30th high school reunion.

Made in the USA
Middletown, DE
22 July 2021